P L MATTHEWS

Poisoned Leaves

A Green Witch Mystery 1

Copyright © 2023 by P L Matthews

All rights reserved. No part of this publication may be reproduced, stored or transmitted in any form or by any means, electronic, mechanical, photocopying, recording, scanning, or otherwise without written permission from the publisher. It is illegal to copy this book, post it to a website, or distribute it by any other means without permission.

This novel is entirely a work of fiction. The names, characters and incidents portrayed in it are the work of the author's imagination. Any resemblance to actual persons, living or dead, events or localities is entirely coincidental.

P L Matthews asserts the moral right to be identified as the author of this work.

First edition

This book was professionally typeset on Reedsy. Find out more at reedsy.com

To my husband. Time is separated between before and after you. You've shown me that soulmates truly exist.

Contents

Foreword	iii
Prologue	1
CHAPTER 1	3
CHAPTER 2	15
CHAPTER 3	29
CHAPTER 4	42
CHAPTER 5	55
CHAPTER 6	69
CHAPTER 7	81
CHAPTER 8	94
CHAPTER 9	106
CHAPTER 10	118
CHAPTER 11	131
CHAPTER 12	145
CHAPTER 13	158
CHAPTER 14	172
CHAPTER 15	186
CHAPTER 16	199
CHAPTER 17	213
CHAPTER 18	224
CHAPTER 19	237
CHAPTER 20	247
CHAPTER 21	257
CHAPTER 22	269

CHAPTER 23	282
CHAPTER 24	296
CHAPTER 25	310
CHAPTER 26	322
Epilogue	333
Notes to Readers	336
Acknowledgements	338
Also by P L Matthews	339
About the Author	340

Foreword

Before you dive into this book, I've got a little confession to make. You might notice that the spelling here is a bit different — that's because we're speaking Aussie English, where "colour" has a "u" and "realise" gets an "s." Plus, it's set in the beautiful city of Sydney, Australia. So, don't be surprised if you catch the occasional "mate" slipping through the pages. Consider it a free lesson in Aussie slang, but don't worry, I'll try to keep the kangaroos and koalas to a minimum. Enjoy the read. Cheers!

Prologue

Bent over the straggly plant, her eyes intensely scanned every wilted leaf. From his hiding spot behind a stack of crates, the Shadow watched her curiously, wondering what could be so important about this plant to keep her here at this time of night.

Her brown hair was loosely tied up in a messy bun, framing her delicate face. Despite her petite frame, she exuded grace and agility, a mix of elf, witch, and dryad blood flowing in her veins.

The Shadow thought that this was all a complete waste of time. After all, she was just a halfling. At thirty-six years old, she was still considered a mere child by elf standards. Her low-level abilities had likely been passed down to her from her mother, and it was well-known that the more diluted the bloodline, the weaker the power.

As the Shadow prepared to leave, he saw the girl suddenly become alert. Though he knew he couldn't have been spotted, he felt uneasy as she glanced toward the crates. Holding his breath, he watched her, waiting for any sign that she had detected his presence.

The girl shook her head and resumed her tending. A soft

glow emanated from her. The glow focused on the plant but soon expanded, touching everything in its path. He watched in fascination as the girl poured her energy, her magic unfurling like tendrils of light, reaching out to the world around her.

As if on command, the plant righted itself, its leaves turning vibrant green and glossy, growing outwards by five inches. The Shadow's eyes widened. It was an incredibly rare and highly prized healing specimen, and the halfling girl had brought it back from the brink of death using her magic. Such an impressive display of power was a feat possessed by very few. The Shadow retreated slowly; his eyes still focused on the halfling girl as the portal silently closed.

"Interesting," he muttered to himself. "Very interesting."

CHAPTER 1

Rhianne woke up to the sun's rays giving her face a friendly nudge. Weird, she could've sworn she'd shut the blinds last night, but perhaps Toto had decided he preferred a sunrise view. She looked around for him but nope, no Toto in sight.

She got out of bed, stretching her arms up high and then bending down to touch her toes - a bit of a challenge after using elf magic the night before. That stuff could really take it out of her, almost like running a marathon or, you know, trying to assemble flat-pack furniture without the instructions. She'd gone to bed at midnight and, elf magic or not, she felt like she could do with a few more hours of sleep.

She sighed. There was always an excuse to use elf magic. Magic she wasn't supposed to have. But saving the Detra orchid was definitely worth it. The orchid could heal a bunch of tough illnesses, help with arthritis pain, and ease Parkinson's symptoms.

After a shower, she wrapped herself in a fluffy towel. She approached the steamed-up mirror, wiping a clear patch with the back of her hand. Peering at her reflection, she gave herself a once-over. Her amber-green eyes, with that sneaky hint of brown at the centre, sparkled back, keeping her earlier anxieties well hidden. She applied some clear gloss to her lips and felt a little better as she took one last look at herself in the mirror. She put on some khaki shorts and a black T-shirt with her landscape business' logo, a simple tea leaf, and slipped on a pair of sneakers.

Grabbing a hair tie, she styled her wet hair in a high ponytail. It wouldn't get in the way and it would soon dry in the heat.

Noticing the time, she poured herself an orange juice and took a banana to go.

But hey, at least she lived right above her workplace. She'd long ago decided she preferred the company of plants to people. Plus, not having to commute was a win-win.

Her apartment was nestled above the private nursery area; a snug one-bedroom setup with a generous bathroom complete with a bathtub for those long, contemplative soaks. The medium-sized kitchen boasted modern appliances, where she occasionally unleashed her love for whipping up quirky dishes. Not that she had a parade of guests over - it was mostly just Nel.

Her employees knew her place was strictly no-go territory. It was an unspoken rule: 'Enter the boss' lair and risk turning into a potted plant.'

She headed down to her enclosed garden to check on the Detra Orchid. Her shoulders relaxed when she saw it was still as bright and healthy as when she'd last seen it. Smiling, she stepped out of the enclosure and locked it up. It wasn't that she didn't trust Carl or Alice, but she had some rare and pricey plants in there, like the Detra. They weren't illegal, but they would definitely grab the wrong kind of attention.

CHAPTER 1

By keeping Carl and Alice out, if anyone asked, they could honestly say they had no clue what was inside. She was pretty sure, though, that they had their guesses. Why else would she have all those extra locks?

She could hear gruff voices and headed in that direction. Carl was lifting several heavy bags of fertiliser with ease. The gargoyle was six foot seven and built like a truck. Next to him his smaller twin, Alice, was lifting just as many. Alice was a mere six foot, which was short for a gargoyle, so she tried to overcompensate at every opportunity. It didn't matter that to Rhianne's five foot three, they both looked like giants. It was like working with a pair of friendly skyscrapers.

"Hey guys," Rhianne called out before approaching them. She didn't want to end up as the unintended target of a flying bag of fertiliser. There had been a few close calls in the past, and she preferred to avoid becoming a "fertiliser casualty."

Carl's grin completely changed his face, transforming him from stern to striking in seconds. With his size and the sharpened features of his kind, he was rather intimidating. Or at least he was to anyone who didn't know him. Rhianne considered him a total teddy bear.

"Hey boss, how are you?" He greeted her in his deep voice.

"I'm good, Carl. Any luck with the ladies last night?" When gargoyles reached the age of one hundred, their families began in earnest to push them to find a life partner. At the age of one hundred and four, both Carl and Alice were being invited to singles parties every month.

Carl's blush was adorable, Rhianne smiled at him and patted his lower arm, which was as high as she could reach.

"Not as such, boss."

Alice flipped her long, blond braid over her shoulder. "To

be honest, most of those events are a complete waste of time," she huffed. "The potential matches are only interested in what you can do for them, whether it's money or connections."

Rhianne frowned at Alice's words. Although her landscape business was successful, she knew she couldn't afford to pay Carl and Alice more than she already did. Sensing Rhianne's hesitation, Alice hurried to add, "I mean, we come from a family that owns a diamond mine on the Victorian border. I'm never sure if guys want me for who I am or for my family's money. Frankly, I'd rather be alone."

Rhianne hadn't known that Alice and Carl's family were wealthy. They had never even hinted at it in all their conversations. Come to think of it, though, most of their chats were work-related.

"Maybe you should try exploring other ways of meeting potential partners," Rhianne said.

Carl, who was busy lifting bags, paused for a moment and looked at her. "What do you suggest, boss?"

Rhianne thought for a moment, realising that she had to offer a solution now that she had brought up the topic. "Well, have you thought about exploring your personal interests outside of work? Taking up theatre classes, joining a lawn bowls club, or maybe even a book club could be a great way to meet new people."

Alice's face lit up at the suggestion. "I've always wanted to take up knitting," she said, her blue eyes sparkling with excitement.

"Knitting, Alice? Well, you never know, you might find the love of your life in a knitting circle." Knitting didn't sound like the best place to meet another gargoyle to Rhianne, but who was she to argue?

CHAPTER 1

Carl, still holding onto the bag of fertiliser, added with a grin, "And imagine the cosy jumpers you could make for your future partner!"

Rhianne offered a bemused smile. "You should give it a go, Alice."

Before Alice could answer, Rhianne's phone rang. Rhianne automatically answered, "Welcome to Tea Leaves Landscapes."

"Is this Rhianne Alkenn?" a flat and hard voice asked on the other side.

"Yes, Rhianne speaking," she answered. She glanced over at Alice, who had raised an eyebrow at her and mouthed, "Who is it?" Rhianne shook her head slightly to signal that she didn't know and walked towards her office.

"This is Detective Senior Sergeant Brett Johannes from the NSW Police. I believe you've done consulting with us in the past. We have a case at the moment. Are you able to come to the crime scene at 205 George Street immediately?" Rhianne stared at the phone for a second and pursed her lips.

"Sergeant, I don't believe we have met." The gall of the guy, he wasn't even asking her if she was interested. "Yes, I've done a spot of consulting for Senior Inspector Rowley. What's this about?"

"Look, I wouldn't be asking a civilian if I didn't think it was important. How quickly can you get here?" His tone was curt, and she could almost imagine the snap of his words like a closing trap.

Rhianne felt her hackles rise at his brusque manner. "Well, this civilian has a full-time job, so unless you can give me some idea as to why you need me, I'd suggest you find yourself another consultant." Okay, so that was harsh, but the police cases always left a bad taste in her mouth and while Inspector Rowley had always been polite, this guy wasn't even making an effort.

The line was silent for a moment before the sergeant replied. "My apologies," he said. "I have a high-profile murder and our forensics team isn't sure about the cause of death. There are some — unusual aspects." His voice trailed off and then firmed up again. "We need to rule out poisoning. I know that with poisons sometimes it's better to act quickly and so I would," and a meaningful pause ensued, "really appreciate it if you could come."

Rhianne took a deep breath. Her professional curiosity and his change of attitude made her mind up. "Okay, what's the address again?"

After telling Carl and Alice she needed to zip off to the city, Rhianne made a beeline for her apartment. While her trusty ute was great for deliveries, for a city jaunt, nothing beat her Energica motorcycle, affectionately dubbed Gee. Parking in the city was about as fun as a game of Tetris on hard mode, and Gee was her cheat code.

She loved any excuse to ride it — the electric speedster could hit zero to a hundred in a breezy 2.6 seconds. Sure, it was summer and hot enough to fry an egg on the sidewalk, but riding in shorts wasn't just a no-go for the bike; it was hardly appropriate for a murder scene. She dashed upstairs, swapped her shorts for jeans, threw on a leather jacket, and slipped into black boots.

Back in the garage, she grabbed her black helmet and gloves, and vroomed off to the city, nudging the speed limit. Finding a paid car park near the building, she parked Gee with a smirk. The sergeant could foot the parking bill.

CHAPTER 1

As she neared the building, her eyes caught sight of police officers in their distinctive uniforms. As she reached out to open the entrance doors, a burly policeman intercepted her, blocking her path. "I'm sorry, but no one is allowed to enter the building, madam." He spread his arms wide.

"I'm here to see Sergeant Johannes," Rhianne said.

The policeman eyed her up and down in a way that made her uncomfortable. "Is he expecting you?"

Why else would she be here? She squinted at the policeman and straightened herself up.

"He told me to hurry, so you can be the one to explain to him why I was delayed. I'll go sit over there until you speak to him." Rhianne turned around.

"Wait!" He raised a finger as his eyes darted to his comm unit. "I'll call him now." The policeman frowned at her as he made the call. Seconds later, though, he bobbed his head.

Johannes should have sent someone to fetch her if this was really so urgent, Rhianne grumbled to herself. Almost as if in answer to her thought, a petite woman in a navy pantsuit exited the lifts. As she approached, Rhianne noticed her hair was neatly tied in a low bun, with a few loose strands framing her face. The woman had a small nose and striking dark slanted eyes, which studied Rhianne with a hint of curiosity.

"Rhianne Alkenn?" the newcomer asked.

"The one and the same," Rhianne said. The woman gave her an assessing glance down to her boots and gave her a nod. Clearly, she had passed the visual appraisal.

"I'm Sergeant Lisa Chen. Thanks for coming. How far out were you?"

Rhianne gave her a brief smile. At least someone was polite around here. "I live on the northern beaches," Rhianne answered. Of course, the northern beaches district was a long stretch of coast, so that could have meant anywhere from fifteen to sixty kilometres from the city.

"Wow, that didn't take you long."

"I have a motorbike and tested the speed limit along the way," Rhianne said and noticed Lisa's eyes spark at that. Recognition hit her in the gut. Lisa was a supernatural of some kind, but it would be rather impolite to ask exactly what type.

"Hence the outfit, then," Lisa said. "It's not just a 'I'm a badass' look."

Rhianne couldn't help the laugh that escaped her lips as they entered the lift. Lisa hit the top floor button.

"I'm a landscape gardener; we are known for being badass. How else would I deal with all the gnomes who tried to eat my roses?" Rhianne tried to keep a serious tone.

Lisa laughed. "Gnomes steal pot plants?"

"Of course, although they prefer roses so I keep those in a separate enclosure." It wasn't a total lie, but Lisa's mirth was spurring her on and so she was exaggerating for effect.

They were laughing as they walked into a dimly lit corridor teeming with police officers. Their laughter echoed through the space, drawing curious glances from the officers milling about.

A dark-haired man in a sharp suit turned around, a deep frown marring what was otherwise a handsome, masculine face. Rhianne could sense his disapproving gaze on them, but she couldn't bring herself to care.

"Are you Rhianne Alkenn?" There was a note of doubt in his voice, one that Rhianne had heard before. She looked young for thirty-six years. Most people expected her to be

CHAPTER 1

ancient-looking if she was going to be an expert in poisons.

Rhianne was determined to divert the conversation from any remarks about her seemingly youthful appearance. Dealing with the 'too young to be good at this' brigade was nothing new for her, and she knew it wouldn't be the last time either.

She was all set to prove that age was merely a number — and in her case, a rather misleading one.

His frown didn't ease off. "Are you squeamish? I'd prefer not to contaminate my scene." He handed over some plastic booties and gloves.

"I guess it depends on how bad it is," she shrugged her shoulders. "Are you Sergeant Johannes?"

"In the flesh." He replied. Was that an attempt at humour? It was hard to tell because his tone remained just as serious, but she could have sworn she saw a brief sparkle in his eyes.

"Lead the way." Better get it over with.

The office was opulent. Sleek glass overlooked the harbour, which sparkled in the morning sun. The desk was made of glass and curved at the edges. The diagonal drawers were slim and crafted in dark timber. She doubted they contained much. On the wall on the left, there was a massive bookshelf filled with books that likely had never been read. They were pristine. On the other wall some bucolic paintings hung. No cushions marred the large taupe leather chairs, which surrounded a light-coloured rug. But it wasn't the rug that caught her eye. A middle-aged man was lying on it.

He was dressed in a suit that probably cost more than her monthly profit. She assumed he was in his sixties and had enjoyed the good life a bit too much if his protruding belly was anything to go by. His eyes were open and staring at the ceiling. She gradually approached him and carefully knelt down next to him. Rigour mortis had set in, so he must have died the night before. His irises were dilated and his skin had a blue tinge. Most telling was the swollen neck. She lowered herself down and from the corner of her eye saw Johannes tensing his body, his jaw jutting out. She ignored him. He was paying for her services, and she needed data. They could get a sample, but she suspected it might be too diluted by then and the forensics team needed to know what to test for.

Aha! There it was, a very faint trace of nutmeg. She slowly backed off, got up and then went walking around the office to see if she could detect it elsewhere.

She approached one of the walls with an interesting landscape painting, when suddenly the wall opened like a door, almost hitting her in the process.

"Ugh," she managed before a guy in jeans and a Pink Floyd T-shirt, looking down at a tablet in his hand, stepped in front of her. "Hey! watch out," Rhianne said, rolling her eyes at the guy's obliviousness. She muttered under her breath, "Must be navigating the digital realm of *The Wall* album cover."

He raised his eyes from his tablet and stepped back, apologising. "I'm sorry, I didn't see you there."

Rhianne noticed his striking stormy blue eyes and the shock of bright red hair. A sudden blush painted his neck and cheeks crimson.

She laughed; she couldn't help it. "Well, you know, secret doors and tablet reading are not conducive to seeing obstacles." At that, he blushed deeper and Rhianne decided he was rather cute.

He blinked and then grinned. "I don't think I'd call you an obstacle. I'm Kai." They shook hands.

"I'm Rhianne, I take it you're with the police?"

CHAPTER 1

He shook his head. "Just a mere consultant," he said. "You?"

Rhianne snorted. "Not sure. What's below mere consultant?"

A decisive cough stopped their conversation. They both turned in unison to look at Sergeant Johannes who didn't look impressed at their banter. Maybe he felt it was cutting into his consulting time.

"What did you find?" Johannes asked seemingly to whoever wanted to answer.

Rhianne and Kai looked at each other and she gestured for him to go first. It pleased her that he didn't argue. Lisa stepped up closer to Johannes and gave Kai a small nod and a slight smile.

Kai looked down at his tablet again. "There are no viruses in his devices, but some emails and files have been recently deleted. And by recently, I mean yesterday. Most people think deleting files is all that's required, but they simply go to the recycle bin."

Rhianne suspected this was a sentence he said often because it was recited in an almost bored tone. Johannes perked up at his words.

"However," Kai continued, apparently unaware of the clear disappointment displayed on both Johannes' and Lisa's faces. "Whoever did this was a bit more savvy than that and also deleted them from the recycle bin."

"So, the information is lost," Lisa said.

"Not necessarily," Kai answered.

"Not necessarily," Lisa repeated. Luckily it was Lisa prompting him because Johannes looked like he was ready to shake Kai.

"I'll run a full scan. It's possible that some things would

have been saved earlier or emailed or there may be drafts. If there are, I'll find them. Of course, it might be nothing. Files get deleted all the time." He looked up at Johannes this time, he clearly knew the drill. "It'll take me at least twenty-four hours and I'll need all his devices."

Johannes shifted his gaze to Lisa. "Get the relevant permissions." Lisa didn't pause to question what he meant. Johannes turned to Rhianne. "Did you find anything?" His tone implied he didn't think she had and his eyes went down to his phone. Rhianne almost smiled but decided that would be unprofessional.

"I did, actually." Johannes' eyes snapped up and Kai locked eyes with her. Lisa paused in her phone call and turned to face them.

"He was definitely poisoned," she said.

"Are you sure?" A deep scowl marred Johannes' face.

"You know, you should try smiling more. Frowning like that will add years to your face — not that your ever-cheerful attitude won't beat it to the punch," Rhianne said. Her remark earned a stifled grin from Kai, who tried to hide it behind his hand, and a full-blown smile from Lisa.

Johannes stared at her, unamused.

"You wouldn't have called me here if you didn't think I knew my stuff." Rhianne crossed her arms. "The poison is likely Romin. It's found in specialist nurseries, mine included." She believed in being upfront. "In tiny doses, it's used for treating certain types of seizures, including epilepsy. But in a concentrated dose? It's fatal in about five minutes." And it wouldn't have been a good way to go.

CHAPTER 2

"Of course, I'm sure forensics will need to confirm but they'd better hurry. The poison will only stay in the blood for another twenty-four hours or so."

Good luck in getting it prioritised. Then again, this looked like it had the attention of some higher-ups if they had called her in so quickly.

Rhianne resumed her search of the office, ignoring Johannes' pulled-up eyebrows and forehead. A diploma on the wall proudly announced Parkes Construction Enterprises as last year's winner of the Industry Construction Award. She moved over to the immaculate desk. No way had Parkes actually worked here. Rhianne appreciated a tidy desk, but hers was a habitat for papers, pens, and even a rebellious stress ball. In stark contrast, Devlin Parkes' workspace was a desert — just his laptop and a small leather-bound journal.

It was Johannes who made the call. "Yes, sir. The poison's expert —" Was there a hesitation in Johannes' voice when he said that? "Has said this is a poisoning case. She also says we'll need forensics on it within twenty-four hours or the evidence will disappear." A pause. "Yes, sir. I'll tell forensics to prioritise it."

Ah, so the guy must be rich and well-connected then. There was a photo on the desk, not, as she had expected, of his family, but of him and the current premier. Hmm, well connected indeed.

That's when she noticed the dainty porcelain cup. There was still a bit of liquid in it. Coffee by the looks of it. Carefully she leaned over and smelt it. It was faint and if it wasn't for her magical senses, she wouldn't have picked it up, but she was certain this cup at least had contained the poison.

"I suggest you test the cup, Sergeant," she said casually. It would not do to reveal she could smell it.

"It's Detective Senior Sergeant and I think I know how to do my job," Johannes snarled.

"You mean, the same way I know how to do mine?" she said with a fake layer of sweetness.

"She's got you there, Brett," Lisa said. "At least now the forensics team knows what to look for."

Johannes snapped out of his mood at Lisa's mild rebuke. "Yes, of course. Thank you for your assistance. We'll be in touch if we need anything further." He waved his hand in clear dismissal.

Rhianne turned to walk away, but something caught her eye on the shelf. "There's another cup here, smaller, but it is an odd place for it," she said. Without waiting for a reaction, she turned and began to walk away. As she approached the lift, she heard the sound of quick footsteps behind her.

"Wait for me," a voice called out. It was Kai, his smile lighting up his face. "It was great to see another professional at work. I could use a cup of coffee. Can I shout you one?"

Rhianne knew she should go back to the nursery, but as the

CHAPTER 2

lift doors closed behind them, she found herself smiling back. "I don't drink coffee, but tea would be nice."

Kai's smile got wider. "I know just the place."

The place was conveniently just a stone's throw away and it was a short and pleasant walk. Rhianne was immediately captivated by the delicate display of teapots in the bay window. They were all so beautiful and intricately designed, each one seemingly telling its own unique story. She admired the craftsmanship that went into each piece.

Kai noticed her staring and walked up beside her, a small smile playing at the corners of his lips. "You like the teapots?" he asked, his voice warm and inviting.

Rhianne tore her eyes away from the teapots and looked at Kai. "They're beautiful," she said.

Kai nodded in agreement. "They are. And the tea here is just as good. I come here often when I need to clear my head."

They walked out the back into a small courtyard with some potted trees against the tall stone walls. Fairy lights hung in a crisscross pattern between the walls. Rhianne smiled. "This place has a good ambience."

"Wait until you taste the tea," he said.

"What do you recommend?" she asked as she looked at the menu. There were so many different kinds of tea; the menu had three pages.

"If you like them sweet and milky, I'd suggest the almond tea. If you prefer soothing, I'd recommend the oolong."

"How can I resist a milky almond tea?" Rhianne smiled. "But how do you know so much about it?"

Kai hesitated for a moment. "I used to come here with my girlfriend."

He looked away and a flicker of discomfort crossed his face.

She didn't want to pry, but the phrase 'used to' piqued her curiosity. It suggested a recent breakup. Not that she was any guru in relationships; her dating life in the past few years was about as active as a hibernating bear. And her last boyfriend? Let's just say he was more of a 'if you blink, you might miss him' kind of fling.

The waitress arrived and Rhianne ordered her milky almond tea and Kai an iced green tea.

"OK, Mr Mere Consultant, what is it that you do? Or should I guess?"

"Guess," he said. "Although it isn't too much of a challenge, given the conversation at the scene."

Rhianne paused. "Tech Mage, high level?"

Kai's eyes sparkled. "What gave it away? I could have been a tech consultant."

She snorted.

"And I'm a level five, not boasting or anything," he hurried to add.

"That's just being honest," Rhianne lifted one shoulder.

"What about you?"

It was a natural question and Rhianne almost flinched, given that she was about to not be quite so honest. "Green witch." Truth. "Level two." Sort of a lie.

Kai's eyebrows rose. "I'd have pegged you for a level three at least. You were quite impressive in there."

She'd fudged the test. Only Toto and her grandfather knew. And although Nel knew about her elf magic, she'd never used it in front of him or anyone else. "Well, I'm a mixed blood," she said by way of explanation.

"Even more impressive then. Your knowledge is superior to other experts I've come across."

CHAPTER 2

An uncomfortable flush of heat surged through her body. She wasn't used to compliments. As a halfling most people would simply assume she was weak or at best avoid the subject altogether. "I like to read and I like plants. I have a landscape business."

"And she owns her own business. Man, I'm so out of my league." Kai looked at her with an intensity that made her blink.

A blush crept up Rhianne's cheeks. "And you are a level five Tech Mage, who can uncover data after a few minutes of interacting with devices," she countered and took a sip of her tea. "This is divine." The taste was sweet but the bitterness of the almonds contrasted nicely.

"What's your take on the case?" Rhianne asked. It was refreshing to have someone to discuss the murder with, given the usual tight-lipped nature of her work.

"Looks like someone went out of their way to off the guy with poison. Is it hard to get?" he asked.

"It's not your everyday plant. Only a handful of specialised plant nurseries stock it because of its healing properties. It's pretty rare and expensive. I'd say maybe five or six nurseries have it, tops."

"And who can get their hands on it?" He took a sip of his tea, leaving a faint green moustache on his upper lip.

She fought the urge to reach over and wipe it away, focusing instead on the question at hand.

"Well, that all depends on how tight security is at the plant nurseries. We do get our fair share of break-ins." Rhianne thought about the gnome gang that hang around her business. Those little troublemakers were shockingly crafty. More than once, they'd outwitted her most intricate security measures.

She recalled one time setting up a mini hedge maze to confuse them, only to find they treated it like their personal racetrack, leaving tiny footprints all over. Good thing they had a taste for roses and carnations only; her orchids were safe.

"My place is pretty secure. High fence, and the rare plants are in a locked section where only I have the key. In the larger plant nurseries, lots of staff could get to it. Or a visitor during the day, if they knew what they were looking for. But I never let anyone into my private garden, not even my employees." She couldn't ignore Kai's tea moustache any longer and gestured towards it, trying not to laugh.

"Right, so it circles back to the employees. But since it's used for healing, anyone with medical knowledge might know about it too." Kai licked his lips and Rhianne's breath caught.

"Apothecaries are another possibility," she continued, regaining her focus. "But they're usually pretty strict with records. The law says they can only sell to certified health practitioners. So, they'd have a detailed log of who bought it and who it was sold to."

"Yeah, but there's always someone who doesn't play by the rules."

"I've never had anyone try to buy it off me on the sly." Rhianne tapped her chin. "But maybe they wouldn't dare because of my mother." Uh oh, she hadn't meant to say that.

"Your mother?" Kai asked.

Oh, here we go; he was either going to bolt or become starry-eyed. "My mother is Esther Broadwater."

Kai cocked his head curiously. "I'm sorry, am I meant to know the name?"

Rhianne chuckled. "You obviously don't read 'Magic Now' or use much social media."

CHAPTER 2

"I don't, actually."

"Isn't that weird for a Tech Mage?" This time she laughed.

Kai made a face. "I know, but I hate social media. It's mostly full of rubbish."

Rhianne agreed. "True, you have to sort through a lot of that before finding little kernels that keep you in the game. I'd like to say that I mostly use it for the landscape business …"

Kai raised his eyebrows and Rhianne laughed again. When was the last time she'd laughed this much?

"Okay. Truthfully, I do mostly use it for my business, but I'll admit to occasionally looking up 'Magic Now' as well as Instagram." She gazed up at him and gave him a coy smile. "I like beautiful things."

Kai blushed and he cleared his throat. "So, who is Esther Broadwater?" Kai asked.

Trying to keep a straight face, Rhianne couldn't help the hint of amusement in her voice. "Don't worry, I'll spare you the horror of sifting through the latest in magical tabloid gossip." Her tone shifted to a more serious note as she braced herself for the revelation. "Okay, here it goes." She took a deep breath. "She's the High Witch, the big boss of the Sydney Coven and one of the state councillors."

The State Council was like a supernatural United Nations, with seven councillors each representing different factions. You had the witches, mages, shifters — usually a werewolf with an attitude — lesser fae, humans, and gargoyles. Then there were the smaller groups, like harpies and ogres, who didn't have the numbers for their own seat but still got a say. They played musical chairs with the Premier position, and her mother was eyeing the federal councillor seat — just a hop, skip, and a jump away from her ultimate goal of presidency. If politics was a game, her mother was playing to win.

"Oh, is that good or bad?" Kai asked.

"You're something else, you know." She shook her head but her light tone gave her mirth away. "Most people think it's all rainbows and butterflies having the Coven leader as a mum. Then there are those who'd assume that being a mere level two green witch in her shadow must be awful."

Kai waited, giving her the floor.

She let out a sigh. "Truth is, it's neither. But it leans more towards the not-so-great side. I'm always wondering if people are talking to me for me, or because of her. So, I keep mum about our connection and steer clear of her in public." She left out the part about avoiding her in private too.

"Well." Kai gave her a small smile, "I had no idea, so I guess I approached you because of you."

His honesty was disarming and charming. She took a sip of her tea to hide her pleased reaction. "I just realised I don't know your surname."

"Kai Wagner. I don't know your surname either. I'm guessing it isn't Broadwater?"

"Well met, Kai Wagner. I am Rhianne Alkenn."

"Well met, Rhianne Alkenn." He paused and opened his mouth only to then shut it again. He cleared his throat. "I'd like to see you again," he finally said.

Rhianne tugged at her pony tail; her fingers and toes tingled. What the heck, she liked him, right? "Do I need to give you my number, or do you already have it?" she waved her phone in front of him.

"I wouldn't dare without your permission." He grinned.

Rhianne's phone beeped with a message. "And now you

CHAPTER 2

have mine too," Kai said, a sparkle in his eyes. She rolled her eyes but couldn't hide the laughter that escaped her lips.

Kai insisted on paying the bill and they walked out together.

It was just a date, with a really nice guy who happened to like her, despite her weak halfling status. Someone who didn't recognise her mother's name.

"Saturday," Rhianne said. "There's a nice Thai place in Manly. I'll text you the address, unless you have something on?" She bit her lip.

"I'll be there with bells on." And he offered her a small bow.

Rhianne walked towards her bike with a spring in her step and rode back to the nursery. As soon as she parked her bike, Toto came trotting towards her with his tail wagging.

"Hey there," she leaned down. "I missed your company at breakfast." She patted the head of the fluffy white dog.

"Hmph!" Toto said. "You hardly eat anything for breakfast."

"Someone came up with the lie that breakfast is the most important meal of the day. Probably the cereal companies," she retorted.

"Look at you! There is no meat on your bones. How can you make a good wife if you are so thin?"

"You're so 17th-century. Besides, I have no intention of becoming a wife any time soon."

"I am merely suggesting that you could encounter Prince Charming and hinder your prospects because of your diet."

"Or I might miss kissing a slimy frog instead."

"That was a total myth. In reality, the prince was turned into a cat and lived his life happily catching mice in the palace, free of the burdens of royal responsibility."

Rhianne often wondered if Toto was teasing her or speaking the truth. He was as old as the hills, but he never divulged his actual age. Toto was a mysterious fae being who could transform into a handful of different creatures, but he preferred taking on the form of a Maltese dog. She had never witnessed him in his full fairy form, and perhaps she never would.

"So where were you early this morning and what was more important than giving me a lecture on breakfast eating?"

"I was out patrolling because I heard a strange noise last night and once again a couple of hours before dawn."

Rhianne frowned. "And what would you have done if it had been an intruder?"

Toto growled. "I can be fierce; I will have you know."

"Uh-huh," Rhianne said. "And did you find this intruder?"

"Had I found him, I would have ripped him to pieces. Or at the very least I would have scared him off with my superior strength and magic."

Rhianne covered her mouth with her hand and simulated a cough. "Well, lucky for him you didn't find him." Rhianne remembered the crime scene and sobered up. The possibility of someone lurking about, particularly, after the murder by Romin poison concerned her. She didn't like nor believe in coincidences.

"I thought I detected something when I was in the private garden last night, like a discordant note or a chilly breeze." She was trying to find the right words to describe the unsettling sensation. "It's probably nothing, but it felt a bit eerie, like a misplaced puzzle piece in an otherwise perfect picture."

"You mean, while you were practising elf magic?"

Rhianne snapped her face towards Toto and stopped abruptly. Toto, who had continued walking, realised she was no longer next to him, and he pivoted towards her.

"How do you know?"

CHAPTER 2

Toto rolled his eyes, which was downright weird for a dog. "Anyone within fifty feet with sufficient magic would have felt it." At her obvious dismay, he softened his expression. "Do not concern yourself overmuch, others would have felt the magic, but neither known the source nor the type of magic you were using."

"Is that so? Then how come you knew?"

Toto sighed. "I have a considerable history and I am both knowledgeable and powerful enough to discern many different types of magic. That includes elf magic."

History, huh? More like a few lifetimes' worth of experience, but she wasn't about to mention that. Rhianne swung open the side gate of the main garden. Could something have gone wrong in that time? She had been away for at least a couple of hours, right in the midst of a busy time. Luckily, she had Carl, a master gardener, and Alice, a whizz merchant, to rely on. Truth be told, they seemed to excel even more when left to their own devices.

Toto's words penetrated the worry swirling in her mind. "Rare only because elves choose not to live in our world." She could taste the bitterness in her words.

Toto placed his paws on her leg when she stopped, seemingly searching the horizon. She bent over to pat his head.

"Creating reliable portals to the elven world is no easy feat, and only a select few elves possess this ability. Portals, in general, are extremely challenging to master, which is why we rarely encounter beings from other realms, like Nel," Toto explained.

Rhianne's eyes widened. "Nel is from another realm?" She felt a bit foolish for assuming he belonged here.

Toto nodded, a solemn look on his face. "Some of the

races of beings inhabiting the Earth realm did not originate from here. While certain populous groups, such as gargoyles, werewolves, witches, or mages, are indeed native to this realm, there are others, demons like the incubi, who hail from different origins. Additionally, we cannot overlook the presence of the lesser fae, whose arrival coincided with one of the great storms, providing them with a temporary advantage in utilising portals." He paused, probably for effect. "As for Nel, that is his story to tell. But back to the elves, remember that, according to the elf queen's policy, elves remain in their home world unless given express permission to leave."

"I haven't seen or spoken to him in over five years, Toto. Surely, he could make an effort to send a message or something." Rhianne's voice broke a little.

"Perhaps there are other reasons —" Toto said.

"No, Toto. I'm not feeling charitable enough to invent excuses for him. Besides I have you and Nel and Tata Angelo. I'm fine," she said with as much conviction as she could muster.

"Let us not forget your mother," Toto sniggered.

"Don't you bring her up! She's more concerned with her coven and political aspirations than anything else." Rhianne spat the words. "And since when do you even pretend to like her?" Rhianne paused and did a facepalm. She had been had, but it had worked. Angel had effectively replaced her pity party. Point to Toto.

"Okay, Mr smarty pants. Did you find evidence of an intruder?"

"Some footprints outside the private garden. And to address your potential inquiry, they certainly did not belong to you, Carl, or Alice. These footprints were unmistakably recent,

CHAPTER 2

and should the need arise, I would be able to recognise the scent of the intruder."

"If they're a customer, they'll be back." Rhianne resolved to check the private garden to see if anything had been disturbed.

Just then the rumbling engine of a bus could be heard coming up to the gates. "Oh no, I forgot the kids' excursion is today." She raced to the front gates and put on her best smile. The school didn't pay her for the excursions, but she loved teaching the kids how to grow seeds and they came every week to visit their 'clients.'

The kids eagerly hopped off the bus, a lively bunch of third-years, jumping and whooping with excitement. Among them, Rhianne detected a couple of werepups, a budding witch and a lesser fae. The little fairy girl was particularly taken with the water lilies. In primary school, supernaturals and humans mingled freely. Rhianne hoped this harmony would persist as they grew older. Unfortunately, as they reached secondary school, parents often segregated supernaturals into separate schools.

As soon as the kids reached the front of the garden with their individual plants neatly lined up, their faces lit up with joy. Rhianne patiently moved from row to row, enthusiastically answering their questions and demonstrating proper techniques for watering and caring for their delicate seedlings. She then led the kids on some enjoyable educational activities. First, they made a game out of plant identification, then they did some bug watching, and finally, using leaves collected from the garden, the kids created beautiful leaf prints.

It was chaos for a couple of hours, and finally, the smiling kids with dirty hands and faces got on the bus.

Rhianne realised it was already three in the afternoon, and

she hadn't had lunch yet. She headed up to her apartment to grab something quick, but as she opened the door, she saw a large shadow moving to her left. Rhianne let out a small squeak, her heart racing as she tried to steady her breathing.

CHAPTER 3

"Hello, darling. You're a bit highly strung today. Were the kids naughty?"

As Rhianne stepped inside, the sunlight streaming in behind her, she was greeted by the sight of Nel. He was, without a doubt, a vision to behold. Standing at a towering six foot two, he had the kind of broad shoulders and narrow hips that didn't just suggest, but rather shouted, that the gym was his second home. His wavy blond hair, pulled back in a casual ponytail, only added to his allure, and his light blue eyes sparkled against his tanned skin.

There he was, leaning against the kitchen bench as if he was modelling for a kitchen appliance ad, a sly grin on his face. Nel, an unabashed incubus, had the art of seduction down to a T. And why wouldn't he? It was pretty much in his job description. In a world teeming with all kinds of supernaturals living alongside humans, incubi like Nel were a rarity. Rhianne couldn't recall ever meeting another incubus. They were even rarer than harpies, which was saying something.

He glided lazily towards her, his gaze full of promise, but

before he could pounce, Rhianne reached out and tickled him in the belly. There were some advantages to not being tall. Nel bent over.

"No, that's cheating!" he complained, but he was giggling. Rhianne continued tickling him, but he started retaliating and soon they were both on the floor out of breath and smiling at each other.

"Did you miss me?" Nel asked her.

"Of course. Who else could I tickle to death?" Rhianne answered.

"Then why haven't you been at the club?"

Rhianne grimaced. Nel was right. She had been neglecting her usual activities. "I know, I've been so busy with work and the business."

Nel shook his head, "You need to take a break, Rhianne. Come on, let's go to the gym and work off some of that stress. I need a partner for capoeira and there's no one else who can give me a run for my money."

Rhianne slapped his arm, "Flattery will get you everywhere. How about I have something light to eat first?" Rhianne could use a distraction and a friendly ear after today. She shouldn't give him the details of the murder, but it wouldn't surprise her if Nel was already in the know. His network was legendary, and not just with the ladies.

"I'll do you one better. Grab your gear and we'll stop at Bethany's on the way." Bethany's had fantastic salads and smoothies and it was conveniently located just a couple of blocks from their gym. Rhianne was already looking forward to a banana, mango, and honey smoothie.

Rhianne went to get her gear and then they headed out.

"I'll meet you there," Rhianne said, heading for the garage.

CHAPTER 3

"Don't want to be seen in my car?" Nel moved his brows up and down.

Nel was driving the red Alfa Romeo, which he treated like it was his first-born child. Rhianne couldn't care less about different car models, and the only reason she knew this was because Nel would go on and on about it, as if the car had its own fan club. Rhianne rolled her eyes. She secretly wondered if the Alfa Romeo had its own social media following and a hashtag like #RidingWithNel. It wasn't his only car either.

"You might pick up a hot chick at the gym and where would that leave me?" she answered. Women flocked to him, like bees to honey, but to be fair, he had never deserted her if he was giving her a lift, she just wanted to ride her bike.

"You wound me, my lady. When have I ever left you for another woman?"

"Last count, about fifty times."

Nel walked to her, grabbed her hand and kissed her knuckles tenderly, "They are only temporary distractions. You are my one and only, my forever."

That's exactly what worried Rhianne. In reality, Nel and her were best friends and had been for the last nineteen years, when she sneaked into the club after a fight with her mother. He found her, took her to a VIP area, and plied her with mocktails. They talked all night and then he took her home. It marked the start of a beautiful and enduring friendship.

Barring his meaningless flirting, he'd never tried anything romantic with her. More weirdly, she had never been attracted to him that way. Sure, he was downright beautiful and charming, but there were no sparks. Maybe that's what appealed to him: a female that didn't fall at his feet.

She shook her head. She wanted him to enjoy a romantic

relationship, but it seemed he had given up. It would be very hard for someone to accept that he physically needed to sleep with many to replenish himself. He had always been upfront about his nature and had never lied to anyone. It was just that most people couldn't handle the truth.

"Indeed," she said. "I'm the only one who can both outfight you and outdance you."

"What?" he sounded outraged. "Well, we need to place a bet on that."

"How much money are you willing to lose?" she asked with a sly grin.

"Only if you don't cheat."

"Ha!" she said. "There's no such thing as a fair fight, mister. It's either hit and run or hit and immobilise."

"True." He smiled, "Okay. I do have an ulterior motive for giving you a lift to the gym."

Rhianne cocked her head.

"I heard you were in the Parkes building this morning," Nel looked around to ascertain no one could overhear, "I heard Devlin Parkes is dead."

"That information's going to cost you."

"You know people offer to pay me for my company. Besides, you're dying to tell someone, Aren't you?"

"In return," she said, "You share with me what you know."

"Deal!" Nel said.

That Nel had agreed to her conditions was no surprise to Rhianne. He was the Sherlock Holmes of the supernatural world, minus the deerstalker hat but with a flair for the dramatic. Secret gathering and gossip trading were his forte, so much so that Rhianne often wondered if his club was just a façade for his true vocation as the supernatural world's top

CHAPTER 3

informant.

Nel was always one step ahead in the gossip game, knowing the latest scandal or secret before it even had time to simmer. Despite his love for uncovering others' mysteries, he was a vault when it came to his own — Fort Knox had nothing on him.

His interest in the murder case was probably like a kid in a candy store — an endless supply of secrets and scandals to uncover.

For Rhianne, though, the case was like a puzzle begging to be solved. Her fascination with mysteries probably stemmed from growing up around her mother's political chess games, a world swirling with plots and secrets. As a kid, it was like being in a real-life detective story, trying to piece together the puzzles around her.

On the way, she filled him in and when they arrived at Bethany's, a cosy diner in the heart of the city, they chose a secluded booth in the back. The place was nearly empty, save for a few regulars sipping coffee at the counter. Rhianne and Nel settled in and ordered some drinks.

"That's quite a shocking way to go." Nel took a sip of his drink.

Rhianne nodded, a shiver coursing down her spine as she pictured the body lying on the rug. "You seem more surprised at the method than the murder. Please don't tell me it's because it's a woman's weapon of choice."

"Darling, you and I know that's a misogynist myth sadly spread with the writings of Sherlock Holmes. In many countries, men make the majority of poisoners in prison. Of course, one could argue that women are smarter and are less likely to get caught. Or that men commit the majority of murders."

One of the most endearing qualities of Nel was that he was a total feminist.

"Devlin had plenty of enemies. I'm only surprised it took this long."

"Then why is poison weird and why were his enemies the kind who would kill?" Rhianne took a good swill of her smoothie.

"Poison is used in a very small minority of murders. My guess would be that you have no guarantee it will work. The good ones are difficult to find, and you have to get close to your victim."

"Yes, the one they used is pretty hard to come by and requires specialised knowledge. It also means he knew his killer."

"Not just knew, trusted. Devlin was a very suspicious character; I doubt he'd have drinks with just anyone."

"So, what made him such a good candidate for murder?" Rhianne asked.

"Let me count the ways, princess."

That was Nel's favourite nickname for her. Rhianne had loved the moniker when she was a teenager, then went through a phase where she rolled her eyes every time he said it. But Nel had persisted undeterred and now Rhianne quietly enjoyed it.

"One thing about climbing the ladder to be a top developer in this town," Nel took a sip of his latte, "you've got to be a bit ruthless. And Devlin? He took that to a whole new level. Picture a guy who'd happily evict old ladies for his next big project, offering them a pittance for their lifelong homes."

He set down his cup with a clink. "Then there was that time

CHAPTER 3

he played dirty over a piece of land meant for a children's charity. The deal was all but done, contracts nearly signed, and in swoops Devlin with a slightly higher offer, turning on the pressure. Made the seller an offer they couldn't refuse, even if it meant leaving the charity high and dry."

Rhianne was pretty sure the downwards set of his mouth wasn't due to the bitterness in his coffee.

"Two, you have to make sure your suppliers are kept on a tight leash. He has probably sent a half a dozen builders bankrupt with his demands and contract clauses. It got to the point where it was hard for him to find builders willing to work with him. Last I heard, he had to up the payments in his contracts. Three, he was a narcissist, who treated others as his servants at best and his slaves at worst. And that's coming from me."

"You're not a narcissist, Nel. At worst, you're — a little hedonistic," she said.

Nel sent a blinding smile her way, "You say that because you love me."

"I say that because I know you," she replied. Although it was true that she loved him. He was the older brother she had always wanted when she was younger and hated her life.

Nel nodded as if he had heard her inner monologue, "In any case, he has two children both in their early thirties with his ex-wife. The ex-wife walked away with far less than she was entitled. Andrea Parkes kept his surname and uses it to her advantage to get invited to parties and places. She's quite the socialite and you're likely to find her at high society events most nights."

That meant Rhianne wouldn't cross paths with her at all. She had stopped attending the events her mother sent her invitations to. Cosying up with her Netflix account and a bag of popcorn was far more entertaining than hobnobbing with the upper crust.

"It gets worse. He also kept the kids and indoctrinated them into his way of thinking and his business. Until relatively recently, they had no contact with their mother. They both work for him."

"Wow, what a nasty character. Are the kids the same?"

Nel leaned closer to her, even though there was no one around to hear. Rhianne loved this theatrical side of him and she felt the curve of her mouth going up.

"Arthur Parkes, dark hair, blue eyes and golden-brown skin. He's COO of Parkes Construction Enterprises and supposedly competent at it. There're rumours Arthur may not have been his father's offspring. He's bisexual, but he keeps that very much under the radar."

"Is that also a rumour?"

Wrinkles appeared at the corner of Nel's eyes. "I'd have said so if that was the case, but I have to say he's a very good-looking man."

"Let me guess, he goes to the club?"

"Princess, all of Sydney's elite up to the age of sixty have been to my club." Nel wasn't being boastful, just factual. "And you know better than to ask me to reveal my clientele." He mimed a zipper across his lips.

"That ship sailed a long time ago. I've been to the club so many times, I'm practically a fixture. But please go on."

Nel shook his head with a smile. "More like my right-hand woman," he corrected. "You've been indispensable to the success of the club."

And to top it off, she still managed the club's books, which

CHAPTER 3

were probably more balanced than her social life.

She had been in a dark place when she first started working for Nel. He encouraged her to study Business Administration and she ended up earning a Bachelor of Science and Business degree. This education gave her the confidence and skills to start her own business ten years ago. She owed Nel a big debt.

"Rita Parkes, natural blonde, blue eyes and on the big side," Nel continued. "She's Human Resources Director and very good at it. My sources tell me she should have been the COO. She's smarter and as canny as her father when it comes to business. But to add to Devlin's fabulous qualities, he is —" He paused and corrected himself, "was, a total chauvinist. Did I mention there is a new Mrs Parkes?"

"Young, right?" Rhianne could have bet she was younger than she was.

"Oh yes," Nel said. "They've only been married for five years, but she was twenty-four to his sixty at the time. I'd like to say she was his mid-life crisis, but Devlin was quite the ladies' man. Ever since his divorce, he has had a young thing on his arm at every event he attended. No particular type, blonds, brunettes, redheads, everyone under the sun. They usually only lasted a few months before being replaced. It's quite a mystery to many as to why he'd choose to end his bachelor's days and marry her." He took another sip of his coffee.

"Sarah Parkes. Not a natural blonde, but you wouldn't be able to tell. I happen to know her very expensive hairdresser. Sarah's quite a looker. Big brown eyes, a toned body that she works hard on with personal trainers, and impeccable makeup are her trademarks. She always looks perfectly put together, whether she's at a social event or running errands. No one knows how they met. She was an aged care worker and from a single-parent household, so it's unlikely they moved in the same circles. Love, of course, has a way, doesn't it, my darling?"

The image of Kai rose unbidden and her lips curved upwards of their own volition. If she thought that Nel missed the expression she was sorely mistaken. He was, after all, a master at interpreting people's moods. Sometimes it was as if he could read minds.

"You're holding out on me." He narrowed his eyes. "Spill, now!"

Rhianne sighed. Now that he was onto her, he wouldn't let it go. "Not much to tell. At the murder scene, there was a tech mage also working there."

Nel's grin nearly threatened to split his face in two. "Details, princess. Every. Single. One."

She told him about Kai, their catch-up and their upcoming date.

"I have to take you shopping," Nel said.

"I have plenty of things to wear."

"Rubbish! You have the dresses I keep for you at the club so you don't embarrass me. This requires a trip to the Mosman boutiques. Something that's sexy, but still casual. It needs to say, 'I like you' but you have to work for it."

Laughter easily burst from Rhianne's lips. "All of that in one dress?" She shook her head emphatically though. "I'm not spending a lot of money on an outfit I may never wear again."

"If I choose it, you'll love that dress and will never want to get rid of it."

She knew she wasn't going to win this argument. "In that case, we will go to a vintage shop. I'm not buying a new dress.

CHAPTER 3

It's a waste of money."

"It's my money to waste," Nel said.

Rhianne crossed her arms.

Nel raised his hands in mock surrender. "Okay, a vintage shop, but I get to choose it."

"Fine. Let's get to the gym so I can wipe that smile off your face."

"I'm also going to suggest you come to the club tonight, and not just because I miss having you around, which I totally do. Thursday night is when Arthur usually comes. Something tells me he isn't going to be too broken-hearted to skip it."

And wasn't that telling.

They headed straight for the gym. After getting changed into leggings and a crop top, Rhianne began her warm up with Nel.

Their usual workout area, a section larger than the size of a ring, with red mats on the floor, had a few people in it. As soon as Rhianne and Nel approached, they moved elsewhere. The conspicuous stools set up around the area for onlookers filled fast because Nel always attracted a fan crowd. Rhianne rolled her eyes at the sudden influx of attention, but she knew it was inevitable. Everyone wanted to see Nel fight.

Rhianne did a few stretches, while Nel charmed some of the people with quick questions about their families and fitness progress. Rhianne caught his eye after a few minutes and with a quick smile and a nod, Nel headed for the mats.

They began their warm-up together. As they did this several times a week, it was almost second nature. They didn't need to look at what the other was doing. They kept in perfect sync: Left leg back, arm forward, right leg back, the other arm forward. The key was treading lightly. You never stayed still; capoeira was all about movement. Swipe right leg around to the right, swipe left leg around to the left and swap. The Brazilians' slaves had hidden the fighting form as a dance, and so long as you were into acrobatics, that's what it looked like. Until you kicked your opponent and flattened them. She had seen fighters render their opponent unconscious in under a minute.

Rhianne grabbed her bottle, feeling the refreshing coolness of the water trickle down her throat. She wiped away some of the moisture that had formed on her forehead and took another long sip, feeling it hydrate her parched throat.

"Are you ready, big boy?" she asked.

Nel moved into position "I'm always ready, princess."

"Best of three?"

"Loser buys dinner at Ralph's next week."

Of course, only the best restaurant in town would do for Nel. "Sure, but I'm getting the Moreton Bay bugs in hollandaise."

"You're very sure of yourself," he said.

"Statistics back me up." Before she had even finished the sentence she had moved in and hit him on the chest, which made Nel stumbled backwards and out of the mats.

"One. Less talk and more action, big boy."

This time Nel moved in and swiped his leg in a long arc. There was a collective intake of breath around her. She managed to avoid the kick to her head by a fraction of an inch. She smiled broadly at him.

"Better."

Nel threw another kick this time aimed at her middle. Rhianne reacted by throwing herself down on a plank, then pivoted sideways and struck his calves. Nel fell on his knees.

"Two and I win!" She did a little victory dance.

CHAPTER 3

"He threw that fight on purpose. There is no way she could have got one on him otherwise," someone in the crowd accused.

Rhianne turned her body towards the speaker, her jaw and fists tensing. Before she could open her mouth, Nel had somehow positioned himself between her and the guy who had spoken. His white teeth were in full display, but his eyes were cold.

"My friend, I'd be very careful about casting aspersions on my character, particularly where Rhianne can hear you. She won't tolerate anyone offending me, and I'm feeling offended. Are you feeling lucky?"

Rhianne had to stifle a laugh, her annoyance evaporating as she struggled to keep a straight face. She tugged at Nel's T-shirt, and he turned to face her, his stern expression melting into a softer one.

"I think the idiot got the message," she said.

Indeed, the 'friend' had already made a hasty retreat. Leaning in, she whispered into Nel's ear, "You missed your chance to say 'punk' at the end."

Nel winked.

CHAPTER 4

After a brief shower at the gym, they hopped in Nel's car and drove to a small Spanish restaurant on the way to the club.

"I was hoping that you would have lost your touch after missing a few days of practice."

"You wish," Rhianne grabbed a garlic prawn with her fork.

"How invested are you in this investigation?" Nel reached for the potatoes 'bravas.'

"I'm curious but also kind of concerned professionally. Whoever did this, knew about the poison and how to get it. That kind of knowledge puts places like my plant nursery under the microscope, making us look bad. If this whole thing blows up, they might start cracking down on us selling and having plants like this."

"I suppose it's possible that someone would commit murder just to increase profits."

Rhianne's fork paused in mid-air. "Yes, but you're forgetting that Devlin knew his murderer, so that indicates a more personal reason."

"Money, power and greed are very powerful motivators."

CHAPTER 4

Rhianne savoured the succulent prawn, deep in thought. "It's quite the mystery. I'm probably more interested in the how than the who, but they go hand in hand, I suppose."

Nel chuckled, his eyes glinting with amusement. "You're hooked, aren't you? I know that look. You've always been curious and puzzles simply fascinate you."

"And Toto would tell you that curiosity killed the cat. You aren't fooling me, though. You also seem to have a particular interest in this. Why's that?"

Nel's gaze shifted upwards and to the side as if recalling a distant memory.

"I was part of the board of that children's charity I mentioned." He sported a sour expression. "We found another site in the end, but it meant an additional four months and extra funds. He didn't need the site that badly."

Rhianne leaned in.

"I'm not overly bothered that he was killed," Nel continued, his tone darkening. "In fact, I seriously contemplated the deed for a while."

Rhianne slapped his arm and narrowed her eyes at him.

"Ouch!" Nel feigned hurt. "I was quite angry at the time, and he certainly isn't much of a loss to anybody."

"His widow might be devastated for all you know."

Nel flapped his hand. "Sure, she is."

"So, let me guess, you're going to grill Arthur tonight?"

Nel looked up at her, a sly smile playing on his lips. "Oh no, I'm not."

Her mouth felt dry all of a sudden. "Uh, oh."

Nel continued, his expression turning serious. "But I do know a thing or two about Arthur. He has a penchant for petite redheads and he gets very talkative after his second glass of whisky."

"I'm not a redhead." She really didn't like where this was going.

"Nothing that a good wig wouldn't fix and I have plenty of those at the club."

"What if he sees me afterwards and recognises me? That would be thoroughly embarrassing."

Nel tapped his chin. "We are due for a mask night for the ladies. Problem solved."

"Nel! I am not good at flirting, let alone seduction." Rhianne's voice took an edge of panic.

"Look, he's not bad on the eyes, and all you have to do is listen, nod and 'Uh huh' at the right times and he'll tell you his full life story."

"You sound awfully confident for someone who isn't going to be doing the deed."

"Good grief, Rhianne, I'm not asking you to sleep with the guy! Just talk to him, and if he gets handsy, leave. And how do you think I get most of my information?"

"I'd have thought that was pillow talk," Rhianne said and regretted it immediately. "I didn't mean —"

Nel flicked his wrist in dismissal. "You know I don't take offence to that, darling. I've come to terms with who I am. But to answer your question, surprisingly, there isn't much talk after the event. It all usually happens before."

Still feeling the embarrassment of her gaffe, Rhianne realised she had lost the argument and would now have to follow through. "Yes, fine. I'll try, but no promises."

"That's my girl!" Nel rubbed his hands. "I have just the outfit for it."

Rhianne sighed and reluctantly accepted that she had no

CHAPTER 4

choice but to surrender.

* * *

"No, absolutely not. No way, Jose, not wearing that —" Rhianne stared at the shiny cloth Nel held in one hand. "That handkerchief," she finally spat out.

Nel's eyes swept over Rhianne's figure. "Darling, you have a fantastic body. Many women half your age would simply die to have a physique like yours."

Rhianne crossed her arms and tapped her foot. "Flattery is your favourite weapon and it isn't going to work this time."

Nel smiled. "It isn't flattery when it's the truth."

"Fine. Give it!" Rhianne was never particularly body conscious around Nel, so she started to undress. As Rhianne slipped into the bandage dress, Nel helped her adjust the fit so that the pleats that ran horizontally looked just right. The royal blue beads that adorned the neckline shimmered in the light as she twirled in front of the mirror. Simple swirls gave way to a thick choker that hugged the base of her throat, completing the elegant look.

Rhianne smiled at her reflection. She had to admit, she looked good in the dress. "What do you think?" she asked.

"You look absolutely stunning. Arthur won't know what hit him. I knew it would fit you like a glove as soon as I saw it."

"Wait! You bought it for me? How long have you been planning this?"

"Tsk. I bought it a couple of weeks ago. No ulterior motive, except to see you looking gorgeous." Nel gave her a pair of blue dangling earrings and a cuff to match. He then produced a pair of diamante heels. "This should go with the dress and they're only three inches, so you should be perfectly comfortable."

"Comfort and heels cannot be put together in the same sentence, big boy." But she let him slip them on. She knew her feet would wage a rebellion by the end of the night, but hey, at least they looked fabulous together.

Nel rifled through a drawer and pulled out an exquisite black Venetian mask. Intricate silver filigrees surrounded the eye openings, and blue and silver feathers adorned the right-hand side, attached by an ornate metal piece that resembled an ivy branch. Rhianne marvelled at the attention to detail in the craftsmanship.

As she admired the mask, Nel picked up a long red wig and began to brush it out. "I thought this might complete the look," he held out the wig for her to inspect.

"It looks very natural," she observed.

"Indeed, it's made of real hair and treated to keep the waves looking soft and natural."

Rhianne made a face. "I meant the mask."

"The mask is priceless, literally. It was made by a friend in Italy, who wanted me to have a memory of our time together. A true maestro."

"Are we talking about the Renaissance here?" Rhianne asked.

She hoped he wasn't insinuating that Leonardo da Vinci had a hand in crafting the mask, but she was too scared to ask. After all, if that turned out to be true, she might be on the verge of putting a priceless work of art on her face.

Nel placed the wig on her and fussed until he was happy with how it sat. He then secured the mask on Rhianne with

CHAPTER 4

straps and pins.

"A gentleman never talks about his age." He winked at her. "Please do not lose it. I'm rather fond of those memories."

Sometimes it was hard to tell when he was joking and when he was serious, but she was sure she detected a wistful tone underneath the lightness.

Rhianne crossed her right arm and placed her fist over her heart. "I will protect it with my life."

Leaning down, Nel gave her a kiss on top of her head. "No, princess, you are far more precious to me than some lovely memento."

"You just want a rematch," she said.

His laughter filled the small fitting room and it gladdened her heart.

"What's the plan?" she asked.

"I'll take you up to the VIP section. I doubt anyone would recognise you like this, but, as you know, my employees are well-trained and paid to be discreet." They walked out the door and towards a set of stairs. "Once there, I'll introduce you and make myself scarce. The fact that you're with me will ensure he'll behave, but will also encourage him to try to win you over."

"Men!" she said. "Besides, you always have a woman on your arm."

"Subtle difference, my dove. I always walk out with a woman on my arm. I never walk in with one."

As Nel led her into the VIP section, Rhianne felt a rush of excitement. Despite having been there during the day, the transformation of the room at night was always striking.

The moody lighting created an alluring atmosphere, and the bass from the club's music could be felt vibrating through the floor. The Devil's Advocate Club, or the Devil's as it was known, was housed in a massive warehouse near the Harbour Bridge, catering to both humans and supernaturals, mostly the affluent ones. The main space boasted a swirling dance floor and blaring music, while the VIP section had a more refined ambience. Soft, pleasant music wafted through strategically placed speakers, and plush sofas occupied most of the area. Against one wall, a sleek bar displayed a large selection of drinks that could satisfy the fussiest of drinkers. Rhianne also knew that if anyone desired something special, the cellar beneath them housed an impressive collection of wines that would make the most serious of wine connoisseurs salivate.

The volume of voices chatting reduced significantly as they entered and many pairs of eyes swivelled in their direction. Nel took on his suave European duke persona. For all she knew, he was genuinely a duke. He certainly played the part to perfection. Even his gait changed as if he was engaged in some slow and sensual dance.

People began approaching and she was quite pleased that, apart from some curious looks, no one seemed interested in engaging her in conversation. Nel affected a slight accent as he smiled at some, nodded at others, and inserted well-placed comments from time to time. So that's what he meant when he asked her to talk to Arthur. She wondered if he had arrived or even if he would turn up. She need not have worried. Nel squeezed her hand lightly and tilted his face to the left. With a skill she envied, he gracefully untangled himself from the current conversation and tugged her across the room. Rhianne tried to guess who Arthur was from the description Nel had given. Sure enough, she spotted him

CHAPTER 4

among a small group. When the group realised who was coming, they magically opened up to allow Nel and her to enter.

"Arthur, my man. How are you?" Rhianne noted Nel made no mention of his father's death, and that made sense, given the police and the family were keeping quiet about it. If Arthur was in the middle of grieving, he was hiding it extremely well. He greeted Nel with a pat on the back in that semi-hug some men seemed to favour.

As she approached, the man's smile widened, revealing a set of blindingly white teeth. Rhianne took a moment to study him, admiring his handsome features. He had a well-built physique, broad shoulders, and nice biceps partially visible beneath his rolled-up sleeves, suggesting that he was a regular gym-goer. His dark skin was a surprise, as she had expected him to have the same pale complexion as his father. Admittedly, the pallor of death would have made it lighter. Nonetheless, she wondered if the rumours were well founded around his parentage. His hair was dark and curly, but his eyes, as he turned towards her with a ready smile, were a light blue.

"Nel, where have you been keeping this gorgeous lady hidden?" Nel smiled in a secretive way.

"Rose is shy, I'm afraid."

Rose? That's the name we're going with? She tried to shoot him a 'you-can't-be-serious' look with her eyes. But Nel was unflappable and just patted her hand.

A server came out of nowhere and whispered to Nel.

Nel straightened up, although he kept his smile. "Arthur, I'm so sorry. I have a bit of an emergency in my hands. Do you mind looking after Rose for a little while?"

Arthur nodded with enthusiasm. "Of course, Nel, she'll be safe with me."

Rhianne snorted, and Nel covered it by brushing a kiss on her lips. "Stay with Arthur." There was merriment in the way his eyes crinkled. "I won't be too long."

Arthur moved to her side, giving his friends the brush, and offered her his arm. "Shall we go and sit somewhere quieter, beautiful Rose?"

Gagging would not go down well, so Rhianne forced a smile. "That sounds delightful." She leaned into his arm.

Rhianne felt a twinge of unease as she and Arthur settled onto the sofa tucked away in a dimly lit corner. She wasn't thrilled about the privacy it afforded them, but she had a job to do and Arthur seemed to be falling for her ruse. She needed to stay focused and keep him interested.

"Call me Art. All my friends do."

Rhianne gave him what she hoped was a wicked smile. "Arthur." She enunciated the syllables. "I hardly know you. In fact, I know nothing about you, except your name."

Rhianne hoped her sassy attitude didn't turn him off. It was hard to pretend to be someone else, especially someone dim-witted and pliable. But Arthur threw his head back and laughed.

"You're very refreshing, Rose. I can see why Nel likes you." He stared at her as if waiting for an answer.

A coy smile was all he was going to get out of that statement.

"What would you like to know?" He studied her as if trying to decide which part of him would impress her the most.

She waited in silence. Most people couldn't handle the vacuum. Arthur was no different.

"I'm the CEO of my own company," he blurted.

CHAPTER 4

"What sort of company?" she asked as if being the CEO was neither here nor there. Interesting that he was already calling himself the CEO when his father's body wasn't even cold yet.

He raised his eyebrows; he probably had been expecting her to be impressed. "A construction development one. One of the largest in the country."

"Have you been the CEO for long?" She crossed her fingers hoping she wasn't pushing too hard.

He blinked a few times and then tried to collect himself. "Not very long at all," he said. "My father passed away recently."

Yeah, like yesterday. She made herself touch his hand. "I'm sorry for your loss."

His confidence was boosted by the gesture and he put his hand over hers.

"Well, it's extremely upsetting. I guess I'm here to drown some of the grief with a drink or two and some good company."

I bet it is. She had to make herself look like she believed him. "Such responsibility on young shoulders. Do you have other family you can rely on?"

He preened at her words. Really, could it be that easy?

"I look younger than I am, and most of the responsibility falls on me. Of course, I have support. I have an excellent technical guy who is my second in command. There's also my sister who works for the company as the Director of Human Resources. She's — dealing with this in her own way."

"I imagine your mother is devastated."

Arthur snorted. "My parents have been divorced for a number of years and it wasn't amicable. In fact, it's only in the last few months that I've reconnected with my mother."

He chuckled. "Imagine, here I am, sharing my life's greatest hits with a total stranger."

"Lucky I don't have to stretch my imagination too far." She offered him a sickly sweet smile. "Do you have a step-mum, then, who can offer some emotional support?"

"My step mother nearly went hysterical with the news, which frankly surprised me."

"Surprised you why?"

"She looks the part of the glamorous wife, but there's nothing dumb about beautiful Sarah. In the five years I've known her, she has never, ever lost her cool. Not even when that silly sausage dog of hers was run over by Dad as he reversed his car. It wouldn't have surprised me if he did it on purpose. I mean, she knew he didn't like dogs and she still went and got it."

"Are you saying she didn't love him?"

"Dad constantly warned us to be wary. That people would only be after the money."

"Do you agree?" Rhianne was genuinely curious to hear his answer. What a sad way of living.

"I agree it's hard to tell, but no I don't think so. My father and I didn't always see eye to eye."

"Do you mean about the business?" she asked.

"Don't lead the witness, counsellor," she thought, suppressing a smirk that threatened to lift the corners of her mouth. After all, this wasn't a courtroom, but a casual conversation that might just turn into a comedy of errors.

"About quite a number of things. My father was — old-fashioned. I thought we should be doing more modern buildings and expanding overseas."

"What about personally? You said it wasn't just business."

CHAPTER 4

"You are a curious one, aren't you?"

"I'm trying to get to know you, Art. I want to know what makes you tick."

Arthur's face lit up upon hearing his nickname, and he placed his hand on Rhianne's forearm. She was, oh so tempted to remove it.

"Unlike my old man, who was all about money and work, I find joy in many things. Like sailing and playing basketball. And hey, I can appreciate the beauty of the world around me too." His hand glided along her arm. "My father hardly ever let himself have fun on weekends unless it was some fancy networking thing where he could rub elbows with the big shots. Funnily enough, my sister ended up taking after him more than I did. He was — disappointed in me." He furrowed his brows before changing the topic. "But enough about me. Let's talk about you, Rose. What's your story?"

Uh oh! Rhianne's heart rate quickened as she struggled to come up with something to say to Arthur. She eventually uttered, "I love nature."

Arthur nodded.

As if summoned by her desperation, Nel appeared and placed his hands on her shoulders. His smile appeared brittle to her and Arthur withdrew his arm. "There you are." He fixed his stare on her. "I know I promised a night of fun, but I'm afraid we'll have to leave."

"Of course." She sighed in relief.

Nel glanced over her shoulder at Arthur. "Thank you for keeping Rose company. I'm looking forward to our next conversation."

"Same here." Arthur tilted his chin down and offered a weak smile.

Rhianne got up and turned to say goodbye. Arthur's lips brushed against the back of her hand. "Until next time," Arthur released her hand.

As they stepped outside, they were greeted by the sight of a large, imposing bodyguard standing sentry at the entrance to the inner sanctum.

Nel nodded to the guard, and they continued on their way.

"How did it go? You appeared ready to bolt." Nel's eyebrows drew together.

"I'm not sure whether to feel relieved or offended by that." Rhianne took off the mask. "He shared a wealth of fascinating information with me. He also gave me a piece of paper when he kissed my hand."

She unfolded it.

It was a phone number neatly inscribed, with 'Art' elegantly scrawled at the bottom.

CHAPTER 5

Nel's office served as the backdrop for their debriefing session. Rhianne, having shed both the wig and the mask, now found herself reclining on the sofa, having abandoned her heels along the way.

"He's totally smitten," Nel declared.

"First of all, no one says 'smitten' anymore. You're showing your age, big boy." Rhianne scowled at him. "Second of all, he was just intrigued because of you. He'll soon forget all about 'little old me'."

"There's nothing old about you," Nel said and Rhianne pointedly ignored the omission of 'little' in that statement. "And I don't think so. It sounds to me like you made quite the impression."

"I thought I'd scared him off."

"Let me guess, you didn't follow the script and went snarky on him."

"I prefer sassy, but whatever."

"You hooked him by being you." His lips curved upwards; he was enjoying himself.

Rhianne shrugged. "I'm not sure we learned anything all

that useful."

"But, princess, we did learn something valuable," Nel exclaimed. "We confirmed that he's not the least bit torn up about his dear old father's untimely demise. And the ex-wife might be celebrating with a happy dance. As for the sister, the jury is still out, but the current wife — she's putting on quite the hysterical act, when that's out of character."

"It sounds like all of them had a possible motive." Rhianne held up her fingers. "Arthur becomes CEO and he no longer has to put up with his father's boorishness and probable bullying. Both children are likely to inherit a large part of his fortune. The ex-wife probably held a grudge a mile long. The current wife is also likely to be up for a nice sum. And that's not even counting any of the people he screwed over."

"Yes, but that takes us to opportunity. The culprit must have been someone intimately familiar with him, someone who could have shared a cup of coffee in his office."

"That means we can discount the ex-wife."

Nel shook his head. "Not necessarily. She could have easily fabricated an excuse, like needing to discuss matters concerning the children. However, I agree that she's less likely to have done it compared to the others."

"That leaves the means. Who knew and had access to Romin?" She paused, considering the situation. "I think if we're in agreement that they are the most likely culprits, we need to dig deeper into their backgrounds."

"The easiest thing is to look into the financial side and confirm a motive. If daddy was displeased with the children, or if his business was on the verge of bankruptcy, that could change the whole picture. I know someone —"

Rhianne interjected, "You know everyone who is worth

CHAPTER 5

knowing in Sydney and beyond."

Nel chuckled softly. "That may be true, but when it comes to financial matters and an ongoing murder investigation, it becomes a bit more delicate. It might take me a few days to gather the necessary information. In the meantime, perhaps you can see what you can glean from your date on Saturday night. Your connections might run deeper than mine."

Rhianne entertained the thought of giving him a good kick, even if it meant sacrificing her comfortable position. Almost worth the effort. Almost.

"I also happen to know that our bereaved Sarah Parkes has a standing appointment at The Belmont's Luxury Spa every Saturday at lunchtime. How do you feel about getting pampered?"

"If she's truly so overwhelmed with grief over her husband's passing, I highly doubt she'll have the inclination to show up at the spa." She admitted that the idea of a spa day held a certain appeal. It had been far too long since she last treated herself.

"I find it hard to believe that anyone, particularly his trophy wife, would genuinely mourn the loss of Devlin Parkes," Nel said. "Sure, she might be putting on a grand performance for the benefit of others, but that doesn't necessarily mean she'll abandon her pampering routine. If anything, the expectations for her to look flawless at the funeral might encourage her to indulge even more. I've been told that she goes to great lengths, paying up to six months in advance, to secure her spot at the spa and ensure she gets her favourite masseur."

"Let's also remember that neither the police nor the family have issued a statement about the death, so maybe she can justify it by saying she's keeping up appearances."

"Worse comes to worse, you'll have two hours to beautify yourself for your date." Nel winked at her. "And then I'm taking you shopping."

"Why am I the one going to the spa instead of you?" Rhianne asked. While the idea of pampering herself sounded appealing, she wasn't entirely sure if she could handle another interview. Tricky gnomes were more her specialty than grieving wives. And given how well she'd been doing with the gnomes …

"You have this uncanny ability to connect with people, especially the ladies. It wouldn't be much of a sacrifice on your part, considering how beautiful you described her to be," Rhianne said.

"She'd be reluctant to speak about her recently dead husband if she wanted to flirt with me," Nel said. "Besides, you did an amazing job with 'Art.'" Nel snickered.

"That could have been a fluke, and I hate to say it, but he was trying to seduce me. Are you saying she is into women?"

"If she is, she keeps it well hidden, but I have a suspicion she would be more open with another well-off woman of the same age." Nel put his hand up to forestall any arguments from her. "I suspect your sarcasm would also appeal to her, so no need to pretend to be ditzy."

"What makes you think that?"

"Anyone who got Devlin Parkes to commit to another marriage and stayed married to him for five years has to have some serious smarts about them. I think there's a lot more depth to Sarah Parkes than she reveals."

Nel gave Rhianne a lift home. She leaned over and planted a kiss on his cheek.

"I'll pick you up tomorrow at ten-thirty," Nel said.

Rhianne stood for a moment watching as the car disap-

CHAPTER 5

peared around the corner before she turned and made her way towards her apartment.

As Rhianne reached the stairs leading to her apartment, she realised she hadn't checked on the private garden to look at the Romin plant. But it was well past one in the morning, sleep was a higher priority.

Toto greeted her with an enthusiastic bark, sniffing her legs. "Did you go to the club today?"

"Why? Do I smell like Nel?"

"Only a faint hint of it. I could detect the scent of leather lounges and an unfamiliar cologne, likely belonging to a male," Toto said, his tone carrying a touch of accusation.

Despite her weariness, Rhianne couldn't help the corners of her mouth tugging upwards.

"Jealous, are we?" she teased.

"No one can ever replace the illustrious Toto," he declared. "However, I would be most delighted if you were to find a suitable husband. Naturally, I would have to grant my approval first. He must possess striking good looks and undeniable charm, radiating an aura of serenity and trustworthiness. A man of impeccable character, respected by all and cherished for his unwavering loyalty and astute intelligence."

Rhianne snorted at the lofty expectations. "Well, Toto, that's quite the list. I'm sure there's a multitude of men out there just waiting to check off every box."

Toto nodded with an air of wisdom, oblivious to any hint of sarcasm. Rhianne couldn't fathom why she bothered.

"No need to worry about that, Toto. I've made it clear multiple times that I have no interest in finding a husband," she said. She had decided to keep her upcoming date with Kai under wraps. Rhianne suspected that Toto might take it upon himself to venture to the restaurant and personally assess Kai if he knew. She deemed it wise to shift the conversation to a different topic.

"Actually, Nel and I were playing detectives." She unlocked the door to her apartment and Toto followed her inside, his tail wagging with enthusiasm.

"It's advantageous not to be actively seeking, as it can create an allure of disinterest that tends to attract men," Toto said. "There's nothing quite like a touch of challenge to captivate their attention."

Rhianne smirked. "You are like a dog with a bone, aren't you?"

"Ha-ha. Not that funny," Toto said, proving he at least understood humour.

Toto's musings echoed Nel's comment about Arthur being attracted to her. Rhianne was pretty sure that his interest primarily stemmed from male-driven competition, though. Nevertheless, she couldn't ignore the fact that Arthur had been willing to defy Nel's authority by pursuing her. Despite Arthur's charm and finesse, anyone acquainted with Nel knew better than to trifle with him. His reputation, built on countless stories, meant no one in their right mind would want to mess with him.

A memory flashed in her mind, recalling an incident during one of the club's VIP events. A senior politician had slapped her butt hard as she walked past. She had spun around, fully intending to unleash a verbal onslaught on him. However, before she could utter a single word, Nel materialised by her side, anger etched across his face. He had told the politician in no uncertain terms that he was not welcome in the club. The man stood there, dumbfounded and flustered,

CHAPTER 5

attempting to assert his importance through incoherent babbling. Rhianne thought he was a complete fool for arguing with Nel, especially when she noticed the muscles in his neck straining against his skin. Eventually, the club's guards had intervened, forcibly removing the politician while he continued to shout insults and threats at Nel until he was finally dragged away.

A couple of months later, whispers of scandal began circulating among the public, unveiling the involvement of the politician with a married woman — a prominent television anchor. The news sparked a firestorm of controversy as both the politician's long-time wife and the husband of the television anchor took to their social media accounts to denounce the illicit affair.

The politician's estranged wife, cutting through the chaos with icy precision, issued a statement declaring that the anchor was more than welcome to the "good-for-nothing cheat." She proclaimed that she and her three daughters were infinitely better off without him.

In a rather symbolic gesture, the anchor's husband opted for a more visual approach. He shared an image on social media, capturing a pile of clothes and assorted belongings strewn across his front yard.

It could have been a coincidence and the gossip might have surfaced regardless, but Rhianne couldn't shake the strong suspicion that Nel had played a role in its revelation. True to his nature, Nel remained tight-lipped, neither confirming nor denying his involvement.

"What investigation are you two embarking upon?" Toto settled himself onto his cherished sofa and curled up, his ears perked.

"The police brought me in as a consultant for a murder case involving a big-shot developer downtown. Turns out, it was Romin," Rhianne explained.

Toto raised his head. "You have Romin in your private garden nursery."

"Yes, indeed. But it's not just our garden; there are half a dozen others, along with a handful of chemists and hospitals." Rhianne twisted a strand of her hair.

"And all of this happened right after that intruder incident. I do not like coincidences."

"That's why Nel and I are on the case," Rhianne grabbed a glass of water. "But honestly, I'm totally beat right now. It's time to call it a night. Tomorrow morning, I'll swing by the private nursery and see if anything looks off."

Toto leapt down from the bed, his tail held high and trailed after her right to her bedroom door. He usually slept on one of the armchairs in the lounge room or any secluded spot where he could vanish into the shadows.

Rhianne collapsed onto the bed. Fatigue washed over her, carrying her into the realm of dreams. However, even in slumber, her mind remained restless, replaying the day's events in an endless loop. The nagging sensation that she was in over her head.

The following morning, Rhianne had barely taken a sip of her freshly brewed coffee when her phone abruptly rang. Alice's voice sounded urgent on the other end. "We've got a situation near the gates. Can you come over?"

Rhianne frowned. "What kind of situation?" Before she could get a response, the call abruptly ended, leaving her with nothing but silence.

Swearing under her breath, Rhianne glanced at the clock. It

CHAPTER 5

was a mere seven in the morning. She couldn't fathom what could have gone wrong.

A large delivery truck occupied a parking spot, and from the other side, Rhianne could hear the sound of raised voices. She trotted around the truck and saw Alice, standing toe-to-toe with the sturdy truck driver. Carl hung back a few feet behind Alice, fidgeting with his cap and shifting from foot to foot. Conflict wasn't his thing, and Rhianne couldn't blame him for it. Alice, on the other hand...

"This is the second time you've tried to pass sub-standard potting mix as seed raising speciality mix. You're nothing but a crook!"

"What would you know? Do they teach you the different tastes of dirt where you come from?" The truck driver's face flushed with anger, his voice seething with contempt.

Alice took a defiant step forward. Before Rhianne could react, Carl interposed himself, wrapping his arms around his sister, holding her back.

"Hey!" Rhianne's voice pierced through the commotion as she strode toward the scene. The burly driver, Joe, snapped his head to look at her.

"You should hire better *people* for your nursery." Joe sneered. "Being around spooks is icky, you know. You watch out or you might catch their nasties." He wrinkled his nose.

Rhianne's gaze sharpened as she locked eyes with him. She counted to ten. "You know what? You're absolutely right."

The truck driver shot Alice a triumphant smile.

"My plant nursery will no longer do business with your company."

Joe's mouth opened and closed. Carl moved Alice to the side and took a step forward. Joe recoiled.

"That's a threat, that is! I'll call the authorities," he warned, his voice cracking.

"You do that, Joe," Rhianne said. "I'm sure the police will be thrilled to hear from such an upstanding citizen like yourself."

Joe spluttered something unintelligible, climbed back into his truck and drove off. Rhianne turned her attention to Alice and Carl, who was rocking back and forth.

"Thank you for standing up for us," Carl said.

Rhianne shook her head. "Well, that certainly wasn't the best way to start the morning."

"I'm sorry, boss," Carl muttered, his gaze fixed on the ground.

Alice, however, continued to glare at the swirling dust left behind by the departing truck. "I'm not sorry at all. Good riddance," she spat.

Rhianne let out a weary sigh. "Indeed, good riddance. But now I'll have to find us a new supplier, and to make matters worse, I have to leave by ten thirty this morning," she said.

There was no point in dwelling on it, though. Rhianne went to her office and started making calls.

She finally secured a supplier who could arrange a delivery later that afternoon at a reasonable price. Caught up in the process, she realised she hadn't had a chance to take a shower or change out of her T-shirt and shorts.

"Tough morning?" Nel asked, leaning against the doorframe of her office. He appeared particularly dashing that morning, donning a white jacket, a baby blue shirt with an open collar, and impeccably tailored navy pants.

Rhianne's attention shifted from her current predicament, and she spun around to face the clock positioned behind her. "Oh no, what time is it?"

CHAPTER 5

"Relax!" Nel sauntered over. He began massaging her neck and shoulders, easing the tension that had built up. "It's only just gone past ten thirty," he reassured her. "I had a feeling you might forget, so I wanted to make sure we had plenty of time to get you ready."

Rhianne felt herself gradually relaxing under the skilled pressure of Nel's hands. "Has anyone ever told you that you have absolutely heavenly hands?" she said. Nel chuckled, causing a blush to rise to Rhianne's cheeks. "Scratch that," she continued, "Of course, they have. What was I thinking?"

Suddenly, Nel's comment registered in Rhianne's mind, breaking through her momentary bliss. "Wait a minute! What do you mean by 'getting me ready'? Aren't I going to a spa where I'll be practically half-naked anyway?"

"Princess, for what we're about to do, I need you to look the part of the pampered girlfriend," Nel explained.

Rhianne raised an eyebrow, observing Nel's attire. "Is that why you're dressed like that this early on a Saturday?"

She was teasing because Nel always dressed up. He never did casual.

"Exactly." Nel grinned. "I'll play the role of the wealthy boyfriend, so smitten that I even accompany my girlfriend to the spa."

"Uh-huh. So, which one of your cars did you bring for that?" Rhianne asked.

Nel had quite the car collection, totalling four, at least the last time she took inventory. She'd often teased him about having just one pair of hands and feet to drive them all, but Nel remained unfazed by such practical concerns. He had a soft spot for his cars.

"A car needs to fit the occasion," he'd argue.

"I'll get you a custom milk bottle holder for the cockpit for Christmas then," she said. "That way you can do the milk run in the Formula 1 racer."

Nel interrupted her thoughts by answering her question. "The Lamborghini."

"And you parked it here?" Rhianne squeaked. The Lamborghini held a special place in Nel's heart, so the fact that he would choose to park it in her unpaved parking lot surprised her.

Nel shrugged his shoulders. "I've got my eye on a new model coming out in a couple of months," he said. "Would you like this one as a birthday present?"

"You bought that one less than a year ago." Rhianne tut-tutted. "Besides, you know I'm not into fancy cars."

"Just motorbikes."

Yeah, yeah. She knew what he thought of her favoured mode of transportation.

Rhianne smirked. "Oh, really? Care to challenge my 'just motorbike' to a hundred-metre race?"

"You'd shatter my fragile male pride, so I prefer to remain blissfully ignorant," Nel said. He then lifted several bags, filled with clothes. "Let's give these a try, shall we?"

The phrase from *The Hitchhikers Guide to the Galaxy*, "Resistance is useless!" echoed in her mind.

"All right," she said. "Let me take a quick shower first."

After her shower, Rhianne dedicated fifteen minutes to trying on various outfits. She wasn't particularly fussy about her clothing choices, but it was Nel who was indecisive, prolonging the decision-making process.

"Look," she finally said, after attempting the same four outfits for the third time. "This one's fine."

CHAPTER 5

Rhianne stood before the mirror, donning a short high-waisted white skirt paired with a matching halter-neck top.

Nel relented. "You won't get off so easily when we go shopping this afternoon," he warned her.

"Why can't I wear one of these outfits for the date?" Rhianne asked. She inwardly winced, realising that she had unintentionally referred to her dinner with Kai as a date. Fortunately, Nel seemed oblivious to her slip.

"These are pampered girlfriend outfits," Nel explained. He handed Rhianne a small box, which she opened to reveal a stunning collection of jewellery. Delicately crafted gold earrings, two necklaces of different lengths, a dainty bracelet, and an elegant ring were nestled inside.

Rhianne hesitated for a moment, unaccustomed to wearing so much jewellery at once. However, Nel insisted. She carefully put on the earrings, feeling their subtle weight against her earlobes, while Nel expertly fastened the necklaces around her neck. The bracelet adorned her wrist flawlessly, and the ring slid onto her finger smoothly.

Hand in hand, Rhianne and Nel strolled into the Spa, with Nel casting an adoring look in Rhianne's direction. Nel had strategically parked their car near the front entrance so that the reception staff would notice the impressive vehicle and the couple's arrival.

"I've made an appointment for my girlfriend for the ultra-luxury package," Nel said.

A wide grin spread across Rhianne's face as she beamed at him. "Oh, you spoil me!"

"Only the best for you, my darling." Nel patted her hand.

The receptionist cleared her throat. "Can I please have a name?"

"Nel Lamont," Nel said, still looking into Rhianne's eyes.

"Yes. I have the appointment right here." The receptionist sent a flirtatious glance in Nel's direction. Her attention then shifted to Rhianne, and with a professional tone, she asked, "And may I have your name, madam?"

"Madam? Argh! I'm not that old," Rhianne grumbled inwardly, feeling a touch of annoyance. "Rose," she replied, omitting a surname. She had no intention of offering it.

Nel leaned closer to her, his voice barely a whisper. "I thought you hated being called Rose,"

Rhianne shrugged, offering a small smile. "Might as well keep it consistent," she whispered back.

As they engaged in their whispered exchange, their attention was diverted by the sound of the front door swinging open.

The receptionist's smile widened, and she greeted the newcomer. "Mrs Parkes, good to see you again. I'll be with you momentarily," she said.

CHAPTER 6

Rhianne realised it was the perfect opportunity to strike up a conversation. She glanced at Nel, who understood her intention and leaned down to give her a gentle peck on the lips. "I'll see you in three hours, darling."

"Thanks, honey!" She cupped his cheek.

As Nel walked out, Rhianne couldn't help but notice Sarah Parkes eyeing him. When Sarah eventually turned around, Rhianne raised an eyebrow but then broke into a playful grin. "He has a great butt, doesn't he?"

Sarah burst into laughter. "It doesn't bother you?"

Rhianne chuckled. "It means you have excellent taste." She winked. "I'm Rose." She mentally high-fived herself for not accidentally slipping and revealing her real name.

Sarah extended her hand with a friendly smile. "Nice to meet you, Rose. What brings you here?"

Rhianne shrugged. "A three-hour treatment of some sort. My boyfriend chose."

The receptionist interjected, "Mrs Parkes, Rose here will be having the same treatment as you."

"Excellent." Sarah's eyes sparkled with enthusiasm. "Jose is the best massage therapist here. How about we share? He can alternate between us for the different treatments."

Rhianne smiled. "That sounds good to me, and it's very kind of you." Perfect for her plans, she thought.

Sarah waved a dismissive hand. "Oh, it's not a big deal. I could use some good company."

Rhianne chuckled. "Well, as long as you don't mind. I've been told I can be quite impertinent."

Sarah's expression shifted. "Is that the hunk of a boyfriend who told you that?"

Rhianne shook her head. "Nope, that was the previous one. We haven't reached that stage yet with the current beau."

"I see. That cinches it. I have a feeling you and I will get along just fine." A warm smile graced her face. "Shall we?" She gestured for Rhianne to proceed towards one of the gold-framed doors. As they approached, a man with a head of dark hair and a golden tan opened the door, revealing an inviting space beyond. Rhianne assumed this must be Jose, the renowned massage therapist.

Jose had an undeniable charm and was quite handsome. He had well-defined cheekbones, and his teeth were a pristine, even white.

Rhianne strode forward, her mind focused on the task at hand. The key was to gather relevant answers, one step at a time, she reminded herself.

As they settled into the plush comfort of the sofa and were handed cups of tea, Rhianne cast an admiring glance at Sarah's stunning emerald and diamond ring. "Ooh, that's a beautiful ring. Is it your wedding band?"

Sarah gracefully lifted her hand, allowing the light to catch

CHAPTER 6

the mesmerising facets of the emerald. "No, this is my five-year anniversary ring," she said.

"Five years, that's quite a milestone. Do you receive a new ring every year then?" she asked.

Sarah's laughter filled the air, brimming with mirth. "Oh, I receive other gifts, mostly jewellery, but this particular ring holds special significance. It symbolises a milestone in our prenuptial agreement."

"Oh?" Rhianne tilted her head.

"See, my husband was loaded, so he insisted we sign a prenuptial agreement," Sarah said. "For each year I get something extra. And now I'll get a cool two hundred grand a month, for life."

"What about his assets?" Rhianne leaned in closer.

Jose interrupted their conversation. "Mrs Parkes and Ms Rose," he addressed them with a Latino accent, gesturing for them to follow him. "Please come with me to the changing rooms. You can undress there and grab towels to bring with you to the massage table." He cast a mischievous smirk in Rhianne's direction. "If you prefer, Señorita Rose, you can leave your underwear on, and I can work around it." Rhianne noticed that he didn't bother mentioning the same to Sarah, as if it was understood between them. She didn't have long to ponder Sarah's stance, though.

"It just gets in the way of a good massage." Her gaze assessed Rhianne. "You have a gorgeous body, and Jose has seen it all before, haven't you, cariño?"

"Thanks," Rhianne returned Sarah's smile.

Sarah walked out fully naked, contrasting with Rhianne's more modest choice of wrapping the towel around her body. Sarah smiled at her when she noticed her looking.

"Like?" Sarah asked with a twinkle in her eyes.

Rhianne's eyebrows shot up at Sarah's flirty comment. She realised she needed to respond. "You're absolutely stunning," Rhianne complimented. "Your husband's very lucky."

A fleeting shadow passed over Sarah's face, causing her smile to waver momentarily. "He passed away recently, so it doesn't matter now." With a renewed smile, Sarah climbed onto the massage bed.

"I'm sorry for your loss." The words fell flat to her ears and sounded insincere even as they left her lips.

Sarah waved her hand in dismissal. "Don't be. I'm free now to do as I please."

"Is that so?" Jose's gaze lingered on Sarah.

Sarah glared at Jose. "No one knows he's dead yet, so I expect you to keep this information to yourself." Her tone had turned cold and unfriendly.

Jose, who had been leaning closer to Sarah, took a step back.

"Of course, Mrs Parkes. Discretion is of utmost importance at Belmont's." His accent had completely vanished. Sarah's instruction had been directed solely at Jose. Did he have loose lips? Rhianne made a mental note to keep this information in mind for later.

"Do you have much family to help you with all the arrangements?" Rhianne attempted to sound concerned.

Sarah let out a sigh. "Oh, I'd expect Devlin's daughter will handle everything. She always does. She's a control freak, just like her father. Emotionless and callous." Her mouth was pinched. "She's already commissioned a bust and a plaque to hang in his old school. My involvement will likely be limited to the flowers, and that's only because Rita couldn't care less about them. I'll also have to find a dress that his side of the

CHAPTER 6

family won't be able to criticise. Apparently, Arthur invited his mother to attend."

Rhianne noted the use of the full name. Not friendly with 'Art' then.

"The only reason she'd come would be to make sure it's him in the coffin. Dev never had anything good to say about her, not that that says much. Dev criticised everyone."

"Including you?" Rhianne dared ask.

"Oh, I made sure I played the good wife." She waved her hand down her body. "I looked beautiful and smiled and nodded at the appropriate times. Even then I wasn't exempt from it. I hadn't been polite enough to a senator's boring wife or I failed to enchant his latest contractor. Still, I did better than most of them. Much to the fury of Rita 'Miss Perfect', who was forever seeking dad's approval, and Arthur, who didn't conform to Dev's idea of the ruthless businessman. Devlin was blind to his daughter's ambitions and skills and the lack thereof from Arthur. At the end of the day, all that mattered to Devlin was what was between Arthur's legs."

It was a scathing assessment.

"Do you have someone from your own family who can offer you support?"

Sarah's eyes clouded over. "My grandmother died quite a few years ago. She raised me from the age of two after my mother abandoned me at her doorstep. I don't know if my mother is alive, but given her addiction to drugs, I doubt it."

"I don't know what to say to that," Rhianne said.

She found herself in a bit of an emotional swirl. On one hand, there was a sense of relief that her own tumultuous relationship with her mother hadn't led to abandonment, which was certainly a win in the family department. On the other hand, a dash of bitterness crept in as she pondered the fact that her mother's support came primarily in the form of material goods — maybe she thought designer dresses were the key to maternal bonding.

Sarah and Rhianne took their places on the massage beds, face down. It was rather warm in the room and Rhianne had decided to follow Sarah's advice and had placed her towel on a chair nearby.

"What about you?" Sarah asked.

Rhianne thought it was best to tell the truth as much as possible. "I have an absent father. He shows up every few years bearing lavish gifts."

"And he probably thinks that makes up for the years in between," Sarah said.

Sarah's perceptiveness took Rhianne by surprise. It was easy to dismiss her, with her gorgeous looks and light banter. She also appreciated the lack of fake sympathy.

Jose poured warm oil on Rhianne's back, and the scent alone was enough to make her shoulders relax. "Just about. There are always excuses, which revolve around family and work obligations."

She was trying to sound casual but her hard tone would have given her away.

"What about your mother?" Sarah asked.

Jose began kneading her shoulders. She had to admit he had very good hands. "Harder or softer?" he asked.

"Softer, thanks."

"I think I would prefer my mother to be absent." There was no heat in her words, the massage was making her drowsy. Maybe she could get a regular treatment here as a birthday present from Nel. It was bound to be cheaper than the

CHAPTER 6

Lamborghini. "I know that sounds heartless, particularly given your experience..." she trailed off, realising she had put her foot in it.

Sarah gave a quiet chuckle. "I was so much better off with Granny Bae. She was the most loving and caring person I've ever met." Her voice held a smile. "She used to take all the strays in the street. Throughout my childhood, our home was a haven for a variety of stray furry companions, including cats and dogs. She also generously provided food to the children in our neighbourhood, even though we didn't have a lot ourselves. She's the reason I ended up working in aged care. I have a deep admiration for old people. They aren't afraid to speak their minds. And boy, do they have stories to tell."

Rhianne noticed that as she was talking, Sarah was relaxing. It probably helped that Jose was now spreading the oil on her back. "I'm guessing your mother isn't the caring type."

Rhianne hesitated, weighing her options. The topic was sensitive, and she could easily deflect or avoid it. But something about the openness and vulnerability Sarah had shown made her reconsider. Maybe it was time to share a part of her story, even if it was with a stranger.

Rhianne chose to open up. "I'm convinced my mother had a whole PowerPoint presentation ready for her life plan. 'Career goals: check. Dream house: check. Precious offspring: oops, surprise bonus round!'"

"Welcome to the club, mate," Sarah said.

Rhianne's tone had an edge to it. "I get it. Other people have had it worse."

"That's not what I meant," Sarah replied.

Rhianne let out a sigh. "I've heard that argument countless

times," she admitted. "But the truth is, my mother saw an opportunity in an unexpected situation. She turned me into her campaign prop."

"Is she a politician?"

"Sort of, everything has been carefully orchestrated. While other kids were mastering the art of mud pies, I was perfecting my curtsy. Instead of playgrounds, I waltzed through ballrooms, dodging judgemental glances like a pro. And forget hopscotch — my game was 'Impress With Your Witty Conversation.'"

"Piano lessons?" she continued. "Tick. And let's not forget deportment. My grandpa was my rock in a life full of fancy parties and events, but he lived far away. Being with him felt like a breath of fresh air, free from the weight of expectations." She paused briefly. "At fifteen, I was done with my mother's expectations. I worked at a local plant nursery and saved every penny. I stopped going to her fancy events. When my father gifted me a motorbike during one of his rare visits, it gave me the mobility I craved. At sixteen, I finally left for good."

With some help from Nel, who found her an apartment that an investor needed to keep occupied for tax purposes. It was only later she found out he owned it. When she confronted him about it, he told her he had got a good deal out of it and to stop pretending she didn't need anyone.

Sarah chuckled and shook her head. "I don't think she's exactly in the running for Mother of the Year."

"Honestly, if she thought it would improve her chances, she'd do it in a heartbeat."

"Do you speak to her?"

"I do. She's still trying to con me into attending functions,

CHAPTER 6

though. Last month, she invited me home for a cosy dinner, which turned out to be a dinner party for seventy of her 'closest' friends!"

"You must admit, she is gutsy."

A small laugh escaped Rhianne's lips. Jose had returned to do her legs and her calves were loving the attention.

"Yes, she's nothing but determined."

"It sounds like the apple didn't fall too far from the tree," Sara said.

Rhianne was about to answer flippantly and then paused. "I hadn't thought of it that way, but I guess you're right. What about you, what's next for you?"

"The plan is to play the grieving wife until everything gets sorted. It suits me to continue living in the big house before all the assets get distributed. Not even Rita's efficiency and whatever expensive lawyers she hires are going to sort all the details quickly. I'm betting it's going to take months." She tilted her head towards Rhianne. "I've been acting for so long, I don't think a few more months are going to hurt me."

"And then what?" Rhianne asked.

"Then I'll do some travelling, probably get a dog or two, and eventually return to nursing older people and listen to their stories. Perhaps I'll write a book."

"Dogs are awesome." Rhianne's smile grew as she thought about Toto. Despite choosing to appear as a Maltese cross, Toto didn't appreciate being labelled as an ordinary dog. She was careful not to tease him; after all, he could be 'fierce' when it came to defending his dignity.

Rhianne didn't manage to extract much more information from Sarah as they hit the pool for a few laps followed by individual saunas. Despite this, Rhianne felt like she had gleaned some valuable insights. The question remained, though: was any of it bringing her any closer to solving the murder?

Nel came to pick her up and she went over and tiptoed to give him a kiss on his cheek.

"Rose!"

It was only Nel squeezing her hand and gently pivoting her around that made her realise that was supposed to be her name.

As Sarah was leaving, she extended a card towards Rhianne. "Give me a call sometime. I have a feeling we could become good friends," she said.

Rhianne smiled and was surprised she meant it. "Will do, Sarah. It was good meeting you."

Nel placed his palm on her lower back and gently guided her out. "How was it?"

"It was fantastic!" Rhianne said. "I'll take a massage over a Lamborghini any day."

Nel threw his head back and laughed. "You always have a unique perspective. But just so you know, one of them is actually worth more."

"As someone very wise said to me once, things are only worth what someone is willing to pay for them. I'd call it value for money. "I'm feeling pretty relaxed."

"Does that mean you are ready for our shopping expedition?" Nel opened the door of the Lamborghini for her.

"As ready as I'll ever be. You know I'm not the biggest fan of shopping." Rhianne sighed, memories of endless hours spent in dressing rooms flooded her mind. The constant scrutiny of her mother as she meticulously chose each outfit, while shopping assistants vied for her attention to showcase the

CHAPTER 6

latest trends. Rhianne's presence was reduced to that of a mere mannequin, silently enduring the ordeal.

"Yes, but shopping with me is a completely different experience."

"Don't tell me you'll ask for my opinion?" Rhianne placed a hand over her heart and opened her eyes wide to simulate amazement.

Nel got into the driver's seat. "You have opinions about fashion?" It was his turn to appear shocked.

Rhianne stuck her tongue out at him.

"Very mature, princess."

"Maturity is overrated. Besides, you're one to talk. And let's not forget about your car obsession."

"It isn't a car obsession; it's a car collection." Nel zoomed past a truck as he sped off.

Rhianne snorted and playfully waved her hand near the side of his face. "Potato, Potahto."

Nel's eyes crinkled. She didn't say anything more as he drove just on the other side of the speed limit. It was hard to believe, but she knew he had never received a speeding ticket in his life.

They pulled up to an upscale area, known for its chic boutiques. The storefronts boasted sleek, modern designs with clean lines and large windows that displayed luxurious goods. "Just so you know, I'm not wearing a dress. I'm taking my bike to this date," she said.

"I'll hire a car to take you there and back so you can wear the right outfit."

Rhianne went to object, but Nel placed a finger across her lips. "Hey, what's the point of having money if you can't use it to treat the people you love?"

"You're playing dirty and trying to guilt trip me."

"Obviously. Is it working?" Nel said shamelessly.

"It's saying something when you're harder to say no to than my own mother," Rhianne said, surprised at herself for the comparison.

Nel gave her a sideways glance as he guided her towards the entrance of a shop. "I'm not sure if I should feel insulted or not," he said. "I want you to dress up to highlight your beauty because I want everyone to see what I see."

"And what do you see Nel?" Rhianne already knew that she would let him choose something for tonight.

"I see a gorgeous human being, who cares deeply about others, but has trouble trusting and allowing herself to love."

"Not true," Rhianne said automatically. "I love you and Toto and Tata Angelo."

"I'm honoured to be part of that exclusive group, but I was talking specifically about partners."

"Kettle, pot —. Besides, I've had boyfriends."

Nel raised an eyebrow and Rhianne blew her fringe up off her face. Her past relationships had been more fleeting than a shooting star, lasting only weeks instead of months. Long-term commitment had always been about as elusive as finding a unicorn in the supermarket. Not that she had a problem with commitment, but you never knew if they'd stick around, so why bother, right?

"You know you've already won," she said instead.

"It isn't about winning. I want you to be happy."

"I know," Rhianne said and resigned herself to wearing a dress tonight.

CHAPTER 7

Thankfully, Nel didn't go overboard with arranging a limousine for Rhianne's transport. Instead, a sleek luxury sedan pulled up to take her to the restaurant. She arrived on time and smiled when she saw Kai waiting for her at the entrance of the restaurant, which had a vibrant neon sign and a lush garden.

"Hi." He roved his eyes over her and blinked. "You look beautiful."

Maybe if someone else had said it, it would have sounded trite or flirty, but Kai saying it sounded like a simple statement of truth. She gave him a coy smile. "Well, if I'd known wearing a dress would have had this effect, I wouldn't have argued with Nel so much about it."

Nel had chosen a dress in peacock blue, with a flared skirt and a form-fitting V-neck top. The colour complemented her skin tone and brought out the green in her eyes.

"Nel has good taste. Should I be jealous?" he asked.

"Nel has excellent taste in clothes as well as friends. He's my best friend. More like a big brother, I guess."

Upon hearing her response, Kai visibly relaxed, his shoulders loosening as a small smile tugged at the corners of his lips.

"Shall we?" Kai's voice was smooth as he gestured for her to walk ahead, his hand lingering on the small of Rhianne's back. The touch, cool against the smooth silk of her dress, sent a delightful shiver down her spine.

"I hope you like Thai food." Rhianne glanced up at him.

"It's my favourite. I adore the bold flavours and spices," Kai said, a genuine smile lighting up his face.

"Ah, so the truth behind accepting my invitation comes out."

"I would have also accepted a hot oolong tea, chocolate-covered strawberries, or a home-cooked meal," Kai smirked.

"Oh my, a cheap date," Rhianne feigned shock and placed a hand dramatically over her heart. "I think I may swoon."

Kai chuckled. "Before you do, let me say that I am more than prepared to make the home-cooked meal, serve the tea, and provide the chocolate-covered strawberries. What do you think?"

"We haven't even started this date, and you're already offering another one? Aren't you supposed to play hard to get?" Rhianne's laughter filled the air.

"Well, you asked me out first, so it's only fair to reciprocate."

"A gentleman, a cook, and a tech genius. Who's out of their league now?" Rhianne's eyes sparkled with merriment, and her face bloomed with warmth.

As they followed the waiter through the dimly lit restaurant, her eyes wandered around, taking in the cosy ambience created by the soft lighting. The glow cast gentle shadows on the walls, creating an intimate and romantic atmosphere that enveloped the small corner where their table awaited them.

"Don't get ahead of yourself, you need to test my food before

CHAPTER 7

you make sweeping statements like that. I couldn't live with you being disappointed in me." A wide grin stretched across his face, revealing charming dimples.

"I have complete faith in any food you made, but even if it was terrible, which I highly doubt, I wouldn't be disappointed," she said. "It would mean you have a flaw and thank goodness for that, or else I'd start feeling self-conscious."

His smile turned coy. "In that case, how about early next week?"

"Sure, which day?" Rhianne asked. She felt both brave and bold, but what the heck, she really liked the guy.

"As a mere consultant, I set my own hours of work and unless there is a crime scene, I'm at your disposal."

"Do you always get invited to crime scenes?" Rhianne asked. This had been her first one. For the other cases she had just reviewed the findings of the forensic pathologist.

"Believe it or not, in about half the cases, they want me to attend. It depends on a number of things." He tilted his head to the side, his stormy blue eyes glistening in the soft light of the restaurant. "High profile cases mean more money and more consultants' budget."

"I'd say this one's definitely a high profile one."

While they were seated in a corner, there were still other people in the restaurant and she wasn't about to say the Parkes' name aloud.

Kai nodded. "And then there are those cases where people suspect there are financial motives involved. It's becoming increasingly difficult to keep financial transactions completely hidden these days. Of course, they can make it challenging, but that's part of the thrill of the job. Cash may be untraceable, but you still have to get it from somewhere, and these days the banks are keeping a closer eye on things. I always follow the money." As Kai spoke, he looked at her expectantly, probably wondering if she recognised the quote.

"*All the President's Men*," Rhianne said.

"You've seen it?" Kai asked.

"It was mandated in our household, given it was about politics."

"Oh?" Kai said.

Rhianne let out a sigh. Everything had been going so well, and then she had to bring up something related to her mother. Why was she doing that lately?

"My mother has always had political ambition," she grumbled.

"You don't seem too taken with the idea."

Rhianne briefly considered changing the subject but it didn't matter. Might as well get it out of the way. "I haven't met any politician yet who doesn't lie to suit themselves or who genuinely cares about the citizens they are supposed to represent, although I'm sure there must be one or two."

"And your mother isn't going to be one of those two." Kai's tone was matter-of-fact, devoid of any judgement.

Her eyebrows furrowed, and a scoff escaped her lips. "Unlikely. I've had my fair share of social schmoozing, and I have no desire to be a part of that whole show." Rhianne shook her head, memories of forced conversations and fake smiles resurfacing.

"Yeah, I agree. It's all excruciating small talk and frantic exit strategies when you find yourself stuck with a total bore." He let out a chuckle.

Rhianne tilted her head. "You've been to some, I assume?"

Kai's eyes lost focus for a second. "Some. It was during the

CHAPTER 7

time when I was trying to establish myself as a reputable Tech Mage. My mentor, the Mage Guild's Archmage and a state councillor like your mother, believed it was crucial to mingle with influential individuals and make the right connections."

"Did it pay off? Was the Archmage right?"

"In a way." Kai had a twinkle in his eyes that accentuated his dimples once again. "During one event attended by top-level executives from various industries, a conversation turned towards a case of significant financial fraud. One executive shared how they had been defrauded out of a substantial sum of money."

Rhianne leaned forward. "And what did you do?"

A smirk danced on Kai's lips. "I offered to help. It was an opportunity to showcase my Tech Mage skills. Within a half an hour, I managed to trace the funds to an offshore account in the Cayman Islands. The culprit turned out to be none other than the executive's own nephew."

"And the executive hired you?"

"No," Kai said. "There was definitely a hint of discomfort due to the family connection. Lucky for me, one of the individuals in our group happened to be the police superintendent, which proved to be quite fortuitous."

"So, he asked you to consult with the police?"

"Yes. While most of my work now comes from the private sector, I prefer aiding the police. In the private sector, justice can often be compromised in favour of protecting reputations. That's why I've made sure to include a clause in all my contracts. If I come across any criminal activities, I report them to the authorities."

"Wow, I guess I'll need to rethink these parties. They may not be as useless as I thought."

"I got lucky." Kai shrugged his shoulders. "And sometimes I wonder if it was worth the sore jaw from the fake smiles."

The waiter showed up to take their orders, and Rhianne decided to go with a red duck curry loaded with lychees. Meanwhile, Kai opted for a Larb Thai chicken salad.

Rhianne asked, "Are we sharing?"

"Of course," Kai said. "Sharing means we get to try a wider variety of dishes."

"So, you enjoy trying new things?"

Kai chuckled. "To my parents' dismay, yes. I would immerse myself in different activities every year. One year it was soccer, the next water polo, and then caving. I also loved taking things apart and putting them back together again. I mean, there was something so satisfying about figuring out how all the pieces fit together. I love challenges and difficult problems."

"Why would that annoy them?"

Kai grinned. "It meant getting a different uniform and equipment every year, especially with my frequent growth spurts. I think what bothered my parents the most was the notion of mastery. They believed that focusing on one subject and becoming exceptional in it was the key to success. But I wanted to do more than just a couple of things. Eventually, they came to accept it when I was tested and proven as a Tech Mage. They let me explore and pursue my interests. Plus, it helped that my older brother chose a different path as a metallurgic mage, so they had to divide their concern between us. That's what parents do."

Rhianne took a thoughtful sip of her coconut water, contemplating the conversation. She drew a comparison to her own situation, where she possessed a range of magical abilities

CHAPTER 7

but didn't excel at any particular one. The words formed in her mind before she spoke them aloud, a hint of irony in her voice. "I don't think da Vinci would have agreed."

Kai's eyes crinkled at the corners. "When you put it like that —"

"I do. Let's drink to Renaissance people. May they live long and prosper." She raised her glass.

Kai chuckled and raised his glass as well. "I think you're mixing your time periods and movies."

"To mixing things up," Rhianne grinned.

"To mixing things up."

They clicked their glasses together. "Johannes called me to follow up, by the way," Kai said.

"Oh?"

"He wasn't being swindled or involved in suspicious transactions. It seems to be related to perfectly legal political donations," Kai took a moment to sip his drink. "However, there was a significant expense recently from a high-end jewellery store."

Rhianne met his eager gaze, her expression softening. She didn't want to burst his bubble, but she was about to anyway.

"That would likely be an extravagant emerald and diamond ring, a lavish five-year anniversary gift for his young and beautiful wife," Rhianne said.

Kai's mouth dropped open. "A mid-life crisis wife?" Kai raised an eyebrow. "And how exactly do you know this?"

"Well, let me tell you, I have quite a story to share."

By the time they had finished dinner, Rhianne had shared all the details about Sarah and Arthur with Kai. Kai suggested they grab some ice cream and take a leisurely stroll along the promenade. They made their way to the ice cream shop and purchased two cones. Rhianne chose a coconut-flavoured one adorned with chocolate chips, while Kai went for the refreshing taste of mango. Finding a cosy bench with a view of the ocean, they savoured their ice creams.

All of a sudden Rhianne felt a sense of unease, and she started scanning her surroundings. People were bustling around, engrossed in their own conversations and activities, seemingly oblivious to any unusual occurrences. But she couldn't shake the feeling that something was off.

As she continued to survey the area, her attention was drawn to a particular spot ahead, where she thought she caught a faint flare of magic and the movement of a shadow. Her heart raced, and she was about to voice her suspicion when Kai's voice interrupted her thoughts.

"Huh, I just realised something," he mused, a thoughtful expression playing on his face. "You're like a magnet for the members of the Parkes family, aren't you? I can see why Arthur finds you fascinating, though."

"I feel sorry for him," she said, "He's been playing hide and seek with his true self his whole life, thanks to his father's master plan." She bit her lip. "And you know what? I can relate to some extent. My mother expects me to fit into this mould of the 'perfect' politician's daughter. But, as my grandpa used to say, the best part about ageing is you start caring less about what's 'in' and more about what's for dinner. So, I've decided I'm all in for growing old, wrinkly, and gloriously carefree."

"I'm pretty sure I'd still like you, wrinkles and all."

"Well, that's a relief! I'll start practising my best 'grumpy old lady' impression now, just to be prepared."

They both laughed.

"So Arthur did not meet his father's expectations. Devlin

CHAPTER 7

Parkes wanted a clone and Arthur was very different to him," he said after their laughter had subsided.

"Yes. Plus, physically, he's nothing like his father. It's hard to believe Arthur hasn't questioned it."

"Ah, the power of denial. People have a knack for it. But you know what?" A glimmer of excitement danced in his gaze. "I can dig into it and see what I find. It's worth exploring that angle. I doubt the police have considered it yet."

Her eyebrows furrowed. "Are you sure you want to spend your time on this?"

Kai waved off her worries. "Are you kidding? This will be fun, something a little different. Besides, I can always share what I learn with Johannes. It would serve to enhance my reputation if nothing else."

"That would be fantastic!" She sat up straighter in her seat. "We still have two other suspects, though." Rhianne had presented her theory that the poison must have been administered by someone close to Devlin Parkes, and he had wholeheartedly agreed. Rhianne's voice grew uncertain. "I'm struggling to come up with a plan to arrange a conversation with the sister or the ex-wife."

Kai's eyes twinkled in the soft glow of the street lights, a glimmer of excitement dancing within them. "I might have an idea on how we can approach the sister."

"I knew there was a reason I liked you!" she nudged Kai's shoulder.

Kai dramatically placed a hand over his heart, feigning a wounded expression. "Ah, so it's only my brain that interests you?" He pretended to pout.

Rhianne's smile widened. "Oh no, don't be mistaken," she said. "I appreciate many things about you, Renaissance man.

Your brain is just one of them."

The full moon had risen and had created a path out to the horizon only briefly interrupted by the waves crashing on the shore. She felt Kai's arm draping on the back of her shoulders with a feather-light touch. Her phone rang. Rhianne's eyebrows lifted. Who would be calling her this late? Her heart raced as she reached for her phone.

"Hello."

"Boss, you gotta come now." Carl's urgent voice pierced through the phone line, accompanied by distant sounds of commotion and voices in the background.

"Carl, where are you? Is everything all right? What's happening over there?" The torrent of questions poured out in rapid succession as she sought to understand the situation.

"We're at the Tea Leaves." Carl abruptly hung up. The suddenness of the call ending was enough to jolt Rhianne into action. She rose from her seat, a sense of urgency propelling her forward.

Kai, holding their ice creams, closely followed her as they started walking. Kai, matched her pace. "What's wrong?"

"That was Carl," she said. "He works for me, and he sounded absolutely frantic. Something bad is happening."

A flurry of scenarios ran through her mind. Vandalism? No, Carl would have handled that on his own. Then it hit her — why were they at the nursery at this late hour? Her thoughts raced, searching for answers until a realisation jolted her. She needed transportation. A car. Should she call for one? Or perhaps hail a taxi?

Before she could decide, Kai's calm voice broke through her anxious thoughts. "My car is parked in the council car park. I'll take you," he offered.

CHAPTER 7

She stopped and hugged him. He grabbed her hand and led her to his car.

Rhianne's intuition was telling her that whatever was happening, wasn't good. Luckily, the nursery was only a fifteen-minute drive away, and with any luck, the traffic would cooperate.

Kai skilfully navigated the route, arriving at the nursery in ten minutes. His focused movements and calm confidence allowed her to focus on the possibilities. Rhianne began to contemplate various potential scenarios. Perhaps there had been a major robbery, and Carl was called in by the police. But then, why was Carl at the nursery? As they drove into her parking area, Rhianne's eyes widened at the sight of four police cars haphazardly parked. The scene instantly heightened her unease.

The moment Kai pressed the brakes, Rhianne bolted out of the car, propelled by a surge of adrenaline. Her feet carried her toward the source of the raised voices, her heart pounding. Amidst the noise, she heard Alice's unmistakable roaring and the distinct, slightly calmer, gruff voice of Johannes. What on earth was going on?

"Hey!" Rhianne shouted, grateful for the voice lessons her mother had once insisted upon. Despite the tense and angry atmosphere, both parties snapped their faces towards her, startled by the force of her voice.

Then, other figures at the scene came into view. Carl was a few steps to the left of his sister, while Sergeant Chen lingered a bit behind. Around them, a group of about ten police officers stood, their stances rigid. Rhianne placed her hands on her hips as she demanded. "What is going on here?"

"This —" Alice spluttered. "Brute," she managed to say,

her fingers curling. "Is throwing accusations at me and demanding to search the property."

Senior Sergeant Johannes' eyebrows furrowed. "You're insulting a law enforcement officer!" he snapped.

Rhianne turned her gaze towards Senior Sergeant Johannes. "Do you have a search warrant?" she asked.

Kai stood steadfastly behind her, his presence acting as a reassuring anchor. Working alongside Nel had granted her valuable insights into the workings of the police, their authority and limitations. Rhianne was well aware that some officers resorted to intimidation tactics, and while she could sympathise with their frustrations with the legal system, she knew her rights and was definitely going to stand up for them.

Johannes' lips formed a tight line, his eyebrow twitching ever so slightly. "Do you have something to hide, Ms Alkenn? I'd have thought a police consultant would value their position with the police and want to cooperate." A self-assured smirk played upon his lips.

Rhianne straightened her posture, her height reaching its full potential of five-foot-three, with the added boost from her heels (for which she silently thanked Nel).

"Senior Sergeant," she enunciated the title with careful precision, infusing her tone with a disdainful edge she had learned from her mother. "As a law officer, you're well aware of what the law dictates, and it clearly states that a search warrant is required to search any premises."

Johannes had opened his mouth to respond, but before he could utter a word, Rhianne interjected, "And I must say, I'm not sure your superintendent would appreciate your using threats to gain illegal entrance."

As Rhianne stood her ground, Kai materialised by her side,

CHAPTER 7

his presence offering support. Her keen gaze caught the widening of Sergeant Chen's eyes, followed by a subtle shift to a neutral expression. She stored that information for later. Turning her attention to the scene, she saw Alice standing in a rigid posture, while Carl fidgeted with his hands.

Johannes' mouth curved into a downward frown; his jaw visibly clenched so tightly that Rhianne could almost hear the grinding of his teeth. "Are you implying that you won't cooperate?"

Rhianne took a deliberate, calming breath. "I simply asked if you had a search warrant, and you haven't answered me. I'll assume that you don't, and therefore I must politely decline the search," she said. "You haven't yet let me know what you're looking for?"

"That's part of an ongoing investigation, and given that you are now implicated, your consulting is revoked until the situation is resolved." Johannes' words hung in the air.

Rhianne's breath hitched. "Implicated in what?" she demanded, her hands balling into fists.

Johannes shifted his attention to Alice. "Alice Vargas, you are hereby arrested on suspicion of the murder of Devlin Parkes."

CHAPTER 8

As Alice let out a furious roar, pandemonium erupted around them. Police officers closed in on Carl, perceiving him as the greater threat. Alice propelled herself forward, aiming for a full body slam. Johannes, displaying remarkable agility, sidestepped the attack, narrowly avoiding the impact. It was a manoeuvre that, under different circumstances, Rhianne might have admired. But in that moment, all she felt was a burning desire to deliver a kick of her own.

Risking personal safety, Rhianne positioned herself directly in front of Alice; her back towards the police.

"Alice, I need you to calm down," she pleaded, her gaze locked with Alice's. Drawing upon the gentlest touch of her magic, she sought to induce a sense of relaxation in Alice.

At that very moment, Toto, barking frantically, made a timely entrance, darting between the legs of the officers. The fluffy whirlwind of activity created confusion among the police, none of them appeared willing to harm the small, energetic dog. His unexpected arrival granted Rhianne precious time.

CHAPTER 8

To her relief, the combination of her subtle magic and Toto's presence had the desired effect. Alice's tense shoulders eased slightly, although her defiant expression remained.

"It'll be okay," Rhianne reassured her. "We'll get a lawyer and have you out in no time. This is nonsense."

Turning away from Alice, Rhianne faced Johannes and Chen, who appeared poised for action. She raised both arms in front of her, briefly considering the idea of taking them down with a good old-fashioned kick. She shook her head, pushing aside the impulsive thought.

"If you don't have enough evidence for a search warrant, I highly doubt you have much to support your accusation," Rhianne said. "All you'll achieve is making yourselves look foolish in the eyes of your superiors."

Chen snorted. "Be that as it may, we're proceeding with the arrest of Ms Vargas. If you interfere, you'll be charged with obstructing an arrest."

"Well." Kai's jaw was tight and his words clipped. "Fortunately, I happen to be a reliable witness who can testify otherwise."

Chen shot him a look that could have curdled milk at twenty paces. "It's still your word against that of professional officers, Kai."

Kai's expression hardened, though he remained composed. "Good point, Sergeant. Luckily, we won't have to rely solely on my word. The judge will have the privilege of viewing video footage of this incident."

"What video cameras?" Rhianne wondered silently.

Chen, sensing the shift in the situation, glanced around, vertical wrinkles forming between her eyebrows. "You do realise it's illegal to record without consent," she said, taking a step back.

Kai stepped forward. "You're standing on Ms Alkenn's property, and she has every right to have security cameras in place. Cameras that were *professionally* installed by a tech mage, and are capable of recording both video and audio."

The layers of underlying tension and unspoken messages swirling in the air were enough to make Rhianne's head spin. It was clear to her that their argument extended beyond the mere legality of the cameras. As she contemplated Kai's words, she realised that he hadn't lied, just used careful wording. Then again, she wouldn't put it past him to have a recording device in place without her knowledge. Given his remarkable abilities, capturing this episode would likely be child's play for him.

Observing the visible shift in Chen and Johannes' demeanour, Rhianne saw that they too recognised the potential implications of Kai's statement. Their aggression gave way to a more stern and serious disposition. However, if they believed that such tactics would work on her, they clearly underestimated her resistance. Years of exposure to her mother's brand of forbidding had rendered her immune, resulting in a healthy disrespect for authority.

Chen and Johannes: 0, Rhianne and Kai: 1. She did an internal fist pump but then sobered up and redirected her attention to Alice. "Please cooperate and go quietly. We'll drive to the police station and meet you there," she instructed. Alice nodded reluctantly.

Taking advantage of the moment, Johannes stepped forward, placing handcuffs on Alice's wrists. The sound of Carl's anguish resonated in the air, causing the surrounding police officers to tense, one reaching for his gun.

CHAPTER 8

Rhianne's voice rang out. "The cameras are capturing not only your intimidation tactics but also your clear prejudice against a supernatural being who has displayed no aggression and is unarmed," she said. Turning her gaze back to Johannes and Chen, she issued a stern warning. "I'll be filing a formal complaint regarding the conduct of your officers today. Tell them to back off now."

"Go back to your cars, officers," Johannes barked at them, his gaze locked onto Rhianne as she stood protectively in front of Carl. The stark difference in size between her and Carl suddenly struck her as absurdly funny, and a giggle escaped her lips. Johannes' face reddened at the sound.

"I'll be back with a search warrant," he snapped. "Cameras or not, I will find what I'm looking for."

They took Alice and piled into their waiting police cars. With tires screeching and sirens blaring, they sped off as if they couldn't wait to escape the scene, leaving a cloud of dust and chaos in their wake.

Rhianne wasn't awarding them any points for the dramatic exit.

Snapping herself out of her anger she began thinking and kicked herself for not having already checked her private garden. Her belly knotted as she realised that she had missed the opportunity. She found it hard to believe that Alice would have any knowledge of Romin, though. There might be some bizarre reason for her to hold a grudge against Devlin, but plotting a poisoning? That was way too extreme and out of character. Alice was the type to confront him in public, maybe even throw a punch or two, but straight-up murder? No, she didn't think so.

Her mind raced with questions. "What were you and Alice

doing here so late, Carl?" she asked. "And how did you get here? Do you know any lawyers? Nel might have some connections."

Carl looked sheepishly at the ground. "Alice has the keys to the truck," he said.

She pinched her lips as she thought about her slow van. It was far from an ideal situation.

"I'll drive you to the police station," Kai offered, cutting through her thoughts. "If we leave now, we might beat them there."

Rhianne hopped into the front passenger seat, realising she didn't feel the urge to argue about who should drive. Well, that was new. For some reason, Kai didn't trigger her usual need for independence. She made a mental note to figure that out later. Glancing at the rear-view mirror, she noticed Carl sitting in the back of the car, hunched over and tapping away on his smartphone.

"All right, come clean, Carl. What were you and Alice doing here?" Rhianne asked.

Carl glanced at his phone before responding. "Don't worry about a lawyer, boss. My mum is sending one," he said.

Carl and Alice's parents were undoubtedly well-connected and knew plenty of people. That was one less thing to worry about.

"You see, boss, it was Alice. She lost an earring earlier in the day, and it's a valuable heirloom. She didn't want to wait until tomorrow to get it. I hope that's all right, boss. She didn't mean any harm by it."

"I wondered what the police were planning to do if there wasn't anyone there to open the nursery," she said aloud.

A grunt caught her attention, and she turned to look at

CHAPTER 8

Kai, who was keeping his focus on the road but had a distinct scowl on his face.

"I hope I'm wrong," he said. "But you know how it goes. Sometimes the police resort to 'legal' break-ins if they can argue there's a crime in progress."

Something in Kai's weary tone hinted to Rhianne that there was more to this than met the eye. She paused for a moment, absorbing his words.

"I see," she said. "So, if I understand correctly, it was fortunate that Carl and Alice were there, preventing the police from finding an excuse to search. Who knows what they hoped to discover." She nibbled her lip. "But that still doesn't explain why they suspect Alice of having a motive to kill Devlin Parkes. In the rear-view mirror, she noticed Carl avoiding eye contact, staring intently out the window.

"All right, Carl," she said. "You need to tell me what you know. If I'm going to help Alice, I need information."

Carl mumbled under his breath; his words barely audible. "It's best if Alice tells you herself, boss. It's not my story to tell."

Rhianne ground her teeth. Stubborn gargoyles! Getting it out of Alice would be even harder. "The least you can do is tell me if she had any connection to Devlin Parkes."

Carl slouched further. "Yes, boss. She did."

Just great. Rhianne groaned inwardly. With Alice's fiery temperament, she was certain that whatever connection existed between them would be public knowledge, and easy for the police to obtain. Her gaze shifted back to Kai. Sensing her intense scrutiny, he risked a quick sideways glance at her.

"Whatever you're thinking," he said, his eyes refocusing on the road as he skilfully weaved through traffic. "Count me in."

A wave of warmth washed over Rhianne, her spirits lifting. "You don't even know what I'm going to ask," she said, a grin forming on her face.

"Doesn't matter," he said. "I'm pretty sure I'll be up for it, whatever you suggest. You know I'm always game for new adventures."

She couldn't resist the urge to reach out and gently touch Kai's hand.

"You sound like a Boy Scout," she said.

A glimmer illuminated Kai's eyes, and a smile tugged at the corners of his lips. "That's because I was."

"Of course you were," Rhianne said.

Kai had a knack for surprising her with his hidden talents, leaving her curious, excited, and challenged. What else was there? The thought sent a tingle down her spine. The desire to delve deeper into their connection lingered, making her smile.

They finally arrived, and by some stroke of luck, Kai managed to find a parking spot a block away — a small miracle on a bustling Saturday night. They hurriedly exited the car and dashed towards the police station. As they burst through the entrance, the officer on duty glanced up, his mouth turning downwards. He watched them from behind the protective partition.

"Can I assist you?" he asked, his tone neutral but guarded.

Rhianne suspected that he'd rather be doing anything else, like arranging his sock drawer by colour, than helping them. Too bad. For him.

"Senior Sergeant Johannes brought Alice Vargas in," she said, slightly breathless from the sprinting.

CHAPTER 8

The officer's gaze scrutinised them, his expression wavering between scepticism and curiosity. "Senior Sergeant Johannes hasn't returned yet." He wet his lips.

"Then we'll wait," Rhianne said.

How much longer would they have to wait? Maybe she had miscalculated and Alice was being processed at a different location. Sensing her distress, Kai touched her arm.

"Are you a relative or her solicitor?" He peered down his nose at her, his posture practically screaming, 'You couldn't possibly be a lawyer.'

"I'm her brother," Carl interjected, positioning himself in front of the officer.

Rhianne smirked as she noticed the officer take a small step back.

"Well, if your sister gets processed, maybe the Senior Sergeant will let you have a chat with her," the officer said, his tone losing some of its arrogance.

"Might?" Rhianne moved next to Carl. "And how long is this so-called 'processing' going to drag on?"

The officer's confidence wavered as he stammered, "Well, uh, it depends on the officer in charge."

Rhianne's eyes narrowed and she took a step closer.

"I'd like to see the officer in charge immediately." A commanding voice boomed from behind them. Rhianne, Carl, and Kai turned to face the newcomer.

A tall woman, standing at six feet, strutted into the room, clad in a striking dark red power suit. In her right hand, she lugged a weighty metal briefcase. Carl's eyes widened, and his jaw dropped open. Rhianne observed the woman's determined stride as she made her way towards the counter. With her darker skin and angular features, she seemed to have gargoyle blood, but her soft blue eyes added a touch of gentleness. It was like encountering an Amazonian warrior with a touch of gargoyle magic. How interesting. A part gargoyle? Now that was something she hadn't come across before.

"Carl Vargas?" The woman asked, and Carl nodded mutely, seemingly speechless. She extended her hand towards him. "I'm Marissa Austin, a solicitor. Your parents contacted me."

Carl shook her hand without uttering a word.

"Hi," Rhianne said brightly. "I am Rhianne Alkenn." She extended her hand and Marissa shook her hand. She had been half-expecting a bone-crushing grip from the formidable-looking woman. To her surprise, her handshake was firm but not overwhelming.

Marissa raised an eyebrow. "And you are?"

"She's our boss at the Tea Leaves." Carl had finally found his vocal cords but was still wide-eyed as he stared at Marissa.

Marissa's lips twitched with amusement. "The Tea Leaves, you say?" She fought back a smile.

"Yep, that's my landscaping business," Rhianne said. "The police decided to show up, probably hoping to find some excuse to search the place. Lucky for me, but unlucky for Alice, Carl and Alice were there searching for a missing earring."

"Did the police have a valid search warrant?" Marissa asked all business again.

Rhianne snorted. "Nope and when I said they couldn't search without it, Johannes —."

"That would be Senior Sergeant Johannes." The officer behind the counter supplied and at Marissa's withering glance, he promptly busied himself with some papers on a

CHAPTER 8

desk. Rhianne noted the officer's attempt to eavesdrop while maintaining a safe distance.

"Anyway, Johannes said he was arresting Alice on suspicion of murdering Devlin Parkes."

"The real estate developer?" Marissa raised an eyebrow.

"The very same," Rhianne confirmed.

Marissa tilted her head. "Interesting, I hadn't heard he'd been murdered."

"No, all of it is being kept very hush-hush by the police and the family. Not sure why." Rhianne shrugged her shoulders.

"Probably to give the police enough time to come up with a viable suspect," Marissa said matter-of-factly. She leaned against the counter, a knowing look on her face. "They don't like it when there's a high-profile case and they can't point a finger at someone. It makes them look incompetent."

"Ah, appearances matter." Kai extended his hand. "I'm Kai Wagner."

Marissa's hand clasped Kai's with a firm shake, her eyes assessing him. "Well, sometimes the looks and the skills align perfectly." A smile tugged at the corner of her lips.

Rhianne appreciated Marissa's directness. She was feeling better about the chances of getting Alice out on bail.

"I'm a Tech Mage and occasional police consultant," Kai said. "I happened to be consulting on the case with Rhianne."

Marissa blinked a couple of times. She turned her gaze towards Rhianne, her eyes filled with curiosity. Sensing the need to be cautious, Rhianne glanced at the hovering police officer, his presence a clear reminder of potential eavesdropping.

"Why were you called on as a consultant?" Marissa asked.

Rhianne hesitated for a second, trying to think of a way to

balance helping Alice and still abiding by her confidentiality agreement. She leaned in closer to Marissa and lowered her voice. "Well, let's just say there are some unique aspects to this case that require a different perspective."

Marissa's eyes narrowed briefly. "Processing will take a couple of hours. There's a great late-night place nearby." Without hesitation, she turned and led the way out of the police station, with Rhianne, Kai, and Carl following closely behind.

The Cuban eatery buzzed with lively conversations, clinking glasses, and the vibrant melodies of Nueva Trova music. Marissa approached the manager, and within moments, they were ushered into a secluded room. Half of the room's walls were solid, while the other half boasted a lattice covered in artificial ivy. Shielded from prying eyes and the boisterous music, they finally had a semblance of privacy.

"I ordered some snacks and drinks. Not sure if you want anything, but being up late always makes me hungry," Marissa said, glancing at Rhianne and the others. She then looked at Rhianne meaningfully.

Rhianne took a sip of her drink. "Well, besides my landscaping business, which involves tending to rare healing plants, I'm also a self-proclaimed expert on all things botanical," she said. "You'd be surprised how much knowledge I've acquired on those plants that can both heal and harm and, sometimes, it's a fine line."

Marissa leaned forward. "Ah, the fine balance of nature. Fascinating," she said. Then she turned to Kai. "And what about you? How do you fit into this intriguing mix?"

Kai shrugged. "With the motive. Always follow the money." Her lips curled into a wry smile. "I'm glad Alice has good

CHAPTER 8

people in her corner." Her focus shifted to Carl. "So, Carl, how's Alice involved?"

Carl nearly choked on his drink, prompting Rhianne to pat his back soothingly. "Well, you see, Ms Austin, I don't think I should be sharing second-hand stories," he stammered, avoiding eye contact.

Marissa studied him intently, her gaze framed by thick eyelashes. "Carl, please call me Marissa. As Alice's solicitor, I need to have at least some information to help her. I understand your concerns, but without some details, it'll be challenging for me to assist."

Carl fidgeted nervously, toying with his drink. "What if it gets her into trouble?" he asked in a small voice.

Rhianne's eyebrows shot up as Marissa's hand landed on one of Carl's fidgeting hands, giving it a reassuring squeeze.

"That's for me to worry about. I will do and say whatever is best for Alice. You can trust me," Marissa said, her tone soft and gentle.

It was a side of Marissa that Rhianne hadn't expected. She glanced at Kai, who seemed to be waiting to see how Carl would respond.

Carl met Marissa's gaze and took a deep breath. "Alice told Devlin Parkes he was a dead man walking a few months ago."

CHAPTER 9

Rhianne cursed under her breath. "Why?" she asked.

Carl's shoulders sagged, and he let out a sigh. "You have to understand, it was in the heat of the moment. Alice has a quick temper, same as our mum. She says things she doesn't mean. You believe me, don't you?" Carl asked in a pleading voice.

Rhianne reached out and gave Carl's arm a reassuring squeeze. "Of course I do. if Alice wanted to kill him, she would have done it in front of a crowd. Sneaking around is not her style."

Marissa's lips twitched. "Remind me not to get you as a character reference."

Carl looked alarmed.

Rhianne nodded. "Exactly, Alice may have a hot temper, but cold-blooded murder? I just can't see it."

Marissa leaned forward; her gaze fixed on Carl. "We need to understand what led up to this. What did Devlin do to provoke such anger from Alice?"

Carl sighed, a hint of weariness in his voice. "It's a complicated story, and I wasn't there for most of it."

CHAPTER 9

Marissa's expression remained gentle, but there was an unmistakable firmness in her tone. "Then you'd better start telling us."

Carl took a deep breath. "About a year ago, Devlin Parkes approached my parents with a proposal. He wanted to buy the land next to their mine to build a golf resort. He had these fancy brochures showing the golf course right where the forest is." He glanced at Rhianne. "I know you have concerns about mines and the environment."

Rhianne pressed her lips together, refraining from interrupting. She had never been shy about voicing her concerns about mines and their impact on the surrounding wilderness. It was one of the reasons she was surprised when Alice revealed that their parents owned a mine. Alice, too, had shown support for environmental protection and had a deep love for her garden business. Perhaps that was why they had kept their parents' mine a secret, not wanting to upset her. While Rhianne believed she wouldn't have been angry, she understood their hesitation.

"It's different, you see," Carl continued. "They mine using traditional methods with axes and picks in the already formed underground caves."

Rhianne shook her head. "You don't have to explain it to me, Carl."

A hopeful expression filled Carl's eyes. "You don't mind?"

She gave him a small, bittersweet smile, recognising the irony in her assumptions. "Why would it matter to me what your parents do? I wouldn't want anyone to judge me based on my own mother."

Marissa, with her arms crossed, nodded, and Carl's face lit up with joy. "Thanks, boss, you're the best!" He reached out to ruffle her hair.

"Hey, no hair messing!" Rhianne protested, trying to put on a stern expression, but her lips betrayed her amusement. In truth, she could never be mad at Carl. He was a peculiar mix of naivety and wisdom that always melted her heart.

"All right, let's get back to the story," Marissa said.

Carl nodded. "Anyway, my parents didn't seem to care much, but Alice was furious about the potential loss of the forest. She tried to convince our parents to do something about it." He rubbed his chin. "But they dismissed it, saying it wasn't their concern. That didn't sit well with Alice, so she took matters into her own hands. She launched a campaign, putting up flyers all over town and speaking at council meetings to rally support."

He briefly paused as his gaze became distant, then continued, "Alice was over the moon when the local council rejected the application. But Mr Parkes wasn't one to take 'no' for an answer. He escalated the matter to the Environment Court. In response, Alice took to social media and started targeting politicians, creating quite a stir. The negative press made the Environment Court hesitate to make a decision."

Carl glanced around the table. "I wasn't present during all of this, so I can only share what I've heard. In any case, Alice received a tip that Devlin Parkes had grown impatient and had arranged for his tree loggers, armed with heavy machinery, to come in the middle of the night and cut down as many trees as possible. Sure, he would have been fined, but once the trees were gone, it would have been too late, wouldn't it?"

Rhianne agreed with Carl's accurate insight and opened her mouth to comment, but Marissa beat her to it.

"Absolutely," Marissa chimed in. "He would have got a mere

CHAPTER 9

slap on the wrist, a few thousand dollars in fines that he would have seen as a small price to pay. And then he would have likely negotiated a deal, agreeing to replace some of the trees on the condition that his plans were ultimately approved."

Carl nodded. "It was headed in that direction, but Alice rallied a group of people and they rushed to the forest to put a stop to it. Some resorted to chaining themselves to the trees to prevent the loggers from cutting them down. Unfortunately, Devlin Parkes decided to show up in person, ensuring the loggers followed his orders."

Rhianne chimed in, "Maybe he thought some of the loggers might have a sudden change of heart and realise what he was truly up to?"

Rhianne knew the type. When money is involved, people have a remarkable ability to turn a blind eye. And in this case, tree logging was their bread and butter.

Devlin Parkes likely wasn't one to gracefully accept 'no' for an answer. Rhianne imagined him as someone who felt entitled, always striving to have things his way. Alice and her group would have been a constant thorn in his side, challenging his authority at every turn. She'd bet against the gnomes that those approval delays cost him more than just a fine. Well, maybe not the gnomes; they were too sharp to take the bet. It probably evolved into a personal vendetta for him. He wanted to prove he could win, and Rhianne could picture him relishing the sweet taste of victory on his lips, particularly when it came to rubbing it in their faces.

Carl toyed with the untouched drink in front of him, his gaze fixed on its contents. "Well, from what I've heard, Alice didn't hold back. She confronted Parkes face to face, shouted at him, and threatened him."

Marissa leaned in; eyes bright. "Do you happen to know what she said to him?"

Kai retrieved his tablet and positioned it at the centre of the table, ensuring everyone had a clear view. It was no surprise that someone had captured a video of the incident. Rhianne figured these days just about everyone under the age of sixty immediately started recording. She paid attention as the images revealed that Devlin Parkes had brought more than the tree loggers. Around him, there were about five beefy guys so he must have been expecting trouble; perhaps even looking forward to the confrontation. Kai upped the volume and she could hear the mixture of the sound of chainsaws and shouting. Alice came into the frame. She was gesticulating wildly, and she walked straight up to Parkes. Before she could get too close, one of the beefy guys stepped in front of him. Parkes snickered behind the guard.

Whoever was filming got closer and the sound of Alice's voice came through loud and clear: "You think you are a big brave man coming here? You're nothing but a coward, a gutless wonder who's hiding behind thugs," Alice yelled trying to move around to see Parkes, but the guard continued to block her.

"That's just stating the facts," Marissa commented.

In the video, Alice continued her tirade. "You may feel safe behind your goon's protection for now, but mark my words, when I find you, I'll tear you apart like you wanted to do with those trees. Let's see how you like it!"

"Well, that could be interpreted as a threat of bodily harm," Marissa said.

"Is that the same as threatening to murder someone?" Rhianne asked.

CHAPTER 9

Marissa pursed her lips. "Absolutely not. It's more of a metaphorical expression, a bit of poetic licence in the heat of the moment, perhaps. I'll make sure the judge sees it that way."

Kai paused the video. "It goes off to focus on a protester chaining herself to the tree. I'll keep looking and see if I can find anything else."

Rhianne gave him a grateful smile.

Marissa stood up, glancing at her gold Longines watch. "I believe I know enough now to secure Alice's release. Let's head back before she loses her composure and inadvertently gives the police ammunition to use against her. They're likely to be watching for any misstep, perhaps even trying to provoke her."

Rhianne went to grab her wallet and noticed that Carl and Kai were doing the same. Marissa shook her head with a knowing smile. "Oh no, this one's on me, and it's all part of the grand expense account," she said, raising a hand to pre-empt any objections. "You've all provided invaluable information. Trust me, her parents will be more than happy to foot the bill for this meal." She winked.

Rhianne hoped this would mean Alice would be back at the 'Tea Leaves' as usual. Both of them were fabulous with plants. It had never occurred to her until now that it was unusual for gargoyles. They had a secret green thumb hidden beneath their stony exterior. Carl could coax the most delicate orchids to bloom, while Alice had a way with hard-to-grow flowers. Life was full of delightful surprises, and the mystery of their green-fingered talents was just another piece of the puzzle.

They all filed back into the police station.

"I am here to see the officer in charge," Marissa announced

as soon as they crossed the door frame.

Rhianne wondered if it was an intimidating tactic. It certainly worked on her. She knew how to project her own voice, but she could take a tip or two from Marissa. She saw the same police officer shrink at the sound and reluctantly turned their way.

"You're back," he said with a hint of resignation.

Rhianne refrained from asking if he'd missed their delightful company. This was Marissa's show.

Marissa simply raised her eyebrows and stared at him. "I'm here to represent my client. If anyone speaks to her without me, I'll raise a complaint to the judge. Is there anyone in there talking to her?" Marissa made a show of taking her tablet out and using the shiny stylus on it.

"I'll go check." The officer said and hurried off.

A few minutes later, Johannes walked out, his brows furrowed deeply. He approached the counter with precise, somewhat rigid movements.

"I'm Detective Senior Sergeant Johannes," he said.

Marissa placed her metal briefcase on the edge of the counter, causing a loud thud.

Rhianne was taking notes: 'get metal case.'

Kai leaned against the wall, seemingly sharing her amusement, while Carl shifted nervously between his feet.

"Marissa Austin, Alice Vargas' solicitor. I'm here to see my client."

Johannes brushed his hand over his head, even though his hair was too short to need fixing. "We're still processing her."

Marissa leaned forward. "I need to know the grounds for charging my client and the evidence supporting it. If it doesn't hold up, you have two options: release her on the spot or

CHAPTER 9

prepare for a judge's order."

Johannes clenched his jaw, his eyes narrowing. "Your client, Alice Vargas, is being accused of the murder of Devlin Parkes."

Marissa stood serenely; her face looked so still it looked like it had been carved out from ivory. "Accused being the operative word. I'm sure the Judge —" She looked up her smartphone and scrolled through it. "Hmm." Her eyes gleamed with mischief. "If it isn't Judge Carruthers on duty. He so detests being interrupted during his bridge game on Saturday nights."

Johannes grunted. "We have witnesses and footage of her violently threatening the victim."

Marissa's smile transformed into a predatory grin. "Ah, the wonders of time-stamped evidence. That footage you're referring to is from eleven months ago. Alice didn't lay a finger on anyone in the forest. And as for her 'threat,' it was nothing more than a clever metaphor uttered in a moment of exasperation."

Johannes' face turned a shade of crimson. "Metaphor?"

"Tell me Detective —" She tapped her long fingers against the counter and appeared thoughtful. "I'm sorry, I didn't catch your name. I will have to put that in my report."

Johannes clenched his jaw. "It's Senior Sergeant Johannes."

"Oh, I'm curious, Senior Sergeant. Can you confirm if the victim was brutally beaten? You see, gargoyle punches leave quite a distinct mark."

Johannes' gaze shifted to Rhianne; his expression filled with warning. "If you've disclosed any confidential information related to the investigation —"

"Now, now, Senior Sergeant," Marissa cooed. "Let's not make accusations we can't back up. Ms Alkenn hasn't disclosed anything about the investigation. But your reaction tells me that the cause of death doesn't align easily with my client, does it?"

Johannes' face turned an unflattering shade of red, his lips thinning into a tight line. "I can't disclose investigation details, even to the accused's solicitor."

"I don't expect you to," Marissa said, her tone shifting to serious and business-like. "But we both know that without solid evidence, Judge Carruthers won't be pleased. He's quite close with your Police Area Commander, so it would be wise for you to consider that before tarnishing any reputation you may have. So, when did you say this processing will be completed?" Marissa waved her phone in her hand.

"I'll go finish it now," Johannes spat out and turned back.

"You do that," Marissa said.

Finally, the side door swung open, revealing Johannes emerging with a disgruntled Alice in tow. He didn't look their way as if their presence was nothing more than an inconvenience. Without so much as a nod of acknowledgement, he unceremoniously unlocked the cuffs from Alice's wrists.

Johannes' gaze shifted between Marissa, Kai, and Rhianne. Marissa met his glare with a calm smile.

"This is not the end," Johannes said.

Marissa's response was laced with equal parts confidence and mischief. "Oh, I can guarantee that it isn't."

They stepped out of the station, leaving behind the stifling atmosphere. Outside, the evening air embraced them, carrying a hint of coolness that provided a brief respite from the lingering summer heat.

"You were amazing!" Carl blurted out. All eyes turned toward him, and a blush collared his cheeks, contrasting

CHAPTER 9

against his dark skin.

Marissa responded with a flutter of her eyelashes. "Why, thank you, Carl." Her teasing tone only deepened the crimson hue on Carl's face.

Meanwhile, Alice remained silent, her eyes stared at nothing. Rhianne placed a comforting hand on her arm. "Are you okay?"

Alice met Rhianne's gaze. "I'm sorry I brought trouble to your door." Her voice trembled.

Rhianne scoffed. "Don't blame yourself for any of this. The police were way out of line, and I know you wouldn't murder anyone."

Kai's voice turned harsh. "Seriously, Johannes went too far accusing you of violating your confidentiality agreement."

It was touching that Kai's anger flared bright on her behalf. "You remember what Li — Sergeant Chen said, right? She threatened to take away your consulting job too. She's got a chip on her shoulder and she's spitting out empty threats and baseless accusations."

Rhianne let it slide, but she was pretty sure that it had mattered to Kai. There was a story there.

"Do we still have our jobs?"

Alice's question caught Rhianne off guard, and she turned her gaze sharply towards her. "What? Why on earth would you think you wouldn't have your jobs?"

"You aren't angry that the police want to search your place, that they arrested me? I know I should have been calmer, but —"

Alice's words struck Rhianne deeply, and she felt a surge of protectiveness for her and Carl. She reached out and grasped Alice's hands. "Alice, I'm not angry at you. I'm furious at the

115

police for their misguided actions and the way they've treated you. You're innocent, caught up in their incompetence."

As the words left her lips, Rhianne felt a renewed sense of determination wash over her. She knew she had to redouble her efforts in finding the real murderer. She was not going to stand by and let the police place the blame on her people.

"Thank you." Alice's downcast expression lightened.

On the other hand, Carl's enthusiasm was hard to contain as he rushed over for a tight hug. Rhianne found herself momentarily caught in a bear hug that threatened to squeeze the air out of her lungs.

"Argh, I can't breathe," she managed to protest, her voice muffled by the sudden embrace. Carl released her instantly, his eyes widening in alarm.

"Did I hurt you?" he asked, holding her shoulders as if she were a fragile vase about to shatter. He searched for any signs of damage.

"No, you didn't. I'm perfectly fine," she reassured him with a smile. "You two are fantastic employees, and I can't wait to see you both on Monday."

"Count on it, boss. We'll be there with bells on," Carl chimed in.

The thought of Carl showing up with bells on triggered a spontaneous burst of laughter from Rhianne, and she noticed Kai's chuckles joining in. Clearly, they shared a similar dry sense of humour.

Marissa smiled. "I think it's best if I get my client out of here and start preparing some documentation. Can I count on you to be a character witness if the need arises?" She paused for a moment, her eyes glinting. "Of course, I'll provide you with a script. You know, just to make sure you give the best possible

CHAPTER 9

character reference. Specific instructions and all."

Rhianne huffed. I mean seriously, a girl says Alice would have been more likely to pummel the guy than poison him and suddenly you need instructions?

After bidding their farewells, it was just her and Kai left standing on the footpath.

They walked towards Kai's car, and he hesitated for a moment.

"Well, that certainly wasn't how I envisioned our evening unfolding," he said.

Rhianne smiled and leaned against the car. "If you plan on sticking around, Mr Expert Consultant, you better get used to the thrill and chaos that seems to follow me wherever I go. Trouble has a way of finding me."

"I could use some excitement, and trouble is underrated." Kai winked at her.

Rhianne laughed. She was tempted to suggest he join her for a drink, but figured they could all use some time to process things.

"I'm looking forward to your home cooked meal next Monday evening," she said instead.

Kai grinned. "No pressure, right? But I have an additional proposal. Let's meet on Monday morning at Rueben's, the French Patisserie on Clarence St."

Rhianne arched an eyebrow. "Oh? And why Rueben's?"

Kai's eyes twinkled. "Well, word on the street is that the forensic pathologist has a weakness for their fresh croissants."

CHAPTER 10

Rhianne slept in on Sunday morning, feeling the toll of the late night catching up to her. She groaned inwardly, realising that she must be getting old if she couldn't handle back-to-back late nights anymore. After a shower, she got dressed and decided it was time to check out the private garden. She doubted they could get a search warrant on a Sunday, but she didn't want to push her luck. Grabbing an apple, she headed downstairs where Toto was snoozing with his paws up. "Morning, sleepy head!" she called out.

Toto jumped up and barked furiously and Rhianne laughed. "Someone is a bit jumpy this morning."

"You would be too if you had undertaken the formidable task of confronting an entire squad of police officers single-handedly." Toto huffed; his tail held high.

Rhianne's lips curled into a smile. "Indeed, Toto, your timely intervention definitely made a difference."

Toto narrowed his eyes. "I must say, your recognition of my courage is a rather unexpected development."

"Oh, your bravery has never been in question," she said. She

CHAPTER 10

just doubted the size of his heroic feats, but she wisely kept that to herself, at the risk of getting her fingers nipped.

Toto harrumphed but was mollified enough to allow her to pat him. "It is indeed fortuitous that Alice has attained her freedom," he said.

Rhianne looked at him. "And how exactly do you know that?"

"It should not come as a surprise that I chose to be actively involved."

Her eyebrow arched in surprise. "You went as an eagle?"

She hadn't seen him or sensed him.

He grinned, clearly pleased with himself. "Indeed, you did not anticipate that, did you?"

"No, I was a bit preoccupied arguing with those rude policemen."

Rhianne retrieved the key to the private garden, a glass greenhouse covered in shade cloth. As she approached the main door, secured with a lock, she was relieved to see no signs of tampering. Entering the plant nursery, she made a beeline for the section where she kept the Romin specimens.

There were only two plants, indistinguishable from orchids by the untrained eye. She assessed their condition, checking the soil's pH and inspecting the delicate stamens where the healing substance resided. With the utmost care, she used long, thin scissors and tweezers, aware that even a touch from her fingers could cause them to wither.

Rhianne pulled out her smartphone, capturing multiple photos of the Romin specimens while ensuring the date and time were clearly displayed. To produce the poison, a minimum of three stamens would be required. She exhaled a breath she hadn't even realised she was holding. The poison had not originated from her own stock.

Toto's bark echoed through the area, a clear call for attention.

"I'm coming!" Rhianne replied.

She made her way towards the opposite end of the expansive space. However, as she passed the door, her gaze was drawn to something unexpected — a shiny black feather caught in one of the vents above. Crows weren't a common sight in the area, leaving her puzzled. "Currawongs, perhaps?" she wondered aloud. Standing on her tiptoes, she carefully plucked the feather from where it was stuck and continued on her way.

Toto was intently sniffing the ground near the bags of fertiliser.

"What's up?" she asked.

"Someone was present at this location. I found footprints," Toto replied, his nose still investigating, a perplexed expression on his furry face.

"In the private garden?" Her hand flew to her throat. "Do you know who it might have been?"

Her mind brimmed with questions. Who was here? To steal something and do what? She tried to remind herself that the Romin plant hadn't been touched, but the mere thought of someone trespassing in her private space was unsettling.

How had they managed to get in without leaving any signs of forced entry? Had they effortlessly picked the triple lock, or was it a display of exceptional skill? The furrow deepened on her forehead, as she contemplated the various possible scenarios.

"Huh? Why aren't there any other footprints leading to this spot from the door?" She knelt down and closely inspected

CHAPTER 10

the ground, scrutinising every inch for any sign or clue. Her gaze then shifted to the glass ceiling, half-expecting to see a broken pane, but it was intact.

Toto grumbled. "They did not enter through the doorway."

She rubbed her eyebrows and bent down to study the footprints. "What do you mean?"

"These footprints belong to an elf," Toto said. "And they arrived through a portal."

"An elf?" Her body tensed. "My father?" she whispered, a flutter in her belly.

Toto shook his head. "No, not your father."

Rhianne's throat constricted. "Are you sure?"

Toto trotted over to her and licked her shin. They said that dogs could sense a person's emotions and in Toto's case she knew it to be true.

"I would be able to recognise your father's scent."

"But how do you know for certain that it was an elf? And isn't using a portal something that only a select few can do?" Rhianne's curiosity was piqued. She had never attempted creating a portal, partly because she was wary of the dangers of attracting unwanted attention, but also because she was frightened she wouldn't be able to do it. That would just be another tick in her own arsenal of self-pity. And her self-pity box was already overflowing.

Toto let out a patient sigh. "Indeed, I can detect their elven signature. It possesses a distinct scent that is unmistakable," he explained. "Nevertheless, I am unable to ascertain their affiliation."

"Wait!" Rhianne exclaimed. "What do you mean by affiliation? And where does my father fit?"

As soon as the words escaped her lips, she regretted them.

Memories of her distant father brought up painful feelings that she had worked hard to bury.

She was about to dismiss the question, but curiosity got the better of her. "I'm just curious," she added.

Toto sat down on his hunches and cleared his throat. "You have the Summer Court, the Winter Court, the Autumn Court and the Spring Court," he said. "Moreover, you have the High Court, where the Queen presides." Toto paused for a moment before continuing, "Your father belongs to the Autumn Court, and both the Autumn and Winter Courts are generally regarded as more inclined towards logic and reason and less driven to emotional displays."

"And is that true?" she asked hesitantly. Was that why her father was so absent from her life? Because he didn't care?

Toto's expression turned serious. "I must acknowledge my previous affiliation with the Summer Court; however, I have since chosen the path of independence. It was hard-won because the Courts regard such independence with disdain. They see it as a weakness."

She sat down on a stool, her eyes fixed on Toto. "A weakness for the independent one?" she asked.

Toto's eyes darkened. "It signifies the absence of allegiance to any Court, and this poses a direct threat to their authority."

She nodded, absorbing Toto's words. She wondered if her father's absence was related to his Court affiliation.

Toto paused. "All courts are powerful in their own right and their strengths and weaknesses are different."

Rhianne's phone rang to the tune of *Winner Takes All*. She groaned inwardly, tempted to ignore the call, but knew she couldn't avoid it forever. With a resigned sigh, she answered, "Hello, Mother."

CHAPTER 10

"Good morning, Rhianne. Did you get my invitation?" Her mother's tone was businesslike and efficient.

Rhianne tried to figure out what invitation her mother was talking about. As she thought about her cluttered desk, she realised she probably had many unopened letters scattered among the mess. She had been so busy with work that she had neglected to go through her mail properly. Darn!

Trying to regain her composure, she asked, "What invitation?" Internally she kicked herself. She had just admitted to an unacceptable faux pas.

"Unless the carrier pigeon got diverted on the way, and my pigeons are very well trained, then it's probably sitting on a pile on your desk. It has my symbol in gold letters, Rhianne, it's not like you could have missed it."

She had, actually, but this time she refrained from saying so.

"It's next Saturday. The dress code is black tie. Given what I know of your wardrobe, please stop by Madame Marchant tomorrow."

"I'm really busy." The answer came by rote.

A deep sigh echoed through the phone line. Her mother had perfected the art of conveying deep disappointment. It didn't work on her anymore. Not much anyway.

"Rhianne," her mother said, "even you can't disagree with this gathering. It's to raise money to build a new school for supernatural children whose parents cannot afford private supernatural schools."

"What's wrong with human schools?"

"Tell me," Her mother said. "What happens when the humans bully a wolf shifter, or when a child fire mage starts experimenting with her powers during Chemistry lab?"

Rhianne pinched her nose. She knew she was losing ground fast. "What about halflings? Are they included or they don't matter?"

This was an issue close to Rhianne's heart; because of their weak supernatural powers, halfling children were often made fun of by supernaturals and humans alike. Not only that, but technically halflings in general weren't really represented by the state council. Only those who displayed sufficient traits were accepted within their packs or guilds, leaving the rest to deal with suspicion from some humans. Rhianne herself was technically part of the coven due to her mother's influence, but she never participated in any of their rituals or events.

Her mother paused as if gathering her patience. "You have this tendency to try to protect everyone. You need to work out what you can and cannot do."

Rhianne had heard this repeated so many times before, she had stopped paying attention. One day, perhaps, she would learn to pick her battles.

"Do you honestly believe it is wise to place low-ability children alongside the fully gifted? They could get injured unintentionally," her mother said. "If they can manage, however, they'll have a spot."

Rhianne stayed silent. This was a game they both excelled at.

"Look," and the exasperation in her mother's voice came through loud and clear. "I'll put forward to the committee a suggestion for a school for halflings."

Her mother's sudden acquiescence surprised her, but she wasn't about to turn down a chance at victory. "You'll have another event to raise money for the halfling school as well?"

"Yes." the sound of finality in her mother's tone, told

CHAPTER 10

Rhianne that the conversation was at an end. "I'll see you Saturday."

"See you then," Rhianne said, but before she could finish her sentence, her mother had already hung up.

Typical! She hadn't even asked if she could bring someone along. In the past, she had occasionally taken Nel to these events, but it was painfully clear that Nel and her mother didn't exactly get along. Maybe this time she could bring Kai. The thought of him in a formal tuxedo, showcasing his broad shoulders, brought a grin to her face. Locking up, she raced upstairs to find the invitation. Knowing her mother, there was probably some enchantment that would alert her if the invitation remained unopened. She definitely wasn't in the mood for another tedious discussion.

The soiree was downtown on the top floor of the Barangaroo Towers. That was the good news, it meant it would likely be a big affair with hundreds of people and she'd be able to avoid her mother. So long as she turned up and was seen she would have done her duty. She searched the bottom of the invitation and luckily it had the requisite 'and guest.'

* * *

On Monday morning, she managed to find a spot for her bike near Rueben's in Surry Hills, one of the city's most bustling culinary neighbourhoods, close to Sydney's downtown. The sweet scent of freshly baked pastries led her to a brick cottage painted in white. She realised there was already a queue out the door and could see no sign of Kai. Her phone beeped and she glanced down to read the message: 'Was early, pastries incoming.'

Then she saw Kai weaving his way around the customers in the queue triumphantly holding a brown box. Rhianne smiled at him as he approached her.

"You look like the cat who got the cream," she said.

"More like the mage who got the last three cinnamon and almond croissants."

This announcement resulted in groans from the customers still in the queue.

"Popular, are they?" Rhianne said, cocking her eyebrows.

"You must have been living under a rock, if you're asking that. And we'd better depart or they," and he pointed behind his back, where people were staring daggers at him, "might decide to steal them and run." His mouth was in a straight line, but the corners of his eyes were crinkling.

"I think we're already in enough trouble with the police, so let's not add fuel to the fire by encouraging a riot," Rhianne said as they hurriedly moved away. "So, where are we headed?"

"I hope you're not squeamish about dead bodies. I'm carrying precious food that I had to fight tooth and nail to protect from the hungry masses and it shouldn't be wasted," he replied, maintaining a brisk pace that made Rhianne struggle to keep up.

"You just want to have enough for yourself," she accused.

"Guilty as charged," he responded with a poker face that was impressively convincing.

"To answer your question, we're headed to the Department of Forensic Medicine's mortuary. Dr Isobel Dupre, the forensic pathologist, has quite the sweet tooth."

"Are you suggesting we bribe a government official?" Rhi-

CHAPTER 10

anne widened her eyes in mock horror.

"I prefer to think of it as providing sustenance to a hard-working government official who needs the right fuel to carry out her important duties," he said with a straight face.

"That sounds like a memorised line," Rhianne said.

"It was Isobel who said it, actually. Here we are." Kai pushed open the glass door. The receptionist was reading the newspaper when they came in but put it down when she heard them.

"Hello Kai," the receptionist said.

She was a middle-aged, heavy-set woman with dark skin and waves of curly hair. "I can smell those from here. You didn't forget Nina, did you?"

"As if," Kai said, opening the box and presenting her with a vanilla slice.

Nina beamed at him.

"You're so wonderful, always remembering my favourite. Go on in. She is in a foul mood, but those pastries there should do the trick."

Kai smiled at Nina and turned to the right towards a set of double doors. The sound of a click told Rhianne Nina had unlocked the doors and she followed closely behind Kai as he pushed them open. The floors were a clean, glossy tile and the smell of bleach lingered in the air.

"Ever been to a mortuary before?" Kai asked.

"No, but this looks and smells just like a hospital."

"You mean the smell of disinfectant and chlorine was a dead giveaway?"

"Hmm, if you weren't such a high-level Tech Mage, I'd suggest becoming a comedian," Rhianne said.

Kai's steps directed them to another door on the left,

Rhianne could hear grumbling on the inside and Kai knocked twice to no response. He opened the door, slipped the pastry's box through the gap and waited.

Rhianne raised her eyebrows.

"Is that a fresh almond croissant?" a hopeful voice said from the inside. "If it is, come in, if not, get lost."

Kai stepped in with a long stride and with little fanfare deposited the box on the desk that dominated the small room.

Rhianne peered in, not sure what to expect. Behind the desk was a small woman with dainty features, her hair a soft brown and her eyes an ethereal blue. She wore a pair of glasses that perched lightly on her nose and she was eyeing the box intently. Rhianne was amazed that Kai had managed to locate a spot on the desk, which was cluttered with piles of folders and stacks of paper.

The woman, presumably Dr Isobel Dupre, got up, grabbed the box and opened it. She took an almond croissant out and bit into it, her face lighting up in ecstasy.

"Marry me," she said to Kai in between bites.

Kai smiled as he would at a cute child and lowered himself onto one of the two plastic chairs.

Rhianne laughed. "I think you'd have to get in the queue." The words slipped out of her mouth before she could stop them.

Kai blushed and heat rose through her body.

Isobel sighed. "All the good ones are always taken." She sat back down after grabbing another croissant and continuing to chew on the one in her hand.

Kai looked at Rhianne apologetically. "It looks like we'll have to share."

Rhianne shrugged and smiled at him.

CHAPTER 10

He hastily plucked the final pastry from the box; perhaps worried Isobel would take it as well. Seeing Isobel attacking the croissants with gusto, she'd say they'd be lucky to hold on to this one.

"Isobel, this is Rhianne Alkenn. She's a friend of mine."

Isobel nodded and little bits of pastry flew in the air. She waved her hand for him to continue.

"We'd like some off-the-record information on a case Rhianne and I are consulting on."

Rhianne wondered if that should have been in the past tense, given their current strained relationship with Johannes and Chen.

"The Devlin Parkes case?"

Kai raised his eyebrows and tilted his head.

Isobel paused in her eating and grinned. "Johannes and Chen have been pestering me and they specifically mentioned not to say anything to anyone outside the force." She looked thoughtful for a moment and there was a sparkle in her eyes.

Was that a flash of light above Isobel's head? But when she blinked it was gone.

"Chen in particular, was quite adamant I wasn't to share information with, and I quote, 'outside consultants who may no longer be part of the case.'"

Kai's body became still and Rhianne pursed her lips, but then Isobel burst into laughter. "Those two can kiss my butt," she said. "They never bother to bring so much as a cup of coffee, and they clearly have no idea how to win a girl's heart. Unlike other handsome," she paused, casting a meaningful glance at Rhianne, "and taken guys. Besides, I already like you much better than Chen."

She took another bite of her croissant, savouring it.

Rhianne leaned forward. "They showed up at my landscape business, demanding to search it without a warrant. They arrived late at night, and I suspect they were looking for an excuse to break in. Instead, they ended up accusing one of my employees of murder."

Isobel scoffed. "Those idiots! So, you have the Romin plant?"

Rhianne nodded in confirmation. "I checked it, and it's untouched."

Isobel shook her head. "It probably wouldn't have mattered anyway. Tell me, do you have a lab?"

"Unless you count my kitchen stove and a collection of cooking utensils, then no," Rhianne said.

Isobel nodded as if she had suspected as much. "Well, then it's clear that Johannes and Chen are barking up the wrong tree. There's no way you or any of your employees could have poisoned Parkes without access to a proper lab and the necessary expertise."

CHAPTER 11

Rhianne and Kai left the mortuary, bidding farewell to Isobel with a promise to return with more pastries another day.

"Well, that was interesting," Rhianne said as they strolled through a nearby park. "Should I tell the police or wait for them to dig an even deeper hole for themselves?"

Kai chuckled. "Best to tell Marissa. She'll relish delivering the news with her signature bite."

"I wish I could be a fly on the wall for that conversation," Rhianne said. "But you're right." She pulled out her smartphone and dialled Marissa's number.

"Marissa Austin speaking," came the sharp voice on the other end of the line.

"Hi Marissa, it's Rhianne. I have some relevant information to share."

She told her, omitting the source of her information and Marissa listened without interrupting.

"Well, this is going to be quite entertaining. I'll call Johannes right away." She hung up.

"She doesn't waste any time, does she?" Rhianne was

impressed by Marissa's efficiency.

"Lawyers are always busy, with invoices to prepare and Senior Sergeants to put in their place." Kai smirked.

Rhianne's lips curved into a smile. "On another note, have you ever wondered what Isobel is?"

Kai arched an eyebrow. "You noticed too? Most people are completely oblivious to it. I only picked up on it because technology sometimes behaves strangely around her. So, how did you figure it out?"

"I thought I saw a brief flash above her head. Did you ask her what kind of supernatural she was?"

"I did. She gave me a reproachful look and said that a lady never reveals her secrets. I haven't brought it up again, but she seemed to like you so maybe you can ask her." Kai suggested.

"You are curious, aren't you? What's your theory?"

Kai stroked his chin. "I'm not entirely sure, and it's been bugging me. I've ruled out some possibilities though. She's not a shifter, mage, or witch. Gargoyles don't have any reaction to her. That leaves a wide range of possibilities. Some demons adapt well to technology, but I'm not well-versed in all the different types. I've also heard that certain fae can't be near electronic devices."

Rhianne nodded. "Some fae have an aversion to iron as it can make them ill, but electronic devices don't seem to have any effect on them."

"You seem quite knowledgeable about the fae?"

Rhianne bristled, her instinctive response triggered by the mention of her mixed heritage. But then she realised that Kai couldn't possibly have known, short of having slightly pointed ears, nothing screamed 'half-elf.' She rarely shared this side of her with others.

CHAPTER 11

Taking a deep breath, she decided to open up a little. "I have some connections to the fae. Toto is a fae of some sort, my grandfather is a dryad, and my father is an elf."

She didn't mention she had hardly seen her father over the years. Because her interactions with him had been so limited, she didn't know as much as she probably should have about elves. To be fair, she also hadn't wanted to learn about them and knew that was a defence mechanism. She braced herself for the typical reactions of disbelief or derision.

Kai nodded. "That's quite unusual, isn't it? I can't say I've had the pleasure of meeting an elf myself, but I've met a couple of mischievous pixies and a helpful brownie. One of the pixies managed to trick me into giving her a pastry, and the brownie kindly took it upon himself to rid my jumper of pesky lint."

Rhianne hid her smile behind her hand.

"Don't laugh," Kai said with earnestness. "The brownie has taken it upon himself to 'see to my wardrobe' once a month."

"Let me guess, he ends up cleaning and organising everything too," Rhianne said, her amusement evident.

"You have no idea. It takes me days to locate some of my stuff after his visits, but I can't complain. He also prepares delicious meals for me and stores them in the freezer."

"Is that one of the meals you're going to feed me tonight?" Rhianne asked.

Kai dramatically placed a hand over his heart. "You wound me! Besides, you might end up liking his cooking better than mine, and I can't have that kind of competition." His eyes crinkled with mirth.

"I'm definitely looking forward to it."

As the words left her lips, Kai's phone rang, interrupting the moment.

He offered an apologetic nod. "Sorry, I have to take this, it's work."

Rhianne nodded and stood up. "I'll see you tonight. Do I need to bring anything?"

"Just yourself," Kai reassured her, his voice turning softer. "That's more than enough."

Rhianne felt a pleasant warmth spreading through her chest. She mouthed a silent farewell to Kai and left him to his call. As she mounted her bike and adjusted her helmet, a sudden realisation hit her — she had forgotten to invite him to the charity soiree.

Rhianne rode back to the 'Tea Leaves', smoothly parking her bike in the garage. She strolled around the main nursery, scanning the area for any sign of Alice. As she turned the corner, her eyes landed on Alice diligently tending to the native fruit trees.

"Hey, Alice!" Rhianne called out.

Alice looked up and greeted her with a smile, though her eyes looked dull.

"Are you doing all right?" Rhianne asked.

"Yeah, just had a chat with my parents. They're not thrilled about us being so far from home. They want us to come back and work at the family mine."

"Oh, I see." She couldn't imagine running the garden nursery without Carl and Alice. The thought left an unpleasant taste in her mouth. She also admitted to herself that she enjoyed chatting with them every day. Alice with her boundless energy and non-stop chatter, and Carl with his gentle and sweet demeanour. With a start, she realised she'd miss them.

Alice continued. "But I told them that the police bail

CHAPTER 11

conditions won't allow me to leave right now."

Rhianne tilted her head. "But why would there be bail conditions? I told Marissa that the Romin couldn't have come from the 'Tea Leaves.'"

"Oh, that was a white lie and it isn't the true reason I'm not going back." Alice grinned.

A noise behind her told her Carl was approaching and about to join the conversation. "It's most definitely not the reason I'm not going," Carl added.

"Oh?"

"I used that as an excuse to get them off the phone, to be honest. Our parents don't understand why we don't want to work in the mine. They believe nursery work is beneath us, and they think the diamond mine business needs fresh talent," Alice said.

Carl raised an eyebrow and cleared his throat, mimicking a deep voice. "Nursery work is not 'suitable' for mountain gargoyles." His voice sounded completely different.

Rhianne glanced back and forth between Carl and Alice.

"That's quite a good imitation of Papa," Alice said, her lips curving into a small smile.

"No gargoyle bride or groom will be interested in either of you if you continue to avoid your responsibilities." His voice took on a different tone again.

Rhianne's jaw dropped, her eyes widening. The unexpected sound of a deep, rough female voice coming from Carl made her do a double take.

Alice's laughter filled the air, breaking Rhianne out of her surprise. The contagious sound caused Rhianne to burst into laughter as well, and soon Carl joined in. Rhianne bent over, clutching her stomach as tears of mirth streamed down her face.

Toto, concerned by the commotion, came bounding over, pawing at Rhianne's leg. "What is occurring, are we under attack? Has someone subjected you to a noxious fume?"

Catching her breath, Rhianne managed to assure him between giggles, "We're fine, Toto. Carl surprised us all with his incredible knack for imitating people. Who knew he had such a hidden talent?"

"He does?" Toto asked, still looking around and narrowing his eyes, a hint of suspicion in his voice.

"I'm the fiercest and bravest of them all," Carl said, flawlessly imitating Toto's pitch and cadence.

The sheer accuracy of the mimicry sent Alice and Rhianne into another fit of laughter.

"That does not resemble my voice," Toto said, puffing up his chest. "I am much more fearsome."

"Then how come you knew he was imitating you?" Rhianne managed to ask, clutching her stomach and attempting to regain control of herself.

"My dear, it takes more than mere mimicry to capture the essence of my fearsomeness. I recognise my own greatness even in the most inaccurate impersonations." Toto held his nose high.

That only fuelled their laughter further. Rhianne felt a wave of relief seeing Alice's smile, even though the exhaustion showed in the bags under her eyes. The arrest had been tough on both Alice and Carl and dealing with disapproving parents added another layer of difficulty. Yet, they persisted in working at the nursery alongside her. Gargoyles typically kept to themselves, rarely interacting with other supernaturals or humans. Their dedication to the nursery spoke volumes about

CHAPTER 11

their resilience and loyalty.

"Hey guys, how about a late lunch?" Rhianne suggested.

Carl looked at her with wide eyes, and even Alice seemed taken aback. "You mean the three of us?" Carl asked.

"Yes, if you're up for it. I think we could all use a little treat," Rhianne said.

Alice hesitated as she chewed her bottom lip. "But what about the Romin plant? What if the police come back —"

Rhianne pulled out her smartphone and deftly tapped on the screen, sending a series of photos to Marissa. "I sent Marissa the photos I took of the Romin. They're date-stamped, so if the police try anything funny, they'll only make themselves look like bigger fools. We've already made it clear that none of us had access to the necessary lab. Their case just fell apart."

Alice let out a relieved breath. "Yeah, that's true."

Carl grinned at Rhianne. "I've always known you were pretty smart, boss."

"Hmph. I have been imparting my wisdom to her, and with my supreme knowledge and outstanding patience, she has improved somewhat," Toto said.

"You're invited too, Toto," Rhianne said, reaching out to give him a chin rub.

"Might they offer fresh fruit?" Toto wagged his tail.

"I'm certain they do. It's strawberry season," Rhianne said with a smile.

Toto's tail wagged harder. "Indeed, I shall not subject myself to that motorised bull of yours. It was not designed with my delicate sensibilities in mind."

Rhianne noticed Alice rolling her eyes and stifled a smile with a quick cough. "Don't worry, Toto. We'll take the delivery van.

"Needs must, I suppose," he said with a sigh. "Do they permit canine companions though?"

"Yes, all good. This place is right by the beach, and they've got outdoor seating where dogs are totally welcome. You can hang out with us."

Toto paused. "Grant me a moment, if you would, please." Without warning, he transformed into a magnificent wedge-tailed eagle and soared into the sky. True to his word, he returned in a few minutes. "I have informed the others to be vigilant and alert me if they spot any suspicious activity, especially those impolite police officers."

"Wait, who are these 'others'?" Rhianne asked but Toto disregarded her question and trotted toward the garage.

"I'll meet you at the café by the beach," Rhianne told Carl and Alice.

As Rhianne turned to head towards the garage, she felt a gentle hand on her shoulder. "Rhianne," Alice spoke softly. "You're more than just a good boss. You're a true friend. Thank you."

Carl nodded in agreement.

Friends? Rhianne had always been a bit awkward in that department. In school, she had the unique talent of not quite fitting in, the curse of being a halfling caught between two worlds. She kept to herself, and dealt with bullies by fighting back fiercely. In her quest to figure out who she was, Rhianne stumbled upon something unexpected — her talent for uncovering mysteries. Like little Lila's pet bunny that went missing. Rhianne took it upon herself to become the pet detective and found the bunny locked away in one of the lab's cupboards. To top it off, she caught the culprit thanks to a candy wrapper left behind. Lila thought Rhianne was a

CHAPTER 11

true hero for saving her beloved pet.

And then there was that time when the teacher's things started disappearing, like Miss Trent's glasses. Before long, she discovered it was a clever bowerbird collecting stuff for its nest. From then on, Miss Trent couldn't stop smiling at her. It turned out that solving mysteries wasn't just a fun game for Rhianne; it became her thing. But despite all her mystery-solving talents, Rhianne was still a bit of a loner. Sure, there were a couple of kids who thought she was their hero, like Lila did. But for the most part, she was labelled as the weird nerd and teacher's pet by the rest. So she kept to herself.

Toto had come into her life when she was six, a faithful companion who had revealed his true nature after a couple of years. Her mother either didn't know or chose to ignore the presence of the odd fae being and Rhianne had never brought it up. Then Nel had arrived, the older brother she had always longed for, and he had become her world for a time. Now, she had two gargoyles who called her a friend, and a potential boyfriend in a Tech Mage. She probably should also add a half-gargoyle lawyer and a mysterious forensic pathologist who might become friends too. Having friends was — strange. But hey, who needs normal friendships when you can have a whimsical crew?

The cafe was nestled by the beach, where the salty ocean breeze danced through the air, providing a delightful escape from the sweltering heat of the day. She heard the faint sound of waves crashing on the shore. As the final days of summer lingered, autumn's chill was nowhere in sight, much to Rhianne's delight. She savoured the carefree spirit of the season.

"Okay, let's shift our focus away from the police case,"

Rhianne suggested as their plates arrived.

Carl and Alice dug into their bean burritos (Were gargoyles vegetarians?), while Rhianne savoured her flavourful chilli cheese empanada.

Toto happily munched on the strawberries and mangoes the waitress had kindly provided, prompting the waitress to comment.

"I've never seen a dog chowing down on fruit before. He's adorable," she said in a bemused voice.

Toto ignored her but preened himself a bit.

"What would you like to talk about, boss?" Carl asked.

"We're having lunch together, Carl, you can call me Rhianne," she replied with a smile.

"Sure thing, boss," he said, his smile widening.

Rhianne rolled her eyes. "How about you enlighten me on the mysterious world of gargoyle dating practices?" She leaned in.

A loud groan escaped both Carl and Alice, drawing the attention of a few nearby customers. But as soon as they caught sight of Carl's imposing figure, they turned their attention back to their own meals. Rhianne smirked. There were definitely some perks to having gargoyles around.

"It's the worst." Alice sighed.

"It's not for the faint-hearted, that's for sure," Carl added.

"All right, you've got me intrigued. Talk to me."

Alice's face turned bright red, while Carl wore a sheepish grin. They exchanged a quick glance.

"The families put forward their eligible offspring from the age of one hundred. They attend these large gatherings that are carefully arranged by the matchmakers," Alice said.

Rhianne took a sip of her fruity and alcohol-free mojito,

CHAPTER 11

the refreshing blend of flavours dancing on her tongue. "Why one hundred? And who are these matchmakers?"

Alice tapped her fingers on the table. "You see, there are gargoyles who specialise in matchmaking. Everyone respects them for it. They start by digging into your family history, going back like five generations. They look at everything — how strong you are, how much you can endure, your height, and even your weight." Alice's hands moved in quick movements. "Some families are very picky about who their kids end up with. Like, one family might only want someone from the mountain gargoyle clan, while another family might be after guardian gargoyles, or maybe they want someone who's not older than two hundred years."

Rhianne's head spun. "There are guardian gargoyles?"

Alice nodded, a glimmer of pride in her eyes. "Yep, Guardian gargoyles hold a special role. They keep watch over our communities."

"When a gargoyle hits a hundred years old, it's a big deal, same as how humans make a fuss about turning eighteen. It's all about celebrating and stepping into adulthood. In our world, kids are really important. Gargoyle parents usually only have one kid in their whole life, so that kid gets a lot of love and attention."

Rhianne nodded.

"And if a gargoyle loses their partner, our rules say they should find someone new within five years. This goes for both the younger and older gargoyles," Alice said.

"Wait, so are you telling me that you're expected to get married before you turn one hundred and five? How old are you now?" Rhianne winced, realising she might have stepped into 'none-of-your-business' territory.

"We turned one hundred and three last November," Carl replied with a smile. "You remember, boss? You got us that incredible cake with layers of chocolate, cherries, and cream. It was absolutely amazing."

"Oh, that was a black forest cake, wasn't it?" She grinned. "I'm pretty sure you devoured half of it all by yourself."

Alice chimed in. "He did too!"

Carl flexed his impressive bicep. "Hey, I'm a big boy. These muscles don't just magically appear, you know."

"What happens if you don't like the match the matchmaker finds for you?"

Rhianne wondered how many potential matches were out there, considering how few gargoyles lived in the city.

Alice's expression turned serious. "There's immense pressure to accept the offers. You can decline up to three, but after that, your parents and family start bombarding you with calls and texts, demanding that you come down from your high horse."

"So, Alice, how many offers have you had?" she asked.

"Carl had four and I've had one," Alice said softly. "It's worse to have less because you are seen as unmatchable."

"Well, you still had the right to turn down the offer," Rhianne said.

Alice's voice dropped to a whisper. "I didn't turn him down," she confessed. "He changed his mind. Apparently, I'm too short and my 'hobbies' are too human."

"What hobbies?" Rhianne asked. Hadn't they recently discussed the idea of pursuing hobbies to meet new people?

Alice sighed. "Working at the plant nursery."

Rhianne's eyebrows furrowed in disbelief. "That's not a hobby, you know. It's more like a calling, a noble mission.

CHAPTER 11

We're like plant doctors, giving TLC to these little green guys that can make people feel better. It's a big deal, not some casual pastime."

"We're on the same page, boss," Carl said.

Rhianne tilted her head. "Why did you turn down your four matches?" she asked.

It was a nosy question, but she'd already put her foot in it. Well, in for a penny, in for a pound. And now she was mixing her metaphors!

Carl let out a wistful sigh.

"They were all wonderful women, strong and fierce. But they all had one condition: they wanted to live in the mountains and for me to work in the mine."

Rhianne's body tensed as she processed Carl's words. "You guys are telling me that working at the nursery is interfering with some major life decisions?" she asked.

The thought of work getting in the way of personal happiness didn't sit well with her.

Carl shook his head. "No, boss, you don't understand," he said. "They weren't interested in me for who I am. It was all about the security and wealth that would come from the mine. They didn't see the real Carl."

"What do your parents say about all this?" she asked, hoping for a glimmer of understanding or support from their families.

"They believe we're wasting good matches and need to grow up and face our responsibilities."

Ouch! Rhianne knew all too well the weight of parental expectations and the pressure to conform.

"Sometimes, the people who are supposed to understand us the most can be the most difficult," Alice said.

Carl's voice shifted dramatically, adopting the tone and accent of an old, gruff woman with an uppity demeanour. "In my time," he said, "children were dutiful and loyal to their families and communities. What matters is not your selfish happiness, but the continuation of a suitable line. Your poor parents! You're besmirching their reputation with your nonsense."

Rhianne's laughter erupted uncontrollably, and Alice joined in, their amusement echoing through the cafe. Their laughter was so infectious that the table trembled, causing Rhianne to quickly grab hold of her glass.

CHAPTER 12

That evening, Rhianne stood before the mirror, her reflection staring back at her. The word "date" hung in the air, creating a flutter of nervousness in her stomach. Should she label it as a dinner at a friend's place instead? But that didn't alleviate the jitters. She frowned as she surveyed the three pairs of jeans and five tops scattered across her bed. She had changed from one outfit to another, yet none satisfied her. Argh, it wasn't like her to be indecisive.

Rhianne's phone rang, breaking the silence in the room. She let out a sigh of relief when she heard the general ringtone, knowing it wasn't her mother or, heaven forbid, Kai calling to cancel their plans. She had assigned a special ringtone for Kai. The chosen tune? *Holding Out for a Hero.* Luckily, Nel hadn't heard it yet.

Rhianne held the green blouse against her face as she answered the phone. "Hello."

"Marissa here. I wanted to know if you are available tomorrow for a character reference at two o'clock. I'll buy lunch as an incentive."

"Uh-huh." Rhianne put down the blouse and picked up a

turquoise halter top. Her gaze shifted to the red one still lying on the bed. Was red too bold?

"I'll then take you to the butchers," Marissa added.

"Eh, what?" Rhianne snapped out of her thoughts.

"Your mind is clearly elsewhere and you're not listening to me. What's up?"

"Oh, sorry."

"Come on, spill it. I won't have your full attention until you get whatever it is out of your head."

Rhianne let out a sigh. "Well, I'm sort of going on a date, maybe a third date, with Kai at his place, and I don't know what to wear." She bit her lip and paused, expecting Marissa to mock her.

But instead, Marissa seemed to consider her words. "Second date, maybe third date at his place calls for a casual yet put-together look. You want to look pretty but not overdone. Show me a video of what you have."

Rhianne switched her phone to video call mode and showed her the three outfits.

"Red is a bit too bold for a maybe third date. The blouse is not quite sexy enough," Marissa said. "Wear the turquoise top with the black jeans and opt for moderately high heels."

Rhianne nodded in agreement, even though Marissa couldn't see her. "Yes, that works, except I'll wear booties. I'm riding," she said. "Thank you for saving me from my indecisiveness. Now you have my full attention for the next ten minutes because I absolutely can't be late."

"I'd be loath to stand in the way of a third date, wouldn't want to be sued for emotional distress," Marissa said.

"You either have interesting clients or you need to stop binge-watching legal dramas," Rhianne said, putting the

CHAPTER 12

phone on speaker and starting to get dressed.

"Watch it, some of those interesting clients happen to be your employees," Marissa retorted.

"Well, technically, their parents hired you," Rhianne said as she squeezed into her skinny black jeans.

"You could have been a decent lawyer if you weren't so passionate about all things green."

"I strive for mediocrity most of the time," Rhianne said, zipping up her jeans.

"Girl, if what I've witnessed is your version of mediocrity, you have a long way to go."

"Mediocrity allows for anonymity," Rhianne said, realising she had inadvertently shared a bit too much. "You mentioned character references?"

Marissa snorted. "Ah, clever redirection tactics. You might have a future in politics with those skills."

Rhianne growled. "Now you're causing me emotional distress."

"Ah, I sense some deep-seated childhood trauma."

"That's a conversation for our third or fourth friendship lunch," Rhianne said as she applied a hint of mascara. "Your ten minutes are almost up."

"Definitely lawyer material. All right, I'll keep it brief. I'll email you a character reference, feel free to make any changes you see fit. We can go over it tomorrow at our lunch. Lunch is at Luna's next to the courthouse. Meet me there at midday," Marissa said, and before Rhianne could agree, the call ended abruptly.

Rhianne glanced at her phone and decided one of these days she would be the one hanging up first. On second thoughts, maybe that was too lofty a goal.

Rhianne jumped on her motorbike and zoomed towards the beach suburb where Kai resided. His terrace house was a few blocks away from the ocean, and the sound of rolling waves filled the air. The scent of sea salt accompanied the gentle breeze. Parking her motorbike in a tight spot, one of the perks of riding, she only had to stroll a couple of blocks to reach his house.

There was a well-maintained garden at the front, with native Lilly Pilly bushes standing at a height of five feet, creating a shield of privacy. Behind them, carefully arranged grass trees and Sago palms formed a pattern, lending a tropical touch to the landscape.

Rhianne approached the door, ready to knock, but before her hand could make contact, Kai swung it open. In that moment, time seemed to pause. Backlit by the soft glow of the hallway lamp, his presence was captivating. She felt momentarily spellbound. A tea towel rested casually on his shoulder, and his fitted t-shirt showcased his strong shoulders and chest. A wide smile illuminated his face, and Rhianne felt her breath catch.

"Hi," she managed to utter, her voice barely a whisper. Her gaze locked with his blue eyes, rendering her speechless.

"Welcome!" Kai's voice had a slight huskiness to it.

A loud truck rumbled past, breaking the spell and Kai stepped aside to let her in. The tantalising aroma of food greeted her as soon as she crossed the threshold. The renovated terrace revealed an open-plan layout. Rhianne's eyes scanned the room, taking in the minimalistic design. The off-white walls were adorned with landscape photographs, adding splashes of colour to the otherwise neutral palette. The modern aesthetic extended to the large light grey tiles on

CHAPTER 12

the floor and the sleek steel hanging lights above. Kai guided her to the lounge area, where a plush brown leather sofa and an elegant ivory chair surrounded a stunning red gum coffee table. A slimline bookcase graced one wall, while a matching hallway table sat against the wall behind the chair.

"Wow," she said, her eyes wandering around the space. "You've created something special here."

"I'm still wrapping up a few details, but the major changes are finally behind me," Kai said, leading her towards the kitchen island. A glass jug of water, filled with lemon slices and aromatic mint, caught her eye. "Thirsty? I have some infused water with lemon and mint. Or if you'd rather, I can pour you a glass of wine."

"Water it is, then," Rhianne replied with a grin. "I'm riding, so wine is probably not a good idea. It smells divine in here! What are you making?"

"You'll have to wait and see," Kai said with a playful wink. He turned around and sprinkled a pinch of herbs into a pot, his movements quick and confident. Rhianne's curiosity grew as the enticing aromas filled the kitchen.

"Can I help with anything?"

"No need, I'm almost done," Kai replied. He plated the food and carried the dishes to the oval table. "Please, have a seat."

Rhianne settled into her seat at the table, and Kai promptly set a plate before her.

Rhianne's eyes lit up with delight as she beheld the beautifully presented dish. Two delectable pieces of golden-brown fritters rested on a simple white plate, accompanied by a pale-yellow sauce. She couldn't wait to take a bite.

"These are crab cakes!" she exclaimed. "It's one of my absolute favourites. How did you know?" She nudged Kai's arm. "Did you stalk my meagre social media presence to uncover my culinary preferences?"

"You mean your thrilling posts about the nursery or the fascinating updates your mother shares about her endless functions where you look like you'd rather be anywhere else?" Kai asked.

"Wait, was I that obvious?"

Kai chuckled.

"Well, you did mention once that you're not a fan of your mother's parties. The photos looked respectable, but your smiles were certainly — restrained."

"My mother used to make me practise in front of the mirror," she confessed. "According to her, a wide smile was a big 'no, no.' It supposedly indicated naivety and lack of class."

She took another bite and her lips curled into a satisfied smile as she licked them. "Is this hollandaise sauce? It's incredible!"

"Homemade hollandaise, my grandmother's secret recipe. So, was the tight-lipped smile the right choice?"

"It was my compromise; I wanted to go for a sneer, but my mother would have never let me hear the end of it."

Before she knew it, the crab cakes had vanished from her plate, leaving only crumbs. Rhianne looked down in surprise. "Wow, those were amazing! I couldn't resist. Your cooking skills are top-notch, Kai."

A warm smile graced Kai's lips. "You certainly polished that off!" He walked over to the fridge and retrieved a plate of chocolate-covered strawberries.

"Oh, you know the way to a girl's heart!" She placed her hand over her heart.

She picked up a strawberry from the plate and noticed

CHAPTER 12

Kai's intense gaze as she purposefully took a bite, savouring it slowly.

Kai's finger brushed against her lips. "You have a little chocolate right here," he said.

She leaned into his touch, feeling a mixture of anticipation and desire. The intoxicating scent of cardamom and dates enveloped her senses. The world around them faded away, and all that mattered was the connection between their lips. Their kiss started tentatively, but the intensity grew. Time seemed to stand still as they melted into each other's embrace. But just as they were lost in the heat of the moment, the loud ring of Kai's phone shattered the spell.

"I think you'd better answer that," Rhianne managed to say, her voice breathless.

Kai's forehead lightly pressed against hers, and he emitted a low growl of frustration.

"This had better be important," he muttered before pulling away to grab his ringing phone. "Wagner speaking," he answered, his voice clipped. There was a pause as he listened. "I should be there in half an hour."

Rhianne sensed his frustration. "Is it a work emergency?"

Kai ran his fingers through his hair, his disappointment reflected in the subtle tension of his movements. "I'm so sorry. It's a large narcotics case, and they believe tonight is when they'll attempt to launder millions of dollars."

"It's all right, I get it," she reassured him.

As they rose from the table, Kai collected his keys. Before reaching the door, he paused, his gaze fixed on Rhianne. Leaning down, he captured her lips in a lingering kiss. "Consider this a promise for more," he whispered.

They remained locked in each other's embrace for a few

moments. Kai took a half step back, breaking the spell. "Darn timing, couldn't be worse. By the way, where did you park?"

"I'm a couple of blocks away, near the alleyway," Rhianne said.

Kai reached out to take her hand. Their fingers intertwined as they left the house and began to walk towards her bike.

As they approached the alleyway, a tingling sensation prickled at the back of Rhianne's neck, causing her to abruptly come to a halt. Following her instinct, she squeezed Kai's hand tightly, and he turned to face her with a questioning look in his eyes.

"Is there a problem?" Kai asked.

She couldn't detect any unusual sounds or smells, but an inexplicable sense of unease washed over her. Her heart raced, and her instincts screamed at her to be on guard. Yet, she couldn't pinpoint the source of her apprehension. She didn't want to appear foolish or paranoid in front of Kai, so she hesitated, shifting her weight from one foot to the other.

Rhianne was torn between dismissing her unease and voicing her concerns. But then she felt it again — the subtle tingle on the back of her neck. Without thinking, she raised her arm in a defensive stance, just in time to block a surprise attack aimed at her head. Adrenaline surged through her veins as she retaliated with a swift and well-aimed kick, causing her assailant to stumble and lose his balance.

He grunted, but his recovery was swift as he unleashed a flurry of punches, his two companions coming at them as well. Rhianne's heart raced as she assessed the situation. These thugs were good fighters, well-built and scrappy, but they lacked the otherworldly aura she had come to recognise in supernatural beings.

CHAPTER 12

She lunged forward, aiming a punch at the first assailant's gut. He deftly dodged her strike, attempting to grab her shoulder. Anticipating his move, Rhianne arched her back, evading his grasp.

Meanwhile, out of the corner of her eye, she caught sight of Kai delivering a powerful kick to one of the other thugs, the impact resonating with a solid thud.

In that split second of distraction, danger flashed before Rhianne's eyes. The thug lunged at her with a menacing knife, aiming for her face. Reacting with lightning speed, she narrowly evaded the deadly strike, but not without a sharp pain searing through her upper arm. She felt blood trickling from the fresh cut.

The pungent scent of sweat and cigarette smoke enveloped the tense air as two of the assailants surrounded her. Adrenaline surged through Rhianne's veins, sharpening her senses. She dropped to a crouched position, unleashing a swift and precise low round kick. The thug wielding the knife managed to evade her attack, but his companion wasn't as lucky. The sickening sound of bones snapping reverberated through the alley as he crashed to the unforgiving pavement.

"You bitch," the thug with the knife grumbled, as he lunged towards Rhianne. As his blade was about to strike, a dark blur streaked between them, diverting his attention. Rhianne seized the opportunity, crouching down and delivering a powerful punch to his groin. The thug doubled over in pain, providing her with a moment to regain her stance.

Rising to her feet, Rhianne followed up with a kick to the wrist holding the knife, sending the weapon clattering to the ground. As she prepared to confront her attacker further, she saw Kai behind him, his hand touching the man's shoulder. In an electrifying display, sparks danced in the air. The assailant convulsed briefly before collapsing to the ground.

Perched nearby, an eagle observed the scene with keen eyes. Landing gracefully beside the defeated thug, it let out a satisfied chirp. "Excellent work," the eagle said. "I was on the verge of incapacitating him, however it appears lover boy here preempted me."

Kai's gaze shifted between the eagle and Rhianne, a bemused expression crossing his face. "Lover boy?" he echoed.

"We get attacked by three armed assailants and all you're concerned about is Toto calling you 'lover boy'?" Rhianne blurted out

Kai raised his eyebrows. "Toto?"

The eagle preened his wings. "That would be me, sir, I'm Rhianne's gu — friend." He finished lamely.

Rhianne noticed the odd slip in Toto's introduction, but she decided to address it later. "Toto, meet Kai. Kai, this is Toto, a fae who usually takes the form of a small dog." She gestured between the two.

"You mean the dog at the nursery?"

Toto chuckled. "Ah, you have indeed caught me, my dear boy."

Rhianne's eyes narrowed, and she shot a warning look at Toto. "Kai, his name is Kai," she emphasised.

Their attention was abruptly drawn back to the thugs sprawled on the pavement as a groan escaped from one of the men. Kai stepped closer to the man and touched his arm. The man twitched and fell silent once more.

"That is quite a remarkable trick you have performed. I must say, I am impressed," Toto said.

"It's part of the Tech Mage's abilities." Kai shrugged his

CHAPTER 12

shoulders. "Think of it as the human version of a taser. I use the tech I carry to power it."

"That's pretty cool. Your kicks were well executed too," Rhianne said.

"As part of my quest to drive my parents mad, I spent a couple of years learning Aikido and Karate. Turns out, it wasn't all for show."

Rhianne made a face. "I guess we should call the police."

"I've already called them," Kai said.

Rhianne raised an eyebrow. Prior to meeting Kai, she had never heard of Tech Mages harnessing the power of their minds to control technology.

"It's a shame we can't interrogate them and find out why they attacked us," she said.

Toto approached from the other side. "They exude the unmistakable scent of fae magic," he said.

"They're fae?" Rhianne's eyes widened in surprise.

"No, indeed not. You would have been aware." Toto cast her a reproachful glance. "However, it is evident that they have been in close proximity to fae magic within the past few hours."

"That could mean anything," Kai said as he searched the pockets of the last guy he'd incapacitated. He pulled out a phone. "Is there a reason you suspect the fae? Do they have any motive to attack you?"

Sirens wailed in the distance, and Rhianne felt a sense of urgency. She hoped Kai would hurry before the police arrived and hindered their access to information. "I don't believe so."

Kai stood up as the first police car arrived, and Toto took to the air, disappearing from sight before the police had a chance to notice his presence.

The scene was illuminated by flashing lights, and a commanding voice rang out from behind them. "Hands where I can see them!"

Rhianne and Kai immediately raised their hands. "I'm Kai Wagner," he called out, "I'm the one who called you."

The police approached with tasers at the ready, pointed directly at them. "What's the situation here?" demanded the officer who had reached them.

Kai remained calm as he spoke up, "Those men attacked us as we were walking past the alleyway."

Rhianne's pulse quickened, but she trusted Kai to handle the situation.

The officer looked sceptical as he questioned, "So the two of you managed to take them down?"

"I'm a level five Tech Mage."

He had shifted the police's attention onto himself and Rhianne was grateful.

"In fact, I'm a police consultant currently working on a high-profile drug case."

A younger officer approached, looking down his nose at them. "As if!"

"You can verify it with Area Commander Johnson," Kai said. His phone rang, almost as if on cue.

The young officer aimed his taser directly at Kai, his finger hovering over the trigger. "Don't make any sudden moves."

As the radio crackled, the senior officer's focus shifted, and Kai's lips twitched. The officer raised the radio to his ear, his expression turning pale. Rhianne strained to catch snippets of the conversation.

"Senior Constable Brown." His pitch had risen. "Yes, sir. I'll take care of it right away."

CHAPTER 12

The senior officer's face contorted as if he had bitten into a sour lemon. "Area Commander Johnson wants you to proceed to the drug crime scene," he relayed.

"What about Ms Alkenn?" Kai asked, pointing towards Rhianne.

The senior officer hesitated for a moment before responding. "He didn't mention anything about her. We'll take her to the police station."

"Then I'm going with her."

The senior officer's face tightened into a frown. "No, I'm afraid the Area Commander explicitly instructed that you proceed to the crime scene without delay."

Kai stood his ground. "I'm going with Ms Alkenn, and I'm happy to tell the Area Commander why I'm going to be late."

The Senior Constable's gaze shifted between Kai, Rhianne, and the unconscious thugs on the ground.

"I'll need your details and hers," the Senior Constable finally said.

"Our names and phone numbers have already been sent to the police station via email." As he finished speaking, Kai reached out, clasped Rhianne's hand and led her away.

CHAPTER 13

Kai and Rhianne walked to her parked bike. Even though the adrenaline from the fight was beginning to subside, Rhianne still felt a restlessness lingering within her, keeping her senses heightened. She couldn't shake the feeling that someone was watching them.

Kai squeezed her hand gently. "You attract excitement wherever you go. Remind me to bring my bodyguard next time."

Rhianne rolled her eyes. "Oh sure, I'm a magnet for trouble. I should start charging admission fees."

Kai grinned. "Hey, you might be onto something there. 'Rhianne's Adventure Tours: Guaranteed Heart-Pounding Excitement or Your Money Back.' It's a business opportunity." He leaned forward, gently brushing a strand of hair off her face. "I'm not complaining."

He pressed his lips against hers. Rhianne melted into the kiss, feeling the heat of his touch. But as his hands brushed her shoulders, she winced in pain.

"You're hurt!" Kai frowned.

Rhianne glanced down at her upper arm and noticed some

CHAPTER 13

blood. "Darn it! I really liked this jacket," she grumbled.

"Do you want to go to the hospital and have that checked out?" His frown deepened.

Rhianne reached up and smoothed out the furrowed lines with her fingers.

"It's a small cut, nothing serious," she said. "I'll clean and bandage it when I get back. No need to make a fuss."

He took a deep breath, his grip on her waist tightening. "I want to see you again soon," he said. "But this money laundering case is going to demand most of my attention in the next few days. But I promise to also dig into the information from those burner phones."

Rhianne offered him a half-hearted shrug. She understood but it didn't mean she wasn't disappointed. She leaned into him, feeling the warmth of his embrace enveloping her.

"That's okay, we can see each other next weekend —" Rhianne's voice trailed off.

"Is something the matter with the weekend?" he probed.

"The opposite. Can I assume you have a tuxedo you can get your hands on by Saturday?"

"Indeed," Kai replied with a wide grin. "Let me guess, your mother roped you into attending a function?"

Rhianne playfully tapped him on the shoulder. "What little confidence you have in me! It's a charity event."

"Hmm. Sure it is."

"OK, so it's likely that there's a political benefit in there somewhere, but it's primarily a fundraiser for a school for supernaturals. I also managed to wrangle a concession out of her," Rhianne said.

Kai raised an eyebrow. "Is that unusual? Getting a concession, I mean."

"Very." She nodded. "Which makes me think there's something else riding on this event, but I haven't quite figured out what part I play in it yet. In any case, she promised to host another fundraiser for a halfling school, so I agreed to attend."

"I'd be honoured to be your plus one," Kai said. "And don't worry, I'll make sure to brush up on my small talk skills. Like nodding in the right gaps of the conversation. Consider me a nodding expert."

Rhianne winced. "Argh! Small talk." She caressed his cheek. "But if you're with me, it'll be tolerable.

"Shall I pick you up?" He glanced at her bike. "It's a beautiful machine, just like you. I'm not sure a tuxedo would survive a ride on it, though."

She chuckled. "Nor the dress I'll be wearing."

Rhianne realised she'd missed today's appointment at Madame Marchant's. She'd have to stop by tomorrow first thing.

"Let's say seven."

"Seven it is. I'll text you if I discover anything interesting," he said, pausing for a moment before giving her another brief kiss. "Actually, I'll text you regardless."

She beamed at him. "I'd like that."

With a wave, she hopped on the bike and took off, the heat of his last kiss still lingering on her lips.

A heady feeling filled her mind, with thoughts of Kai's words and touch swirling within her. When she hopped off the bike, the pain in her arm served as a stark reminder of the fight.

Up at her apartment, Toto, now in his dog shape, sat in his favourite spot.

"Thanks for the help today," Rhianne said as she took her

CHAPTER 13

jacket off. "What made you decide to follow me?"

Toto continued grooming himself. "You spent an awful long time getting ready so I surmised that whomever you were meeting was significant enough to you to warrant an assessment."

She couldn't help but chuckle. "Assess, huh? So, what's your verdict?"

Toto glanced up. "He's powerful, composed, and quite skilled in combat. A worthy candidate, if I may say so."

Her eyes crinkled at the corners. "Do you have a little crush on Kai?"

She retrieved the first aid kit from a kitchen cupboard and started tending to her wound.

Toto straightened himself, feigning indignation. "I beg your pardon! It is purely an objective analysis of his qualities."

Their banter was interrupted by the sound of a vehicle pulling up outside. Rhianne made her way to the window to see who had arrived.

"I called Nel," Toto said before she could even catch sight of the approaching car.

"You called Nel? Why would you do that?"

"In case you didn't notice, you were assaulted by three armed humans earlier. I thought it was important to inform Nel immediately about the danger you faced. Additionally, we need to figure out the reason behind the attack."

"Good grief." Rhianne sighed. "This could have been a random mugging, and now Nel is going to get all protective and bossy."

She shook her head and placed a large band-aid on her cut. It stung but she'd live.

"It may have seemed like a random occurrence, but the

distinct scent of fae magic clung to them. Not merely any form of fae magic, but specifically, elven magic," Toto said.

"Elf magic?" Nel asked, standing in the doorway. "Elves rarely venture into our world, and they certainly don't concern themselves with our politics."

"I thought I locked that door," Rhianne said, settling back onto the lounge and crossing her arms.

Nel joined her on the sofa, taking a seat beside her. "Locks don't mean much to someone like me, especially when I'm invited," he said and gave her a peck on the cheek.

"You're not a vampire," Rhianne grumbled.

"It's not only vampires who need an invitation to enter a supernatural's dwelling," he said, his touch gentle as he held her chin. "You're upset."

"Duh!" She rolled her eyes, trying to mask the hurt in her voice. "Just learned that my dear old dad apparently has a hit on me. How's that for a family reunion?" She blinked back the tears threatening to escape

"In all certainty, it was not your father," Toto said. "If his intentions were indeed malicious, he could have made his move long ago. Moreover, he would never cause you harm."

She narrowed her eyes at that, but let it go. "The footprints at the nursery tell us that someone was there, targeting me. But who?"

Nel's gaze shifted between Rhianne and Toto. "What footprints are you talking about?" His words were clipped.

Toto let out a soft bark and covered his eyes with a paw. "Ah, how could I have momentarily overlooked that!" He sat up, his expression focused. "I stumbled upon a set of footprints within the private garden and the indication of an elven portal. However, a notable complication arises." Toto paused. "I

CHAPTER 13

am certain that the elf responsible for the aforementioned footprints is distinct from the individual who orchestrated the assailants' attack."

Rhianne raised her hands in exasperation. "Great, so now we've got a pair of elves in this mix. One's sneaking into my personal space like a nosy neighbour, and the other's playing puppet master with those goons. And to think, the only elf I've ever known is my father!" She stood up and started pacing. "If they can waltz into my garden, what's stopping them from having a party in my apartment next?!"

Nel shook his head. "Don't worry, your place is safe because of the protective wards I set up, plus it has your signature. Only people you let in can get through, and they're linked to you, making it virtually impossible for anyone to bypass the security."

"Hang on. Wards, what wards?

Nel tightened his grip on her shoulder. "Princess, the wards are part of the security measures I installed in your apartment. They provide an extra layer of protection against intruders. I'm sorry I didn't mention the wards before."

Rhianne narrowed her eyes at him, but then her shoulders relaxed as she thought it through. "But wards are usually reserved for places that require extra protection, right?"

"I have them in my apartment," Nel said.

Rhianne took a deep breath. "That's because you're a high-profile businessman who knows everyone's secrets! I'm nobody."

"You're not nobody. For starters, people know you're important to me, and that makes you a target for anyone who wants to get to me. Secondly, you have some unusual powers that could make you interesting to certain circles."

"Except for the two of you, people are unaware of that fact."

"Maybe, but if they did find out…" Nel's voice trailed off.

"Do you really think that's what's going on? I've been so careful with using my magic," Rhianne said.

"No, I don't think so, or at least I hope not," Nel answered.

"There is an alternative possibility," Toto said.

"Well, spill it out, old thing," Nel said, a teasing glint in his eyes.

Toto feigned offence. "Are you insinuating that I am old? Isn't there a human proverb that goes, 'The pot calling the kettle black'?"

Nel chuckled. "We could compare dates, if you'd like. I'm sure you've got a few more decades under your belt."

Rhianne raised her hand to interrupt them. "All right, enough of the jokes. What's the other possibility?"

"Indeed, it's not uncommon for elven factions to engage in power struggles and use individuals as leverage against their rivals. Your father's position and influence could be the reason behind these attacks on you."

"Well, if they think they can manipulate him through me, they're in for a surprise. He won't care."

"If your father truly didn't care about you, he wouldn't have defied the queen to visit you," Toto said.

She blinked and wished the sting of her arm would provide a better distraction to her jumble of emotions. "He may have had another reason for being in our world," she mumbled.

"If that was the case, why bother coming and seeing you at all? I don't think things are black and white when it comes to your father, princess," Nel said.

Her eyes glistened with unshed tears. She held them back, determined not to break down and shifted the conversation.

CHAPTER 13

"You haven't explained what you meant by my signature."

Nel shot her a knowing glance that said he decided to play along, for now. "Ah, yes, your signature," he said. "In the world of magic, everyone has their own special magic print, a bit like a fingerprint. Even though your magic powers might not be top-tier for a witch, the mix of all your different skills makes up a unique and strong magic signature."

"I've never heard of a halfling having multiple magical abilities. It doesn't make sense."

"Most halflings don't have multiple abilities," Nel corrected. "But in your case, you have a unique blend of magics. It's rare, and I must admit, I've never come across a combination quite like yours before."

He glanced at Toto.

"The amalgamation of diverse magical lineages often proves to be complex, not only due to prejudices, but also because of fertility. This is why you primarily encounter halflings who are half-human; it is more practical in terms of both genetic compatibility and magical potential. The limited manifestation of magical abilities in halflings probably arises from having only a single magical lineage," Toto said.

Rhianne's mouth formed an O shape as Toto's words sunk in. She had always considered herself the same as every other halfling, but now she realised the uniqueness of her situation. It dawned on her that she couldn't recall any other halflings who came from two different supernatural backgrounds, except for herself and her mother. Marissa's parentage hinted at a gargoyle-human pairing, but Rhianne had never asked her. The thought of discussing such a personal matter with Marissa made her slightly uneasy. But now she was really curious.

"I hadn't considered it from that perspective. It's surprising that no one has ever brought it up before," she finally said.

"Probably due to the disapproval of inter-supernatural marriages," Toto explained. "To many supernaturals, the emphasis lies in safeguarding their heritage, preserving the integrity of their magical lineage, and upholding the purity of their magic. It's a way to ensure the survival of their species."

"I don't recall ever having a conversation with my mother about this," she said.

Nel arched an eyebrow. "Does your mother talk about your grandfather often?"

Rhianne's voice wavered. "She sent me to spend time with him during the school breaks —" She hesitated. "But I've never heard her mention him to anyone outside our inner circle."

That made her wonder — was her mother ashamed of what her own father was? Rhianne's voice filled with realisation and frustration. "Wait, my mother's magic level is five!" Her eyes widened as the pieces started to fall into place. "I can't believe I didn't make the connection before. I've been avoiding anything related to my mother, but it should have been obvious. We had a discussion about halflings, and I didn't even consider her as an example. She acts and behaves as if she's a pureblood."

"Indeed!" Toto's face lit up like a teacher who finally sees a student grasp a difficult concept. "She, too, is a halfling, yet her mastery of power is truly exceptional."

"She probably hides her halfling heritage to avoid people questioning her leadership abilities," Nel explained. "Your grandmother was a powerful witch, and that family background means a lot to her."

CHAPTER 13

Toto nodded. "The compatibility between dryads and green witches is widely acknowledged. If her lineage were known, her power levels would probably be attributed to that very connection."

"You know, it's strange," Rhianne said. "When I took the levels test and the results came in, I thought my mother would say something. Maybe question it or offer some insight, but she remained silent. It was as if it didn't matter at all."

Rhianne didn't tell them she'd been oddly hurt by that.

"In all honesty, I must commend your remarkable ability to deceive both the Mage Testers and even your own mother," Toto said.

Nel's interest piqued. "You cheated?"

"Duh! I did it partly as a way to defy her," Rhianne admitted. "I was tired of being manipulated and controlled. At twelve years old, all I wanted was some peace and independence." She paused, collecting her thoughts. "I also had a fear that my fae magic would surface, so I willed it to remain dormant."

Nel planted a soft kiss on her cheek. "You're truly remarkable, princess."

"What?" Rhianne raised an eyebrow. "Why do you say that?"

Nel and Toto exchanged a meaningful glance, and then Nel's smile widened. "It's incredibly difficult to cheat on the test. Many have tried in the past, but very few have succeeded."

"Bah! That's probably because most of them were attempting to achieve higher scores, not lower." Rhianne crossed her arms.

"No, princess, the test is designed to catch cheaters in either direction. It doesn't only detect attempts to do better; the spell they employ nullifies all forms of deceit," Nel said. He leaned in closer, his hands holding hers. "I must admit, I'm genuinely fascinated by how you managed to fool them."

"Our young lady possesses extraordinary qualities, Nel, even if she's hesitant to admit it," Toto said. "But we must turn our attention to the current threat."

Nel's expression turned serious as he gently patted Rhianne's hands and leaned back in his seat.

Rhianne noticed the tension returning to Nel's shoulders. "You still haven't explained about my signature. What does it mean?"

"Your magic signature is strong. There's no need to worry," he reassured her. "They won't know it's yours specifically, they'll just sense the magic."

"Wouldn't they suspect it's mine because it's in my home?" Rhianne asked.

"Chances are, they'll assume I'm the one who placed it there. I have enough of my own protective wards in place to effectively mask its origins."

"Is it the signature of an elf?" she whispered.

What would it mean if it was? Her whole identity had been that of a green witch, albeit with minor powers. She'd thought her elven side dormant at best. I mean, she wasn't much of an elf at all, in looks or in power.

Toto fixed his gaze upon her, contemplating for a moment before answering, "Only those who truly understand what they're seeking would be able to identify it as an elf signature."

"Another elf would," Nel pointed out. "You mentioned picking the scent of elf on the attackers."

Rhianne curled up, hugging her knees tightly as a surge of emotions swept over her. The idea of elves spying on her and organising an attack on her filled her with a deep sense of anger. How dare they invade her world?

CHAPTER 13

She hated that Kai had been caught in the middle. On the other hand, it had given her the opportunity to watch him in action. He'd defended himself, and her, really well. Plus, the hand-taser thing had been rather cool.

"No, not all elves possess the ability to do so," Toto said.

"What do you mean?" she asked.

"Only those among the Shadows and select members of the nobility possess the capability."

She felt a pang of regret for choosing to remain ignorant about her heritage. It dawned on her that this decision was fuelled by spite towards her father.

In other words, it was entirely her fault. What was that saying again? Oh yeah: 'Revenge is the poison you drink, while you wait for your enemy to suffer.'

"What exactly is a Shadow?" she asked.

Nel's arms crossed, and his mouth opened briefly before snapping shut. His furrowed brows and downturned mouth revealed his concern. In a silent but unmistakable warning, he cast a pointed glance at Toto, a message not lost on Rhianne.

"Nope, you don't get to shield me by keeping things from me," Rhianne said. "I'm an adult now, and I have the right to make my own choices." She pointed her finger at Nel, wagging it back and forth for emphasis.

Nel sat there, still and tense, resembling a magnificent Greek sculpture. She mirrored his defiance by crossing her arms and leaning forward, refusing to be shut out. No freaking way.

"You might think you're all grown up, but that's just human thinking," Nel said, pausing for emphasis. "And let's not forget, you're not human."

Rhianne pursed her lips. "That's right. I'm a half-witch,

and in the world of witches, I am most certainly considered an adult," she said. "I'm thirty-six years old, Nel. I run my own thriving business and earn a substantial income." Her pitch and volume rose. "For goodness' sake, Nel! I've been managing the club's accounts for years and you've been perfectly content to let me do it!"

Nel shook off his stiffness, his gaze briefly drifting to the ceiling as if seeking guidance before returning to Rhianne. "Ouch! That was a low blow."

"The truth hurts," she volleyed back.

Toto leapt off the couch and made his way over to Rhianne. He licked her foot affectionately before placing his paws on her knees. "She is correct," Toto said. "She can defend herself, as she so aptly demonstrated earlier today. Even in the absence of Kai, she would have defeated those thugs. You should have witnessed her in action, a true embodiment of a graceful warrior!" Toto turned to face Nel. "You and I may still perceive her as the headstrong child she once was, and we struggle to see beyond that perspective. However, from an elf's standpoint, she is on the cusp of a profound transformation."

Nel ran his fingers through his hair. "A Shadow? That seems rather extreme."

Rhianne scooped up Toto, cradling him in her arms as he dangled his paws. "I appreciate your vote of confidence. Can we take this step by step and address things one at a time? It seems there are things I should have learnt ages ago," she said.

Toto tilted his head.

"I know, it's my fault," she said. "You did try to tell me things, but I wasn't ready to listen. Now, whether I like it or not, it's time for me to be better informed."

CHAPTER 13

She placed Toto back on the cushion beside her.

Toto closed his eyes momentarily, a shudder passing through him. "A Shadow is an assassin."

CHAPTER 14

"An assassin?" Rhianne shrieked.

Nel snorted. "Do you have to be so melodramatic?" He rolled his eyes. "That's just one of the roles of a Shadow."

"I must confess," Toto said. "My mother used to recount tales of the Shadows to my sisters and me, intending to instil discipline and obedience." He placed a paw over one of his eyes. "They are incredibly mysterious. They move with uncanny agility, blending seamlessly with the shadows, hence the name. They can slip in and out of places undetected, like whispers in the night."

Nel patted Rhianne's knee. "It's Okay. They can't get into your apartment."

"Thanks to the wards you've set up?"

Nel shook his head. "While my wards might slow down a Shadow and trigger the alarm, they'd eventually figure out how to bypass them."

Nel had always been pretty confident in the security his club's wards offered, often bragging that they were impenetrable. However, his admission that Shadows could possibly

CHAPTER 14

break through those defences surprised her. It appeared that when he said "no one," he didn't mean these Shadows.

As if he'd heard her unspoken question, Nel added, "They might be able to get into the club but they wouldn't be able to get into my apartment for the same reason they couldn't get into yours."

That reminded her of what Nel had said earlier. "Your signature."

"It's the same with your apartment," Nel said.

"But they can obviously get into the garden nursery," Rhianne said.

Nel's apologetic look spoke volumes. "I didn't expect to need wards in the nursery. I should fix that," he said. "I'm not sure about your signature there, though."

Toto nodded. "Indeed, it might be feasible. I will consult relevant scrolls to ascertain the required procedures."

"I could ask Kai to set up cameras and a perimeter alarm system. I'm guessing their presence would trigger the technology, but even if not, it would help in detecting any other intruders," she said.

Nel feigned puppy eyes. "Are you implying that you trust him more than me?" he waggled his eyebrows. "Ah, I see. Your date must have gone swimmingly." He smirked.

"Actually, it was our third date," Rhianne corrected him reflexively, her face flushing with a deep shade of crimson as she realised her slip-up.

Nel's smile broadened. "I believe it's high time I meet this Tech Mage of yours, don't you agree, Toto?"

Toto's head bobbed up and down. "He is indeed worthy," Toto affirmed with a wag of his tail. "A true gentleman who fearlessly defended Rhianne and stood up to those foolish police officers who wanted to take her to the station. He put them in their place, he certainly did. And not to mention, he possesses impressive power reserves."

Nel's eyebrows shot up at Toto's glowing assessment.

"He has a man crush," Rhianne said with a grin and a wink.

"I don't think he's the only one." Nel said.

A blush crept up Rhianne's neck once more as she admitted, "True. And if you raise your eyebrows any higher, they might disappear."

Nel raised his hands in a defensive gesture, a playful smirk forming on his face. "Offence is the best defence."

"Tsk, were you not throwing accusations about maturity before?" Toto fired back. "You might want to take a good look in the mirror, my friend. However, let us not be swayed from our purpose. We must remember that we are yet to confront the troublesome Shadow issue. Time is of the essence."

Nel's demeanour instantly shifted as he sobered up.

Rhianne held up her hand. "If this Shadow truly wanted me dead, I'd be six feet under by now."

Nel tapped his fingers, while Toto barked once in agreement.

"In fact," Rhianne said, "I don't believe whoever is behind this wants me dead."

Nel threw his hands up in the air. "Seriously, which part of being attacked by three armed men did you happen to miss?"

"The part where they only drew their knives after realising they were losing the fight. I think that initial punch they aimed at me was meant to disable, not to kill," Rhianne said.

"Are you suggesting a potential kidnapping attempt?" Toto asked.

"There is another possibility we haven't considered," Nel

CHAPTER 14

said. "What if this has nothing to do with Rhianne's powers or her elven origins?"

Toto directed a sidelong glance at Nel. "What precisely are you suggesting?"

"You think this is connected to Parkes' murder?" She stretched her neck to relieve the stiffness. "All we've done is ask a few questions, and I'm pretty sure neither Sarah nor Arthur recognised me."

"No, I don't think they made the connection," Nel said. "But the fact that you've been actively involved as a key consultant on the case may have spooked the murderer."

"First of all, let's not forget that I *was* a consultant. I highly doubt the police are eager to see me again anytime soon. In fact, considering our last encounter, 'ever' might be a more accurate timeframe."

"You don't know that. Johannes may consider himself Superintendent material, but he lacks the necessary influence. If the family demands answers and your expertise is deemed necessary, they'll have no choice but to call you back onto the case."

She wagged her finger at him. "You know something!" she accused.

Nel's smirk widened. "I know a multitude of things. You'll have to be more specific."

"Argh, you're impossible!" Rhianne said.

She rose from her seat and made her way to the sink, filling a glass with water. Turning back to face Nel and Toto, she raised an eyebrow and asked, "Drink anyone?"

Nel and Toto shook their heads in unison.

"All I know." Nel paused, a sly smile playing at the corners of his lips as he studied his fingernails, "is that the Superintendent is catching heat from his superiors. They're desperate for an expert in Romin, and there aren't many of those around."

"You know what the forensic pathologist pointed out? To kill Parkes, the killer would have needed access to a lab," she said. "It's frustrating that I didn't think of that myself. I already shared this information with Marissa, Alice's lawyer, so the police would be aware of it by now."

"Wouldn't the forensic pathologist have already shared that information with the police?" Nel asked.

Rhianne's smile grew. "Let's just say that according to the pathologist, Johannes and Chen haven't exactly earned themselves a spot in her good books."

"Oh?" Nel tilted his head to the side.

"According to her, Johannes and Chen don't even bother to bring her coffee," she said. "But our little bribe, on the other hand, was well received."

"Bribing an officer of the government, now that could get you into trouble," he teased. "But I must admit, I'm quite curious about this bribe of yours. Do tell."

Rhianne snorted as she blew a strand of hair away from her face. "Oh, you'd be an expert on bribes, wouldn't you, big boy?"

"Darling, I've elevated the art of providing high-quality entertainment to a whole new level," he said, a smirk dancing on his lips. "But let's not confuse that with bribes. That's a whole different thing."

Toto barked, interrupting them. "If you would kindly redirect your attention to the matter at hand and refrain from needling each other. Let us not overlook the elf connection. Remember, I detected the distinct scent of elf on those thugs." His gaze shifted between Rhianne and Nel. "It appears we

CHAPTER 14

may be facing three potential adversaries: a Shadow, an elf with mysterious and possibly malicious intentions towards you, and a murderer who may be prepared to strike again."

"Is there a possibility that these parties are somehow connected?" she asked. "What else do Shadows do?"

"Shadows, princess, are the ultimate spies," Nel said. "Their primary role is to gather information. If a Shadow made an appearance, it suggests their interest in either you or the plants you have here."

"I have some rare healing specimens," she said, rubbing the back of her neck. "They're incredibly difficult to grow. It's possible that someone could be after them."

Toto chimed in. "Alternatively, they could be targeting the individual who possesses the ability to cultivate those specimens. Contrary to what the forensic expert mentioned, obtaining the healing potion doesn't necessarily require a laboratory."

Nel leaned forward. "Do you have the ability to develop the poison yourself?"

Her gaze sharpened on Nel. "Yes, or rather, no. I haven't and I wouldn't." She crossed her arms across her chest.

"Mere curiosity, my beloved princess," he said.

Rhianne narrowed her eyes at him. Developing a poison went against everything she believed in. She remembered what her Grandpa Angelo told her when she wrote her initials on a tree. She'd been five, and she'd never forgotten the look of disappointment on his face. It was a lesson she'd carried with her ever since: "Don't ask, can I? Ask, should I?"

"Toto's theory makes sense. In the elven world, poison is often seen as a go-to weapon for getting rid of people they don't like."

"Shadows are exceptionally rare and command exorbitant fees. Only those with significant wealth are able to afford their services," Toto said. "In fact, the queen herself keeps a Shadow on retainer."

Nel's lips curled up. "I highly doubt the queen would have any need for Rhianne's poisons. She's renowned for having an extensive collection herself."

"Okay, let's put the Shadow character on hold for a minute," Rhianne suggested. "Do elves typically resort to hiring thugs for their tasks? I always thought they were a proud race."

Rhianne didn't identify herself as an elf, notwithstanding the slightly pointed ears she often hid with her hair. Her ambivalent emotions regarding her absent father played a part in this. But mostly the magic scared her. It called to her. It wanted her to use it. Rhianne didn't want to fall prey to its addictive nature.

"It's a plausible scenario. The magic had a faint resemblance to compulsion magic. It would have been potent enough to influence the thugs to target you or orchestrate your abduction. In the unlikely event that the authorities were to investigate any supernatural involvement in the attack, any traces of it would have vanished. The thugs would be clueless," Toto said.

"It still might be worthwhile to interrogate the thugs." Nel stroked his chin which boasted a six o'clock shadow.

"Wait, are you suggesting that we simply march into the police station and demand to speak with them?" Rhianne gazed at Nel with disbelief. "You can bet Marissa would have a field day if I told her we planned to pull off such a move."

"Marissa?" Nel asked.

"Alice's lawyer. I've got a lunch meeting with her tomorrow

CHAPTER 14

to go over Alice's character reference."

"I could reach out to my contacts in the police or try to charm the officer in charge at the station, but I believe it would be more effective if you asked your lawyer friend."

Rhianne blinked rapidly. "She's not my fr — Ask her what, exactly?"

"If she can arrange for us to talk to them." Nel leaned back with his arms casually resting behind his head.

"She'll probably just laugh at me," Rhianne said.

"If you don't ask…"

"You don't get," she finished his sentence with a sigh. Perhaps Nel had a valid point. It was the only lead they had, after all. "What about the Shadow?" she asked, shifting the focus back to their original topic.

Toto tilted his head and scratched his left ear. "I could conduct some inquiries, although I must admit my prospects appear rather slim. If he indeed utilised a portal, it is improbable that he engaged with anyone during his presence here."

"We know of one visit," Nel said. "But it's possible there were more visits. I must admit, I'm surprised that he left any evidence behind. They take pride in their ability to remain almost invisible. It's careless. It's like leaving breadcrumbs for someone to follow."

Toto grinned, his expression so endearing that Rhianne couldn't resist patting him on the head. "Arrogance, no doubt," Toto said, nudging into her hand for more affection. "It probably never crossed his mind that anyone would investigate such a matter. He likely remained oblivious to the fact that very few individuals enter the private garden. Even then, there are plenty of footprints within the enclosure. And he certainly didn't anticipate my superior olfactory senses coming into play."

Arrogance indeed.

"But that doesn't change the fact that he might have been around before or since," Nel pointed out. "And that he'd have a reason for coming."

"Not to mention, gaining permission to enter the human world would have been necessary," Toto said. "I'll make sure to pass that information along to my contacts. If he did inquire about the 'Tea Leaves', people might recall any peculiar behaviour he exhibited. Despite their ability to wear glamour, elves often find it challenging to navigate the human realm without drawing some attention to themselves."

"I'll do the same around my less illustrious contacts," Nel said.

"Didn't know you had any contacts who weren't?" Rhianne said.

Nel widened his eyes in an exaggerated display of mock outrage. "I'll have you know I'm acquainted with some truly seedy characters."

Rhianne threw her head back and erupted in laughter, the sound filling the room. "Only you would be proud of that fact," she said when she had managed to curb her laughter.

It was a welcome relief to let go of some of the tension that had been weighing on her shoulders and neck.

Rhianne recognised the familiar sarcasm in their dynamic, often a shield for uncomfortable emotions. The "Hey, let's not get too deep here." It was sobering that she was as adept at using humour to sidestep deeper emotions as he was.

"There's also the possibility that someone is specifically targeting me through you," Nel said. "They could be searching

CHAPTER 14

for vulnerabilities to exploit."

"Now you are calling me a vulnerability, which sounds awfully close to a liability." She pouted.

A wry chuckle escaped from Nel's chest.

Toto cleared his throat, redirecting the focus of the conversation. "Nel, may I inquire about the frequency of your encounters with the elven court?"

"I haven't had many, but some might have been enough to make some elves want some — retribution," Nel acknowledged.

"Spousal jealousy?" Rhianne asked.

"Nothing as trivial as that." Nel tugged at his cuffs.

Rhianne contemplated whether to press further, but her attention was diverted by something black — a feather. It was the one she had found on the day Toto discovered the footprints. It lay innocuously near the fruit bowl on the benchtop. She examined it as she turned it in her fingers.

Nel rose from his seat and walked over to inspect it. "What's this?"

"I don't know, but I found it lodged in the door of the private garden on the same day we found the elf's footprints."

"We?" Toto interjected, jumping down from the sofa and leisurely making his way over.

Rhianne bent down and positioned the feather near his nose.

Toto took a few sniffs and grumbled. "Raven shifter," he finally said. "You should have informed me about this sooner. The scent feels somewhat familiar as if I have come across it recently."

"You're suddenly quite popular." Nel extended his hand for Rhianne to pass the feather over.

Nel examined it closely, smelling and licking a corner.

"Eww!" Rhianne cringed. "You have no idea who that feather belongs to or where it's been."

Nel nudged her shoulder. "It belongs to a female shifter."

"How on earth do you know that?" she asked.

Toto huffed.

Nel grinned and his eyes were full of mischief. "I could claim that I detected it through pheromones or that the distinct colour pattern is exclusive to female Ravens."

Rhianne reclaimed the feather and swatted Nel with it. "Enough with the teasing! Spill it!" she demanded.

"You're no fun!" Nel pouted. He took another sniff of the feather. "The feather smells like Chanel No 5."

"That's one of the most popular perfume brands. My mother wears it." Rhianne sighed. "All right, then. We now know that our culprit is a female raven shifter who wears Chanel No. 5. I have a feeling our paths have crossed before, and it's likely they will again."

Nel's eyes lit up.

"I can't sense raven shifters other than recognising them as supernaturals. I can pick up werewolves mostly." Rhianne turned to Nel. "What about you?"

"I can sense they're shifters, but identifying their exact species is hard," Nel said. "I agree werewolves are easier."

Rhianne gazed down at Toto. "How can you tell, Toto?"

Toto puffed up his chest. "I can teach you to detect feathered beings, it is a more sophisticated ability. However, we can certainly make an attempt. Close your eyes."

Rhianne blinked. "Are we really doing this right now?"

"Seize the moment, for you never know when you'll cross paths with this person again, and it's vital to remain alert

CHAPTER 14

when that happens," Toto said.

Rhianne dutifully closed her eyes.

"Now, I invite you to awaken your senses," Toto said in a tone, infused with a gentle, resonant hum.

"I sense your presence, both Nel and you?" Rhianne said.

"Very good. Take a few moments to steady your breath." Toto paused. "Now, when you next inhale I would like you to extend your senses outward."

Rhianne squinted, peeping at him. "What exactly do you mean by 'sending my senses out'?"

Following his own advice, Toto inhaled deeply. "Close your eyes, my dear." He exhaled. "Envision yourself as if extending tendrils of energy outward."

Rhianne made another attempt, and this time, a vivid image emerged in her mind. It resembled a towering tree, gracefully extending its slender roots deep into the earth. As she focused on Nel's presence, the roots retrieved a distinct flavour, rich and smoky. "Medium roasted coffee," she said.

Nel chuckled

"Very well, now direct your focus towards me." Toto coaxed.

She extended her awareness downwards and replicated the process. However, this time proved more challenging as the taste carried a fruity essence with a hint of sharpness. After a moment of contemplation, she finally said, "Sour cherries."

"Hmph! Delve deeper," Toto urged.

As she inhaled and exhaled a faint headache emerged at the base of her skull. She experienced the familiar fruity taste but shook her head. "Perhaps sour cherries with a subtle hint of basil?"

"Again!" Toto's tone brooked no argument.

Rhianne heard a whistling sound that quickly faded, leaving

silence in its wake. She clenched her teeth and made another attempt, but to no avail. The taste of sour cherries dominated her senses, leaving her frustrated. "Sour cherries, I guess, without basil?" she hesitated, feeling like she was grasping at straws. "Or maybe — sesame seeds? Ugh! I honestly don't know." She opened her eyes, and saw that Toto had transformed into his eagle form.

With its sharp, piercing gaze, the eagle locked Rhianne in place.

Rhianne threw her hands up. "I tried!"

The eagle shook its wings and parted its beak, breaking the silence. "You fared better than my initial expectations. For a first attempt, it is commendable," Toto said. "The fruity taste you perceived is likely your association with the fae, although each fae race may exhibit slight variations. The earthy flavour you detected from Nel aligns with your interpretation of Demons."

Rhianne's expression twisted into a grimace. "This doesn't get me any closer to recognising the raven shifter."

Toto tilted his head. "Your interpretation of magic is largely untrained," he said.

Rhianne winced internally, knowing she had resisted learning about elven magic or accepting Toto's guidance. Most of her magical abilities had developed unintentionally.

"On the positive side," Toto said. "The herbal taste you're experiencing is likely tied to the unique essence of the shifter you're seeking. To identify them, you must discern the primary 'taste' associated with shifters and separate it from the herbal flavours, which could provide clues about their specific shifter type."

"Wait, are you saying I have to go around testing every

CHAPTER 14

shifter I come across until I get a sense of their taste? That would take ages!"

Toto tutted. "You had better begin then."

CHAPTER 15

The next morning, Rhianne sipped on a vegetable and fruit juice before heading to the main garden. The prospect of a hectic day ahead made her shoulders slump. She had paperwork to catch up on, deliveries to check, a trip to town for lunch with Marissa, a dress fitting and several mysteries to investigate. Her life had certainly taken a weird turn. "Argh, I need to shake off this mood," she muttered.

She caught sight of Carl fertilising the larger trees. "Hi, Carl!"

Carl turned, his face breaking into a full smile. "Hi, boss."

"Any idea where Alice is?" Her question was interrupted by a beep from her phone.

"She's at the back, getting the deliveries ready," Carl replied. "And she's in a much better mood today. She was singing in the truck on the way here."

"Looks like I've got to leave you guys to hold the fort while I head into town for a few things and meet Marissa." Rhianne put on her gloves.

"You're meeting Marissa?" Carl's face blushed and he

CHAPTER 15

stopped in his tracks.

Rhianne hid a smile. "Would you like me to say hi from you?" she asked. She didn't want to tease him too badly; he was just so adorable.

"No, I mean — maybe you could just check in to see how she's doing?" Carl stepped back a few paces, mumbling under his breath, before returning to his tasks.

Uh oh! Carl clearly liked the lawyer. She made a mental note to gauge Marissa's feelings.

Unlocking her phone, a smile formed on Rhianne's lips as she read Kai's message: "Good morning, battle angel - worked through the night on the case. Will tackle burner phones after some rest."

Rhianne's fingers danced across the screen. 'Good morning, alpha geek. Sleep first!'

Alice was indeed busy preparing the deliveries.

"Good morning," Rhianne said. It was great to see Alice smiling again.

"Morning." Alice attended to the plants that were scheduled for pick-up later. "We have two delivery trucks coming this morning for the major landscape job at the heights."

"Can I help with anything for the next two hours? I need to head into town after that."

Alice brushed her gloved hands on her pants and turned towards Rhianne. "Yeah, Marissa told me you're doing a character reference for me. Thanks a bunch for that! But don't worry about helping out, I've got things handled here. I just need to choose a couple of ornamental trees for the delivery, and then I'll be good to go."

Rhianne's shoulders relaxed. "I feel kind of redundant," she admitted, her smile growing wider.

187

"Nah, you can handle all the admin stuff yourself." Alice grinned.

"How about a bonus for taking care of the admin?" Rhianne suggested only half-jokingly.

"Not a chance." Alice winked at her.

"Can't blame a girl for trying," Rhianne shrugged her shoulders and she made her way back to her office. The mountain of paperwork wouldn't tackle itself.

A couple of hours later she parked her motorbike in the designated spot at the back of Madame Marchant's. The shop's expansive front windows boasted stunning floral displays. Inside, two chic mannequins struck poses; one lounged while the other leaned casually against a pillar, anchoring the showcase.

Stepping forward, she braced herself, and as she entered, a delicate chime of a crystal bell resounded, announcing her arrival.

A woman with an elegant blonde up-do emerged to greet Rhianne. She looked somewhere in her forties, although Rhianne knew she was older. Dressed in a pristine white pantsuit, not a single wrinkle in sight, Rhianne couldn't help but wonder if Madame Marchant had cast a spell on the fabric. The woman approached with a graceful stride, her high heels making no sound on the plush carpeted floors.

"Ma chérie, cela fait si longtemps!" she exclaimed upon seeing her, moving closer to plant a kiss on one cheek, then the other.

Rhianne's childhood memories of visiting this place involved enduring seemingly endless hours standing still while her measurements were taken and fabrics were pinned against her. She had despised those moments, except for Madame

CHAPTER 15

sneaking palmiers or madeleines to her whenever her handlers were distracted. Rhianne had always admired Madame's effortless elegance. The French cadence of Madame's words now, after all these years, still held a soothing quality.

"You recognise me?" Rhianne asked.

"Bien sûr, child. You have grown, but that fiery spirit remains, non?" Madame Marchant said, giving Rhianne's cheeks an affectionate pat. "Why haven't you visited Madame in so long?" Her face radiated warmth and kindness.

Rhianne winced in spite of herself. Madame had always been kind to her.

"Never mind, ma chérie, life often gets in the way. Come!" Without waiting for a response, Madame grabbed Rhianne's hand and eagerly pulled her further inside, leading her into the dressing salon.

"Your maman gave me a call and mentioned a soirée on Saturday," Madame said, her eyes scanning the rows of hanging dresses as they walked along. She stole quick glances at Rhianne, assessing her with a discerning eye. "Hmm, pastels won't do for you." Madame plucked a navy-blue dress off the rack. "She told me you would be coming yesterday." Rhianne bit her lip, but Madame didn't give her a chance to apologise. In a swift motion, she grabbed another dress, this time a dark burnt orange. "It is going to be my pleasure to dress you. You are très belle! With your figure, the possibilities are endless." Her eyes shone with excitement and delight. Suddenly, Madame's attention was captured by another dress — a deep burgundy piece that glistened under the lights. "Your maman said a conventional dress, mais non! You, ma chérie, shall be the belle of the ball. Come on, try these on," she urged, handing the dresses to Rhianne.

Rhianne slipped into the navy-blue dress, appreciating the way the satin fabric lent a graceful sway to the A-line skirt. The strapless top emerged from a wide belt, forming a fan-like structure adorned with delicate pleats. Stepping out of the dressing room, she encountered a slightly impatient Madame.

"Hmm, that would be lovely for dancing, but considering your complexion — yes, we can do better. Please try on the burnt orange dress." Madame waved her hand imperiously.

Rhianne obediently retreated to the dressing room and slipped into the next dress. It showcased a Grecian style, featuring a wide belt that accentuated her waist and elegant folds draping gracefully around her figure. The colour of the dress complemented the light brown hues in her hair.

Before she had a chance to open the door, Madame peered in. "Better," Madame murmured. "Now, please try the burgundy dress." With that, she closed the door.

The burgundy dress boasted a mermaid style, adorned with a pleated bust and elegant off-the-shoulder sleeves. Madame swung open the door, her eyes sparkling with satisfaction. "Oh la-là. That's the dress for you!" she exclaimed, practically trembling with enthusiasm. "Come out, ma chérie. I will make the necessary adjustments!"

"It fits fine," Rhianne protested.

"Mais non, it must be absolute perfection!" Madame guided Rhianne to step up onto the fitting stand and called out, "Marie, the pins please." With a wink directed at Rhianne, Madame added, "And some madeleines."

Marie, a petite young woman, entered the room carrying a large pin cushion. With a deferential nod towards Rhianne, she positioned the cushion within Madame's reach.

As Madame skilfully pinned the dress, her words were

CHAPTER 15

muffled by the pins in her mouth. "It's been quite a busy week with this soirée," she mumbled. Kneeling down to adjust the hem, she continued, "Just the other day, a client came in. I had already made her a lovely gold dress." Madame placed another pin. "But she insisted on having a black one, claiming, 'My ex-husband is dead.'"

Rhianne's mind, which had momentarily drifted off, snapped back to attention.

"Can you imagine? I said to her, 'You must still love him.' And you know what she replied?" Rhianne shook her head in silent curiosity. Madame's gaze locked with hers. "She said, 'I hated him. I wished I had seen him thrashing in his dying moments.'"

Rhianne's head jerked down towards Madame, her eyes widening. "Thrashing? She used those exact words?"

"Please maintain your posture, ma chérie," Madame said. "Oui, she used those very words."

Rhianne's eyes flickered as she leaned forward. "Was that Mrs Andrea Parkes, by any chance?"

"Well, yes, indeed, ma chérie. Do you happen to know her?" Madame asked, rising to her feet with a few pins still held between her fingers.

"Not yet," Rhianne replied, a slow smile playing on her lips. "But I'm looking forward to meeting her at the party."

Rhianne started to piece together various details. By Friday, Andrea Parkes had already been informed of her ex-husband's death. It was possible that one of their children had shared the news with her right away. Did the police inform Arthur and Rita that the cause of death was poisoning on that very night? It seemed unlikely. Not all poisons lead to violent reactions; some acted quickly, while others immobilised the victim.

However, considering that Parkes would have struggled for breath while the Romin closed off his airways, it was likely he had experienced convulsions. Maybe Andrea had watched one too many crime shows; or maybe she knew more than an innocent party should.

She left Madame's with a promise to come by on Thursday for a final fitting.

Arriving at Luna's five minutes late, Rhianne found Marissa already seated at a table near the window. As she approached, Marissa's wave beckoned her in. Rhianne entered Luna's to the symphony of ambient sounds — murmured conversations, clinking glasses, and soft background music. The enticing aroma of freshly brewed coffee and aromatic spices enveloped the air.

"May I help you?" A waiter materialised before her. Rhianne realised he was a supernatural of some sort. She took a deep breath and closed her eyes for a moment, allowing her senses to reach out. A distinct taste of gaminess, reminiscent of roasted venison, reached her nose.

"She's with me." Marissa's commanding voice sliced through Rhianne's concentration. Rhianne sighed, relinquishing her hold on the magic and opening her eyes. The waiter bowed his head.

"Allow me to show you to your table, madam," the waiter said. Marissa gestured towards the seat beside her. As Rhianne settled in, the waiter approached and deftly placed a napkin on her lap.

"Give us a moment to decide, please," Marissa said, casting a brief glance towards the waiter. The waiter vanished as swiftly as he had appeared.

"He's fast," Rhianne fixed her gaze on the spot where the

CHAPTER 15

waiter had stood just a moment ago.

"Of course, he's fast; he's a cheetah shifter," Marissa said, a wry smile playing on her lips. "Hello to you too."

Rhianne rolled her eyes. "You usually don't bother with pleasantries. How do you know he's a cheetah shifter?"

"True. Politeness costs money and my rates are quite high."

Rhianne arched her eyebrows at her.

Marissa threw her head back and laughed. "To answer your question, I make it my business to know. When I bring clients to a place on a regular basis, I always make sure the food is delicious and the service is top-notch. It helps to have a connection with the owner and chef, who, by the way, is a gargoyle and also a client of mine."

"Do you bring all of your character witnesses here? I must say, I'm impressed," Rhianne said.

It was her first time at Luna's, but the opulent surroundings spoke volumes. The classical décor, the plush chenille padded chairs in a rich mustard yellow, and the impeccably uniformed waitstaff all pointed to an upscale establishment.

Marissa's eyes sparkled with delight. "Actually, I brought you here because I like you."

"I'm flattered," Rhianne said. "What about Alice and Carl? Do they qualify?" She did her best to keep her expression neutral.

Rhianne's eyes were drawn to Marissa's subtle blush. She observed Marissa's reactions while putting on a show of browsing the menu.

"Alice is my client, and while liking clients isn't a requirement, I think she's a good person." Marissa's fingers tapped against her glass and her gaze momentarily drifted to the window before returning to meet Rhianne's eyes.

Marissa fidgeted in her seat. It was fascinating to watch the terrifying lawyer at a loss for words. "Hmm, Carl's a lovely guy. He's quite different from other gargoyles I've met."

"Oh? How so?" Rhianne leaned in, propping her elbows on the table and placing her chin on her entwined hands.

Marissa let out a sigh. "It's tough being a halfling, like us. We never really belong to one world or the other. You've got to shine, or they'll chew you up and spit you out without a second glance."

Rhianne nodded. This she understood well. "Yeah, I get it. When you decide to stand out and live life on your own terms, it can be freeing, but it can also get pretty lonely."

The admission surprised her and she realised how lucky she was to have Nel and Toto as friends. Now, there were these new people stepping into her little bubble and it stirred up a whole jumble of emotions inside her.

Marissa beamed, showing all her teeth. "My dad's the head of the gargoyle clan. He drove me hard, nearly to breaking point." She gave her head a little shake. "But he made sure everyone knew they'd have him to answer to if they picked on me. So, I carved out my own space, where everything's pretty and polished on the surface."

"But?"

"But when it comes to gargoyle males, it's often a tale of extremes," Marissa added with a wry smile. "They're either overly aggressive, constantly trying to assert their dominance and prove they're in charge, or they become too intimidated by me."

Rhianne snorted. "I have a feeling those aggressive ones got what was coming to them, didn't they?"

Marissa's smile turned fierce. "You bet!" Her expression

CHAPTER 15

then softened, and she gazed into her crystal glass for a moment before meeting Rhianne's eyes. "Carl is different. He's shy but not scared of me. He's more interested in plants than people, but he finds joy in life, and he's a really nice guy."

"You want to have a relationship with him."

Marissa's jaw tensed and she lifted her chin up. "You say that like it's a bad thing."

Rhianne reached out and grabbed Marissa's hand. Marissa stared at their joined hands, then back at Rhianne, blinking.

Rhianne couldn't contain her excitement as a big smile bloomed on her face. "That's so cool! I can't believe two of my friends might get together! We definitely have to set you up on a date!"

Marissa's eyes opened up and she backed off looking panicked. "No, I mean, you can't and I can't!"

"Huh?"

"It's a gargoyle thing. The male gargoyle is expected to be the one to make the first move," she said. "If I initiated anything, it would come across as too bold or mean that I'm only looking for a casual fling."

"But you are bold!" Rhianne argued.

Marissa vehemently shook her head, the intensity of her motion causing Rhianne to worry it might detach. "No, absolutely not! I can't be the one making the moves in this situation. If our relationship is going to work, I need to take a step back. If word gets out that I'm interested and pursuing him, it would only embarrass him."

"I don't think Carl would care."

Marissa sighed. "You don't understand how our society operates. It wouldn't just be his reputation at stake, but his entire family's."

Rhianne pressed her lips together. She couldn't argue against something she didn't fully understand. She felt a twinge of regret for not having dived deeper into her friends' customs and traditions sooner. "I guess I need you to give me a crash course on all this." She exhaled. "But isn't there always a loophole?"

The waiter reappeared. This time, Rhianne was prepared and managed to keep her heartbeat steady.

Marissa sat up straight in her chair, brushing away an imaginary strand of hair, and offered the waiter a polite smile. "I'll go with the lasagne, please, and a glass of pinot gris," she said.

"I'll take the Gnocchi with Gorgonzola Dolce, and could I get a lime water too, please?" Rhianne hadn't glanced at the menu but hoped they served what she asked for. Thankfully, the waiter nodded and left.

Marissa regarded Rhianne with a puzzled expression.

Rhianne offered her a small, triumphant smile. "It has a gamey taste with a hint of grassiness."

Marissa raised her eyebrows.

"Never mind, private joke. Let's get back to discussing that loophole so we can do something about Carl," Rhianne said.

Marissa perked up. "What do you mean by a loophole?"

"Okay, let's think about this logically. You're saying you're not allowed to ask him out, right?"

Marissa nodded, and began to chew on her bottom lip.

"Carl's quite shy, and he probably believes you aren't interested in him."

Marissa frowned. "What are you saying?"

"That Carl likes you, but his shyness and self-doubt make him believe that you are out of his league."

CHAPTER 15

"But that's not true." Marissa's voice cracked. "I'm the halfling here."

"Carl doesn't judge based on appearances or social status. To him, you're simply a beautiful, smart, and strong woman."

Marissa leaned forward, her voice barely above a whisper. "Do you really think he likes me?"

Rhianne's head bobbed up and down. "Oh, absolutely! When I told him we were having lunch together, he blushed like crazy. He genuinely cares about you, but he couldn't even muster up the courage to ask me to say hello."

"So, he's too shy to make a move, and I can't do anything about it?" Marissa twisted the simple gold ring on her right hand, her shoulders slumping

Rhianne's heart went to her. "Wait! I have an idea! I can organise a get-together and create the perfect chance for you and Carl to connect."

Marissa was on the verge of opening her mouth, but then her gaze sharpened and her expression shifted. Rhianne recognised the familiar pose that she had internally dubbed "the lawyer look."

"We could have dinner at your place. You'd be there so there would be a chaperone," Marissa said. "But what about Alice?" her eyes narrowed. "Carl would never do or say anything in front of her, and she can't find out about this either," she warned.

"Don't worry, I'll take care of it," Rhianne said. "But the challenge for you, my friend, is to find a way to show Carl that you're interested, while staying within the boundaries of those silly rules."

Marissa's smile sharpened, exuding a predatory air. "Leave it to me. I've convinced reluctant juries and stubborn judges for years. I'll find a way."

CHAPTER 16

The mouth-watering scent of Italian cuisine wafted through the air, signalling the arrival of the waiter. Rhianne's nostrils caught a whiff of the fragrant herbs, the rich tomato sauce, and cheese, making her stomach growl in anticipation.

They quietly enjoyed their meals, each deep in thought. The Gnocchi was amazing, super soft and melting in Rhianne's mouth like butter. The mix of sweet and tangy cheese gave it the right amount of zing.

"By the way, something happened on Monday night." Rhianne suddenly remembered she needed to ask her about interrogating the guys who attacked her.

Marissa smirked. "Ah, you mean your so-called 'maybe third date'."

"The date was amazing," Rhianne said. "But we had a little run-in with three thugs when we left the house."

Marissa nearly choked on the food in her mouth. "Wait, what? Did they hurt you or Kai?"

Rhianne shook her head. "Oh, they got way more than they bargained for," she replied. "But here's the thing — I need a favour, and I'm not sure if you're able or willing to help."

"You want legal advice?"

"More like legal interference."

Yep, Marissa's smile definitely looked like a shark's. "Ooh, my favourite kind."

"I want to question those thugs about why they targeted me. I'm sure the local police will question them, but I don't expect them to cooperate or disclose anything meaningful. And even if they did, I doubt the police would share that information with me."

Marissa's fingers tapped rhythmically on the table. "If they don't already have legal representation, I can make a move and get involved," she said. "Hold on! Are you suggesting that they were targeting you or Kai specifically? What makes you think that?"

Rhianne's lips formed a slight pucker as she weighed how much to disclose to Marissa. Despite liking her, her inherent mistrust held her back. Opting for a partial truth, she decided on a simpler explanation. "I suspect there was some fae magic involved," she said, her voice measured.

"I see." Marissa studied her under half masted eyes. She'd have plenty of experience with people evading the truth, heck, lawyers may not have invented evasiveness, but they surely had elevated it to an art.

"To be honest, I can't see why anyone would want to harm me," Rhianne mused. "But Kai's work might put him in the line of danger more than me."

Marissa's eyes narrowed as she speculated. "Well, there's one thing you both have in common - being key consultants in the Parkes murder case," she said. "The Fae rarely pop over from their realm. They were human, right?"

CHAPTER 16

Rhianne nodded. "Yes, how did you figure that out?"

Marissa leaned back, a thoughtful expression on her face. "Well, if those thugs were fae, they wouldn't be held in a regular police station. They would have been transferred to a specialist facility, unless they were minor fae," she explained. She twirled her empty glass. "It's quite intriguing, and I love a good mystery. Do you happen to know which police station they're being held at?"

"They're being held at the same police station where Alice was," she said. Then, changing the subject, she added, "Speaking of which, what's your rate? My budget is kind of limited, so I can't afford too many hours of your time."

"Nonsense. This is going to be fun, and besides, you're helping me with my case," Marissa countered. Pausing for a moment, she gazed out the window before turning back to Rhianne with a shy smile. "And you know, friends help each other out, right?"

A rush of warmth filled Rhianne's heart and a broad smile spread across her face as she looked at Marissa. "Yes, that's what friends do."

They nailed down the plans for the dinner, finding a time that worked for both of them. Marissa agreed to head to the station later, knowing the thugs would likely be relocated soon. But now it was time to sign the character reference.

They approached the courthouse, a grand old sandstone colonial building with a rich history. The entrance, once adorned with thick wooden doors, had now been replaced with sleek glass doors that slid open automatically as they approached.

Once they cleared the security screening, they made their way up the marble staircase. Rhianne couldn't help but be impressed by Marissa's brisk pace, and in heels. As they approached the counter, they noticed four clerks engrossed in their work, their attention glued to the screens in front of them, completely oblivious to their presence.

Marissa cleared her throat. Loudly. Startled, one of the clerks glanced up, wearing a scowl that vanished when she saw Marissa. The middle-aged woman's complexion turned pale, and she immediately adopted a polite tone.

"Can I assist you, Ms Austin?" Her grip on the stylus tightening so much that her knuckles turned white.

As soon as she mentioned Marissa's name the other clerks hunched their shoulders and feigned busyness, desperate to avoid any potential interaction. Marissa responded with a smile that revealed a mouthful of teeth, but rather than offering reassurance, it had the opposite effect. The intimidated clerk shrank further, seemingly attempting to retreat from their presence.

"We're here to file a character reference," Marissa said.

The clerk rose from her seat and approached the counter, holding a form in her hands. Marissa placed her hefty briefcase on the counter with a clank, causing a collective flinch from those nearby. "No need, just make sure you identify the witness."

It only took a few minutes and all the documents were signed and returned to the still pale clerk.

As they walked away from the office, Rhianne heard the sighs of relief coming from behind them. She turned to Marissa with a grin. "You know you are quite terrifying, don't you?"

"Oh, I've worked hard to cultivate that reputation. It definitely comes in handy when dealing with my colleagues

CHAPTER 16

and the judges."

As they stepped out, their cell phones simultaneously rang. Marissa waved at Rhianne, bidding her goodbye, before answering her own call.

As the familiar tune of *Holding Out for a Hero* echoed from her phone, Rhianne answered with a soft "Hey." "Did you manage to get some sleep?"

"I slept like a log." A yawn belied his proclamation.

"But not for long." she chided.

"Long enough."

She swore she could hear the smile on the other side.

"Hey, I've got some news. You want the good news or the bad news?" Kai asked.

Rhianne let out a weary sigh, adjusting the phone to her other ear. "All right, hit me with the bad news first."

"The burner phones were purchased two days ago by someone in a hoodie at a local convenience store," Kai said. "Not our thugs, though. The person looked male, but the baggy clothes made it hard to be certain."

"Sure it wasn't one of our thugs?" Rhianne asked, her voice carrying over the background noise of a bustling street as she awaited the signal to cross.

"The guy was surprisingly tall and skinny, despite wearing those baggy clothes. Our thugs are on the wider side, definitely not that height," Kai said. Anticipating Rhianne's question, he added, "And get this — he paid with cash, but it was clear he wasn't used to handling money. Had to get help from the cashier."

"I know teenagers who would consider cash a relic from a bygone era."

"Exactly my point. Teenagers these days wouldn't bother

with cash, and if they did, they'd know what to do. No, I have a hunch that this is our enigmatic elf."

Rhianne nodded, only to realise that Kai couldn't see her gesture. Doubt crept in, causing her to gaze at the screen for a moment. "Are you watching me?"

Kai chuckled softly. "I didn't think of it, but if you'd like, I could," he said, sounding hopeful and causing Rhianne's heart to flutter.

"I'm crossing the street now, so I should focus. By the way, was that the good news or the bad news?" She started to walk as the pedestrian lights turned green.

"That's the bad news," Kai said. "Are you busy on Thursday afternoon?"

"I thought the case was going to tie you up for a few days?" Rhianne asked. Her lips curled into a smile and her eyes crinkled with delight. Seeing him sooner than expected was definitely a pleasant surprise

"I am, but here's the good news part — I've been hired by Parkes Construction Enterprises to dig into some encrypted files, and guess what? I've got a meeting with none other than Rita Parkes herself to discuss it." Kai sounded smug about it.

"How did you pull that off?" Caught off guard, she stumbled momentarily on a rough section of the pavement.

"Ever heard of the algorithms social media uses to keep people endlessly scrolling?" Kai posed the question but did not pause for a response. "It's surprisingly straightforward. You identify their interests, then entice them with posts catered to those interests, subtly nudging them towards specific actions. All the while, they believe it's entirely their own choice. Besides, Rita Parkes was already looking around cyber security topics and money transfers. I just pointed her

CHAPTER 16

in the right direction."

Rhianne abruptly halted in her tracks, her jaw slackening as she stared at the phone, momentarily rendered speechless. "Wait, I thought you didn't do social media," she managed to say.

"I don't, and that's precisely one of the reasons why," Kai said. "But just because I don't use social media doesn't mean I don't understand how to use algorithms to subtly influence someone."

"Alpha geek indeed. I'm not sure whether to be thoroughly appalled or completely blown away."

"I'm voting for the latter," Kai said.

"A bit of both," Rhianne said and chuckled. "How will you explain my presence at the interview?"

"Ah, well. People with money always expect assistants. But I must admit, I don't have any disguises handy. Unless you happen to have a secret stash of wigs somewhere?"

Rhianne groaned, realising that altering her appearance for the Parkes family was becoming a regular occurrence. "Nel has wigs. I'll ask him."

"Your best friend?" Kai's tone remained largely unchanged, yet a hint of reservation seeped into his voice.

"My best friend and for all intents and purposes, brother," Rhianne clarified. "He's excited to meet you." She didn't want Kai to think he had anything to worry about.

"Then I'd like to meet him too." Kai's voice came through a yawn.

"Okay, so what time shall we meet?"

"The interview is scheduled for three. How about we meet at the coffee shop across from the building at two?" Kai suggested. "That way, we can discuss and strategise how we're going to approach it."

"Sounds like a plan to me. Now, go and get some more sleep," Rhianne said.

"I will, but promise me you won't get into any fights without me."

"What, you think you need to protect 'little old me'?" Rhianne teased.

Kai laughed. "It's not just about keeping you safe, Rhi. I want in on the action that seems to tag along with you."

Rhianne's smile widened, her heart skipping a beat. The way Kai called her "Rhi" sent a pleasant shiver down her spine. It was a name she had never embraced before, but with him, it felt good.

"Your idea of fun needs revisiting." Rhianne said.

"I've led a sheltered life." There was a hint of a shrug in his voice.

"See you then," Rhianne said, a giggle escaping her lips. Unbelievable! Kai had managed to make her giggle. Lucky neither Toto nor Nel were here to make fun of her.

Rhianne suddenly had the distinct feeling of being watched. She discreetly scanned the people around her, but no one stood out as suspicious. Still, there was something about the atmosphere that felt off. And then, she caught a faint flare of magic and noticed an eerie play of light and shadows. But just as quickly as it appeared, it vanished, leaving her questioning her own senses. Was she simply spooked and imagining things? She chuckled to herself, all this talk about the Shadows was getting to her.

She shook it off and dialled Nel's number. "How about a fight, big boy?"

"What, no hello? Although, I must say, I do appreciate a

CHAPTER 16

woman who knows what she wants."

"Where are you?" Rhianne asked, noticing the excessive noise in the background, which seemed out of place for the early hours at the club.

"I've just met with some of my shadier connections," Nel replied, his voice underscored by a grunt and the crash of something heavy hitting the floor. Rhianne could almost see him ducking a punch as he continued with a hint of annoyance, "They don't even have a clue what shady means," he complained.

"They may not understand the words, but they certainly recognise the contempt," Rhianne said. "You have no sense of self-preservation."

"If I didn't, I wouldn't still be alive, would I?" Nel said.

"No, you're just exceptionally lucky," Rhianne countered.

"You know what they say, princess: you make your own luck." Nel invoked an old argument between them.

"No, you take advantage of opportunities when they arise," Rhianne said.

"You're too young for such a pessimistic view of the world." Nel tutted. Another thump resonated in the background.

"Are you having a fight without inviting me? What kind of friend are you?"

"It's a rather dull one, though you might find amusement in the dirty tactics," Nel said amidst the sounds of chaos and destruction. He didn't even sound puffed.

"Don't tell me you're resorting to dirty tactics?" Rhianne feigned scandal.

"Not in your wildest dreams! I'm an honourable warrior," Nel's words dripped with mock righteousness.

A loud crash prompted Rhianne to move the phone away

from her ear, shielding it from the cacophony. "Can you speed up your honourable ways and meet me at the gym in half an hour?" she asked.

"Oh, fine," Nel said. "But only because I'm missing you," he added, a final metallic thump marking the end of the chaos, and a blissful silence ensued on his end.

"Don't even think about using this as an excuse when I thoroughly beat you later." Rhianne grinned.

"Well, someone's in a good mood," Nel said. "Does this new-found cheer have something to do with your tech warrior? I'm starting to feel superfluous."

"You're one of a kind, big boy, irreplaceable, and you know it! So, don't go fishing for compliments."

"Ah, was there a hint of fondness hidden in that insult?" Nel mused.

She blurted out, "Kai wants to meet you." She held her breath, waiting for Nel's reaction.

"He does, does he?" Nel's tone took on a mischievous undertone. "Is he not jealous of your tall, dark, and handsome best friend?"

"Not in the slightest." Or at least not after Rhianne had explained it.

"Well, as it happens, I'm dying to meet the man who is competing with me for your affections," Nel teased.

"There is no competition, you're my brother," Rhianne said. "And he is — someone I want to get to know much better." Her words trailed off lamely as she struggled to define her evolving feelings for Kai. In such a short time, he had become much more than she had initially expected.

"I see," Nel said. "Then I'd like to meet him as well. See you soon, princess."

CHAPTER 16

Rhianne swung her leg over the bike, turned it on and gripped the handlebars. With a determined turn of the throttle, she shot forward, blending into the bustling streets. As she navigated through the city, her mind continued to conjure images of Kai.

As Rhianne arrived at the gym, she spotted Nel engaged in conversation with an attractive blonde woman, who was gazing at him in adoration. Without interrupting, she tapped Nel on the shoulder while passing by, heading straight to their designated fighting corner. Glancing back for a moment, she caught the woman shooting her a venomous glare. Rhianne snorted, having grown accustomed to the jealous looks of Nel's conquests.

To say that Nel was commitment-phobic was like saying the ocean was a bit damp. He never went beyond a second date. She figured he did it to soften the blow when he called things off. Still, there was that one time a woman lost it over a one-night fling.

As soon as Nel caught up with her and they were out of earshot, Rhianne asked, "Have you slept with her?"

"Not yet, but I'm starting to think I won't," Nel shrugged his shoulders. A sidelong glance from Rhianne prompted him to continue, "She seems too clingy already."

Rhianne's curiosity, perhaps fuelled by her own budding relationship with Kai, gave her an edge of boldness. "Don't they all get clingy?" she asked, her words direct and unfiltered.

Nel winced. "It's my innate charm." He attempted to brush it off.

"Innate or magical? And does that apply to humans only, or does it affect all supernatural beings too?"

Nel's head snapped towards her, his brows furrowing.

"You've never asked before. Are you worried that I might be influencing you?"

Rhianne paused, suddenly aware of the topic's delicacy for Nel. How had this escaped her before? She knew he rarely spoke of his incubus traits, assuming his silence stemmed from their sensual implications. The idea that he might fear his own influence on others had never occurred to her. And it should have.

"As if, big boy!" She strived to keep her tone light. "Otherwise, I'd be too afraid to fight dirty, for fear of damaging the crown jewels, and that would never do."

Nel threw his head back, letting out a genuine laugh, and the tension that had been in his eyes dissipated. "So that's the reason you can beat me."

"Even if I didn't, you'd still lose."

He wagged his finger, his cockiness resurfacing, and although Rhianne liked this lighter side of him, she was more resolved now to dig into what scared him.

"Here's the deal: If I win, you spill," Rhianne proposed.

"And if I win, you'll let me get you a decent car," Nel countered, cracking his knuckles.

His quick, confident response sowed a seed of doubt in her. Could he have been holding back all this time, despite his denials? Was she about to be thoroughly outmatched? She narrowed her eyes, sizing him up. She knew his fighting style well — his size and strength — and she was aware she couldn't outmatch him in a straightforward battle. If he had been holding back, she'd need to switch up her strategy, but how?

As they began their warm-up, the onlookers gathered at the edges of the mats, a sight that irritated Rhianne. The crowded

CHAPTER 16

surroundings spooked her. She needed to focus. Perhaps that had been Nel's intention all along, and if so, he had succeeded. She needed something to anchor her thoughts, to shake off the unease creeping within her.

Slowly rotating her arms, she used the movement as an excuse to search for a focal point. The woman from earlier had positioned herself front and centre with a nasty grin on her face, clearly convinced that Nel was about to give her a beating. Rhianne narrowed her eyes, refusing to give her the satisfaction of looking worried.

Then, her gaze shifted to a small pot plant perched on one of the high windows. It was a hanging fern, delicate leaves trailing down at least two feet. Rhianne extended her magical senses towards it, sending a tentative greeting. To her surprise, the plant responded, as if offering a gentle caress and a comforting warmth in return. The soothing sensation washed over her, instantly revitalising her energy levels. Closing her eyes, she allowed the feeling to permeate her being, maintaining her movements as she went through the warm-up routine by muscle memory and intuition.

"Ready?" Nel's voice broke the silence, as if only seconds had passed since they started warming up, though it must have been the usual allotted twenty minutes.

The sound of his voice gently echoed in Rhianne's mind, prompting her to open her eyes. Her vision had sharpened, allowing her to see Nel in all his magnificent glory. He had taken off his shirt, revealing his well-defined six-pack and glistening pecs under the gym lights. However, what truly caught her attention was the radiant aura surrounding him, a shimmering glow she had never witnessed before.

"Pretty," she said, only then realising she had spoken aloud.

Nel cocked his head, and Rhianne could hear a snort from the nasty woman. She fought back the urge to laugh, settling instead for a grin. The energy coursing through her was exhilarating, and she positioned herself in a poised and balanced stance. "Bring it on," she said, initiating her attack with deadly precision, executing a high leg sweep — an unexpected move she would have never employed as an opening gambit. The element of surprise ensured she landed a hit on his side.

"Best of three?" Rhianne's grin stretched wide.

Nel hesitated, as if sensing that something was amiss. His narrowed eyes locked onto her, his casual reply betraying the tension in his jaw. "Sure."

Rhianne took a step back, executing a seamless somersault, she tapped Nel on the shoulder hard and gracefully landed in a roll on the other side. Rising to her feet, she couldn't help but wear a triumphant smile on her lips, revelling in her successful move.

However, her elation vanished as her eyes locked with the hanging fern. Where once it had been vibrant and green, it now appeared withered, reduced to a brown, dry mess.

CHAPTER 17

Rhianne's mouth hung open as the shock of what she'd just done shook her. She could feel the shivers running through her, and her eyes started to fill up, tears on the brink. Then, someone's comforting hands were on her shoulders, steadying her.

"Nice one, princess," Nel called out, his voice cutting through the silence so everyone could hear. "Time to head off and celebrate." His tone was that easy, cool kind that could settle the most frayed nerves. Rhianne felt like her body was made of lead all of a sudden, and just thinking about moving was a chore.

Nel's hands left her shoulders, and she missed their steadiness instantly. But then, in no time at all, she was wrapped up in a firm hug, giving her the comfort and strength she needed. Rhianne let herself relax into the support, the contact snapping her back into the moment.

She shot a regretful look at the wilted fern, aware that with everyone watching, there wasn't much she could do right then.

With an act of deliberate will, Rhianne marshalled her

concentration "Great idea," she said, attempting to infuse her voice with cheerfulness, though it came out brittle. "I'll go get changed and meet you at the front."

She rushed through her shower, got changed and left. Nel stood waiting, his eyes holding a mix of questions and quiet support.

"Let's get out of here," she said, sidestepping any conversation. Not here with the many eyes and ears likely fixed on them.

Without a word, Nel placed his arm in the crook of hers and guided her out. She didn't resist when he led her to his parked car and opened the door for her. She slid into the passenger seat, lost in thought as they drove in silence. She watched the world outside morph from vivid blues to the dusky greys of evening, signalling their arrival at Nel's place. Getting out of the car, she trailed behind him to the lifts, the quiet bubble of their isolation a small comfort amidst the chaos in her head.

In a quiet voice, Rhianne finally asked. "Did you see the fern?"

Nel nodded, his expression neutral. "I didn't sense any magic happening."

Rhianne's thoughts were a whirlwind of magical theories. Green magic? Yeah, that left a clear trace. But then there was the fae magic - the stuff Toto claimed he'd felt in her. That magic had a certain sweet smell to it, at least to Rhianne. But the question was, could Nel pick up on that scent, or was it a fae-only kind of thing? And that odd energy she got from the fern — it didn't quite gel with the rest.

"I can't put my finger on what kind of magic that was. I was looking for something to focus on, and the fern just — gave off this comforting warmth. I didn't mean to hurt it." Her

CHAPTER 17

voice wobbled.

"Since I didn't sense anything familiar, I suspect it might be connected to your dryad magic."

She let the thought roll around in her mind a bit before speaking. "I can't tell the difference between green magic and dryad magic. I mean, I don't think I've ever purposely used dryad magic before," she confessed. "My green magic has this certain feel to it. And that ... wasn't there this time."

Curiosity sparked in Nel's eyes as he asked, "So have you used dryad magic before?"

Once they emerged from the lift into Nel's apartment, Rhianne found her way to the chaise lounge and sank down. "I remember walking through the forest with Tata Angelo back in the day. He'd always tell me to listen to the trees, to connect with them. I never got the hang of it though."

She left out the silent fear of failure and exposure that got in her way. Even when she practised her green magic, she was careful, not entirely sure how her different magical abilities might interact. Staying under the radar had always seemed the safest bet.

She rubbed her eyes tiredly, letting out a soft sigh. "I really wanted to heal that fern afterwards. But with all those watchful eyes around, it wasn't on the cards. Felt like the fern ... it sensed I needed a boost, and it gave me its strength. But all I did was drain it,"

Nel pulled out his smartphone and typed a message. "Something bothered you today, and you seemed off. What happened?"

For a fleeting moment, Rhianne toyed with the idea of steering the conversation away and not answering. "I started thinking — perhaps you've been going easy on me all this while, because, well — you love me." Her words spilt out in a sudden rush.

Nel let out a sigh. "The last time I defeated you, you were nineteen. Why would I suddenly decide to boost your ego now? I've never treated you with kid gloves."

Rhianne snorted. "You've spoiled me rotten, as everyone can attest. Expensive gifts, financial support for my studies, helping me set up my business…"

Nel's expression turned tender. "I love you, princess. That's always been out in the open. Sure, I've spoiled you with stuff and watched out for you like any brother would, but I've never held you back. You stood up to those attackers because you're strong, not because I've sheltered you. Even if a part of me will always see you as my little sister, I know you're all grown up."

She fixed him with a pointed look. "All right, if you mean that, then give me a straight answer about your powers, will you?"

Nel passed a hand through his hair, a gesture of resignation, and leaned back against the bookshelf. "You're right, you've earned that much. I don't keep quiet about my powers because I think you can't handle it. Truth is, they frighten me," he confessed.

He hauled himself up and trudged to the chair opposite Rhianne, flopping down with a dramatic exhale. For a second, Rhianne just blinked at him. Nel and scared? They went together like oil and water. He was the guy who'd wink and dive into the deep end while everyone else was still dipping their toes.

Nel settled deeper into the chair, his tone threading a line between surrender and worry. "I've been around a while, and

CHAPTER 17

with age, our kind get stronger," he said. "It's odd, you know, you're the first woman in centuries who my charms haven't touched. Heck, there are guys who find me irresistible, and it's got nothing to do with who they fancy. Humans can get tangled up in a heartbeat with just one touch. Other creatures, though, they can shake it off better, especially the ancient or powerful ones."

Rhianne cracked a smile, trying to cut through the tension. "Don't you mean they fall in love? I've seen the letters and poems, you know."

Nel let out a humourless chuckle. "Exactly," he said. "They mistake that lust for love. It's always about what they want from me, not about me as a person. Sure, I need that physical connection to keep going, but it's been a long time since I've felt a real closeness with anyone." He paused, taking a breath that seemed to hold a lot of unspoken things. "That's why I was always careful not to touch you when we started hanging out."

Rhianne shifted uncomfortably, her mind racing. She had thought Nel's distance was about him being mindful of her youth, trying not to give her the wrong idea. "So, I have like some sort of … immunity to you? Is that why you kept me around?" Her voice wavered a bit with the question, unsure if she wanted to hear the answer.

Nel's head gave a gentle shake as a smile, warm and genuine, surfaced. "No, you've been different right from the start. It wasn't just about the immunity, though that puzzled me for the longest time." A glint of reminiscence danced in his eyes. "I think it hit me that day I came to help you move out."

Rhianne's face lit up with sudden understanding. "Oh, you mean that day I had the massive blow-up with my mother and

I rang you in a panic to come over?" she asked, the memory clicking into place.

Nel's grin grew. "That's the one," he said, a warm note in his voice. "You were all fire and spirit, even back then. Standing up to your mum, making it clear you weren't anyone's pawn. I was so impressed." His eyes took on a faraway look. "When I turned up, you didn't hesitate, jumped right in for a hug, head tucked in against me."

Rhianne couldn't help but smile at the memory, a moment when she'd felt truly supported. "Yeah, I remember," she echoed. "Off to the studio flat you whisked me, claiming some favour from the owner. You made it sound like I was doing them a big favour, taking over that space to spruce it up."

Nel's smile softened, the lines of stress relaxing around his eyes. "That hug was my moment of truth," he confessed. "You touched me, but you didn't fall all over me. Instead, you practically shooed me out once you got your bearings in the new place. I tried to stick around under the guise of grocery shopping, but you weren't having any of it." A chuckle escaped him. "You know, nobody had ever managed to send me packing quite like that. It was refreshingly nice. So, I kept an eye on you after that, and not once did you act like you were under some spell. That's when I knew for sure."

Rhianne stood up and walked over to him, enveloping him in a hug. "I found you fascinating, just not that way," she said. "Wait, is that why you don't pursue long-term relationships? Because you think others are only after one thing with you?"

Nel simply nodded in response and Rhianne's throat tightened. Rhianne empathised with Nel's feelings to a certain extent.

CHAPTER 17

That's exactly why Rhianne had a tough time making close friends, except for her solid connection with Nel. High school for her was full of fake friendships — people being nice to her just to get magical help or to benefit from her family's status. This kind of thing happened so often; it made her pretty wary of making new friends.

So, Rhianne found her comfort zone in the library, hanging out with books instead of people. But she couldn't stand by when she saw younger kids getting bullied. She became their defender, standing up to the bullies for them. In doing this, she found some realness — these younger students didn't want anything from her; they needed her help, and that was refreshingly simple and honest.

"Maybe," Nel said, bringing her back from her reverie. But in an instant, his attention shifted back to Rhianne and a mischievous grin spread across his face. "Or maybe no one can truly compete with you, princess. So, I don't even bother trying."

She playfully pinched his forearm. "Oh, come on, don't try to deflect. I know your tricks, mister. You can't fool your baby sister." Rhianne tucked away the thought to bring up with Toto later. With his access to old archives and his vast knowledge, he might have a trick or two up his sleeve that could help Nel tone down his powers.

Nel's laugh was light, his smile genuine and bright. "You know, you should take some of that advice yourself, princess. When are you going to see just how incredible you are? You've got your own successful venture, and you're unbeatable in the ring. You've got nothing to prove."

Rhianne exhaled slowly, feeling the weight of his words. She knew Nel was right, yet there was always that inner battle, that nagging doubt fuelled by not living up to her mother's high standards and the ache of her father's aloofness.

Now, though, she was surrounded by people who appreciated her for who she was, quirks and all. She offered a half smile. "Yeah, I get it, but it's harder to shake off the doubt than you think."

Nel smirked. "Well, it's not easy being this good-looking, talented, and smart either. It's a burden I bear every single day."

Rhianne burst into laughter. "Oh, the cocky and flippant incubus I know and love." She bumped his shoulder and planted a friendly peck on his cheek.

"Talking about love, Art has been asking about you at the club. Discreetly, he thinks."

Rhianne snorted. As if anyone could do or say anything in Nel's club without him finding out about it.

"He was rather taken with you," Nel added.

"He was taken with the *idea* of someone and titillated by the forbidden fruit." Rhianne waved it off. She paused, mulling over her options. "But if I need more information. It might mean Rose needs to make another appearance at the club on Thursday night."

Nel raised an eyebrow and then leaned forward, "Maybe I can make a spy out of you yet."

"Oh, please. You're a secret agency all on your own, big boy. You don't need my help."

"I'll always need you." He tugged at a soft wave of her hair and then turned searching eyes on her. "But the idea has merit. Having a female spy opens up more possibilities."

"No way. You're not involving me in your extra-curricular activities."

CHAPTER 17

"Don't dismiss it so quickly. You have a talent for extracting information from people, and your insatiable curiosity is a valuable asset. That's the currency I deal in."

"And use to your advantage."

He flashed her a wide smile, his eyes sparkling with mischief. "Of course, but I use it to keep the right people on their toes."

Rhianne's eyes narrowed as she studied him. Just how deeply involved was Nel in politics? Could that be the reason her mother wasn't particularly fond of him? "What exactly do you mean by keeping the right people on their toes?"

Nel raised a finger, a playful gesture. "All I ask is that you think about it. "Once you have the information, it's up to you how to use it. But let me give you a little sneak peek - I've gathered solid evidence against a notorious fairy trafficker and a few others."

A mischievous glint danced in Rhianne's eyes as she leaned closer. "How about a butt-slapping politician? Did you orchestrate that?"

Nel looked smug. "Oh, he definitely deserved it."

Rhianne wanted to roll her eyes, but her mouth twitched and a soft chuckle escaped before she could contain it. "I knew it! You sneaky, vengeful, and brilliant demon! Why didn't you tell me about this before?"

Nel's gaze dropped, his hands suddenly the centre of his world. "I didn't want to lose any respect in your eyes," he said. "A lot of this goes back to my younger days." He paused, lost in thought for a moment. "You know, being young and trying to figure out who you are can be tough. You're not sure of your own worth, and there are always those waiting to take advantage of that doubt." There was a brief shadow of a frown on Nel's face as he mentioned his past, a whisper of old memories. "That's part of why I got into the secrets game. Knowing what makes others tick gave me some clues about myself," he said. "And now, I've got a taste for the hidden and the unknown. There's something about secrets and puzzles that pulls me in."

A warmth spread through Rhianne, and she reached out to gently squeeze his hand. "I could never think any less of you, you silly oaf."

Nel met her gaze and offered a wry smile. "So, does that mean you'll consider my offer?"

Rhianne suppressed a laugh. "All right, Nel, I'll consider it. In fact, I may need your help with yet another disguise."

Nel tilted his head. "Oh? And what kind of disguise are we talking about this time?"

"Kai has managed to secure an interview with Rita Parkes, and he's invited me along."

Nel whistled in admiration. "Impressive. How did he manage that?" Rhianne told him. "That tech mage of yours is quite resourceful and smart, isn't he?"

Rhianne wagged her finger at him. "Don't you dare start thinking about recruiting him either."

Nel feigned innocence and tapped his chin. "I wouldn't dream of it. At least not without your consent, of course."

"I know that look." Rhianne frowned. She was treading carefully, not wanting to mess up the delicate early stages with Kai. Falling for someone came with its own cocktail of thrill and nerves, and she was all in to see where this ride with Kai would take her. She loved Nel, truly, but he was devious and tricky. With a plan always up his sleeve, she sometimes wondered if he was the human equivalent of a chess game — always three moves ahead

CHAPTER 17

Nel shifted the conversation to the upcoming mission. "You'll have to come up with a strategy to bring up the murder," he pointed out. She hadn't thought that far ahead. Perhaps Kai would have some ideas, but Nel was right — they needed a strategy. "Don't sweat it. People always want to talk; you just need to steer the conversation." He grinned. "And since Parkes wasn't exactly Mr Congeniality, you'll probably find people more than ready to dish out dirt. That's your in."

Rhianne nodded. As an assistant, she'd be overlooked, and people would be more likely to share information with her. "So, what do you think an assistant to a Tech Mage should look like?"

Nel grinned. "We're going shopping."

Rhianne groaned.

CHAPTER 18

The shopping trip had turned out to be more fun than she'd expected, but that was a secret she'd keep under wraps. It wasn't just aimless wandering through aisles; they were on a mission, piecing together a persona crucial for their investigation. It gave the whole shopping adventure a thrilling edge.

Nel had picked out a sleek dark grey suit for her. The knee-length skirt had a straight cut, while the hip-length jacket gave off a professional vibe. Completing the look was a crisp white blouse with a charming bow at the front. Nel insisted on getting a pair of black shoes with low kitten heels to match.

Back at the club, Nel delved into his collection of disguises and unearthed a short blonde bob wig. Rhianne, trying it on, couldn't help but acknowledge the drastic change it made to her look. Then, Nel brought out a pair of thick reading glasses from another stash.

"Are these going to mess with my vision?" she asked.

"Try them," Nel nudged.

To Rhianne's relief, the glasses were just for show, no prescription involved. Her vision stayed perfectly clear. Check-

CHAPTER 18

ing herself out in the mirror, she was genuinely shocked. The wig had already morphed her appearance significantly, but the glasses? They were the cherry on top. She barely recognised the woman staring back at her.

"Are these custom-made or something?" Rhianne held up the glasses.

"You'd be surprised at the kinds of fantasies people have. The whole secretary look? Big hit in the club. Glasses like these can really boost a dancer's tips."

Rhianne shook her head, still fixated on her new look in the mirror. "Some things, I'm better off not knowing."

Nel raised an eyebrow. "Everyone's got their thing, princess."

"Yeah, especially if there's money in it, right?" She gave him a playful glance.

"Money makes the world go round. Can't fault a guy for playing the game well."

"Or for spending it like it's going out of style." Rhianne mused, half-wondering if his lavish spending was his way of balancing things out.

Nel chuckled. "What's the point of making money if you don't enjoy it?"

Their conversation was veering into one of those uncomfortable territories they occasionally stumbled into, but Rhianne couldn't resist. "Last time I checked, money doesn't give hugs."

"Really? You didn't feel embraced by the leather seats in the Lamborghini?" Nel replied with a playful arch of his brow. "Besides, your hugs are more than enough."

Rhianne rolled her eyes. "Sure, sure. I should get changed and head out. My bike's still at the gym."

Nel flashed a grin, his teeth a stark white contrast. "Already sorted. Your bike's in the club's garage."

Rhianne gave him a playful shove. "You know it's not exactly legal to tow someone's bike without asking, right?"

He chuckled. "You could just say thanks, you know."

"Thanks, but next time, maybe ask first?" Rhianne shot back, half-teasing, half-serious.

Nel put his hands behind his back, looking a bit deflated. "Not sticking around?"

"Don't look so down, big guy. I'll catch you at the gym tomorrow. And hey, thanks for the help with the shopping and getting the disguise sorted." Rhianne was trying to keep things light, especially given the puppy dog look Nel was giving her, which made leaving a tad harder than she'd admit.

"There," Nel said, a smirk on his lips. "Was that so hard?"

Rhianne managed to squeeze the secretary outfit and wig into her bike's pannier bag before heading home. She had a few things to run by Toto.

As she entered her apartment, she found Toto sprawled on the sofa, seemingly asleep. "Hey, sleepyhead," she greeted, flicking on the light and heading to the kitchen to unload her bags. She was parched and peckish.

Toto stirred, nearly tumbling off the couch, and gave a single bark in protest.

"I wish to clarify that I was not engaged in sleep; rather, I was in a state of meditation. You should consider meditation. It offers insights and wisdom."

Rhianne chuckled as she grabbed a glass of water and a slice of brie from the fridge. "Why bother with meditation when I've got you around to dish out all the wisdom?"

Toto gave her a slightly miffed look before puffing out his

CHAPTER 18

chest. "I have aimed to be a superior teacher. Many seek my unparalleled knowledge. They travel from afar to come to this world for my words of wisdom."

Rhianne bit into the cheese, relishing its creamy flavour as it melted on her tongue. "Exactly what I need," Rhianne said, "You're a walking encyclopedia. If you don't have the answer, you'll know where to find it."

"Hmph, I have forgotten more than most will learn. Ask away!"

Rhianne paused, cheese halfway to her mouth. "What can you tell me about incubi?"

The look Toto gave her was loaded with understanding. "What is it about Nel that's puzzling you?"

She sighed, putting down the cheese. "Is there no way to counter an incubus' powers? Does it affect everyone?"

Toto sat upright, paws fluttering. "Ah, but you, my dear, seem immune to his charms."

Rhianne, careful not to reveal too much of Nel's personal issues, kept her response vague. "Yes, I am. But Nel is unaware of anyone else like me, and I was just — wondering."

Understanding crossed his face and Toto licked one paw thoughtfully before continuing. "His influence is particularly potent on females of any kind, except for you, of course." Toto paused. "There exists a correlation between the potency of a female's power and her level of resistance against the charms of incubi. The greater the strength of her power, the lesser the sway they hold over her."

Rhianne mulled over her own immunity. She didn't consider herself particularly powerful, so why was she unaffected?

Toto must have read her mind. "You are an exception

perhaps attributable to your unique lineage."

"But are there any species that are naturally resistant?" Rhianne pressed

Toto took a moment before answering. "Some elves are known to possess a higher degree of resistance, which could partially account for your immunity. which might explain your situation. But remember, resistance does not mean total immunity. There are other factors at play."

"What about other demons?" Rhianne asked.

Toto shook his head. "No, however, many train intensively over years to build up a resistance to such influences."

"Can you do some research? I'd be happy to help."

"Hmm, I will need to consult some ancient tomes," Toto said.

"Thank you, Toto. I appreciate it."

Rhianne finished her nightly routine and climbed into bed, but her mind was far from ready to rest. Questions and theories buzzed around like restless bees, pushing sleep further away. Who was the killer? Art or Sarah Parkes? She couldn't imagine Art committing murder; he seemed lost and lonely, but not cruel. But what if his domineering father had pushed him over the edge?

Then there was Sarah, who looked more capable of planning something so cold and precise. Wasn't it often the spouse in these cases? Sarah had the intellect and the will, she'd shown as much when she confronted the masseur. And the motive? Money was a powerful one.

But the method kept bothering Rhianne. How would either of them get their hands on Romin poison? And what about the attack on her? No news from Marissa yet — could there be a link between the murder and her assault? The shadowy

CHAPTER 18

figure that had been following her, could it be connected? For a fleeting moment, she wondered if her father was behind it, but that was far-fetched. He'd never cared enough to spy on her.

The involvement of elves was another puzzle. The magic used by her attackers, the Shadow's elven nature — why were elves suddenly cropping up in her life?

Rhianne grabbed a pillow, pressing it against her head, trying to muffle the relentless onslaught of thoughts. Sleep, when it finally came, felt like a distant, hard-earned victory.

She woke up before the alarm went off, still feeling unsettled. She had the strong feeling she was missing something important but couldn't figure out what.

Determined to shake off the unease, she hopped out of bed, showered, and dressed for the day. She chose practicality over comfort: cargo pants and a T-shirt, despite the heat. Working with plants meant braving thorns and bugs, so shorts were out of the question.

Making her way to the main garden nursery, she spotted Alice cleaning one of the water fountains nestled within the area known as the grotto. Large trellises surrounded the space, with native climbers all through. The sandstone fountain was in the centre, with pot plants creating meandering pathways.

Rhianne approached Alice, who was scrubbing the fountain. "Running a garden nursery isn't always as delightful as it sounds, is it?"

Alice looked up with a smile, sending droplets of water flying. "Yep, no fairy serenades while cleaning."

Rhianne grinned. "Just be careful of those crafty gnome thieves lurking around."

Alice chuckled as she scrubbed away. "Yeah, I've already

lost three trowels this week. I'm starting to suspect there's a black market for garden tools run by gnomes."

Their shared laughter lightened the mood. After a moment, Alice wiped her brow and turned more serious. "Hey, thanks for the character reference with Marissa. It really means a lot." She hesitated. "Any chance I could leave a bit early today? My parents want me over for dinner."

Rhianne nodded. "Sure, that's fine. But is Carl tagging along? I might need to close up shop early if both of you are out."

Alice gave a small shake of her head. "Nope, it's just me this time. I'm pretty sure it's another of their 'find Alice a partner' missions. I can't really say no, not with all the help they're giving me." She then flashed a mischievous smile. "Doesn't mean I have to say yes to whoever they throw at me, though."

Rhianne tilted her head, considering. "Who knows? Maybe you'll click with this one. Why not give it a shot?"

Alice's smile turned into a pondering look. "Let's just say my parents and I don't exactly see eye to eye on what makes someone 'suitable.' And, to be honest, I don't exactly fit the typical gargoyle bride mould."

Rhianne couldn't help but smile, trying to inject some humour back into the conversation. "Hey, who wants 'typical' anyway? It's the quirks that make things fun."

Alice's eyes twinkled as she laughed. "You know, you're right. I'd much rather find someone who gets why I love knitting at 2 a.m. or why my sock drawer is full of mismatched pairs."

Rhianne joined in with a playful tone. "Exactly! Someone who gets the thrill of untangling a stubborn ball of yarn, or doesn't mind your ever-growing collection of knitting

CHAPTER 18

needles."

Alice gave Rhianne a playful nudge. "And if it doesn't work out, at least I'll have an endless supply of hand-knitted scarves for those chilly nights." Their laughter echoed around the grotto, bouncing off the stone fountain and climbing plants.

Rhianne's phone blared out Lady Gaga's 'Born This Way', signalling a call from Marissa.

"Hi Marissa," Rhianne answered, moving away from the fountain and Alice's amused look.

"I managed to secure a meeting with them," Marissa said without preamble.

"Wow, how did you pull that off?" Rhianne said placing the phone on her ear while walking away from Alice.

She could almost hear the smirk on the other side. "Well, criminals are like anyone else — they can't resist a freebie."

"So, they fell for it?"

Marissa chuckled. "Oh, absolutely. They weren't the sharpest tools in the shed. I'm pretty confident they don't know much."

"I'm guessing you can't share details because of client confidentiality?" Rhianne strolled towards the nursery's tropical section.

"I didn't officially take them on as clients, so I'm not bound by that. But there's not much to tell. I think they were glamoured to target you."

"What makes you say that?"

"Their reasons for targeting you were foggy at best. More like an impulse than a well-thought-out plan."

Rhianne took a deep breath. "Not sure whether to be relieved or horrified."

"You could also go for flattered. Glamours aren't easy to

come by, let alone afford."

Rhianne half-laughed. "I guess it's all about perspective."

"Impressive work by the way. They were big guys and you left them barely able to move."

"Kai helped a lot. I think they weren't expecting us to fight back, which worked in our favour." Rhianne's gaze drifted over the tropical plants as she spoke, her mind still processing the conversation.

As Rhianne caught sight of Carl working in the distance, an idea sparked. "Hey, Marissa, you free for dinner tonight?"

Silence greeted her on the other end of the line, causing Rhianne to question if the call had dropped. "Hello? Marissa?"

Then, with a burst of excitement, Marissa's voice erupted from the phone, her words stumbling over each other in a rush. "Tonight? You mean with Carl? Oh, I'd have to go shopping and I won't have time for the hairdresser's —"

"If it's not a good time, that's totally fine," Rhianne interjected, walking faster towards Carl, needing an answer to set her plan in motion. She lowered her voice. "Honestly, he'll think you're beautiful regardless, and I don't know when we can set this up again."

"I'll be there at seven "Marissa said, her tone steadier.

"Good, see you then," Rhianne replied, but Marissa had already hung up.

Rhianne turned her attention to Carl, who was cleaning the leaves of a dwarf palm. "Hi, Carl."

Carl glanced at her, a smile playing on his lips. "Hi, boss."

"I heard that Alice is going out for dinner with your parents tonight," Rhianne began, testing the waters.

"Yeah," Carl said, returning to his task but with a broader grin. "I'm not invited. Third wheel problems, you know."

CHAPTER 18

She hesitated, searching for the right segue. "Well, I've got this mountain of paperwork back at the office ..." She let her voice drift off.

Carl perked up, standing tall as he faced her. "Need some help with that?" He had a knack for paperwork, a rare love for the task that Rhianne appreciated.

"Actually, yes," Rhianne said. "I was thinking we could tackle it together later. Maybe order some pizza? I'll cover the overtime, of course."

Carl's face lit up. "I'm in! And don't forget the anchovies, right?" Alice can't stand the smell, so it's a rare treat for me. And don't worry about overtime," Carl added cheerfully.

Rhianne wrestled with a twinge of guilt over her little plot but reminded herself that sometimes a gentle push was necessary. "Great, we'll dive into the paperwork and have some pizza. And a heads up, we might have a few extra people dropping by later."

Carl chuckled. "As long as they're down with anchovies, I'm cool with it."

Relieved, Rhianne confirmed, "Anchovies will be the star of the show. Let's meet up at the office later this afternoon."

"Got it, boss," Carl said with an agreeable nod, his gaze already returning to the tasks at hand. "I'll probably be wrapped up here by late afternoon."

"That works for me," Rhianne said, smiling. "Just come and find me when you're done." She then turned and headed towards the private garden section of the greenhouse.

At lunch, Rhianne opted for something quick but satisfying — a cheese toastie and a side of sweet mango. While eating, she thought about updating Nel and Kai on Marissa's findings. She drafted a message to each and hit send.

Soon after, her phone buzzed with a reply from Kai. "Figures. I'm looking into other security footage for clues. Miss you." Rhianne's smile was instant as she replied, 'Disguise ready. Can't wait for tomorrow. Miss you too.'

After brushing off the last of the crumbs, her phone chimed again. This time it was Nel. 'Disappointing but expected. See you tomorrow Gym and then club?'

Rhianne typed. 'Yes gym. Maybe club.' And sent it with a hug emoji.

Toto was sprawled out on the sofa, his eyes closed. "Hey there, mister," she called out.

Toto slowly opened one eye and glanced at her. "I was not sleeping," he grumbled.

Rhianne held back a smile. "Just meditating, right?" She told him what Marissa had said.

"Well, it was worth the attempt, I suppose. Hopefully, Kai will uncover further information, "Toto mused.

"Oh, and by the way, I've invited Carl and Marissa over for dinner," Rhianne added.

Toto raised an eyebrow. Are they aware of each other's arrival?

"Marissa is in the loop," Rhianne replied.

"I understand. Perhaps you should consider enhancing the ambience by introducing some candles." Toto suggested feigning indifference, although his wagging tail betrayed his excitement. Who knew? Toto was a closet romantic.

Before she knew it, closing time had arrived, and Rhianne joined Carl as he closed off the gates. "Hey, ready to tackle the mountain of documents?" She wiped her hands on her apron.

Carl brushed the dirt off his overalls. "Mind if I take a quick

CHAPTER 18

shower first? I'm covered in dirt and leaves."

Rhianne nodded. She had designated a separate breakout area that featured a compact kitchenette and a full bathroom.

"Good idea. I'll do the same and meet you in the office in twenty minutes."

When Carl entered the office, Rhianne was already staring at the daunting stack of papers on her desk.

He chuckled, picking up on her visible frustration. "Why don't you start with the correspondence, and I'll tackle the chaos that is this desk?" he suggested, gesturing towards the piles of paper that seemed to have a life of their own.

Rhianne let out a sigh that was half relief, half exasperation. "At this rate, we might uncover the lost city of Atlantis under these papers," she joked.

Glancing at the clock, Rhianne was surprised at their progress. "Wow, look at the time. I better order those pizzas before we turn into paper zombies." She stretched her aching muscles and then dialled the pizza place, requesting one with extra anchovies. "For the anchovy aficionado."

The amiable voice on the other end promised a delivery in less than half an hour, anchovy overload and all.

Twenty minutes later, a knock echoed through the office door, and Carl got up to answer it. "That must be our delivery guy," he said. "If your friends don't hurry, they'll miss out on the pizza."

As he opened the door, Rhianne's attention was drawn by Carl's sudden intake of breath.

Marissa greeted them with a soft hello, her voice barely more than a whisper. Rhianne tried to peer around Carl's broad shoulders, but he was frozen in place, resembling a granite statue. Sensing the awkwardness, Rhianne tapped

Carl on the shoulder and said, "Aren't you going to let Marissa in?"

Carl snapped out of his trance, closing his mouth, and moved aside to let Marissa enter.

"Hi Marissa, come on in," Rhianne said, mustering up some forced cheerfulness. "We should probably stop working now and head up to the apartment."

To her surprise, neither Carl nor Marissa said a word or made a move. Rhianne looked up at the ceiling, taking a deep breath to steady herself. She took a step forward, grabbing Marissa's arm and gently pulled her along. "Carl, don't just stand there! Close the door and come up."

Marissa was dressed in a cream cross-over bodysuit and a calf-length fitted skirt, paired with nude high heels. Marissa and Carl hadn't said a single word since they entered the apartment. Rhianne could feel the heavy tension in the air, so she decided to take matters into her own hands. With a hopeful smile, she blurted out, "Hey, doesn't Marissa look absolutely lovely?" She was hoping to get a positive response from Carl and inject a bit of positivity into the atmosphere.

To her dismay, Carl only grunted in response, and Marissa's lips quivered. Rhianne let out a loud sigh.

It was going to be a long and awkward night.

CHAPTER 19

The pizza delivery guy arrived with three steaming hot pizzas, but Rhianne soon realised that food alone couldn't salvage the awkward situation. She should have thought ahead and grabbed some wine to help break the ice. As it stood, she felt like she was single-handedly filling the silence, desperately trying to keep the conversation afloat. Carl and Marissa sat across from each other, doing their best to avoid any meaningful eye contact. Rhianne threw out various topics, but all she got in return were short, monosyllabic responses. The evening was quickly turning into a disaster.

Carl and Marissa reached for the same slice of anchovy pizza; their hands unintentionally colliding. The suddenness of the touch startled them both, causing them to retract their hands as if they had touched a hot stove. Their faces turned crimson, matching blushes spreading across their necks. Rhianne wanted to give them a good smack.

The sound of loud barking broke the silence. "That's Toto, I wonder what got him so worked up. Maybe it's another intruder."

Carl locked eyes with her. "What do you mean, another intruder?"

Marissa piped up. "You mean other than the thugs who attacked you?"

"Thugs? What thugs?" Carl asked, his eyes darting from one to the other.

Rhianne rubbed her eyes and got up. "That's a long story. I'd better go check what's got Toto in a tizzy."

"I'm coming with you." Carl stood up, his shoulders and jaw rigid. "And I want to hear about this attack."

"I'm coming too," Marissa said using a napkin to dab at her mouth. "I doubt that those thugs would have been let go from the police station since I visited this morning."

Carl cocked his head and gave Marissa a sharp look. "You visited those thugs by yourself?" His voice boomed, the closest to anger Rhianne had ever heard him.

Marissa tossed her mane of hair to the side as she joined them at the door. "I'm a lawyer, I deal with worse types than that. And those are just the other lawyers; don't get me started on some of my clients."

Rhianne raised her eyebrows. "Is that where the term 'cut-throat lawyer' comes from?"

Marissa snorted. "As a lawyer, you need to be a master of intimidation, and equivocation. And if you're a female lawyer, you also need to be thick-skinned, both literally and figuratively."

Rhianne would have been glad they had finally found something to talk about, except it wasn't particularly romantic and she still needed to find out what was wrong with Toto. It wasn't like him to go off barking like that. Ignoring them, she skipped down the stairs. She was not surprised to hear

CHAPTER 19

two sets of heavy steps behind her. She shook her head; she hadn't even succeeded on getting them to have alone time.

She sprinted towards the spot where Toto had been barking, only to realise he had suddenly stopped. Her heart raced in her chest. When she arrived, the area was eerily silent, and a wave of anxiety gripped her. "Toto? Where are you?" she called out.

A faint sound reached her ears from her left, causing her to skid on the gravel. "Toto?" she called out once more, her voice shaking.

Under the wooden entrance arch, she spotted a small ball of white fur. She rushed over, her eyes fixed on his motionless form, fear clutching her heart. "Are you hurt?" she asked.

There was no answer.

Carl crouched down next to Toto. "Is he okay?"

Toto's chest rose and fell in a slow, steady rhythm. Rhianne felt a huge wave of relief wash over her — thank goodness he was alive! But amidst the relief, a sense of urgency still gnawed at her. As she carefully examined Toto, she couldn't spot any visible injuries, which only heightened her worry. The question crossed her mind: could it be poison? The mere thought sent a chill down her spine.

"I'll go ahead and pick him up," Carl said in a gentle tone. With care, Carl scooped Toto into his arms, then turned to face Rhianne. "Where should we take him, boss?"

Dread twisted in her gut, but she needed to keep it together for Toto. "To the private garden. I have all the healing plants there." She started striding towards it.

She took the keys out of her pocket and with trembling hands she attempted to place the key in the lock. She swore when the key didn't seem to want to go in. She grunted in frustration and took a deep breath. Then placed the key in, and this time the lock clicked open. She swung open the gate and made her way towards the corner, where she nurtured her healing plants. It was here that she worked her magic, using these plants to concoct potions that could mend and soothe. The table was cluttered with pots, seedlings, and tubes.

"Quick, grab a towel from the apartment," she instructed, aware of her brusque tone. But in that moment, her sole priority was Toto's welfare. Marissa didn't need to be told twice and dashed off without wasting a second. She began moving things off the table to make room, as her brain madly tried to work out what kind of treatment to try. She didn't have a clue what the problem was and if she gave him the wrong stuff — she usually gave out medicine for regular humans or lesser fae who couldn't afford doctors and hospitals, mostly for everyday minor issues. Regardless of how Toto looked, Rhianne was certain that he wasn't just some ordinary lesser fae.

Marissa placed a few towels on the cleared space, her face etched with worry. Rhianne bit her lip, drawing blood. Marissa and Carl stood there; their eyes fixed on Rhianne as if she held all the answers in the world. It made her want to scream out in frustration. Carl shuffled, while Marissa's hand rested on his forearm.

Rhianne gritted her teeth, her words coming out sharper than she intended. "Just go," she urged, her focus solely on helping Toto. Their presence only served as a distraction, hindering her thoughts. Her gaze remained fixed on Toto's small, still form.

His breathing had become more laboured, and she feared his heart was slowing down further. Tears welled up in her

CHAPTER 19

eyes, but she wiped them away with the back of her hand. Crying wouldn't save Toto; she needed to focus. She heard rather than saw when Marissa and Carl moved away and when the gate was shut behind them. A thought had planted a seed in her brain. It was desperate and it could backfire, but she didn't know what else to do.

Rhianne laid her hands on Toto's chest, feeling the slow rhythm of his heartbeat. She tried her best to steady her trembling hands. She closed her eyes, picturing herself in a peaceful forest, finding comfort beside a towering tree. It wasn't like she was actively trying to tap into her dryad magic, but she was seeking a connection with nature.

In her mind, a gentle melody began to form, a tender invocation. Her magic responded eagerly, a warmth building in her belly. She sang to the warmth, coaxing it, guiding it upwards through her chest, and down her arms. This was a delicate process, reminiscent of healing plants, where the right balance was crucial. Uncertainty gripped her, she had never used her powers to heal a living beings.

She continued to sing, the warmth responding to her call, growing and expanding. Yet doubt lingered, creeping into her thoughts. What if she failed? What if she made things worse? Pushing these doubts aside, she persisted, maintaining a rhythm in her mind.

Failure was not an option. She would not allow it.

The warmth reached her fingertips, a glimmer of light emanating from her hands as she opened her eyes.

Her gaze travelled over Toto's form, spotting a pulsating red mass, no larger than a five-cent coin. She directed her hands towards it, guiding the light to cleanse and heal. The light emitted a soft hissing sound, and the red mass began to shrink, gradually disappearing. Rhianne released a breath she didn't realise she had been holding, her attention focused on Toto. Despite the reassuring beat, he remained unconscious.

Relieved that the red mass was gone, Rhianne ceased her inner melody, allowing the light to dim and the warmth to retreat. The cool night breeze brushed against her face as she leaned on the table, bowing her head in exhaustion. Toto would hopefully awaken soon.

She picked him up, cradling him against her chest. A small whimper escaped him, causing her heart to ache. With gentle steps, she carried him back to the apartment.

Carl and Marissa looked up with equally tight expressions when she walked in and she gave them a tired small smile. "I think he'll be all right but he needs some rest to recover."

Rhianne set up a comfortable space for Toto on the sofa, making sure to place cushions around him for added safety in case he woke up feeling a bit dazed. As she kept an eye on him, fatigue began to creep in, causing her thoughts to get a bit muddled. She rubbed her eyes, trying to shake off the tiredness and regain her focus.

"I can't say for sure, but it definitely feels like a nasty magic spell," she murmured. "If Toto were a regular dog, or even a lesser fae, things could have turned out much worse."

The idea made her fists clench, her nails digging into her palms. Who on earth would deliberately harm Toto? Or maybe poor Toto found himself in the wrong place at the wrong time, caught off guard by the intruder. The possibility only fuelled her anger. Whoever was behind it had no qualms about causing collateral damage. It became clear that someone had set their sights on her or her business, but the burning questions remained: who and why?

CHAPTER 19

"They hurt Toto to keep him from alerting me. Cowards!" Rhianne clenched her fists.

"Well, talk about overkill, pardon the pun, boss," Carl said.

Rhianne shot him a quick glance and then sighed. "Yeah, true," she admitted. "Using a magic spell to kill a dog during a break-in shows sloppy work. So maybe the witch who created the spell gave it to someone else." Her fingers tensely tapped on the sofa's arm; her eyes fixed on Toto.

Marissa chimed in, "Chances are, the attacker is a supernatural themselves."

Rhianne raised an eyebrow. "Oh? What makes you say that?"

Marissa scrunched her nose. "Supernaturals tend to stick together. Sure, you might find witches who dabble in selling minor spells to humans, like beauty enhancements or weak love potions. But a spell that could kill a minor fae? That's crossing a line. They'd be in hot water, facing serious consequences like banishment or worse."

Rhianne reclined on the sofa and closed her eyes for a moment, letting Marissa's words sink in. The idea struck a chord with her —witches were known to be highly secretive when it came to sharing their spells, preferring to keep their knowledge within their trusted circles. Especially when it came to powerful spells like that.

"I think you're right. They are a supernatural, but I don't think they are a witch."

Marissa cocked her head and waved her hand, urging Rhianne to continue with her theory.

"I know a thing or two about covens." Rhianne grimaced. "To cast a spell like that, you need some serious magical prowess. We're talking at least a level four, if not more. That kind of power only comes with experience and skill."

Marissa scoffed but Rhianne raised a hand to forestall her. "A witch like that wouldn't use such a powerful spell to silence a dog's bark. It's like using a gun to kill an ant."

"Could they have known he was more than just a dog, or been targeting him specifically?" Carl asked.

Both Marissa and Rhianne turned to him sharply, blinking in surprise.

Rhianne bit her lower lip, pondering his words. "If they were targeting Toto specifically, they would've used something more potent. Toto might not look powerful, but I'm pretty sure he's not to be underestimated."

There was a whole lot more to Toto than he let on. He had this knack for dodging direct questions about his nature. The day was coming when they would have to sit down and have a proper heart-to-heart.

First things first, she had to make sure Toto was okay. Once she knew he was safe and sound, she could start playing detective and figure out who the heck was behind the attack. It was time to put an end to their nonsense because, seriously, she wasn't going to let anyone else she cared about get hurt in the crossfire.

A pang of guilt hit her square in the belly, twisting and turning. The weight of responsibility for putting Kai and now Toto in harm's way bore down on her. Rhianne wrapped her arms around herself. Darn it all! This was happening right in her own backyard! The guilt transformed into searing fury, her face growing warm as she clenched her jaw tightly.

Carl had slipped into the kitchen and returned with a glass of water, offering it to her. Rhianne flashed him a half-smile. As she sipped, her thoughts turned to Toto's ability to mask

CHAPTER 19

his power. Even in her mother's house, a gathering place for powerful witches and mages, he had managed to go under the radar. Considering that most supernaturals could sense each other's presence to some extent, it was remarkable. She drank from the glass and felt the coolness of the water slide down her throat. Yep, a conversation with Toto was way overdue.

"Do you think this is all connected?" Marissa asked.

Carl raised his hand and settled into a wooden chair beside Toto. "Can we start from the beginning?"

Rhianne suppressed a wince as the chair groaned under Carl's weight. "Well, there's not much to it, really," she started, but Carl's focused gaze encouraged her to elaborate. "Three humans ambushed Kai and me near his place. Initially, they just used their fists, but when we fought back…" She shivered at the recollection. "They pulled out knives."

Carl frowned.

"It was no big deal; Kai and I handled them, with a bit of assistance from Toto." She tugged at her hair, coming to the most perplexing part. "Toto detected fae magic on the thugs and Marissa suspects they were glamoured to target me."

Carl's eyes narrowed to mere slits.

"Or possibly Kai," she added.

Carl crossed his arms. "And you were going to tell me when?"

"Um, well…"

Carl turned to Marissa, staring daggers at her. "You knew as well and didn't think it was relevant for me to know?"

Whoa! This was not good.

Marissa gave him a slow smile full of promise. "The boy has claws, who would have guessed?" she all but purred.

Carl widened his eyes for a minute, but then his jaw set in

a tight line and he pointed a finger at Marissa. "You, I will deal with later." Marissa's eyes lit up, but she wisely kept her mouth shut.

He then zeroed on Rhianne. "Boss," he said. "I'm a gargoyle, which means I'm pretty tough, but it also means no one messes with my family or my friends. From now on. I want in."

A lump formed in Rhianne's throat, making it difficult for her to speak. She simply nodded.

CHAPTER 20

The next morning, Toto woke up as Rhianne was preparing her breakfast. Seeing him stir, she made her way over, kneeling to examine his eyes.

"Hey there, how are you feeling?"

Toto stretched out, extending his front legs in a fluid motion. "I must say, I feel quite rested. The healing you performed was quite remarkable."

Rhianne rubbed her sore neck to try to release some tension from her shoulders. "How did you know it was me who healed you?"

Toto let out a soft chuckle. "Well, your magic has a distinctive feel to it, and I've been around it long enough to recognise it. Moreover, healing magic of that strength is rare, and there are only a few who can wield it with such proficiency."

Rhianne furrowed her brow. "Was the spell designed to kill?"

Toto corrected her, "It was a potent hex, but your healing prowess surpassed what was needed. That's the reason for my prolonged slumber."

Rhianne felt her chest constrict. "I'm sorry, I didn't mean to overdo it."

Toto moved closer, licking her chin affectionately. "Do not fret, child. You performed admirably, and I must say, I feel considerably better than I have in quite some time. Merely keep in mind to exercise a touch of restraint in future."

Rhianne placed her hand on Toto's back. "I was so worried about you."

Toto shrugged. "Pfft! I am made of sterner stuff. The shifter may have landed a fortuitous blow to the centre of my chest, but rest assured, I would have regained my strength naturally within a day or two."

"Shifter?" Anger rose in her like a tide.

"The very same raven shifter as before. This time, I caught her in the act of snooping."

"But why would she attack you? She could have simply flown away."

"I managed to bite one of her wings and began barking to alert you. She must have panicked. "

"Do you think she recognised your true nature? That spell was vicious." Fury vibrated through her.

"Only high-level elves possess the ability to perceive my true form unless I decide to reveal it to others. The silver lining is that she is likely to wake up with a rather sore arm this morning."

Rhianne patted his head. "I hope so." If that made her sound callous. Too bad.

Toto responded by licking her chin once more. After giving Toto his favourite breakfast: a bowl of strawberries, she left him and made her way downstairs to her office.

It was proving quite difficult for her to focus on her work.

CHAPTER 20

Fiddling with her earrings, she took a quick glance at the wall clock. Lunchtime had sneaked up on her, and she realised that she wouldn't get much more done. Instead of settling for a sad desk lunch, she made a spontaneous decision to head into town early and pay a visit to Isobel Dupre. Something was nagging at the back of her mind about the poison, and her best bet for finding answers lay with the forensic pathologist.

As Rhianne reached for her helmet, her phone started ringing, playing the catchy tune of *Hey Big Brother*. Balancing the helmet under her arm, she answered the call. "Hey, big boy!"

"Just wanted to confirm if we're still on for our gym date. You've been bailing on me lately," Nel teased.

"Someone has to keep you grounded," she retorted.

"Oh, you're my one and only; you're breaking my heart."

"Uh-huh. Well, I'm heading into town right now." She wasn't sure how long this visit with Isobel would be and she didn't want to be late for the meeting with Rita Parkes.

"Ah, so you're cheating on me with lover boy?"

"Oh, come on! Not you too. Yes, I'm seeing Kai later, but at this moment, I'm on my way to the mortuary to get some information from the forensic pathologist."

"Why don't I meet you there, and then we can grab a quick lunch afterwards?"

"I see right through you, mister. You want to meet Kai, don't you?"

"How could I resist the chance to meet lover boy?"

"Stop calling him that, or Toto will get jealous. He's already Team Kai."

"Toto may be easily swayed, but I'm not. Not when it comes to my little sister's happiness," Nel said.

"Hey! I'm just dating the guy, and you're not allowed to scare him away."

"If he's easily scared off, then he's not worth your time," Nel said.

"Uh huh. By the way, do you know where the mortuary is?"

"I'll find it."

"Wait," Rhianne interjected, remembering Isobel's fondness for sweets. "Meet me at Rueben's in Surry Hills."

"Dessert before lunch, really, princess?"

"Hush, big boy. The way to this forensic pathologist's heart is definitely through Rueben's pastries."

"I could just use my charm. No need for bribes when you have me."

"Oh, please. Your charm has its limits. Pastries, on the other hand, do not."

"Well, if you insist. I'll meet you at Rueben's. Prepare yourself for a feast of both sweets and charm."

Rhianne grinned. "Deal. See you there in twenty."

Rhianne ended the call, sliding her phone into her pocket. With the helmet securely on her head, she zoomed out of the parking lot, heading towards town.

Nel arrived shortly after her at the café. "That's a long queue!"

She raised an eyebrow. "Haven't you ever had to wait in line before?" She facepalmed. "Who am I kidding? Of course you haven't. You can wait over there, I won't be long."

A few minutes later she emerged with her precious pastries. Rhianne had managed to snag the last almond croissant, swapping the vanilla slice for a tempting brownie instead. Hopefully, Nina would still appreciate it. She glanced around for Nel and found him in conversation with a trio of attractive

CHAPTER 20

women. One brunette had the audacity to cling to his shirt collar, fluttering her lashes. Nel responded with a charming smile, clearly relishing the attention.

With an exasperated eye roll, Rhianne picked up her pace and approached the group. "Hey there, ladies. Hate to interrupt, but we've got a meeting we can't miss," she interjected. The brunette shot her a hostile glare and maintained her grip on Nel's shirt, refusing to back down.

Rhianne sighed, contemplating whether she should just head to her meeting with Isobel alone. But before she could decide, Nel stepped back. He flashed the women an apologetic smile.

"Sorry, ladies. Duty calls," he explained. The brunette moved to grab him again, but Nel straightened his posture, causing her to hesitate. With a nod, he spun on his heels and took hold of Rhianne's elbow.

"I don't know how you tolerate some of them," Rhianne said.

Nel offered a theatrical shrug. "They're just part of the daily menu — think of it as dealing with overly enthusiastic waiters at a restaurant."

"More like waiters who won't stop refilling your water glass, even when it's already overflowing," she retorted.

Reaching the mortuary, Nel held the door open with a flourish, gesturing for Rhianne to enter ahead of him.

"Hi Nina," Rhianne called out to the receptionist, who looked up and greeted her with a smile.

"Now, love, if you're bringing sweets again, you and I are going to become besties," Nina's eyes twinkled. Her gaze then shifted to Nel. "Hello, handsome." She gave him a playful wink.

"You sure know how to attract the good-looking men." She sighed wistfully. "If only I were twenty years younger and twenty pounds lighter."

Nel leaned over the desk, offering a smile that was both charming and disarming. "I'd say any man would be fortunate to catch your eye."

Nina fanned herself. "Oh, you better keep an eye on this one."

Nel's smile remained dazzling, and Nina matched it with enthusiasm.

Clearing her throat, Rhianne said. "They didn't have a vanilla slice, so I took a chance and got you a macadamia brownie. I hope that's all right."

"Girl, that's more than all right. Anything from Rueben's will do." Nina accepted the bag, placing it on her desk.

"Can we go in?"

Nina gestured them forward. "Off you go, and good luck! Although, with enough of those pastries, you won't need it."

Rhianne waved in thanks and headed towards the side doors, hearing the click as the doors unlocked. She entered the mortuary, with Nel closely following behind. "It's been a while since I've been in a mortuary," Nel said.

"Do I want to know why you were in one before?" Rhianne asked, as they walked down the corridor toward Isobel's office.

Nel chuckled softly. "Probably not, unless you're up for a 'Tales from the Crypt' night with a side of tequila shots."

Rhianne knocked on Isobel's door, only to be met with a gruff yell from inside. "Go away!"

Nel raised an eyebrow, and Rhianne cautiously opened the door, holding the pastry box in front of her as a peace offering.

CHAPTER 20

"I said —" Isobel's words trailed off as she caught sight of the pastry box, her expression softening instantly. "Bring it over." She waved Rhianne inside.

Rhianne placed the box on Isobel's desk, and the forensic pathologist couldn't tear her eyes away from it. As soon as it landed, she opened the box and let out a contented sigh. "They always run out of croissants by this time. How on earth did you manage to get one?" Isobel plucked the croissant from the box, took a bite, and closed her eyes in bliss. "So good." She savoured a few more bites before opening her eyes again. "Hello, Rhianne. It's great to see you."

"Me or the pastries?" Rhianne said.

Isobel chuckled. "Can we go with both?" Her eyes twinkled. "Have you ever considered becoming a detective full-time? I could definitely get used to this treatment."

Rhianne shook her head. "I'm not detective material and quite content running my own business, but whenever I'm in town, I'd be more than happy to bring you goodies. Maybe you could step out and grab them fresh from the oven from time to time," she suggested, her lips twitching at Isobel's wide-eyed reaction.

"Do you see this Everest of paperwork? I swear it breeds when I'm not looking." She threw her hands up and loose papers fluttered around her. "Who in their right mind thought a forensic pathologist should juggle all this admin? There are actual bodies waiting for my attention!" Her last words came out as a half-groan, half-sigh.

Rhianne nodded. "I totally get it. Maybe Kai could whip up some tech magic to ease your load."

Isobel looked at Rhianne as if she had offered her a lifeline. "That might be better than your croissants, though it's a close call. I usually ignore everything but the most urgent documents, and even then, only if my boss is breathing down my neck."

"So, you're telling me all of these," Rhianne gestured at the multitude of papers scattered across Isobel's desk and floor, "are potentially urgent?"

Isobel lifted a shoulder. "Hard to say. I spend half my time hunting for the urgent papers, and the other half creating new ones, only to misplace them again."

"And your boss doesn't mind?" Rhianne wrinkled her nose in disbelief. Isobel's smile turned predatory, revealing all her teeth. Rhianne felt a slight urge to step back. "Oh, he keeps moaning about budget cuts and how he can't afford an assistant for me. Well, let's see who blinks first." Rhianne's mental bet was solidly in Isobel's corner.

Nel cleared his throat, drawing Rhianne's attention. He was leaning against the wall, his gaze fixed on Isobel.

"Ah, right." Rhianne gave Nel a narrowed-eye glance. "Isobel, this is Nel Lamont. Nel, meet Dr Isobel Dupre."

Nel stepped forward, extending his hand towards Isobel's desk. Isobel looked at it briefly, then shook it with an expression that remained stoically neutral.

She shifted her attention back to Rhianne. "I'm guessing you didn't come here just to hear me rant about my paperwork nightmare?"

"Yep." Rhianne picked up a stack of folders from a nearby chair to clear a spot for herself.

Nel remained where he was, squinting his eyes.

"When Kai and I were here last, you mentioned that crafting the Romin poison would require a proper lab."

Isobel nodded and took another bite of her croissant.

CHAPTER 20

"Mmm."

"Just how sophisticated does this lab need to be?" Rhianne asked.

"You could give Sherlock Holmes a run for his money. The other two? They wouldn't know a clue if it danced in front of them wearing a tutu."

Rhianne glanced at Nel, who was still leaning against the wall with his arms folded, head tilted as if deep in thought. "Nel, you look like you're trying to solve the mysteries of the universe over there," she joked.

Nel simply raised an eyebrow.

"Can I assume that a school lab could suffice?"

Isobel sobered up. "Yes, it would likely do, but they would still need to know how to use it."

Rhianne nodded, her suspicion confirmed. "That opens up the possibilities, doesn't it?"

"It certainly does," Isobel agreed. "Does that disrupt your theories about the murder suspect?"

Rhianne's grin widened. "No, the opposite. It narrows down our suspects to a specific circle. Now, the real challenge is pinpointing the right one."

"Well, I'm relieved someone with a brain is on the case. The arrogance and overconfidence of those detectives are more blinding than a lighthouse in fog. And hey, don't be a stranger — do drop by again — with a croissant or two."

"I will, and I'll chat with Kai about your paperwork situation," Rhianne responded. She paused, then added with a mischievous glint in her eye, "Unless, of course, you're enjoying your little tug-of-war with your boss?"

"Ah, am I that transparent?" Isobel's eyes twinkled. "It must be the croissant effect."

Rhianne winked and turned to leave the room. Nel, however, remained stationary against the wall, looking unusually stiff. Rhianne shot him a puzzled glance, and when he failed to respond, she reached out, tugging at his arm. After a moment, he emerged from his trance, blinking rapidly. Without a word, he followed Rhianne out of the room.

As they reached the reception area, Nina greeted them with an enthusiastic wave. Rhianne noticed that the macadamia brownie was now just a smattering of crumbs.

"Don't be a stranger, love!" Nina called out with a bright smile.

"Seems like I'm popular here. Isobel said the same thing." Rhianne returned the wave.

Nel, meanwhile, had his gaze fixed forward, his lips pressed together in a tight line. Once they were outside the building, Rhianne turned to him, throwing her hands up. "What's the matter with you? You didn't even say goodbye."

Nel's distant look finally cleared. "What is she?"

She narrowed her eyes. "You mean Isobel?"

He nodded.

"Well, apparently, she could tell us, but then she'd have to kill us," Rhianne said, a playful smile tugging at her lips.

Nel's expression remained pensive, his brow furrowed.

"All right, big boy," Rhianne turned to face him directly. "What's bothering you?"

Nel opened his mouth to speak but then hesitated, shutting it again. "She didn't react," he finally said, a hint of surprise in his voice. "She didn't react to me at all."

Nel's eyes sparkled, and a small smile crept onto his lips.

CHAPTER 21

Rhianne widened her eyes. She couldn't recall ever seeing Nel look so surprised or delighted before. "Maybe she's a type of fae halfling?"

Nel gazed into the distance, lost in contemplation. "No, she doesn't give off an elvish aura, and she's definitely powerful. Quite the puzzle."

"Uh oh, I know that look. You can't approach her, bother her, or dig into her background. I have a feeling she'd know if you did the latter. I need her on my side for the investigation."

"What do you mean?" Nel batted his eyelashes.

"That innocent routine has got the same chance of working with me as with her, big boy, so drop it. She's off limits until I solve this murder. Besides, I like her."

"Fair enough," Nel conceded. "I'll have to up my game with the investigation. The quicker we solve it, the quicker I can start my research on her."

Rhianne let out a weary sigh. Arguing with Nel was like trying to teach a cat to swim — a pointless endeavour given his stubborn streak. But at least he had semi-agreed to put a pin in it until the case was wrapped up. That, of course, depended on her solving the murder, which at this rate seemed as likely as her winning a lottery with a ticket she never bought.

While Johannes and Chen may be competent, Rhianne suspected their focus was closing the case quickly rather than seeking the whole truth.

Glancing at her watch, Rhianne frowned. "Oh gosh, I have to go or I'll be late." She grabbed Nel's hand and tugged him along, as he kept casting longing glances back at the building. She didn't like the idea of leaving him loitering outside; his promise to wait felt as sturdy as a house of cards. Clearly, Nel was more than just a little intrigued, but thankfully, her mention of meeting Kai pulled him back to the here and now.

"Does that mean I finally get to meet lover boy?" he asked.

"Only if you're on your best behaviour and not for too long. Kai and I need to discuss how to approach Miss Parkes."

"I'm always on my best behaviour." Nel placed his hand over his heart.

Rhianne nearly choked on that statement. "Resorting to lies now? Oh my! How low can we go?"

"I *am* on my best behaviour," Nel insisted, a mischievous glint in his eyes. "I could behave much worse."

"On that, we agree," she said. "I'll meet you at the coffee shop across the road. Look for me in disguise."

"I wonder how long lover boy will take to recognise you. Care to make a bet?" Nel asked.

Rhianne let out a loud exhale and scowled at him. "Really? That's a bit childish. It didn't turn out well for you last time you bet against me."

"Ah, come on! What happened to your sense of fun? I'm not betting against you this time. I'm betting against him. Let's keep it simple: if he doesn't recognise you within ten minutes,

CHAPTER 21

I win."

"Oh fine! What do you want to bet?" Rhianne asked.

"If I win, I'll have the freedom to, as you so eloquently put it, 'dig' into Dr Dupre's background."

"Fine, but If I win, you'll be nice to Kai and Dr Dupre. No digging into their backgrounds, at least until the case is solved." Rhianne said.

"I never said I wouldn't be nice to Dr Dupre," Nel replied.

"My definition of nice, Nel. Not yours."

"Ugh. You take all the fun out of it."

"Sometimes I wonder who's the older sibling in our relationship," Rhianne muttered.

Nel threw his head back and laughed. "I think that was established when you turned twenty. You were born an old soul."

"Ha, you'd better remember that next time you're trying to 'protect me,' especially without telling me."

"Don't think so, princess. I still remember that wide-eyed sixteen-year-old desperately trying to pass for an adult at my club."

She stuck out her tongue as they reached her bike. "You'll never let me live it down, will you?"

"Not a chance. See you soon."

She hopped on the bike and zoomed off towards her destination, feeling the exhilarating rush as the wind tousled her hair. She needed to find a spot to change into her disguise.

Once she arrived, she found a nearby restroom. As she stood in front of the mirror, she checked her reflection, making sure that every detail of her disguise looked natural and convincing. Adjusting the wig to sit perfectly and putting on the glasses as a final touch, she nodded at herself, satisfied with the outcome. She felt confident that even her own mother wouldn't be able to recognise her.

Arriving a few minutes early, she decided to enter the café and wait for Kai there. She ordered tea and chose a table near the window. Nel was already seated at one of the back tables, engaging in conversation with the waitress. The café was bustling, with most of the tables occupied.

The scent of cardamom caught her attention as the door swung open. Kai entered, scanning the café. Nel subtly waved a finger at her, silently urging her not to give herself away. Rhianne suppressed a smile and pretended to be engrossed in her phone. Within seconds, Kai took a seat in front of her, a wide grin on his face.

"Wow, that's an amazing disguise, Rhi!" Kai said.

Unable to resist, Rhianne tilted her body slightly to shoot a teasing glance at Nel and with a flourish waved her fingers. Kai furrowed his brows and turned around to see who she was messaging. Nel rose from his seat, catching the hovering waitress off guard, and sauntered over.

Nel extended his hand to Kai. "Hi, I'm Nel Lamont."

Kai shook his hand. "Ah, yes, the big brother. I'm Kai Wagner." He then turned his attention back to Rhianne, raising an eyebrow inquisitively.

"You know, Nel was keen to meet you. He just happened to lose a bet with me. Again," Rhianne said.

"Piece of advice, friend. Don't bet against Rhianne, she almost always wins." Nel took a seat.

Rhianne rolled her eyes.

"What surprises me is that knowing her so well, you actually took the bet."

"Well, to be fair, the bet was my idea, but it wasn't against

CHAPTER 21

her as such," he confessed.

"Oh?"

"I bet against you. I didn't think you'd recognise her in this getup. You're not a shifter, so it couldn't be your sense of smell. How did you do it?" Nel asked.

"Ah, but revealing that would spoil the mystery, wouldn't it? A magician never reveals his secrets." Kai maintained a poker face.

Rhianne watched the back-and-forth between them, feeling like she was at a tennis match. Nel was brimming with confidence and a natural flair for reading emotions, while Kai was the epitome of cool and collected. It was like witnessing the relentless ocean trying to wear down an immovable cliff.

"You didn't even hesitate for more than a second or two," Nel said.

Nel employed that charming, soft tone he often used when fishing for information. It was a tone few could resist, laced with just the right amount of charisma and intrigue.

"Indeed," Kai said.

Rhianne sighed. This could go on for a while, so she decided to cut to the chase. "Well now that we have the introductions out of the way, how about we discuss the case." She injected a dose of faux cheer into her voice.

Two sets of blank stares swivelled her way.

Kai was the first to recover and offered her a small smile. "As I said, that's a fantastic disguise, but I've got to say, I prefer the real you, Rhi."

Nel sputtered. "Rhi?"

Rhianne kicked him on his shin under the table.

"Ouch." Nel gave her a hurt look.

"Thanks, I like being myself too. But the little assistant

needs to be as invisible as possible."

Rhianne's words were interrupted as a waitress arrived to collect Kai's order, her eyes lingering flirtatiously on Nel, oblivious to her attention.

Kai ordered a green tea. "In their world, assistants are part of the background, but the glasses? They're a cool touch," he said.

Nel preened at the compliment and shot Rhianne a smug look. "See, I told you the glasses would work."

"Yeah, yeah. I guess I can count myself lucky that those glasses don't have prescription lenses or I'd be tripping all over myself. So, what's our game plan for the interview?"

"Rita Parkes knows I've been helping the police with the case."

"Wait, does she want you to investigate his death?"

"Not exactly. She wants someone to conduct a forensic analysis of the financials. She's after someone to do a deep dive. I think she's got a hunch that there's something off there, but she didn't outright say it."

"Hmm, that's interesting. I wonder what made her suspicious and who she suspects," she mused.

"That's what I plan to find out. People often let slip more than they intend when they believe you're on their side, ready to help. Sometimes, they even overshare." Kai said.

The waitress returned, placing Kai's green tea on the table with a small smile directed at Nel as she left.

Nel leaned forward, resting his elbows on the table. "So, you're into technical financial audits?"

Rhianne shot Nel a sidelong glance. "What, you think I can't handle the accounts"

Nel laughed and held up his hands in a gesture of peace.

CHAPTER 21

"No, no, not at all. We need someone to scan for spyware. There's been a leak of confidential info, and I'm trying to figure out how it got out."

"It could be an inside leak. It's quite common," Kai sipped on his tea.

"Maybe, but I have my own methods of recruitment, and I don't believe that's the source. Are you up for the challenge?" Nel asked.

Rhianne shot Nel a suspicious look. This was the first she'd heard of any leak. Either the leak was recent or he was making it up as a way of checking Kai. She made a mental note to grill Nel about it later — there were definitely going to be words.

"Sure," Kai responded with a casual shrug. "But how urgent is this? My schedule's pretty packed right now, and that includes sorting out who's behind our alley thugs." His voice was steady, but Rhianne detected a hint of challenge in his tone.

Nel nodded understandingly. "Rhianne's case is the top priority, of course. But when you find some time, I'd appreciate your help." He handed Kai a business card. Kai snapped a quick photo of it with his phone and handed the card back.

Nel raised an eyebrow but didn't say anything as he took his card back.

Round one to Kai.

Kai shifted his attention to Rhianne. "You know, Rita Parkes has a whole team of assistants, or 'business managers' as she calls them," he said. "Maybe you could try talking to some of them, see if you can dig up anything extra."

Rhianne acknowledged the suggestion with a smile. "That's a good plan," she said. "Although I've no idea what we are looking for. I doubt she'd have the poison sitting in one of her drawers."

Kai rubbed his chin. "If we did see something like that. Would you be able to identify it if you saw it?"

"Not without opening it. The smell is quite distinctive. I assume the police would have done their job and conducted a thorough search."

"Maybe, but you have to consider the sheer size of the building. It's practically impossible for them to have gone through every nook and cranny, but let's play it by ear and see what we find."

"Okay." Rhianne looked at her watch and saw it was ten minutes to three. Better make a move on. It probably wouldn't do to make Ms Parkes wait for them.

Rhianne and Kai left Nel at the café and crossed the street. At the reception of the building, they were given visitor badges and told to head up to level twenty-nine. Rhianne couldn't help but think it was interesting that they were going to be one floor below where the murder had happened.

When they got off the lift on level twenty-nine, they saw another reception desk. The woman sitting there, her hair in a neat bun and minimal makeup, gave them a professional smile as they walked up.

"You're Kai Wagner, right?" she said to Kai, then gave Rhianne a curious once-over.

"Yes, that's me. And this is my assistant, Raine," Kai replied.

Rhianne mentally kicked herself for not thinking to sync up on fake names earlier. Kai had clearly picked something close to her real name, probably to make sure he didn't slip up.

"Hello, Raine. I'm Susan." The woman introduced herself

CHAPTER 21

with a warm smile.

"Hi, Susan. Nice to meet you," Rhianne returned the smile.

Susan's attention then shifted back to Kai. While her smile stayed in place, it lost a bit of its earlier warmth. Rhianne found herself wondering what that meant. Maybe Susan wasn't too keen on management and their associates, or perhaps she was worried Kai might dig up something she was involved in. She didn't look the part, but then again, they rarely did.

"Ms Parkes will be with you shortly. Please have a seat," Susan gestured towards the elegant tan leather sofas behind them before picking up her phone to announce their arrival.

After five minutes, the door to the office opened, and Rita Parkes emerged, extending her hand towards Kai without even acknowledging Rhianne's presence. Both Kai and Rhianne stood up, and Kai shook hands with Rita as she scrutinised him from head to toe. Rita, about five feet seven with light blonde hair and a fair complexion, bore a striking resemblance to her father in terms of colouring and physique. As Nel had mentioned, she had a plump figure with a defined waist. With a more flattering haircut, she could have been quite attractive. As it was, the short pixie cut, and pursed lips gave her an irritated air.

"This is my assistant, Raine," Kai introduced Rhianne.

Rita offered a brief nod but made no attempt to shake Rhianne's hand. Her focus immediately shifted back to Kai. "Shall we step into my office to discuss my requirements?" Her words were presented as a question, but they carried an undeniable tone of command.

The siblings couldn't be more different in appearance and character. Rita turned and walked into her office without checking if they were following, clearly expecting immediate compliance. Kai followed suit, while Rhianne made a conscious effort not to make a face and entered at a more measured pace. She caught a fleeting glimpse of what appeared to be a hint of dislike on Susan's face, quickly replaced by a vacant and pleasant expression.

"Please have a seat," Rita said, her piercing light blue eyes fixed on Kai.

Rhianne felt a bit unsettled by Rita's intense gaze, but at least it wasn't directed at her. Kai settled into the luxurious leather armchair in front of Rita's desk, exuding an air of professional composure.

Rhianne took the seat next to him, trying to look the part of a dutiful assistant ready with her tablet. In reality, she was busy taking in the details of the office, taking in its clinical appearance. It reminded her of Rita's father's office, with dark wood desks and stainless-steel frames. The bookshelves and the style of the furniture was eerily similar.

She wondered if it was a deliberate homage to her father or simply a coincidental touch. As her eyes roamed around the office, she noticed the modern art gracing the walls, adding a touch of sophistication to the ambience. Among the art pieces, she also spotted two university degrees, prominently showcased in gold edges. Unlike her father's office, there was a photo frame on Rita's desk, although Rhianne couldn't make out the photo from her vantage point.

Kai broke the silence that had stretched on for a moment too long. "How can I help you?"

Rita fixed her gaze on Kai, her eyes filled with intensity. "What I'm about to disclose must remain strictly confidential, and I expect both you and your assistant," Her lip curled

CHAPTER 21

as she briefly glanced in Rhianne's direction, "to sign a confidentiality agreement regarding any information you uncover in our files. Absolute discretion is paramount." She leaned forward. "Officially, your role will be portrayed as assisting with our cyber security measures."

Kai gave Rita a cold smile. "The contract I sent you yesterday clearly states that if I come across any criminal activities during my investigation, I am obligated to report them to the police. Would that pose a problem for you?"

Rita placed her elbows on the desk and loosely clasped her hands. "What if it's something like embezzlement?"

"As this is a private company, it's within your discretion to decide whether to press charges if funds have been stolen," Kai said.

So that's what Rita suspected, the question was, who did she suspect?

Kai must have read her mind. "Only people with sufficient financial access are able to do that. I assume you have controls in place?"

Rita nodded, her fingers tightening around each other, causing her knuckles to turn white. Her eyes remained devoid of emotion. "We run a tight ship here."

Rhianne wasn't sure who she was trying to convince.

"Only key people, mostly family members, have access to approve transactions," Rita said.

Rhianne sneaked a quick glance at Kai, who was maintaining a flawless poker face. She redirected her attention to her tablet, not wanting to let her surprise show. Given that her father was dead, Rita Parkes must suspect her brother.

Kai got straight to the point, but in a polite way. "I'm going to need your go-ahead for complete access. Is there anyone

267

else who has to sign off on this?"

Rita pursed her lips. "No, my authority as the Human Resources Director is sufficient for this matter."

Hmm, somehow Rhianne doubted that Arthur would see it that way, particularly if he was guilty as she seemed to suspect. Or even if he wasn't. Rita was almost acting like she was the one running the show now.

"I'll need you to sign the necessary consent forms, as per the contract," Kai said.

Relaxing back into her chair, Rita opened her laptop and typed something. "I have accepted the contract." A glimmer of satisfaction flickered in her eyes.

Rhianne watched, puzzled. What exactly was Rita expecting to uncover?

Kai bent down and touched some buttons on his smartphone. Rhianne was pretty sure it was just for show; she'd seen what he could do without even touching devices. "Then I'd like to get started if that works for you."

"Perfect," Rita said. "What do you need?"

CHAPTER 22

Kai glanced at his smartphone as if checking something "Who should I consult regarding the technical equipment and controls?"

Rita appeared to be scrolling through a document on her laptop, "I'll give you a list of our tech equipment."

"We'll need a full list of all the technical equipment to identify any gear that shouldn't be there. It's important for making sure our investigation is thorough." He sat back.

He had cleverly put Rita in a bit of a bind. If she said no, she'd be getting in the way of the investigation she wanted in the first place. And really, she couldn't argue against the need for what he was asking. But why was she reluctant for Kai to speak to anyone else? It was possible that Rita was trying to cover for her brother, or she had something to hide herself

You could almost hear the gears turning in Rita's head. Her jaw had that subtle tightness of someone trying not to grind their teeth, and her lips were pinched together like she was holding back words. She picked up her desk phone with a sigh. "Susan, can you come in here, please." The "please" sounded like it had to take a running jump to make it into the sentence, probably added because Rhianne and Kai were there.

Within moments, Susan entered the office. Rhianne noticed her sensible shoes and wondered if she frequently ran errands for her boss. "Can you please show…" Rita's voice trailed off, her brows furrowing as she waved her hand vaguely in Rhianne's direction.

"Raine," Susan said, smoothly adding the name to the conversation.

Rita's tone turned clipped. "Mr Wagner's assistant. She needs to conduct a visual inventory of equipment."

"Of course, Ms Parkes," Susan replied, casting a quick look at Rhianne.

Rhianne rose from her seat, giving a nod to Kai before following Susan out of the office.

As they walked through the corridors, Rhianne said, "Thanks for remembering my name."

Susan, leading the way with a quick pace, glanced over her shoulder and replied with a hint of a smirk, "Well, it's not rocket science if you make an effort."

Rhianne, keeping up with Susan's brisk stride, raised an eyebrow in question. "So, Ms Parkes doesn't make the effort? Isn't that kind of the point of Human Resources?"

Susan slowed down for a moment, her expression faltering slightly, before she nodded confidently. "You'd think so. But when you're using HR as a stepping stone, it becomes more about the bottom line."

Curious, Rhianne asked as they turned a corner, "A stepping stone to what, exactly?"

With a knowing glance, Susan continued walking. "Straight to the top. And her brother being next in line? She probably sees that as just a minor obstacle."

CHAPTER 22

Rhianne's eyes widened, playing up the innocent assistant part. "But in this day and age, gender shouldn't be a factor, right? Someone must see her potential to have put her in charge of HR."

As they approached the lift, Susan's voice dropped to a more confidential tone. "Oh, she's definitely clever. Her dad knew that too, used it to his advantage. It's a bit sad, really," Susan said. "Rita idolised her father. We've all sat through her countless tributes to his business savvy. But I don't think I've ever heard him give her any credit. She's poured her life into this company. I can't recall her going on a date."

Realising she might have said too much, Susan hastily cleared her throat as they exited the lift. She led Rhianne through a pair of double doors into a cramped room full of cubicles. Computers and tech gear littered the place. Everyone was glued to their screens, headphones on, immersed in their own world of keyboard clicks. Not a single head turned as they walked by.

"I wasn't sure which areas you wanted to visit, but I thought the IT department made sense." Susan shrugged. "Ralph, the CTO, was one of the few people Mr Parkes seemed to respect."

Rhianne played along, feigning ignorance. "CTO?"

Susan lowered her voice, although the surrounding employees paid no attention to their conversation. "Chief Technical Officer. Rumour has it that Ralph was being prepped for Deputy CEO."

"What about the male heir?"

Susan waved her hand dismissively. "The plan, as far as I know, was to have him work alongside the kid." She appeared oblivious to Rhianne's slight wince at the casual reference to Arthur as 'the kid.' "Clearly, Mr Parkes didn't see him as the top dog." Mid-sentence, Susan paused to flick a piece of lint off her sleeve, then abruptly changed the subject. "Anyway, here we are."

"Thanks," Rhianne replied, a slight awkwardness creeping into her voice as she tried to come up with a convincing task to occupy herself. She reached for her tablet, jotting down some notes and snapping a few photos of the equipment.

"I think I've got what I needed. By the way, do you happen to know where I can grab a cup of coffee?" She didn't crave coffee, but she hoped it would provide an opportunity to casually overhear conversations in areas where people gathered and relaxed.

"Sure," Susan said. "So long as the ogr —" she interrupted herself and covered her slip with a fake cough, "boss lady doesn't call me back."

Susan guided Rhianne towards the lift, exchanging casual hellos with a couple of people they passed. They entered an open area adorned with functional yet attractive tables and chairs. The aroma of freshly brewed coffee mingled with the chatter of patrons seated in the booths near the expansive windows, enjoying their drinks.

Adjacent to the inviting seating area, a circular counter beckoned with its array of treats. Three diligent servers hustled to prepare aromatic coffee, warm sandwiches, and serve tempting cakes to the short queue of customers. As Rhianne and Susan joined the line, a hurried young woman joined behind them.

"Hi Susan," the petite redhead greeted, her voice breathless.

Susan responded with minimal enthusiasm. "Hello, Anne."

"Did you receive my note about the changes Mr Parkes wants for the investors' celebration party?" Anne asked.

CHAPTER 22

Susan scowled and shot a disdainful glance at Anne before composing herself. "I passed it on to Ms Parkes. I don't think she was particularly pleased with the additional requests."

Anne, seemingly oblivious or unfazed by the snub, maintained a bright smile. "Well, Mr Parkes is the CEO now. Should I let him know there's a problem?"

"Lower your voice," Susan hissed, causing Anne to widen her eyes and nod. "You can tell him that Ms Parkes will be in touch regarding his request."

"Will do. Hey, mind if I skip ahead of you? Art is in a rush." Without waiting for a response, Anne moved ahead of Rhianne and Susan, proceeding to order two coffees.

Rhianne's phone rang with Kai's ringtone. "Excuse me," she said to Susan, stepping aside. "Yes?"

"I have what I need. How about you?"

"Yep. I'll meet you downstairs."

"See you then." Kai hung up.

"I'm heading downstairs, Susan. Nice meeting you." Rhianne waved and disregarded the questioning look Susan directed at her.

As the lift doors opened in the foyer, Rhianne's eyes caught sight of Kai standing near the entrance, completely engrossed in his phone. As she was about to call out to him, another voice beat her to it.

"Kai!" Rhianne turned to see a familiar face making a beeline for him. Sergeant Lisa Chen halted a foot away from Kai, and Rhianne slowed her pace, silently observing the unfolding scene.

Kai looked up, his expression registering surprise. "Lisa?"

Lisa's next words, "Miss me?" were delivered with a flirtatious undertone that didn't sit well with Rhianne.

Rhianne's eyebrows knitted together. This was a side of their relationship she hadn't seen, or even suspected. Was there a history between them she was unaware of? The sudden revelation stirred a sudden tightness in her chest.

Kai folded his arms across his chest. "Was there something you wanted?"

"You've been ignoring my texts and calls. How would you know if I wanted anything?" Lisa pouted, reaching out to touch Kai's arm. "It's been two months since you last warmed my bed."

"Is that what you want? A warm bed?" Kai's response was curt, his body tense and coiled. He withdrew his arm from Lisa's touch. "We broke up for a reason."

"No." Lisa adjusted a loose strand of hair behind her ear. "You broke up with me because you got a little upset but we've always got back together before. Why haven't you called me back? Is it because of that green witch?"

Rhianne bristled at the disdain in Lisa's voice.

"It's just a fling, and you know it. It can't compare to what we have."

Well, wasn't someone Miss Confidence? She mentally awarded Lisa ten points for audacity, even as she wondered how Kai would respond to such a bold claim.

Kai narrowed his eyes, his voice cutting. "You're right," he said, and Rhianne's heart skipped a beat. "What I have with Rhianne is far better than anything you and I ever had."

Rhianne let out a slow exhale, contemplating whether she should step in or not. Then it hit her: she was still in disguise. Lisa wouldn't have a clue who she really was, but speaking up might blow her cover.

"Two years, you practically lived in my apartment!" Lisa's

CHAPTER 22

voice grew louder. "How can you say that?"

Rhianne took a step back, her mind reeling with the revelation. Two years? They had only broken up two months ago. Her hands trembled as she tried to steady herself, biting the inside of her mouth in an attempt to regain control. Summoning strength, she forced herself to walk around Kai and Lisa, making her way towards the exit. Each step felt like a struggle as she focused on creating distance between herself and the emotional turmoil unfolding behind her. As she neared the door, their voices reached her ears once more.

"I've made myself clear, Lisa. We're done," Kai's voice rang out. "Please don't contact me unless it's related to an official case."

"Oh, is that so? Then what the hell are you doing here?" Lisa's tone underwent a swift transformation, shifting from seductive to aggressive.

Rhianne kept walking, her mind swirling with conflicting thoughts and emotions. She resisted the urge to look back, knowing it wouldn't change anything. Right now, she needed to find a way to clear her head.

Overwhelmed with the need to blow off some steam, hitting the gym sounded like a good idea. She was supposed to meet Nel there later anyway; getting there a bit early wouldn't hurt. With her thoughts still racing, she picked up her pace

When Rhianne arrived, Nel was nowhere to be found. Undeterred, she headed to the changing rooms and put on her gear. Emerging from the changing rooms, she was eager to dive into her workout and shut out the world. Engaging in her warm-up routine, she focused her attention solely on the movements. Breathe in, breathe out. Sidestep, jump back. High kicks, low kicks. She kept her body in motion, maintaining a steady flow. Moving and allowing the exercise to fully engage all her senses brought a sense of momentary peace.

Somewhere along the way, Rhianne became aware of Nel's presence. He had quietly joined her, mirroring her every move.

"Something's bothering you," Nel said.

She chose not to respond, shrugging and offering him a shaky smile instead.

Nel narrowed his eyes, his expression shifting. "Trouble in paradise already?"

Rhianne took a deep breath, pausing to reflect on her reaction as she observed Nel's protective anger. Was she overreacting? Sure, it would have been nice to know about Kai and Lisa's past relationship. It would have been even better to have a clearer timeline of their breakup. But did it really change anything? Kai had been crystal clear about their status. Then it hit her. She was scared. Things had been going so smoothly between her and Kai that she had a lingering fear that something might go wrong.

She wanted to talk this one through with someone but Nel would overreact. She wasn't exactly a pro at lying, but she hoped that some of her mother's lessons on maintaining a poker face had stayed with her.

"Actually, we interviewed Rita Parkes," she said instead.

Nel glanced at her his lips pressed flat.

"Turns out, she suspects Arthur of stealing money, and that's why she hired Kai. From what I gathered through office gossip, she was definitely daddy's girl, but it was a one-sided affair. She's got some serious ambition; I'll give her that. But it's making me think I should have another chat with Arthur,"

CHAPTER 22

she spoke fast, hoping to mask her inner turmoil.

Nel raised an eyebrow. "So, why does that put you in such a mood?"

"Because it means I have to pretend to be interested in Arthur, and that doesn't sit right with me." It was the truth.

Nel's nod was slow and thoughtful, accompanied by a curious look "Oh, I see. Are you sure that's all?"

Offence was the best defence. "What do you mean, 'is that all'? It feels terrible, and I'm not even sure if I can pull it off."

"You'll be playing a role, princess, putting on a wig and a mask. Once you've transformed, you can remind yourself that it's all just an act." He gave her a wry smile. "Your reluctance might make you more desirable. He'll pick up on the lack of interest."

"Argh! Anyone mentioned you're ruthless?"

"No, but I've been called shameless and charming, though."

Rhianne threw her hands in the air. "You're impossible!"

Seeing Nel's cheeky grin brought a touch of warmth to Rhianne's heart. It nudged her to push aside her worries, at least for now. A part of her was kind of excited about chatting with Arthur again, curious about what new info she might uncover. Plus, she had successfully steered both herself and Nel away from the real issue at hand and that that restless negative energy she was secretly eager to channel into something... less dramatic. And a good sparring session seemed like the perfect way to channel it.

"You up for a fight?" she asked.

As Rhianne and Nel sparred, she found herself fighting more than just her skilled opponent. Her mind kept drifting away from Nel's swift moves and right back to the messy situation with Kai and Lisa. She was annoyed, not just at the

277

whole thing with Kai, but also at herself for not dealing with it head-on. Fear of what might happen next was messing with her head, making it hard to concentrate on her sparring. She landed kicks and manoeuvred around Nel's attacks, but internally, she wrestled with a mix of emotions — frustration, a sense of betrayal, and uncertainty about the future. It was as if she was in two fights at once, and the emotional one was proving to be as challenging as the physical sparring.

After her shower, Rhianne dried off and reached for her bag. She checked her phone and found it full of missed calls and messages from Kai, which set off a whirlwind of emotions. Was she ready to talk to him? What if she messed up her words, or what if he said something that made things more complicated? Maybe he'd been rethinking things and …

An image of Kai popped into her head. She remembered his stormy blue eyes and how he always seemed to have her back. Funny, kind, unflappably calm, and an absolute nerd to boot. She couldn't help but smile at the thought. For all his quirks, Kai had a way of making complicated situations seem a little less daunting.

She picked up her phone and dialled.

"Hey," she said. It felt inadequate, the weight of unspoken words lingering in the air, but she couldn't find the right words to express everything she was feeling. She had disappeared without a word, leaving him without a chance to explain.

"I'm sorry," he said.

"So am I," she replied softly.

"I should have told you." His voice was husky.

"Maybe," she said. "We've been busy."

"She's not relevant." It was a plea.

CHAPTER 22

Despite herself, Rhianne felt the corners of her mouth twitch. Lisa would be livid if she'd heard him say that. "Ouch!"

"It's the truth."

"I know." And she did. One day she'd ask him what had caused the breakup, but today was not that day. She felt lighter, though, a sense of readiness to move forward. Changing the subject, she added, "By the way, did I mention Nel owns a club?"

"The one where you met Arthur?"

"Yep, one and the same. "I'm planning to head back there tonight, try to get some more info. How about you? Any luck with your part of the investigation?"

"There's definitely money going missing, and all signs seem to point to Arthur," Kai admitted.

"But you're not convinced," she said.

She heard a deep exhale on the other side. "No, I'm not. There are two sets of transactions and they don't add up, pun intended, I need more details." There was a brief pause, and Rhianne could hear the sound of movement, as if Kai had settled into a chair. "Could you maybe find out how much Arthur knows about finances?"

"How do you suggest I figure that out?" she asked. Accounting wasn't the angle Kai seemed to be aiming for, which is what she was familiar with.

"Maybe you could casually bring up that you're looking into different investment opportunities, or that you're seeking financial advice. Pay attention to how he reacts and what he says. It could give us a clue about how much he knows about finances," Kai suggested.

"Ugh. I feel thoroughly unprepared for this." She worried at her lower lip.

"Well," Kai paused. "What about if I helped you?"

"Help me how?"

Kai's voice quickened with excitement. "Well, like suggesting the topics and the right direction to steer the conversation. I can give you cues to help draw out the information we need."

"How would we do that?"

"I can set you up with some discreet communication devices, like an earpiece and a microphone, and then I can guide you as I listen in on the conversation."

"Whoa! You're talking about setting me up with spy tech?" The idea made her feel a little giddy.

"Well, not exactly spy tech, just a simple communication system. I would need to be within two hundred metres of your location for it to work smoothly."

"That means you'd have to be in the club with us." As soon as she said it, Rhianne decided it was a good idea. Working together on this mission felt like a step in the right direction for them. "Oh, and you'll have to meet the dress code." She grinned at the brief silence that followed on the other end of the line.

"What dress code?"

Rhianne's grin widened. "When was the last time you went to a nightclub?"

"Does a bar downtown count?" Kai asked.

"Nope. Wear nice jeans and a long sleeve shirt and Nel can provide something else if need be. The Devil's Advocate is a high-end nightclub and pretty exclusive. How about we meet at the club at nine tonight? It's down on the Walsh Bay Arts Precinct."

"If it's that exclusive they won't let me in," Kai said.

"Don't play coy with me, Mr Consultant. I've heard you

CHAPTER 22

have friends in high places."

"Hmm," Kai said. "I'll be there with bells on."

"I'm pretty sure that's not acceptable club attire." She laughed and it felt good to let go.

"I hear in some places anything goes. The respectable people need to let their hair down after all," Kai deadpanned.

Rhianne burst into laughter, trying to catch her breath. "Uh-huh. I'll catch up with you later," she managed to say between giggles.

"See you, Rhi," Kai replied, his use of her nickname causing a delightful flutter in her stomach.

CHAPTER 23

At five minutes to nine, as Rhianne sat finalising the club accounts, her mobile rang.

"I'm at the back of an endless queue, stretching all the way to the promenade. It's not moving," Kai's voice sounded exasperated.

Rhianne chuckled. "That's nothing. On Saturdays, the queue can extend all the way to the bridge. Just go up to the bouncers and tell them Rhianne is expecting you. I've already given them your name and description."

"I saw them. They look pretty intimidating. Plus, I'm carrying some expensive kit with me," Kai said.

"Don't worry, they won't even think about touching your kit. Go on through, and I'll meet you at the entrance."

Rhianne felt the excitement bubbling up inside her. She hurried downstairs, her heart racing with anticipation.

As Rhianne reached the doors, Kai emerged from the crowd, holding a metal briefcase. She came to a sudden stop, locking eyes with him. Those stormy blue eyes bore into her as if she was a treasured prize he had somehow won. She offered him a shy smile. "Hello, alpha geek."

CHAPTER 23

"Hello to you too, Rhi. Did I get the dress code right?" Kai's arms opened wide as he spun around, his question sounding mundane, but the intensity in his gaze made her cheeks flush.

Rhianne reached for his free hand and pulled him closer. He didn't hesitate, bending down to give her a brief and tender kiss.

"You're absolutely perfect," she whispered into his ear, her words causing a delightful flush to colour his cheeks, visible even in the dimly lit ambience of the club. "Let's get out of here. We're in the way."

As the bouncers ushered more people inside, the place buzzed with the energy of enthusiastic club-goers. Rhianne tugged at his hand, leading him to a quieter area and up the stairs that led to the offices.

Guiding Kai into the treasure trove of a costume room, Rhianne watched as he took in the sight. It was a large space filled with wardrobes and shelves proudly showcasing a dazzling assortment of hats, wigs, and all sorts of accessories. Right in the middle, a cosy nook was fashioned with a couple of comfy armchairs and a welcoming coffee table.

"I see what you meant about Nel providing clothes if I needed to blend in." Kai scanned the room.

Rhianne grinned. "Welcome to the backstage world of The Devil's Advocate."

"Nel has quite the collection. This is not the only room, but it's where he keeps his favourite pieces. He should be along shortly," she said.

"Do we need to talk some more about this afternoon?" His arm wrapped around her waist.

"We've done enough talking. Let's move to the making-up part." She wrapped her arms around his neck, pulling him closer. The kiss was fuelled by a cascade of emotions held back. How could she have doubted him? In that single kiss, he set her entire body alight, sending tingles racing up and down her spine. But it wasn't just a physical response; her mind felt perfectly in sync with his, as if they were on the same wavelength in every way possible. There was an instant, mutual deepening, a silent recognition of their connection. His kiss felt like a luxurious, spiced hot chocolate — rich and warm, with a hint of spice that awakened all her senses.

"Ahem!" Nel's voice interrupted them.

At some point, he must have entered the room without them noticing. Reluctantly, she ended the kiss. With Kai's arms still around her waist, she turned to face Nel.

Nel offered a subtle nod to Kai, though the stiffness in his shoulders and neck betrayed his distrust. Either their earlier discussion hadn't fooled him, or he was in overly protective big brother mode.

Neither of the men bothered with extending their hands for a shake. The whole situation was starting to feel a little ridiculous.

"Hello Nel." Rhianne gave him a bright smile.

"Thanks for allowing me to come to the club." Kai took the high road.

Rhianne squeezed his arm in silent gratitude.

Nel eased the tension in his shoulders as he approached them, openly assessing Kai from head to toe. Starting with a discerning gaze at his shoes, his eyes travelled up, taking in every detail along the way. "I have a jacket that will complement the shirt and jeans."

"Thanks." Kai nodded. "Do you also have a secluded table where I can discreetly listen and give instructions to Rhi?"

CHAPTER 23

Nel flinched at the nickname but quickly recovered. Without skipping a beat, he reached for a navy-blue jacket hanging on a nearby rack. "I'll get the waiters to set up a table for you. If anyone sees you talking to yourself, they'll probably think you're in a business meeting. And I'll make sure you're not disturbed."

Nel handed the jacket to Kai, who slipped it on.

The jacket fit like a glove, which didn't surprise Rhianne in the slightest. Maybe this was Nel's subtle way of showing he was starting to warm up to Kai ... or maybe he just couldn't stand the thought of anyone looking less than sharp. It was a toss-up.

Interrupting her train of thought, Nel continued, "I suggest we get you situated first, separate from Rhianne's entrance. Arthur just arrived with a group of friends."

"I need to set up the equipment first." Kai placed his heavy metal briefcase on the coffee table. He cast a sideways glance at Rhianne. "It might be better if you change so I can conceal the microphone in your clothes."

"Well, I guess wearing the same dress as last time is completely out of the question?" Rhianne glanced at Nel, who had already started rummaging deeper into the room.

He emerged a few seconds later with a green ensemble. "Put this on. I'll find a matching mask for the dress."

"Are we still going with the masked look?"

"We need to keep you a bit of a mystery, and it's important that your face isn't easily recognised. Especially if you're going to do more undercover stuff in the future." Nel handed her a mask from one of the shelves.

Rhianne's attention then turned to the green dress. It was two pieces — a stylish crossover top that sat off the shoulders, and a long, elegant skirt with daringly high slits on the sides.

"Don't worry, I'll make sure I keep a low profile. It'll make your job of getting information easier," Nel said.

"We should establish a safe word for Rhianne," Kai interjected.

"Excuse me?" Nel's voice came out strained.

Kai disregarded his evident outrage and continued. "Look, if Rhianne feels uncomfortable, all she needs to do is use the safe word, and I'll signal you immediately. That's your cue to step in and escort her out."

Rhianne struggled to keep a straight face at Nel's comically surprised reaction to Kai's suggestion. She coughed a bit to hide her growing smile. "Yeah, I agree with Kai. Although things were okay with Arthur last time, it's always smart to have a quick way out just in case."

Rhianne grabbed the dress and found a quiet spot in the corner to change. Nel kept an eye on Kai, who seemed completely absorbed in setting up his gear, unaware of Nel's watchful gaze.

She needed to have a word with Nel about giving her some space, especially when it came to her personal life. His overprotectiveness was starting to feel more fatherly than brotherly. This thought made her reflect briefly on her own father's lack of involvement. Shaking off these thoughts and any residual annoyance, she slipped into the dress.

Kai's attention shifted from his equipment, his eyes sparkling with appreciation, and a gentle smile played on his lips. "You look beautiful," he said; his words filling Rhianne with a comforting warmth.

Nel handed her a pair of high heels. "Kai has impeccable taste. You look stunning."

CHAPTER 23

Was that an olive branch? Rhianne glanced at Nel, noticing a softening in his eyes and a faint smile on his lips.

Kai stood up and attached a microphone in the form of a jade pin to her top. He then proceeded to place a lovely ear cuff adorned with Zirconia butterflies on her left ear. "When is an earpiece not an earpiece?" he said with a lopsided grin.

Rhianne couldn't help but groan, but her matching grin betrayed her amusement. "When it's a beautiful earring given to me by my boyfriend," she replied.

Kai paused while adjusting the earring, and for a brief moment, Rhianne grew anxious, wondering if she had said the wrong thing. Maybe it was too soon. But Kai continued with the adjustment, his fingers gently caressing her earlobe. Leaning in closer, he whispered, "I must be the luckiest guy around."

Kai leaned back; his eyes filled with a promise that sent a thrill of anticipation through Rhianne.

She touched the earring. "How about 'butterfly' as the safe word?"

Nel's face softened. "Perfect. Are you both ready?"

Kai glanced at Rhianne once more before turning to Nel. "Lead the way, please."

Rhianne mentally crossed her fingers, silently hoping that one day Nel and Kai would find some common ground, or at least agree to disagree without the dramatics. She felt a flicker of hope. Kai was fast becoming someone significant in her life, and it would be nice if her team could get on board with that. At least Toto was Team Kai. That was something, right?

As Rhianne waited for a text from Nel, her mind was a whirlwind of theories and suspects. Among them, Sarah stood out. She had this savvy, tough vibe about her, and Rhianne had to admit there was something about her she liked. But how much would Sarah inherit? How much would be enough to drive someone to murder? Sarah's blunt admission about using her late husband for financial gain raised more questions. Did she have the means to pull off something like this? Sure, working in aged care meant she knew a thing or two about medicines, but that didn't mean she could whip up a poison.

Rhianne's thoughts then drifted to Rita. Calculating, cold — she fit the profile of a suspect. The meticulous planning needed for the murder was up her alley. But there was a hitch in that theory — Rita had practically worshipped her father. Killing him just didn't add up.

Then there was Arthur. Too caught up in his own insecurities and loneliness to plan a murder, let alone execute it. Yet, what if his dad had caught him embezzling funds? Or maybe Arthur wasn't working alone.

And then there was the ex-wife. Their estranged relationship made it seem unlikely, but who knew?

Rhianne paced the room, feeling like she was missing a crucial piece of the puzzle.

A beep from her phone jolted her back to reality. It was Nel, giving her the go-ahead. Standing in front of the large mirror, she adjusted the red wig and put on the mask. It was time to refocus and get her head back in the game.

As Rhianne stepped out of the room, she spotted Nel waiting for her with a grin on his face.

"I love the look."

She tilted her head and considered his casual stance. "What? The mysterious masked redhead?" She paused as she suddenly

CHAPTER 23

realised something. "You know what's weird? I feel like a completely different person when I'm wearing this disguise."

Nel offered her his arm. "It's called 'getting into character' and it's what all good actors do."

"I'm clearly not cut out for acting. Remember how I fumbled when Arthur bombarded me with questions? You practically had to play the hero and rescue me."

"Well, most men just like having someone to listen to them," Nel said.

"Most women do too," she countered.

"Can't argue with that," Nel agreed, his tone light. "Listening is my secret weapon for gathering intel. It's amazing what people reveal, especially when they're ... let's say, in a good mood." He flashed her a cheeky grin.

Rhianne poked him in the ribs. "You're hopeless."

His smile widened. "Guilty as charged."

They stepped into the VIP area and Rhianne began immediately looking for Kai. Nel must have noticed.

"Kai is in the north corner, doing his best not to look your way," he informed her. Rhianne turned her head in that direction and caught sight of him. Kai seemed totally lost in his own world, and Rhianne felt a twinge of disappointment. But just then, her earpiece buzzed.

"I see you, battle angel. Go get him!" Kai's voice rang in her ear.

She couldn't help the smile that blossomed from her lips and the disappointment faded as if it had never existed. With a lighter step, Rhianne followed Nel. "So, are you going to lead me straight to Arthur?" she asked.

"No, not directly. All eyes are already on us, so we'll use that to our advantage. He won't be able to resist taking the bait." He led her towards the bar area and found a stool for her to sit on.

Rhianne lightly brushed her fingers against her mask, feeling a twinge of self-consciousness. "No one else is wearing a mask. Do you think he might find it a bit odd?"

"He'll find it intriguing," Nel replied with a smirk. "And speaking of the devil, he's just abandoned his entourage and is making a beeline for us."

"Show off," Rhianne mumbled, though her words lacked their usual bite.

Her heart raced, and she dug her nails into her palms, trying to steady herself. She had been less nervous during their previous encounter. Maybe it was because of Kai's presence, throwing her off her game. Or perhaps her gut instinct was telling her to be wary of getting too close to a potential murderer.

Nel positioned himself towards the bartender, intentionally turning his back to the approaching Arthur. "Nel, my old friend, how are you?" Arthur's eyes immediately sought Rhianne's.

Rhianne offered him a small smile.

"My dear Rose, it's so good to see you!" Arthur placed his palm over his heart.

"You actually remember me?" Rhianne's voice quivered slightly.

"How could I forget?" Arthur's gaze lingering on her.

"You're not flirting with my girl, are you?" Nel interjected with a cross tone.

What was Nel playing at? He was going to scare Arthur off. If she could have got away with it, she would have kicked Nel in the shins.

CHAPTER 23

"Wouldn't dream of it, but I must say she's a sight for sore eyes." Arthur winked at Rhianne.

He had leaned close enough for her to pick up a hint of alcohol on his breath. His sense of self-preservation had clearly been dulled.

"You don't own me, Nel," Rhianne snapped. At least some of that anger was real. Why did he have to switch things up on her without warning?

"Is that right, Rose? Then who's going to cover the cost of your expensive habits?"

"I think you've had one too many," Rhianne said.

Nel didn't get drunk. He had once confided in her that it would take too much alcohol for that to happen. No one knew though, and it was a tool he occasionally used for cover. Nel had better play along, given he had backed her into a corner.

"Are you presuming to dictate what I can or cannot do in my own club?" Nel narrowed his eyes at her, his body swaying slightly as he discreetly gestured with his left hand.

One of Nel's staff members appeared.

"Sir?" the man asked.

"Yes?" Nel replied.

"There's someone waiting for you in your office, sir."

"I don't recall an appointment."

"Well, sir, with your busy schedule, it's possible it slipped your notice. This way, please, sir." The man positioned himself as if ready to assist Nel as they exited the room.

"Are you okay, my dear Rose? I've never seen Nel quite like that,"

He may have been curious but he was clearly more interested in taking advantage of the situation.

"He'll be fine. He always bounces back." She had to be

cautious now. She inwardly groaned, hating the acting part. It felt like trying to walk in high heels on a tightrope — not exactly her idea of fun.

"Let's find a spot to sit over there," Arthur suggested, his hand resting lightly on her elbow. Out of the corner of her eye, Rhianne caught him signalling his friends, who promptly vacated the seats they had occupied. The area ahead was arranged with comfortable sofas in a semicircle, bathed in gentle, dim lighting. Despite the temptation to steal a glance in Kai's direction, Rhianne kept her focus straight ahead.

"Seems like your friends are abandoning you."

Arthur offered her a rueful smile. He had a boyish charm. "They just care about what's important to me."

"You can't be that desperate for female companionship," she challenged. The image of the women in the group, especially the fiery-haired woman who might be his secretary lingered in Rhianne's mind.

"I'm desperate for yours. You never called me." He gave her a puppy-eyed look as he helped her settle onto one of the sofas.

Rhianne casually lifted a shoulder and placed her drink on the table before her. She wasn't entirely certain if it contained alcohol, but she didn't want to take any chances. "You didn't call either," she said in an indifferent tone.

Arthur inched closer to her, careful not to make physical contact. "I didn't have your number, and no one here knew how to reach you."

"Nel probably didn't want me to be found." Which was the truth just not in the way Arthur was imagining.

"You don't have to stay with him; I could take care of you."

It was lucky Rhianne hadn't been sipping from her drink;

CHAPTER 23

she was sure she would have choked on it.

Suddenly, Kai's voice resonated in her ear, prompting her to touch her earring. "This is the perfect opportunity, ask him what he knows about investment opportunities."

"I don't need anyone to look after me." Rhianne flipped a strand of hair over her shoulder. Was she overdoing it? "I have investments in various places."

"You are an investor?" Arthur said.

"You seem surprised."

"I could use help with that myself."

"Oh, really?" Rhianne said. "Surely you have your own extensive portfolio."

"I do, but it was all managed by my father, and it's terribly conservative. I've been considering venturing into riskier investments," Arthur said.

"Such as?" Kai's voice echoed in her ear, and she relayed his question.

"Well, I've heard art collections and rare cars can bring in some serious cash. But you know my father always believed in having physical assets, things you can actually hold."

Rhianne leaned back. "What about foreign investments? I've heard some countries offer attractive tax benefits."

"Wow, you're quite the risk-taker," Arthur said. "I'd be worried that might raise some red flags with the authorities."

"Hey, why not claim a trip to the Cayman Islands as a tax deduction?" Rhianne pretended to sip her drink.

Arthur tilted his head, then reached out to take her hand. "You know what? I can fly you in a private jet to wherever you desire. We could spend some quality time on an island, getting to know each other better. Actually, my father, or rather I now, own a small island in Hawaii."

Once again, Kai's voice broke the silence in her ear. "I believe that's all I needed to hear."

Rhianne flashed a smile at Arthur, feeling a twinge of guilt for leading him on. "Oh, I've heard they have beautiful butterflies there." She clapped her hands in delight.

Arthur beamed at her as if he had finally heard something that made sense.

Nel tapped Arthur on the shoulder. "You have a way with words, Arthur." Nel bared his teeth.

Arthur flinched at his touch, pulling his hand back from Rhianne's. Seizing the opportunity, she stood up. Leaning in she planted a friendly peck on Arthur's cheek. "It was nice talking to you, Art. Catch you later,"

Arthur wore a dazed expression, his lips slightly downturned. Rhianne gave him a dainty wave and joined Nel as they made their way out of the VIP area and back to the costume room.

As they entered, Rhianne noticed Kai already seated in one of the chairs, waiting for them. "Well, I'm pretty sure he was telling you the truth. His heart rate remained steady when he answered your questions."

"And?" Rhianne settled down next to Kai on the sofa, removing her mask and slipping off her high heels. With a sigh of relief, she bent down to massage her tired feet.

"Arthur withdrew some money from the company a few months ago. It wouldn't surprise me if he had incurred some gambling debts. I can trace the transactions and confirm. But he repaid the amount the day after his father's death. The second, much larger sum was sent to the Cayman Islands a few days prior to the murder," Kai said.

"Oh?"

CHAPTER 23

"Someone's deliberately trying to frame him."

CHAPTER 24

"His sister," Rhianne said.

"Likely, but I can't say for certain just yet. Give me a few days, and I'll have a clearer answer," Kai said.

There was something comforting about his quiet confidence.

Changing gears, Rhianne turned to Nel. "What was that little act you pulled?"

Nel tilted his head from side to side, eliciting a series of cracks that made Rhianne wince. "Well, if I'd left you there with him, he might've got suspicious. I had to improvise."

"That could have easily backfired," she scowled.

"But it didn't, and you played your part brilliantly. You have more talent for this work than you give yourself credit for."

"What work?" Kai glanced up from his phone.

"He's talking about detective work," Rhianne clarified.

She wagged a finger at Nel. They'd talk about this later. Why did he have to go and blurt it out like that? She hadn't had a chance to think about it let alone tell Kai.

"You already have a successful business," Kai pointed out.

CHAPTER 24

"It's called diversification," Nel answered with a casual shrug.

Rhianne glared at him.

"Nel wants me to help him some more with his business. I promised to think about it," she said.

Kai said nothing. Loudly.

Nel, in an obvious but effective change of subject tactic, asked, "Does that mean Rita Parkes murdered her father?"

Rhianne sighed. "That doesn't necessarily point to guilt. She might've wanted Arthur out of the picture for a bit. Maybe she was trying to show her father she was the better choice for running the business, especially since he thought men were more suited for the job, despite her being super qualified."

Kai nodded. "She definitely doesn't lack achievements. She's got a degree in business, a master's in finance, and she was top of her class in everything. Science, maths, you name it. She was even a school captain, and she's got a Duke of Edinburgh award under her belt too."

Nel backpedalled. "If she did all that to convince her father, killing him just days later would be counterproductive."

Rhianne threw her hands up. "Ugh! This case keeps getting more convoluted."

"I'll have more details soon. We can't forget about Sarah and Andrea Parkes. I'm going to look into the will, see what Sarah could gain from his death. That might give us some more clues." Kai said.

Rhianne sighed again. "She implied to me that it wasn't much."

"She could be lying." Nel settled down on one of the sofas.

"Why would she?" Rhianne removed her wig.

Kai cast her an appreciative look. He hadn't voiced it, but

she suspected he preferred her as a brunette.

"From her perspective, she was speaking to a complete stranger. She could have easily boasted about the inheritance instead of downplaying it," she said.

"People have committed murder for far less. Human nature never ceases to amaze me."

Kai ran a hand through his hair. Rhianne resisted the urge to do the same; she loved the sensation of his curls between her fingers.

Nel nodded. "It's possible that she stood to gain more as a widow than through a divorce."

"That's a valid point," Kai acknowledged, giving Nel a nod. "I'll look into it. The will isn't public yet, so it will require some finesse."

Seeing Rhianne's glance, Kai added, "Don't worry, I'm not going to do anything dodgy. You'd be amazed at what people accidentally let slip on social media. Sometimes, all you need is a few posts and their algorithms to connect the dots."

As he leaned back, looking a bit on edge, Rhianne reached over and took his hand, hoping to ease any concerns. She hadn't meant to make him feel like she was questioning his methods.

"I prefer to stick to the law," he said.

"The law can be a real pain in the butt sometimes," Nel grumbled.

Kai shifted his gaze, his eyes locking with Nel's. "You know, a lot of cops would agree with you. But there's a thin line there. Too much authority mixed with a casual attitude towards the law can lead to trouble."

Nel blinked rapidly and Rhianne tilted her head. There was something more beneath the surface of Kai's words. It made

CHAPTER 24

her wonder if she had brushed off the subject of his breakup with Lisa too hastily. She made a mental note to bring it up again later.

"We'll have to see what we can get out of Andrea on Saturday," she said.

"Saturday?" Nel asked.

"My mother is hosting a fundraiser party, and I've got some solid intel that Andrea Parkes will be gracing the event with her presence."

"You're attending one of your mother's parties?" Nel raised an eyebrow.

Rhianne flicked her hand. "Long story, but yes. But more importantly, it will give us the perfect opportunity to meet Andrea."

Nel brought up his smartphone and typed, then looked up with a grin. "What do you know, I have an invitation too, and I think I'll also attend."

"My mother invited you?" Rhianne couldn't hide the disbelief in her tone as she leaned forward.

"I may not be her favourite person, but I support a few charity causes. Just because she's not a fan of mine doesn't mean she'll turn down a chance to benefit her own interests," Nel said.

"Fair enough." Rhianne relaxed back into her seat. "But I have to ask: why do you want to go?"

"Because attending the event gives us not one, but two golden opportunities to get some useful information from Mrs Parkes."

Rhianne scrutinised his face. "Are you sure about this?"

Nel shrugged. "As an incubus, I have to feed, might as well get something more out of it."

Rhianne narrowed her eyes. Did he say that to shock Kai? She understood Nel's nature, but she'd never get used to his superficial attitude to intimacy. Rhianne couldn't shake the feeling that there was a mask hiding Nel's true emotions. She had this nagging feeling that underneath all his bravado, Nel was lonely and unhappy. It was like he was stuck playing a part, torn between the real him and the version he thought he had to be.

Rhianne shifted her gaze towards Kai, noticing his apparent immersion in his smartphone. Was he genuinely occupied, or intentionally avoiding sharing his opinion? While she hadn't explicitly disclosed Nel's true nature to Kai, she had a hunch that he might have figured it out on his own. Perhaps Nel should consider hiring him instead. The thought brought a smile to her face, picturing the likely clashes that would ensue between Nel and Kai. They were both strong-willed and that could easily lead to some entertaining showdowns.

"I'm aiming to track down the flow of money and get into the contents of the will by then. If we can do that, it could give us some crucial clues and help us figure out exactly what we need to ask." Kai proved that he had indeed been paying attention.

Rhianne crossed her fingers, both literally and figuratively, hoping Kai would hit the jackpot with some solid leads. At this stage, she felt like she was playing a game of 'Clue', where everyone was a suspect. Sure, there was a tiny chance that some random outsider could be the culprit, but she seriously doubted it. The odds were high that the murderer was someone from Devlin's inner circle.

They wrapped up and Kai agreed to pick her up at seven sharp. The party was supposed to start at seven thirty, and

CHAPTER 24

Rhianne had to make sure she was on time. While the guests could afford to be fashionably late, the same couldn't be said for the host and her daughter. Rhianne had earlier picked up the dress at Madame's. When she had tried it on at the boutique, Madame had insisted on ensuring everything was perfect. Rhianne's eyes had sparkled at her reflection. The dress was simply exquisite and she had said so to Madame. Madame had demurred and told her it was the wearer who made it so.

Now dressed in the gorgeous wine-red gown and complemented by nude pumps, Rhianne had styled her hair into an elegant high bun. She had adorned herself with long gold earrings and a simple gold chain. The sound of Kai's car announced his arrival. Shortly after, she heard a knock on her door.

"It's open!" she called out, grabbing a light tan clutch and heading for the door. She paused as Kai entered, looking incredibly handsome in a dark navy tuxedo and a cobalt blue bow tie. A smile spread across her face.

He stood there, seemingly frozen, his gaze fixed on her face before freely roaming over her body. His lips were slightly parted, and his pupils dilated.

"You look absolutely beautiful." His voice was husky. "You *are* beautiful."

Closing the small distance between them, he planted a kiss on her lips, his hand resting gently behind her neck as his thumb caressed her throat. Rhianne leaned into the kiss, her fingertips brushing against his cheek. Reluctantly, she broke away, but she remained just inches from his face.

"You look pretty amazing yourself, alpha geek." Her words were accompanied by a soft laugh. "Though, I must warn you, if you keep looking at me with those 'puppy dog' eyes, we'll be so late Nell will send out a search party."

They strolled hand in hand, their fingers intertwined.

A voice emerged from the shadows of the trees. "You look stunning, my dear."

It was difficult to spot him in the darkness. "Thanks, Toto. I'll raise a glass for you."

"No need, human alcohol cannot compare to fairy wine. But enjoy yourself! And Kai, please take good care of our girl," Toto said.

Rhianne briefly considered objecting to being called 'girl,' but she decided it wasn't worth the effort. Sometimes, you simply had to choose your battles.

"Will do, Toto. She's pretty special to me as well." Kai smiled.

Kai's sleek white Tesla gleamed under the glow of the nearby lamppost as he opened the passenger door for her.

Luckily, the traffic was relatively light for a Saturday night, allowing them to arrive at the venue's car park early.

The party was hosted on the top floor, and as they stepped into the spacious room, Rhianne's gaze was immediately drawn to the breathtaking harbour view visible through the expansive windows. The twinkling lights of boats and yachts created a spellbinding display on the glistening water, accompanied by the soft murmur of conversations.

Taking a deep breath, Rhianne tightened her grip on Kai's hand. It was time to locate her mother, or she would never hear the end of it.

"Rhianne, there you are!" her mother's voice rang out, drawing her attention. Rhianne turned around, finding her mother's gaze. She was wearing one of Madame's creations, a

CHAPTER 24

long purple dress with embroidered sleeves. Rhianne noticed a fleeting twitch of her mother's lips as she spotted Kai. Either she wasn't thrilled that Rhianne had kept a relationship from her or she had other plans for the night that didn't align with this unexpected guest. Too bad.

"Hello, Mother." Rhianne pulled Kai gently to her side. "This is Kai Wagner."

Her mother's blue eyes bore into them, assessing and calculating.

Kai nodded. "Nice to meet you, Esther."

"Indeed, this is a surprise," her mother said, giving Rhianne a pointed glance that promised a discussion later. She pivoted to Kai and offered him a small smile while locking eyes with him. "Tell me about yourself, Kai. What do you do for a living?"

Rhianne bit her lip, but Kai was unfazed by her mother's scrutiny. Not many could withstand Esther Broadwater's penetrating gaze, but it appeared Kai was one of them. Rhianne silently cheered for him.

"I run a Technical and Financial Forensic business."

Her mother tilted her head, a hint of interest reflected in her eyes. "Ah, so you're a Tech mage." It was a statement not a question. "Wagner," she snapped her fingers, "are you the son of Anna and Martin?"

"Yes," Kai said.

"Am I remembering correctly that you achieved one of the highest recorded levels for a Tech Mage?" Her mother feigned uncertainty.

As if! Her mother was like a human encyclopedia — an eidetic memory that filed away every detail, especially the juicy ones. She wasn't just the kind of politician who greeted everyone by name; she'd also remember their kids' names and their favourite sports, and probably the last time they scored a goal or tripped over their own shoelaces.

If he was taken aback, he didn't let it show. Score one for Kai.

"You're well informed," Kai said.

Then it hit her. The highest score? Rhianne's eyes widened and she silently scolded herself for the visible reaction. Her mother wouldn't have missed it. After all, she was the one who had often reminded Rhianne never to reveal her emotions to opponents. Rhianne had no doubt that Esther Broadwater was already dissecting her emotional display, storing it away for future use.

"Welcome. It's a pleasure to meet you, Kai," her mother said. "Rhianne, there are some friends I'd like you to meet later, please stay until I have the opportunity to introduce you." Without waiting for her daughter's agreement, she pivoted and sashayed away.

"I didn't know you held one of the highest recorded levels," Rhianne said to Kai as soon as her mother was out of earshot.

"It was the second highest ever recorded, but the mage who achieved the highest is now dead," Kai said.

"How long ago was the other record set?" Mages lived for several centuries.

"Over three hundred years ago," Kai replied. "The testing methods have evolved over time with technological advancements, so it's hard to compare accurately."

"No wonder my mother was impressed," Rhianne mused.

"If that's her impressed expression, I can only imagine how intimidating her disappointed face must be."

"Trust me, It's not fun. I've lived with her disappointment

CHAPTER 24

all my life." Rhianne tried her best to mask the pain in her voice. Her mother had managed to get under her skin once again. "Do you have any idea what Andrea Parkes looks like?" Rhianne asked, eager to shift the focus.

Kai pulled out his smartphone and showed her a series of photos featuring Andrea at various events. "By the way, I was right about Arthur not being responsible for the second withdrawal of funds. They did a meticulous job using multiple shell companies. Their plan might have succeeded if they hadn't tried so hard to make him appear guilty. I have a strong hunch that Rita is behind it all."

"In moments like these, I'm relieved to be an only child," Rhianne said, though a part of her wondered if having a sibling would have eased some of the burden.

"I also dug into the details of the will. Legal secretaries should be more discreet on social media. But it simply confirms what Sarah told you. She's entitled to an annual allowance of two hundred thousand for each year she was married to him. And if she wants, she can opt for a lump sum instead. Plus, she gets to keep any gifts Devlin gave her during their marriage."

"That must have been one tight prenup," Rhianne commented.

Considering the immense wealth amassed by Devlin Parkes, the sum seemed rather meagre.

"Most of his assets are tied up in a complex trust fund, so even without the prenup, she wouldn't have received much more."

"What you're saying is that he was worth more alive than dead to her," Rhianne said. And Sarah was definitely someone who knew which side her bread was buttered on. "Well, at least that means we can eliminate —" Her sentence trailed off as Kai squeezed her hand twice.

Rhianne turned her gaze towards the doorway, and there, making her grand entrance was Andrea Parkes. Andrea appeared youthful and could easily be mistaken for a woman in her late thirties. Clad in a dusty pink gown that accentuated her slender figure, her honey blonde hair elegantly styled in a French braid bun, she projected an air of sophistication. Adorned with dazzling long earrings and a necklace, she was a vision of glamour.

Rhianne released Kai's hand and approached Andrea as she took a glass of champagne from a passing waiter. Putting on her best polite society smile, Rhianne greeted her, "Welcome, Ms —?" As they came face to face, the veneer of youth faded, revealing a woman who had clearly taken measures to preserve her appearance. Still, she was definitely good-looking, something that seemed common in their family.

Andrea responded with an instinctive smile, though Rhianne could tell she was trying to figure out who she was. "Andrea Parkes." She extended her hand.

"I'm Rhianne, Esther Broadwater's daughter." Rhianne shook her hand, feeling the limpness of Andrea's grip.

Recognition sparked in Andrea's eyes. Glancing back, Rhianne noticed Kai had hung back, probably thinking a one-on-one chat would loosen her lips a bit more.

"So, how are your children holding up?" Rhianne asked, adopting a caring tone. It was a risky move, but Rhianne was banking on the fact that her mother had her finger on the pulse of everything happening in town and everyone knew it.

Andrea's voice lowered. "Oh, they each have their own way of dealing with it, you know. Rita, always a daddy's girl, is

CHAPTER 24

throwing herself into the business, saying it's what her father would have wanted." A wry smile tugged at Andrea's lips. "And she's not wrong, you know. Devlin never let anything get in the way of business. She was going to join me tonight, but had other commitments." Andrea gestured towards the venue with her hand adorned in flashy gold rings. "She's got a real passion for education and sits on the board of her father's old school."

Rhianne nodded, offering an encouraging smile. "How wonderful of her."

"And then there's Arthur, bless him. He defied Devlin's wishes to reconnect with me and helped me reconnect with Rita. It's been such a joy to be a part of their lives again."

Rhianne felt a twinge of unease as something in the back of her mind started nagging at her.

Andrea eyed Rhianne in speculation. Whatever thought she had must have pleased her, because Andrea's smile widened. "You should meet Arthur. He's now the CEO of Parkes Construction Enterprises. He's a handsome boy who's happy to let others lead him."

"I'd love to meet him." Rhianne mustered an air of sincerity. She mentally gave herself a pat on the back. Maybe she was improving at this whole 'feigning interest' game. "Is he here tonight?"

Andrea's smile faltered momentarily, but she quickly regained her composure. "No, he's not here, but if you give me your phone number, I can arrange for him to call you," she offered.

"Rhianne, my dear." The sound of her mother's voice came as a welcome interruption. Rhianne had to give her credit, she had impeccable timing. "Hello, Andrea. It's lovely to see you," Her mother approached, extending a hand for a brief handshake. "Please do let me know if there's anything I can assist with, or if you have a preferred address for flower deliveries."

It was a close call, but Rhianne managed to suppress a snort. Her mother took hold of her elbow and steered her away. Given that she'd saved her from having to fend off a mother set on finding a suitable match for her son, she went along without complaint.

Her mother led her to a small group, and Rhianne found herself facing three men who bore a striking resemblance to each other. It was clear they were all part of the same family. "Rhianne, you may remember Senator Norton," her mother said.

Nope, definitely not, but she offered him a tight smile nonetheless. The grey-haired senator nodded his head in acknowledgement.

"And this is his son, Stewart, and his grandson, Brett."

Stewart sized her up, while Brett extended his hand. He had a friendly smile. As she shook his hand, Rhianne's senses tingled, capturing the distinct aroma of forest and musk that enveloped him.

They were werewolves. Figures! Rhianne couldn't help but let out a sigh. Her mother was pulling out all the stops to find her a suitable match. Having struck out in the powerful male witch department, she had apparently moved on to setting her up with shifters for a bit of political matchmaking. Rhianne wondered if a vampire was next on the list.

"Esther, my dear, so wonderful to see you," Nel's voice resonated around them as he draped a strong arm around Rhianne's shoulders. "Stewart, it's been a couple of weeks

CHAPTER 24

since I last saw you at the club. I hope you'll drop by again soon." A perplexed expression formed on Senator Norton's brow. "I do apologise, but I'm afraid I need to whisk Rhianne away for a few moments."

Her mother's stern gaze promised repercussions, but Nel's cheery demeanour didn't crack. He deftly guided her away from the group and towards where Kai stood.

"Thanks for the rescue," Rhianne said.

Nel offered her a small bow. "I always aim to please." He casually adjusted his cufflinks. "Besides, not only am I derailing Esther's machinations, but as a bonus, I'm also helping raise funds for a halfling's school."

The words reverberated in the depths of her mind, and suddenly everything clicked into place. Rhianne snapped her fingers, causing both Kai and Nel to blink in surprise.

"That's it!" A wide grin spread across her face. "I know who did it."

CHAPTER 25

Nel and Kai fixed their curious gazes on her.

Nel spoke first. "Okay, out with it."

Rhianne glanced around, taking in the bustling atmosphere of the party. There were too many prying ears. "Not here."

"My place," Nel suggested. "It's closest."

Without hesitation, the three of them made their way out, Rhianne feeling the weight of her mother's disapproving gaze burning into the back of her neck. She resisted the urge to look back.

They drove through the city, the streetlights lighting up their way. Soon, they were in Nel's building's underground car park. Going up in the lift, Rhianne's mind was buzzing, putting together all the pieces of what she'd figured out, a jittery energy coursing through her, her nerves tingling with excitement.

As they stepped into Nel's apartment, he headed straight for the kitchen and came back with a bottle of wine, a jug of water, and some glasses. He arranged them on the coffee table, creating a makeshift bar.

CHAPTER 25

Nel leaned back in his chair. "I must admit, I'm a bit disappointed that I couldn't offer more help with the investigation."

Rhianne shot him a sideways glance. "Is that because you feel left out or because you missed your chance with Andrea?"

"Why not both?" He grabbed a glass of wine for himself.

Kai, on the other hand, opted for a glass of water, just like Rhianne. Smart move. They needed him sharp and focused.

"Or was it missing out on the thrill of getting intimate with a potential murderer?" Rhianne said.

Nel choked on his wine, resulting in a fit of coughing. He hastily retrieved a handkerchief from his pocket and wiped his lips, trying to regain his composure.

Rhianne laughed, and a subtle twitch appeared at the corner of Kai's mouth.

"For the record, she wouldn't be the first one," Nel said once he'd recovered. "Did Andrea do it?"

She shook her head. "No, but I need proof."

She turned her gaze towards Kai.

"You know I'm happy to help." He held up his palms.

Rhianne smiled. "Don't worry, I'm pretty sure you can get most of what we need without breaking any rules."

Kai scratched his chin. Rhianne held her breath, waiting for his reaction.

"No time like the present. Let's get to work."

Rhianne wrapped her arms around him in a hug. "Thank you," she whispered, planting a soft kiss on his cheek. The warmth that filled her heart was gentle and soothing.

"Thank me when we find the data." He rolled his shoulders.

Nel took off his jacket and loosened his bow tie. "Tell me what you need."

"I might as well head back unless you've got some high-powered computers here?" He gave a half-shrug.

Nel grinned. "How many do you need?"

It turned out that Nel had an office equipped with three computers, which Kai deemed sufficient. Rhianne couldn't help but stifle a budding grin, while Nel huffed and grumbled at the assessment.

As the clock approached five in the morning, Kai lifted his head from the computer, his fingers kneading the back of his neck.

"Got what we need," he announced.

Rhianne's eyes fluttered open at the sound of his voice, and she rubbed them, having dozed off in her chair not long ago. Then his words registered in her mind. "You've got it?"

She shot up, her breathing quickened as she leaned over his shoulder to catch a glimpse of the frozen image on the screen.

Nel sauntered over, looking annoyingly chipper, completely oblivious to how Rhianne was barely keeping her eyelids propped open. Nel had his hands clasped behind his back as he studied the image. A smile flickered across his face. "I believe you should contact Ms Austin and have her arrange a meeting with the police."

"It's a bit early, isn't it?" Rhianne yawned.

Nel gave a short and amused laugh. "Lawyers don't sleep, they bill by the hour."

In the end, Rhianne figured they could all use a good breakfast, so Nel took the lead and ordered some food. By the time Rhianne dialled Marissa's number, it was the more civilised hour of six in the morning. On the second ring, Marissa answered. "Good morning, Rhianne." Her tone was brisk as ever.

Rhianne wondered if Nel was right about Marissa never

CHAPTER 25

sleeping. "You're up early."

"Rise early, work hard, strike oil," Marissa said.

Rhianne raised an eyebrow but decided to cut straight to the point. "We know who the murderer is, and we have proof."

"Where are you?" Marissa asked, and Rhianne provided the address. "Ten minutes," Marissa ended the call.

Rhianne glanced at her smartphone. One day, she swore she'd be the one hanging up on Marissa.

Twelve minutes later, the concierge informed Nel that their visitor had arrived.

Marissa entered, a heavy briefcase in tow. She surveyed the surroundings, taking in the tasteful furnishings and the view. Her gaze settled on Nel. "Nice place you've got here. Looks like you can afford a top-notch lawyer." She handed Nel her card.

Nel's lips curled into a sly smile and he extended his hand, which Marissa shook. Rhianne winced and held her breath, knowing Nel was testing Marissa's boundaries with physical contact. She made a mental note to have a serious talk with Nel about not using his charms on her friends.

"I'm Nel Lamont."

Marissa stiffened momentarily before stepping back and smoothing down her skirt.

"Marissa Austin," She took a deep breath and straightened her posture. She then turned her gaze to Rhianne and Kai, nodding decisively. "So, where's this proof you mentioned?"

Maybe gargoyles had some resistance to the incubus lure but Rhianne still gave her points for a quick recovery. Then again Marissa was as tough as nails, so she probably had developed her resistance to anything.

Kai handed over the printouts he had gathered while

Rhianne walked Marissa through the intricate details of the case — the who, the how, and the why. Granted, the "why" was mostly speculative on Rhianne's part. It was hard to put herself in the shoes of someone willing to kill in cold blood.

"This is premeditated murder." There was a hint of surprise behind Marissa's cool gaze. She then switched to a look of impressed curiosity. "Nice job. You cracked the case while the police were busy running around in circles, and you've got enough proof for the prosecutor to start slapping handcuffs."

Rhianne closed her eyes and let out a sigh of relief. "You think we have enough?"

"Are you kidding? The prosecutor will love you. It doesn't get much better than this. But in the end, it's the jury that determines who the better lawyer is — the defence or the prosecution."

Rhianne shot her an alarmed look. "Would you defend a murderer?"

Something like pity crossed Marissa's face and she patted Rhianne's hand. "Murderers deserve a defence too, but in this case, even if I wanted to, which I don't," she said with a wry smile at Rhianne's frown, "I shouldn't. My client has also been accused of the murder, so it could be seen as a bias or, at worst, a conflict of interest."

"What's our next move?" Kai's tired voice cut in, putting a pause on any comeback Rhianne might have had.

"Now I organise a meeting with Senior Sergeant Johannes, you, Rhianne and myself." She paused, turning to Nel with a knowing smile. "Sorry, but you'd be too distracting."

Nel let out a chuckle. "Noted. I'm sure Kai will capture it on video for me to enjoy later."

Marissa wagged her finger in admonishment. "Not without

CHAPTER 25

the police's consent, and I highly doubt they'll grant it."

Nel and Kai exchanged a quick glance. Rhianne didn't think Kai would break the rules just to please Nel, but she knew he had a knack for finding alternative solutions. A yawn escaped Rhianne's lips, and Kai yawned as well.

Marissa furrowed her brow. "I'll schedule the appointment for later this afternoon."

Rhianne started to protest, eager to hand over the evidence to the police as soon as possible. But Marissa cut her off.

"Don't even think about it. You and Kai need rest. You have to be sharp for the interview. Detective Johannes won't be happy that you beat him to it, and he'll be tough to handle. You'll need all your wits about you."

"You can both stay here; I have plenty of space."

Nel surprised Rhianne with his offer and she looked at Kai.

Kai rubbed his shoulder, clearly worn out. "If you have a spare room where I can crash, that would be safer than me driving."

Exhaustion had taken the shine out of his eyes and his hair stood on end in disarray.

Marissa nodded. "I'll arrange the appointment and send you the details. Get some rest." With that, she gathered her briefcase and saw herself out.

"You can take your usual room, Rhianne. I'll show Kai to his."

"Thanks, wake us up at lunchtime so we don't miss the appointment."

Nel made a non-committal grunt and Rhianne headed straight for the room. She was too exhausted to bother with a shower. "Later," she thought, as she collapsed onto the bed.

"Later" ended up being three in the afternoon. Rhianne

cursed under her breath and reached for her smartphone. Marissa's message was concise: "Northern Beaches police station at five o'clock. See you then."

Rhianne breathed a sigh of relief, glad they hadn't missed the appointment. She took a shower and changed into a set of clothes she had stashed in Nel's apartment.

She followed her nose to the kitchen where wonderful aromas were emanating, expecting Nel. Instead, she saw that Kai was cooking. His hair was still wet and he was wearing different clothes. Either he'd gone home and changed or Nel had lent him some clothes.

Kai must have sensed her because he turned around, frying pan in hand. "Hello, sleepy head. How are you feeling?" His eyes were once again bright and his smile was relaxed.

Rhianne stretched her arms above her head. "Slept more than I thought. I was worried we had missed the meeting with the police."

"Nel got a message earlier from Marissa, so he knew we had time. He wanted to give us a chance to recover." He turned back to the stove and flipped a pancake. "I've made pancakes, so feel free to add whatever toppings you like."

On her way to the cupboards, she paused to plant a kiss on his cheek and give him a tight hug. "I'll burn the pancakes," he warned her.

"Where's Nel?" She pulled out strawberry jam and honey.

"He said he had a meeting with a client," Kai said.

She frowned, puzzled. Nel rarely met clients in the early afternoon — he probably needed to feed. Letting out a sigh, she rubbed her temples, remembering she hadn't checked in with Toto about the incubus lure. The recent attack on Toto had thrown her off, and she'd been wrapped up in trying to

CHAPTER 25

figure out something about the raven shifter. As if that wasn't enough brain gymnastics, linking her attackers to the murder case was getting more complicated by the minute. And the elusive elf with the portal? That was a mystery she figured she'd crack around the same time pigs started their flight training. Lost in her thoughts, she realised she'd gobbled down a whole pancake without even noticing. Glancing at Kai, she saw him patiently watching her.

"A penny for your thoughts." He smiled.

She grinned back. "Just thinking these pancakes could've used a seatbelt."

He chuckled, his eyes twinkling. "You made them vanish like a magic trick. I've never seen pancakes stand less of a chance."

Rhianne felt her ears heat up.

Kai reached over and gently held her hand. "Looks like I'll need to make you another round of pancakes. They're the ideal breakfast, right?" He wiggled his eyebrows, drawing a bright laugh from Rhianne.

"Count me in!"

After finishing their breakfast, Kai offered to give Rhianne a lift to her apartment. On the way, they talked over their plans for the day. They agreed that Rhianne would take her motorbike to the police station later on. With the Parkes case taking up so much of his time, Kai had his own tasks to get back to after their police meeting.

Marissa was waiting for them at the entrance to the police station. She rubbed her hands with glee. "This is going to be fun."

Rhianne made a face. "Your definition of fun needs looking into."

"Johannes was in a total snit about this. He demanded an immediate meeting," Marissa's hard eyes told her how well that had gone over with her. "I told him to cool his heels. After all, they haven't made much progress themselves."

Rhianne could only imagine the sour mood Johannes would be in, and she licked her lips nervously. It was time to face the music. They were escorted inside by a young constable who seemed relieved to be rid of them as they entered the conference room. Her eyes scanned the room, and she noticed Kai's reaction upon spotting Lisa at the table. His body tensed, and his face hardened. In return, Lisa met Rhianne's gaze with a glare full of hostility.

Johannes sat a few seats away, his jaw clenched tightly as he sneered at them. He gestured for them to take their seats, adjusting his jacket lapels with irritation.

"Good afternoon, Senior Sergeant and Sergeant." Marissa's tone teetered on the edge of disdainful, but then again, that could be her default setting when dealing with the police.

"Shall we dispense with the pleasantries?" Lisa leaned back in her seat and crossed her arms. "We are busy conducting our investigations so I sincerely hope you're not wasting our time."

"Wouldn't dream of it, officer," Marissa said. "After all it's our taxes that pay your salaries."

Kai settled into his seat, placing a thick folder and his laptop on the desk before him. He glanced at Rhianne, who took a deep breath to steady herself. "We have reason to believe that Rita Parkes is responsible for her father's murder, specifically by poisoning him in his office."

Lisa snorted loudly. "Belief is a fool's wager."

"Like your belief that Alice was the murderer?" Rhianne

CHAPTER 25

retorted sharply.

"We had strong suspicions." Her voice lacked any hint of apology.

"We have evidence, not just suspicion," Rhianne said.

Johannes perked up, a glimmer of interest shining in his eyes, while Lisa fixed her with a piercing glare.

Kai chimed in, "Recently, I discovered that Rita Parkes was orchestrating a scheme to implicate her brother Arthur in embezzlement."

Lisa leaned forward, poised to interrupt. But Kai held out his hand, pre-empting her. He extracted a document from the folder and slid it across the table. His tone remained professional, yet icy.

"Before anyone suggests I was hacking," he said. "Let me be clear: Ms Parkes hired me for this investigation. Our agreement specifically permits me to reveal any evidence of criminal behaviour."

Lisa's jaw snapped shut.

"And a crime was committed. Rita Parkes attempted to set her brother up with not just embezzlement but also tax fraud. She thought she could outsmart us, but even the cleverest criminals leave behind traces. Her overconfidence proved to be her downfall. She should have hired a less competent tech mage." Kai said.

One corner of Rhianne's mouth twitched.

"That doesn't make her a murderer." Despite Johannes' gruffness, there was curiosity in the statement.

"No, it doesn't," Rhianne agreed. "But it does raise the question of why she would go to such lengths." She paused for emphasis. "The staged embezzlement took place a week before her father's murder, carefully designed to force Devlin

Parkes' hand." She interlocked her fingers and rested her elbows on the table. "Devlin Parkes was an old-fashioned sexist bigot, convinced that women were incapable of running a business. Rita spent her entire life trying to prove to him that she was worthy of being his rightful successor. By all accounts, she's incredibly accomplished and as ruthless as her father. She's definitely got the skills and determination to be a successful CEO."

Rhianne cleared her throat, and Marissa stood up to fetch a water jug and glasses, which she filled and placed in front of Rhianne and Kai.

Lisa saw an opening during the brief silence and couldn't resist voicing her opinion. "So, she was jealous of her brother, big deal. She could have simply worked harder and eventually achieved her goals."

"She wouldn't have, not in her father's company anyway. Devlin Parkes had this thing for keeping it all in the family. He was paranoid and didn't trust outsiders. That made her think if he found out Arthur was embezzling from the company, he would disown him."

They had talked it over and agreed not to mention that Rita had attempted to prove that Arthur wasn't Devlin's son but she had been unable to find any proof.

"I think that Devlin laughed in her face and told her he'd speak to Arthur and correct the mistake. After all, Arthur had taken money in the past and paid it back."

Whether Arthur had intended to pay back the money or been forced by Devlin's intervention, they'd never know for sure.

"He probably told her that even if Arthur wasn't around, the CEO job wouldn't go to her." Rhianne could almost see

CHAPTER 25

the scene playing out in front of her.

Johannes crossed his arms, a sceptical expression on his face.

Lisa snickered. "You're contradicting your own argument. If she was so confident that her embezzlement lies would convince her father, why would she have needed the poison?"

Rhianne lifted her chin and met Lisa's gaze head-on. "Because the intended victim was Arthur."

CHAPTER 26

The room fell into stunned silence as Rhianne's declaration hung in the air. Johannes and Lisa exchanged disbelieving glances, their faces displaying a mix of shock and surprise. They both erupted with a barrage of questions, their voices overlapping in a chaotic symphony. Johannes stood up and leaned forward, using his massive frame to loom over them.

It was Marissa's booming voice that cut through the noise. "Sit down!" She hadn't moved from her seat, yet Johannes sat back down. "Let her finish."

"You see, Rita Parkes is quite smart. A person like her always has a plan B," Rhianne continued. "If her father didn't come around to her way of thinking, she had a plan to take out Arthur and step into his shoes. But it turns out, her conversation with her father probably made it clear that he wouldn't let a woman lead the company, Arthur or no Arthur. Devlin Parkes had already lined up another man from within the company, someone he thought could fill Arthur's shoes if needed. It was the final blow."

"That's just speculation," Lisa spat.

CHAPTER 26

Rhianne tilted her head slightly. "Yes and no. The fallback successor is Ralph —" She glanced at Kai.

"Johnson," Kai supplied without even glancing at his notes.

Lisa refused to let it go. "Still speculation."

Rhianne gave her a wry smile. "The fact that he had another successor waiting in the wings? I think you'll find that Ralph's latest contract confirms it." She held up her palm, fully expecting Lisa to raise another objection. "It's amazing what people discuss on social media," she added drily. "Even cybersecurity-conscious CTOs like to boast."

According to Kai's findings, the announcement of the Deputy CEO position was scheduled for the week Devlin had died. Rhianne had no doubt that Arthur would disclose the appointment to the market as soon as possible, perhaps after the funeral.

Johannes looked pensive as he rubbed his chin. "The forensic pathologist said that making the poison required a lab."

Rhianne nodded, acknowledging his point with a small smile. She mentally reminded herself to get Isobel some extra pastries next time. "Like I said earlier, Rita was pretty accomplished. She aced advanced chemistry and biology in high school. All she needed was a decent lab, and a school lab would have done the trick." Rhianne had to tread carefully now. "Rita Parkes is on the board of her late father's old school and visits regularly." She found it both pitiful and sad how Rita had desperately sought her father's approval. "Somehow, she got her hands on the keys to the school's lab, and that's where she concocted the poison."

Lisa's eyes gleamed dangerously. "You can't possibly have proof of that." She shot Kai a glance that screamed 'gotcha.'

Rhianne didn't react. "Actually, we do." She disregarded Lisa's gasp of surprise and indignation. "We have CCTV footage from the building opposite that shows her going into the school late at night, a few days before her father was killed."

Lisa slammed her palms down on the table, glaring at Rhianne and then Kai in turn. "That's illegal."

Marissa casually inspected her fingernails and didn't even bother looking at Lisa as she responded. "It's not if you have the permission of the building owner for the footage."

The police would never discover that Nel owned the building through a series of companies. It was a stroke of luck, assuming Nel hadn't somehow bought it last night.

Marissa continued in a monotonous tone, "The camera was aimed at the street, which is perfectly legal. It so happens that it also caught a view of the school's exterior — a lucky break."

Lisa's face and neck flushed red with frustration.

"Given it's the summer holidays, there's a fair chance of finding her fingerprints in the lab, maybe even some evidence of what she was up to," Rhianne suggested.

This part was more of an educated guess, but she was pretty sure Rita hadn't expected anyone to pinpoint the poison that killed her father. Maybe Rita thought the post-mortem would take a while, long enough for any traces of the poison to disappear. That was where she miscalculated. She might have bounced back from this if she hadn't been so set on removing her brother and taking over as CEO.

"I'd get on that as soon as possible if I were you."

Johannes drummed his fingers on the table, his gaze fixed unwaveringly on Rhianne's face. "We haven't placed her at the scene of the crime." It wasn't so much a question as it was

CHAPTER 26

a challenge, demanding more evidence to support the claim.

Rhianne glanced at Kai, who cleared his throat. "During my investigation into the false embezzlement, I had complete access to the employees' movements in the building, including CCTV footage." Rita had not specified a timeframe for the investigation, which meant Kai could freely conduct his tech searches up until the time of their meeting. "The codes for transferring large sums of money were kept in the safe in Devlin's office, so I focused on identifying individuals who could have accessed them. On the day of his murder, Rita went up to his floor at eight in the evening and returned to her floor below at eight twenty. She then left the building shortly after. No one else entered or exited Devlin's office until his secretary discovered Devlin Parkes' body the following day."

She left out the part about Rita trying to wipe the footage but Kai had recovered it.

Lisa bristled. "Why would she kill her father?"

Despite the mounting evidence, it was clear that Lisa's personal feelings were clouding her judgement. She simply didn't want to accept that they had been beaten to the solution.

"She had nothing to gain."

Rhianne leaned forward. "With her father deceased and her brother discredited, she thought she'd become the CEO."

Her belief was that Devlin's refusal to acknowledge Rita as a capable successor had pushed her over the edge, causing all logic to fly out the window.

Letting out a low whistle, Johannes' face broke into a slow smile. He looked quite handsome when he wasn't being so condescending and overbearing. Clasping his hands together, he turned to Lisa, who had tightened her lips. "Okay, go ahead and get the search warrant for the school. With any luck, we'll uncover some useful evidence before the cleaners clear everything away."

Lisa stood up, trying to maintain a defiant look as she made her exit.

Johannes turned to face Rhianne and Kai. "Just a heads-up, when you're sending in your invoices, drop my name as you forward them to the department. I'll handle the approval. And, could you also include electronic copies along with the hard copies? That would be really helpful."

"Already done for mine." Kai didn't bother to reach for his smartphone.

Johannes didn't seem surprised by Kai's prompt answer. "We appreciate your help on behalf of the police department. Do you prefer to keep your involvement anonymous?"

Rhianne's throat tightened at the mere thought of her name being plastered all over the news in connection with the case. The last thing she wanted was the scrutiny and attention that would come with it.

"Keeping our names out of the spotlight is key for our work down the line." Kai cast a sidelong glance at Rhianne.

She met his gaze with a firm nod.

"Great!" Johannes was likely pleased he could take full credit, at least outside of his superiors.

Marissa must have had the same thought, as she snorted. "I'll also be sending my invoice for today."

Johannes' smile dimmed. Marissa wouldn't come cheap.

Rhianne felt a wave of relief wash over her now that it was all over. She said goodbye to Marissa, promising to meet for lunch the following week.

Kai took her hand and pulled her closer by her waist. "I wish I didn't have to work tonight."

CHAPTER 26

"Tomorrow night. My place."

Kai flashed her a lopsided grin. "That's a date!" He leaned in, their lips meeting in a slow and tender kiss, a promise of more.

Feeling a mix of fatigue and exhilaration, Rhianne hopped on her motorbike. The day had been a whirlwind of triumph and accomplishment. Mystery number one was officially solved. With a satisfied grin, she rode towards the nursery.

As she parked her bike and stepped off, she was greeted by the sight of Toto bounding down the stairs, wagging his tail.

Bending down, Rhianne greeted him with a smile. "Hello, Toto. We did it!" She pumped her fist in excitement. "We gave all the evidence to the police. Rita Parkes will probably be arrested within the next few days."

Toto wagged his tail and danced around her legs. "Excellent. Shall we proceed upstairs? I have procured everything for the trap."

* * *

Rhianne was roused from a deep sleep by a persistent alarm. She rubbed her eyes and reached for the bedside lamp, casting a dim glow across the room. Hastily slipping into a pair of jeans and a t-shirt, she grabbed a lantern and made her way down to the private nursery. As she approached the locked entrance, her gaze fell upon a large cage. The bars glistened in the lantern's light, reflecting a metallic sheen. Inside the cage, a raven was furiously pecking at the metal bars, its feathers bristling with agitation.

Rhianne leaned against the door, setting down the lantern beside her. The raven made another futile attempt to bite the cage, only to recoil from the bars.

"I wouldn't advise doing that," Rhianne warned. "Those bars are made of silver." Just where Toto managed to get the cage from was a mystery. "The more you bite it, the worse it's going to be for you." The raven tilted its head, and Rhianne crossed her arms. "Let's skip the games. You've disturbed my sleep, and honestly, I'd much rather go back to bed and sort this out in the morning."

The raven let out an indignant squawk.

"The silver will weaken you, and by then, you might be more willing to talk." Extensive exposure to silver was damaging to shifters, but a night would do nothing more than tire her out. Rhianne found herself not caring all that much. She hardened her voice. "You hurt my dog badly." She stumbled slightly on the word "dog," hoping Toto wouldn't be upset with her for using it. "You tried to spy on me, invading my home. So, here's what we'll do: you turn back into your human form, and we have a chat."

The raven glared defiantly, its eyes narrowing. Rhianne shrugged, picked up the lantern, and began to walk away.

She had only taken a few steps when a female voice called out from behind her, "Wait! You can't leave me here all night."

A triumphant smile crept across Rhianne's face as she spun around. Confined uncomfortably within the cage, with her legs bent in front of her body, was a naked Sergeant Lisa Chen.

"Well, well, if it isn't Lisa," Rhianne said with feigned cheerfulness. "What a surprise to have you drop by." She approached the cage. She wanted to pump her fist; her suspicions had been right.

Lisa growled. "Let me out! You're illegally holding a police officer. As soon as I get out and tell the department, you'll be

CHAPTER 26

arrested and thrown in jail."

Rhianne clucked her tongue disapprovingly. "I don't think you're in any position to be making threats. First off, you came onto my property uninvited. That's home invasion, unless you have a search warrant?" She smirked at Lisa, who squirmed uncomfortably within the confines of the cage. "And you're assuming I plan to let you go."

Lisa's eyes widened. "You wouldn't!" She had tried for an indignant tone but her shaky voice gave away her fear.

Rhianne fixed a piercing glare on Lisa. "Why would you attack my dog? That spell you used was seriously nasty. And I'm pretty sure it wasn't legal."

Lisa responded by flipping Rhianne the middle finger and accidentally smacked the cage bars she had been carefully avoiding. "Ouch!" she yelped.

"I'm sure I don't need to remind you that the longer you stay in that cage, the more susceptible you'll be to silver burns."

Lisa pulled her hand back and curled up, hugging her legs. Rhianne almost felt a pang of sympathy, but pushed it aside. Lisa had hurt Toto and could've killed him — that was unforgivable.

"The dumb dog wouldn't quit barking, and in my rush to shut him up, I accidentally cast the wrong damn spell."

Rhianne knitted her brows, the dumb dog comment wasn't winning Lisa any points. "Seriously, how many offensive spells do you carry around with you? And how on earth did you get your hands on them?"

Lisa must have recognised it was pointless keeping silent. "As a police officer, I come across all sorts of people from various backgrounds."

"So, they pay you off to ignore their illegal activities?"

Rhianne countered.

Lisa choked out a response, indignant. "Some of them are crucial informants. I've solved more than a few cases with information from those connections.

"Save those excuses for your senior officers. I'm not buying it. Why?" Rhianne demanded.

Lisa defiantly jutted her chin out. "Why what?"

Rhianne's scowl deepened. "Why are you spying on me? Who are you working for?"

Lisa touched the base of her neck and squinted at Rhianne. "What on earth are you talking about? I'm not working for anyone." The fury on Lisa's face was evident as her features contorted with anger. "You've charmed Kai, haven't you? I haven't been able to prove it, but I'm certain you've put some spell on him. There's no way he'd be so infatuated with you otherwise!"

Rhianne couldn't contain her laughter and it erupted from her with such force that tears welled up in her eyes. "You're absolutely bonkers." After struggling to regain her composure, she looked at Lisa and a surprising wave of pity washed over her. "You've been hanging around with all those dodgy characters for too long, and it's starting to show."

Lisa shook her head, still glaring at Rhianne with accusation in her eyes.

Rhianne sighed. "I suggest you have a word with your contacts. The love spell you believe I've cast? It's not possible. Only incubi and succubi can make someone fall madly in love, and I'm neither." Rhianne took a deep breath, knowing she had one final question that needed to be asked. She directed an intense gaze toward Lisa. "You'd better be truthful with me, did you set those thugs on me?"

CHAPTER 26

Lisa swallowed hard and nervously bit her lip. "I — I didn't mean for them to hurt Kai. My intention was only to frighten you."

"They had knives, Lisa!" Rhianne's voice rose with a mix of anger and disbelief.

Lisa's shoulders slumped, and she shrank in on herself.

"And what about the elf?" Rhianne pressed, her eyes narrowing.

Lisa's face froze for a second. "What elf? I have a shifter contact. He organised the whole thing. He has lots of contacts so maybe he subcontracted."

Lisa may have been a skilled actress, but she sounded like she was telling the truth. Rhianne let out a weary sigh and pushed herself off the wall. Either way, it seemed unlikely that she would get any more useful information from her.

"Listen carefully. I'm going to open the cage," Rhianne said. Lisa's eyes widened with anticipation. "But here's the deal: you're going to leave right now and stay away from my place for good." A cunning expression crossed Lisa's face. Rhianne noticed and smirked. "Oh, and by the way, our heart-to-heart tonight? It's been recorded. It's currently enjoying a cloud vacation." Behind her back, Rhianne crossed her fingers, hoping that Toto had managed to capture the entire conversation. She would definitely ask Kai to install surveillance cameras soon. Lisa's face fell as she glanced around. "If you think of crossing me or anyone I care about again, that recording is going straight to your superiors. Got it?" Rhianne's voice took on a low, almost growling tone, her teeth bared in a warning.

Lisa gave a single nod. "Will you tell Kai?"

"None of your business."

Lisa swallowed and nodded. Rhianne stepped back and the cage unlocked itself. It took a few moments for Lisa to transform into her raven form, and she stumbled as she walked out of the cage. Without casting a glance back, she took flight, soaring into the night sky.

Unbeknown to Lisa, an eagle soared high above, keeping a vigilant watch on her. Toto would ensure that Lisa caused no further trouble tonight.

She still didn't know who the elf was who glamoured her attackers, but his race might have been a coincidence. Nor did she know the identity or motive of the Shadow who had been spying on her private garden.

There was always tomorrow for doing more detective work. It had been surprisingly satisfying working it all out. Huh! Maybe she should take Nel up on his offer and become an information detective.

Rhianne looked up to the sky. The stars shone brightly and a quarter moon took centre stage. She'd sleep on it.

Epilogue

Marissa remained tight-lipped about whether she had been approached to take on Rita's defence. Regardless, a swanky law firm had taken up the case, all funded by Arthur. It went to show that family, whether by blood or otherwise, sticks together.

Personally, Rhianne believed that Arthur was being too forgiving. She was pretty certain that Rita had not only contemplated killing him originally but would have made another attempt if he stood in her way.

Andrea Parkes was capitalising on the publicity, making appearances on television and oscillating between portraying herself as the distressed mother of a child driven to murder by her own ruthless father and boasting about her philanthropy to the audience.

Arthur had also enlisted the help of a formidable PR firm to salvage the reputation of Parkes Construction Enterprises and portray his sister as a victim. Arthur was proving that he was much more than the flaky, irresponsible person everyone had pegged him to be.

According to Marissa, given the calibre of the law firm

representing Rita, she might end up with a shorter jail sentence than she deserved. It was going to take a few months for the case to go through the court's system though.

Rhianne had spoken to Nel and agreed to undertake investigative work for him on an ad hoc basis. It turned out that Nel was more than just a titan of information currency; he also took on "investigations" when he deemed them worthwhile. The specifics of his operations remained vague, and she had made it clear that she wouldn't give up her own business. Nel had readily agreed. She still had her doubts about the whole thing, but it was, after all, just a trial.

She gave Kai a bare-bones version of her confrontation with Lisa. Kai wanted to show the footage to the superintendent, but Rhianne was against involving the police. She didn't want them probing into the silver cage, Toto, or her plants. He had pursed his lips, nodded once and then never brought it up again. Shortly after, he installed a comprehensive system of cameras throughout the nursery and around her apartment, along with an alarm system.

She was eager to slip into a cosy cardigan and start preparing dinner. As she opened the door, a strong magical presence tingled her senses and she froze in her tracks. Leaning against the opposite wall, the silhouette of a man became distinct. She switched on the light, and he blinked. He wore a traditional green elf vest, tights, and long boots. Leather bands crisscrossed his strong arms, but they were otherwise bare. A long single braid of blond hair hung over his shoulder, and his emerald green eyes shone.

His beauty was ethereal and Rhianne bit her cheek. "What are you doing here?"

EPILOGUE

"Hello, Daughter."

Get ready to dive back into another mystery or two with Rhianne and her eclectic crew in Pack of Lies, Book 2 of the Green Witch Mystery series.

Notes to Readers

Dear Fantastic Reader,

I hope you enjoyed this book. If you found it entertaining, then please consider sharing your thoughts with a review.

Your feedback helps other readers find their next literary adventure.

So, grab your metaphorical pen (or keyboard) and unleash your inner critic, comedian, or motivational speaker in your review. Your words might just make my day!

With gratitude and a virtual high-five,

P L

Mailing list

If you would like to receive fun updates from me, subscribe to my newsletter. Don't worry, I won't overload your inbox; it's just monthly. I'd love to connect with you! As a thank you, you will receive the prequel to the Green Witch Mystery series.

Losing your head just got a lot more literal

Green witch Rhianne Alkenn has her hands full with not one, but two puzzling cases. A leak of confidential information threatens the Moonshadow pack, putting her best friend, incubus Nel, in a tight spot! And the elven queen's best friend has been murdered. Rhianne's hoping to solve the murder and quickly, because the phrase 'Off with her head' is playing on repeat in her mind!

With the help of the enigmatic coroner Isobel, and her tech mage boyfriend Kai, Rhianne sets up to find out the truth.

Her mission? Clear Nel's name and keep her head firmly on her shoulders. Sounds simple enough, right? What could possibly go wrong?

Continue the adventure in Pack of Lies

Acknowledgements

Writing this book has been a labour of love, made possible with the unwavering support of many. My husband, who believes in me unconditionally (and read the story from beginning to end), my mum, who instilled in me a love for the written word, and all my friends who offered encouragement and cheered me on; a big hello to the 'Trio."

I'd like to extend special thanks to Percy, who doesn't read fiction but read my manuscript anyway, and even said I had done *him* a favour by broadening his horizons.

And, last but certainly not least, to my readers, I extend my heartfelt gratitude. It is my sincere hope that you derive as much joy from reading this story as I did from crafting it. Thank you.

Also by P L Matthews

The Green Witch Mystery Series
Poisoned Leaves
Pack of Lies
Blood Debt
Deadly Forest
Courting Danger

The Digital Detective Mystery Series
Murder by Code (Dec 24)

About the Author

In Sydney's urban jungle, this wife, mum, and hopeless romantic once herded corporate cats as a project director—a job that sharpened her skills in intrigue and (non-lethal) murder. Now she's busy plotting the demise of fictional characters in her enchanting urban fantasies and murder mysteries.

When not infusing her stories with humour, light and a touch of romance, you'll find her attempting to ride waves and embracing the art of the wipeout, jamming tunes with her husband, or valiantly trying to restore order to the delightful chaos that is family life.

You can connect with me on:
- https://plmatthews.com
- https://www.facebook.com/profile.php?id=61551925178512
- https://www.instagram.com/pl_matthews_author

Subscribe to my newsletter:

✉ https://plmatthews.com/index.php/newsletter

Printed in Great Britain
by Amazon